'Catnip to horror fans, complete with meddling kids, doppelgangers, dimensional fissures, demons, and ghosts; it's a prototypical edge-of-your-seat plunge into real terror.'

Kirkus

'In the tradition of Stephen King's Dark Tower books, Wendig views the cosmic and terrifying through the lens of the domestic, anchoring his visions of the sublime in the grit of the familiar. The result is a novel to ramble around in, to get lost in.'

John Langan, author of *Children of the Fang and Other Genealogies*

'A bold, impressive novel with fierce intelligence and a generous, thrumming heart . . . It's intimate and panoramic. It's humane and magical. It's a world-hopping, time-jumping ride that packs a deep emotional punch.'

Library Journal (starred review)

BY CHUCK WENDIG

Wanderers

ZerOes

Invasive

THE HEARTLAND TRILOGY

Under the Empyrean Sky

Blightborn

The Harvest

MIRIAM BLACK

Blackbirds

Mockingbird

The Cormorant

Thunderbird

The Raptor & The Wren

Vultures

ATLANTA BURNS

Atlanta Burns

Atlanta Burns: The Hunt

NONFICTION

The Kick-Ass Writer

Damn Fine Story

STAR WARS

Star Wars: Aftermath

Star Wars: Aftermath: Life Debt

Star Wars: Aftermath: Empire's End

Praise for *The Book of Accidents*

'Move over King, Chuck Wendig is the new voice of modern horror. *The Book of Accidents* is a masterwork, and Chuck is only just getting started.'

Adam Christopher, author of
Stranger Things: Darkness on the Edge of Town

'Wendig combines cosmic horror and human heroism with his continuing theme of the traumatic effect of abusive relationships handed down from father to son; this is a rich, rewarding tale.'

Guardian

'With a story both universally horrifying and viscerally intimate, Wendig brilliantly uses *The Book of Accidents* to explore a painful truth: in the end, we all haunt ourselves. I couldn't get through the pages fast enough.'

Kiersten White, *New York Times* bestselling author of
The Dark Descent of Elizabeth Frankenstein

'A gruesome, compelling, bloody yarn complete with serial killer, mysterious landscape of shifting stones, abandoned mines and an interdimensional twist that turns the suspense up to 11 and beyond. Goodness prevails, but what a ride.'

Daily Mail

'The dread, the scope, the pacing, the turns – I haven't felt all this so intensely since *The Shining*.'

Stephen Graham Jones, *New York Times*
bestselling author of *The Only Good Indians*

'A full-blooded rural haunted house chiller with something for everyone: ghosts, doppelgängers, numerology, parallel worlds, demons and more.'

Financial Times

THE

BOOK

OF

ACCIDENTS

CHUCK WENDIG

PENGUIN BOOKS

PENGUIN BOOKS

UK | USA | Canada | Ireland | Australia
India | New Zealand | South Africa

Penguin Books is part of the Penguin Random House group of companies
whose addresses can be found at global.penguinrandomhouse.com

First published in the US by Penguin Random House in 2021
First published in the UK by Del Rey in 2021
Published in Penguin Books 2022
001

Typeset by Jouve (UK), Milton Keynes
Printed and bound in Great Britain by Clays Ltd, Elcograf S.p.A.

The authorised representative in the EEA is Penguin Random House Ireland,
Morrison Chambers, 32 Nassau Street, Dublin D02 YH68

A CIP catalogue record for this book is available from the British Library

ISBN: 978–1–529–10109–6

Penguin Random House is committed to a sustainable future
for our business, our readers and our planet. This book is made
from Forest Stewardship Council® certified paper.

Hell with it, this one's for me

A father, Steven said, battling against hopelessness,
is a necessary evil.

—James Joyce, Ulysses

May the forces of evil become confused on the way
to your house.

—George Carlin

THE
BOOK
OF
ACCIDENTS

Ride the Lightning

Edmund Walker Reese was a man of numbers. Not an accountant, or a mathematician, but, rather, a man of simple interests, and it was here and now, in the Blackledge SCI—State Correctional Institution—that he sat strapped to an electric chair, running the numbers.

Three guards walked him here.

They passed seven other prisoners on Death Row, each in his own cell.

There would be one executioner, too: an anonymous man who would throw the switch, the man who would end Edmund Reese.

It was ten P.M. on a Tuesday. Second Tuesday in March, 1990.

(Time, after all, was a number, too.)

But there were details he did not yet know, and so he asked the older guard who was slitting Edmund's prison jumper up the calf to make room for the electrodes. (The leg had already been shaved that morning, right before Edmund Walker Reese—Eddie to his friends, of which he had none—ate his last meal, a simple bowl of wholesome chicken noodle soup.)

The older guard, a man named Carl Graves, had sideburns so gray and wispy they were like bits of fog clinging to his jowls. (Though the top of his hair was dark, not yet taken by age and drained of color.) He was in his forties, maybe early fifties, it was hard to tell. A whiff of sourness on his breath: cheap whiskey, Walker thought. Carl was never drunk, not really, but he was always drinking. (Smoking, too, though here the whiskey seemed to mask the smell.) The drinking was why Graves always seemed to hover somewhere between weary and angry. But the whiskey made him honest, too, and that's why Edmund liked him. As much as he could like anybody, anyway.

Reese chided the guard slicing the leg of his jumpsuit: "Be careful of my left leg. There's an injury there."

"That where the girl gotcha?" Graves asked.

But Reese didn't answer. Instead, he said: "Tell me more. More numbers. How many volts in the chair?"

The guard sniffed and stood up, saying, "Two thousand."

"Do you know the dimensions of the chair? Weight. Width. And so on?"

"Don't know, don't care."

"Is there an audience? How many?"

Graves looked to the window that Edmund faced—a window that had metal blinds pulled down over it. "Got a big audience today, Eddie." Graves used his nickname even though they were not friends, not at all, but Edmund did not object. "Seems people really want to watch you cook." Cruelty flashed in Carl Graves's eyes like a lit match. Edmund recognized that cruelty, and liked it.

"Yes, yes," Edmund said, unable to conceal his irritation. His skin itched. His jaw tightened. "But how *many.* The number, please."

"Behind the window, twelve. Six private citizens invited at the behest of the warden and the governor, and six journalists."

"Is that all?"

"There are more watching on closed-circuit TV." Carl Graves pointed at the camera in the corner, a camera whose vigilant eye watched the chair intently, unblinking, as if afraid to miss what would come. "Another thirty."

Reese did the calculation. "Forty-two. A good number."

"Is it? If you say so." Graves stepped aside as the other guard, a big slab of meat with a lawnmower buzz cut, stood with a grunt and began affixing the electrodes to Edmund's shorn scalp. Carl sniffed. "You know, you're special."

I am special, Edmund thought. He knew it to be true, or did once. Now, he wasn't so sure. He'd once had a mission. Been given life and light and a quest. A sacred quest, he was told. Blessed, consecrated, *holy* and *unholy* in equal measure, and yet, if that were true, why was he here? Caught like a fly in a slowly closing hand. Foiled at Number Five. Only Number Five! He had *work yet to do.*

"Special how?" he asked, because he wanted to hear it.

"This chair, Old Smokey—most electric chairs have names, a lot of them are called Old Sparky, but here in PA, it's Old Smokey— well, it's been in storage since 1962. Last fucker who fried in this thing was Elmo Smith, rapist and murderer. And then they stopped using it. Been nine death warrants since Elmo, but all of them got by on appeal. But then, you came along, Eddie. Lucky number ten."

Numbers flashed through Edmund Reese's mind, doing a do-si-do square dance—again, nothing mathematical. But he was looking for something. Patterns. Truth. A sacred message.

"Number ten isn't classically lucky," Edmund said, twisting his lips into a grimace. "What number am I?"

"Number ten. I told you."

"No, I mean, how many before me? Died? In this chair?"

Graves looked to the big ginger guard for an answer. Big Ginger provided, saying, "Before him, three hundred and fifty fried in the hot seat."

"Makes you three-fifty-one," Graves said.

Edmund considered that number: *351.*

What did it mean? It had to mean something. Because for it to mean nothing, for all of it to have added up to the sum total of a bucket of piss and shit, would kill him. It would kill him in a way this chair would not. Kill him in a way worse than those girls—

No, he chastised himself. *They were not girls. They were just things. Each a number. Each a purpose. Each a sacrifice.* Number One with the pigtails, Number Two with the painted nails, Number Three with the birthmark just under the left eye, Number Four with that scrape on her elbow, and Number Five—

Rage throttled him and Edmund tensed up in the chair as if he were already being electrocuted.

"Settle down, Eddie," Graves said. Then the older guard leaned in and again, there glimmered that flash of nastiness in his eyes. "You're thinking about her, aren't you? The one that got away."

For a moment, Edmund felt truly *seen*. Maybe Graves did earn the right to use his nickname. "How did you know?"

"Oh. I can tell. I've been a guard here on Death Row for a while, and in Gen Pop for a long time before that. Started when I was eighteen. At first you hold it all back. Keep it at bay. But it's like water in the tides, washing up on your beach, pulling a little bit of your sand away, day after day. Soon you're pickling in it. Brining like pig meat. It gets in you. So you get to recognizing it. Evil, I mean. You know how it thinks. How it is. What it *wants*." Graves licked his lips. "You know, your hunting ground? Where you took those girls—"

Those things.

"It was near my house. Scared my wife. Scared my kid."

"It wasn't them I was after."

"No, I guess not. Just the girls. Young girls. Four dead. And as for the fifth, well, she got lucky, didn't she?"

"Number Five got *away*," Edmund said in sorrow.

"And when she got away, you got caught."

"I wasn't supposed to get caught."

A mean grin crossed Graves's face. "And yet, here you are." With that, the guard slapped him on the knee. "One thing you ought to know, Eddie, is that what goes around, comes around. You get what you give."

"You also give what you get."

"If you say so."

They cinched all the belts, checked the electrodes one more time, and informed him of what was to happen. They asked him one last time if he cared to have a chaplain present, but he'd already refused that opportunity and did not beg for it now, for as he told them, *I have a patron in this life, and the demon is not here.* They explained, almost jokingly, that on the other side of the door was the prison superintendent, on an open line with the governor's office just in case of any (and here Graves snort-laughed) "last-minute reprieves." They explained that his remains would go into a potter's field, for Edmund Reese had no family left in this world.

And with that, they opened the metal shades.

Edmund saw the witnesses and the audience that had gathered to watch him die. They sat, equal parts horrified and eager, held rapt by those polar forces like ball bearings between two strong magnets. The executioner turned on the voltage, then the amperage, and then went to the power panel to flip the switch—which was not a comical Frankenstein-making switch on the wall you could pull down dramatically, but, rather, a simple white switch, so small you could flick it with a thumb.

And then the thumb moved and—

Edmund Reese felt the world light up around him, big and bright. All things washed out in the wave of white. It felt suddenly like he was falling—and then, the opposite, like he was being picked up by invisible hands, the way a cow must've felt when sucked up into a tornado, and next thing he knew, he was gone from the chair, gone from that world, not dead, no—

He was something, and somewhere, else.

The Boy Is Found

The hunter, Mike O'Hara, was not a fancy man, but he dreamt of pheasant under glass. It was a family recipe, passed down from his grandmother to his father and now to him and his brothers, Petey and Paul. But they didn't give a shit about pheasant under glass, or hunting like Dad did, so Mike hunted alone. Again. Today of all days: his father's birthday. Or would've been. *Rest in peace, old man.*

Mike was not a great hunter, and pheasant was a hard bird to find here, nowadays. So he wandered farther and farther afield in search of a nice cockbird to startle out of the fields and fencerows. Worse, he didn't have a hunting dog with him, either. The work was his own, so he did it slow and methodically, as his father had taught him.

But as he did, his mind wandered. He thought about his dad, dead from a stroke—a blood clot shot like a bullet into his brain. He thought about Petey's debts and Paul's liver issues from drinking. He remembered being a kid and swimming in a quarry not far from here. And as his mind wandered, so did his feet, not paying much attention to where he was at or where he was headed—until he came upon a row of dying ash trees, poor things eaten up and half-killed by ash borer beetles, leaving once-lush branches looking like bones stripped clean. Beyond, he spied the crumbling white frontispiece of the Ramble Rocks mine. Overgrown with grape vines and poison ivy, nature coming to reclaim the space.

Mike kept walking. The brush crackled underfoot as he crept

along. He wanted dearly to get a bird, if only to honor his father. It felt right.

Step by step, he went. Mind still lost in thought—

Just as something shot up out of the collapsed thicket.

The flutter of wings filled the air and a dark shape moved east to west. Mike saw the telltale patch of red around the eyes, the white ring around its neck. He juggled a step backward, cinching the gun to his shoulder as he brought the twelve gauge up to fire. A tug on the trigger—

Shit, the safety! he realized.

A quick click and he swung the gun ahead of the arc of the bird's flight and—

Boom.

The bird twisted in midair, corkscrewing through open space before plunging beak-first into the dry field grass.

I did it!

Pheasant under glass.

His ears ringing, the eggy stink of expended powder in his nostrils, Mike blinked past the haze of shotgun smoke and—

He saw the small person standing there in front of him.

"Christ on a bike!" he barked, blinking. There, in front of him, stood a boy covered in blood. His first thought was, *I shot a kid,* but that didn't make sense, did it? He sucked in a sharp breath, saw that the blood on the boy wasn't fresh. Gone dry. Crusty. It covered half his face, closing one eye behind a hard cake of scab.

The kid wore a simple white T-shirt, half of which was nearly black with old blood. His lips were so chapped, they looked salted. His skin had gone yellow with jaundice.

"Hey," Mike said, not sure what else to say.

"Hi," the boy answered. His voice cracked. He smiled a little, like he was pleased with himself for some reason.

"Are you okay?"

A stupid question, he knew—this kid wasn't okay. But maybe it would be good to get him talking, to make him not realize that he was all fucked up. His own daughter was like that—Missy was accident-prone and one time she'd gashed her head on a glass coffee table so bad she needed three stitches. The trick was, you never let her see that you were upset. Pretend everything is okay, and she thought it was okay. She never cried because they never let on how bad it looked, what with her face a mask of blood.

The boy was like that. A mask of blood.

Just don't spook him. Maybe he doesn't know.

Mike asked again. "You okay, kid?"

"I'm out."

Those two words made Mike's stomach sink, though he couldn't say why. And he wouldn't get the chance to figure it out.

"Out of where?"

"The mine."

Mike blinked. The realization hit him. He *knew* this kid. Or, at least, knew who he was. He forgot his name, but he lived around here. Went missing, what, three, four months ago? No, even earlier. Before school was out. Early May. That's when the posters went up, when his phone got the Amber Alert. People talked about it, but kids went missing all the time, and there was talk, too, that this boy had a shitty family life so maybe he just ran away . . .

Now, Mike had a different idea. Maybe he did run away.

Maybe he got lost down there in the old coal mine.

But how the hell did he survive all this time? That wasn't possible.

Mike eased the shotgun down on the ground. He held up both hands. "My name's Mike. You remember your name?"

"Maybe."

"Okay." He took a step forward. "You been missing a while, huh?"

The boy's one good eye lost focus as he looked off at the horizon. Or maybe, beyond it. Like he was fixated on a point beyond time and space.

"Here's what we're gonna do," Mike said. "I'm gonna come over there, okay? Gonna help you get out of this field. I got my pickup about a quarter mile from here, not far, a short walk. Get you to a hospital."

The boy didn't say anything. He didn't even seem to hear the question. So, Mike kept on creeping forward. Step by step. A small part of him thought, *Shit, I wish I could find that cockbird I hit.*

Pheasant under glass . . .

Closer, closer, he crept.

He bent a knee and reached for the boy. "Okay. C'mere. We're gonna get you somewhere safe, kiddo, just relax—"

The boy's hand twitched.

Something was in it. He twisted his hand, flicked his wrist, and that's when Mike saw the pick-ax. It hadn't been there before. Couldn't have been. Was the boy hiding it behind his back? Had he brought it out of the mine? Sure looked like a coal miner's pick. Should've been too heavy for the boy's hand. But the kid white-knuckled it pretty good.

"Whatcha got there?" Mike asked.

The boy moved fast.

Mike felt a hard pressure against his temple. He tried to cry out, tried to backpedal, but he couldn't make either of those things happen. He felt wetness dribbling down his jawline. His head felt heavy, and it drooped down and to the left.

Boy, it's hot as hell out here, he thought, *so goddamn humid for October,* and then his legs went weak and he tumbled backward onto his ass bone. Brush crackled underneath him.

As he began to bleed out, the boy stood in front of him. Lording over the space like a little king. The pick-ax wasn't in his hand anymore.

Pheasant under glass. Mike reminded himself to buy a bottle of brandy on the way home. *Sure gonna taste delicious,* he thought, smacking his lips as blood filled his mouth, as the boy stood over him and the darkness of dying swept him away.

PART ONE

A ONE-DOLLAR DEAL WITH THE DYING

The Darr Mine disaster at Van Meter, Rostraver Township, Westmoreland County, Pennsylvania, near Smithton, killed 239 men and boys on December 19, 1907. It ranks as the worst coal mining disaster in Pennsylvanian history.

An inquiry carried out after the disaster determined that the blast was the result of miners carrying open lamps in an area cordoned off the previous day by the fire boss. The mine's owner, the Pittsburgh Coal Company, was not held responsible.

—Wikipedia entry, Darr Mine disaster

Tinnitus

This was Oliver:

The boy, fifteen, knelt on the ground, his chin against his chest, the soft undersides of his forearms pressing into his ears even as his fingers dug into the thatch of messy hair at the back of his head. His ears rang sharply—not the tolling of a bell but a shrill whine, like that of a dental drill. To one side of him: yellow lockers. To the other: a water fountain. Above: a waterfall of bright fluorescence. Somewhere ahead were two gunshots, *bang, bang.* Each made his heart jump. Somewhere behind him were the murmur and rustle of students moving from classroom to classroom, seeking safety. Oliver imagined them dead. He imagined his teachers dead. Blood on linoleum. Brains on chalkboard. He imagined weeping parents on the news, and the suicides of survivors, and the thoughts and prayers of uncaring politicians—he could see the pain like a little ripple that became a wave, that met other waves and became tsunamis roaring back and forth over people until all were drowned underneath.

A hand grasped his shoulder and shook him. A word spoken as if through a fishbowl—his name. Someone was saying his name. "Olly. Oliver. Olly!" He gently rocked himself back on his ankles, sitting partly upright. It was Mr. Partlow, his BioSci teacher. "Hey. Hey, lockdown drill's almost over, Oliver. You okay? Come on, kiddo, let's get you—"

But then the teacher let go and took a half step back. Mr. Partlow stared down at the floor—no, not at the floor. At Oliver. Oliver took a look, too. His crotch was wet. Fingers of liquid were spreading down his pant legs. Ahead, he saw a few students gather and stare. Landon Gray, who sat behind him in homeroom, looked sad. Amanda McInerney—who was in all the plays, and chorus, and student council—made a gross face and giggled.

Mr. Partlow helped him stand up and took him away. Oliver wiped tears from his face, tears he didn't even know he'd spilled.

The Lawyer

This was Nate:

That same day, Nate sat in a lawyer's office in Langhorne. The lawyer was round and grub white, like the inside of a cut potato. In the window of the office, an AC unit grumbled and growled, so that the man had to raise his voice in order to be heard.

"Thank you for coming," the lawyer, Mr. Rickert, said.

"Uh-huh." Nate tried to keep his hands from balling into fists. Tried, and failed.

"Your father is sick," the lawyer said.

"Good," Nate answered without hesitation.

Rickert leaned forward.

"It's cancer. Colon cancer."

"Fine."

"He'll be dead soon. Very soon. He's on hospice."

Nate shrugged. "Okay."

"Okay," the lawyer repeated, and Nate couldn't tell if the man was surprised by his reaction—or prepared for it. "Mr. Graves—"

"I know you expect me to be broken up about all this, but I'm not. Not one little bit. My father was—or, is, I guess—a tremendous piece of garbage. I have no love for him. I have only hatred and disdain for that monster masquerading as a man, and truth be told, I've been dreaming of this day for the better part of twenty years, maybe longer. I've imagined how it would go. I've prayed to whatever god that would listen that my father, the piece of shit that he is, would go painfully and miserably, that it wouldn't be fast, wouldn't be a quick sprint to the end, but, rather, a slow, stumbling marathon, a . . . a clumsy run where he's painting the walls with his lung blood, where he's drowning in his own fluids, where he's gotta wear some, some *bag* on his side to contain his own f— his own mess, a bag that breaks on him or that pops out of its port every time he moves to adjust his ruined, dying body. You know what? I was *hoping* it'd be cancer. A crawling, steady cancer, too, not fast like pancreatic. Something that eats him up from the inside sure as he ate up our family. Cancer for cancer, tit for tat. I figured it'd be lung, given the way he smoked. Or liver, given the drink. But colon cancer? I'll take colon. He was . . . he was always full of shit, so that is a fitting end for that semi-human sack of septic excrement."

The lawyer blinked. Silence passed between them. Rickert pursed his lips. "Are you done monologuing?"

"Go to hell." He paused, regretting being so angry at this man who probably didn't deserve it. "Yes, I am."

"Your speech doesn't surprise me. Your father said you'd say those things." He laughed a little, a high-pitched titter, and he gesticulated with both hands so it looked like his fingers were little moths taking flight. "Well, not *those* things, exactly. But the gist."

"So, what's the point? Why am I here?"

"Your father, before he passes, wants to offer you a deal."

"No deal, whatever it is."

"It's a favorable deal for you. Don't you want to hear it?"

"I don't." Nate stood up, kicking the chair out behind him. It juddered louder and more aggressively than he'd intended it, but it was what it was and he wouldn't apologize.

He turned to leave.

"It's the house," the lawyer said.

Nate's hand paused on the doorknob.

"The house."

"That's right. Your childhood home."

"Great. He can leave it to me in the will."

"It's not in the will. He will sell the house to you, instead. The house, and the thirteen acres of land on which it sits."

Nate shrugged. "Sorry. I can't afford it." The house—as the lawyer noted, Nate's childhood home—was in an area that had, over the decades, become prime real estate. Upper Bucks County. Used to be just farmland and swamp, but these days, prices were up, taxes were up, rich people had moved in from Philly or New York. Gentrification wasn't just for the inner cities. "Tell him to sell it, then. He can use the money to pay for a really fantastic casket."

"Surely you can afford the cost of a single dollar."

Nate turned his narrowed gaze toward Rickert. He ran a hand through his beard and winced. "A dollar."

"A dollar, that's right."

"If I have it right, the idea there is so I avoid . . . what, some sort of taxes? I pay a dollar, and it's a free-and-clear transaction."

"That is the perception."

Nate nodded. "The 'perception.' Uh-huh. I'm a city cop. I'm not too caught up on white collar stuff, it's mostly blue collar for me, but I know a con when I smell it. Dad could just gift the house to me and it'd be good to go. Or I could inherit it like most people do—and I'd only be on the hook for taxes if I sold it and made more money than the fair market value of the house. But this, and correct me if I'm wrong, means that if I buy the house for a dollar and sell it for any amount over that dollar, I get whopped with a capital gains tax on top of it being income. I have that right?"

An unhappy smile stitched between the lawyer's plump cheeks. "That's likely correct. The IRS usually demands its pound of flesh."

"I'm not buying the house. I'm not buying anything the old man is selling. I wouldn't buy a cup of water from him if I was dying of thirst. I don't know what his game is, except to saddle me with a house I don't want. Please tell him to take his offer and shove it up his rotting, cancerous behind."

"I can convey that message." The lawyer stood and offered a hand to shake. Nate looked at it like the man had just blown his nose into it, no tissue. "The offer will remain on the table until Carl passes."

Nate walked out the door without saying another word.

3

The Box Has Eyes

This was Maddie Graves:

She had short-cropped hair the color of silver mist—dyed that way, because she thought it looked cool. (And it did.) She was long and lean, arms and legs stretched tight like bridge cables. That, from her work: Maddie, or Mads, was a sculptor. Mostly worked with found materials. Which is exactly what sat before her, now: a cardboard box, this one from Amazon, cut apart with an X-Acto knife and reconstituted into the shape of a little box-faced and box-bodied man. The Box Man's cardboard limbs were fixed to the body with wire stolen from an old chain-link fence, twisted with a pair of needle-nose pliers.

In his one hand, she had placed the X-Acto knife.

As if he were a little monster. A threatening Chucky doll, ready to stab-stab-stab with his blade.

She stared at it.

And stared.

And *stared* some more.

"The fuck," she said.

Behind her, other artists worked dutifully at projects—tables, easels, laptops—a buzzing beehive of art co-op creation. One of them, a friend named Dafne (punky grandma, butch as hell, fifty-five years old, acrylic rainbow one-inch-diameter plugs stretching out her earlobes, septum dog bone piercing, *Welcome to Night Vale* ALL HAIL

THE GLOW CLOUD T-shirt fringed ragged at the bottom, shitkicker construction boots spattered in a barfy rainbow of paint), swaggered up behind Maddie, hands on hips.

" 'Sup?" Dafne asked.

"I, ahhh . . ." Maddie started, then stopped.

"I can see it being a little hackneyed, if that's your worry. Like, as a critique of crapitalism, it's a little simplistic—like, okay, Amazon is this big-box online retailer and it's destroying the world, but kind of an obvious target. Plus, yeah, no, I think you can think bigger than just a little knife in his hand, right?" Dafne's voice lowered to a mutter. "I mean, *I* still use Amazon, sometimes, I dunno."

"No. No!" Maddie said, furrowing her brow. "That's not—that's not the problem. It's . . . it's a lot of things. Something's wrong. Something's weird with it."

"Nothing wrong with weird."

"I just, uhh." She swallowed. "It's not just weird. It's crazy."

"I specialize in crazy. I take lithium. What's the sitch?"

Maddie laughed a little. "Okay. See these eyes?"

She used a pair of pliers to indicate the Box Man's eyes—which were wire, like the rest of it, coiled up like little metal millipedes, and gently screwed into the box.

"Yeah."

"I didn't make them."

"Didn't make what?"

"The eyes."

"You didn't make the eyes?"

"That's what I'm fucking telling you—I didn't put, or don't remember putting, them there. Is that weird?"

Dafne shrugged and grunted with amusement. "Hon, I don't remember what I had for breakfast, much less the shit I'm painting as I paint it. I go into a Bob Ross fugue state. It's like ASMR, some hypnotrance hallucinogen shit. My brain goes off, my arm starts dancing with the brush as its partner, and off we go."

Maddie bit her lip, nearly hard enough to draw blood.

"That's not *me*, though," she clarified. "I'm, you know, I'm in control. I know it. Every movement, every piece, it's purposeful. But I swear I didn't put those eyes there." *And I swear they're looking right at me.* It wasn't just that. There were other things bothering her. The way the eyes seemed to be *looking* at her. The way she was sure, too, that what was supposed to go in the Box Man's hand wasn't a blade—but, rather, a pair of scissors. Something about all of it felt eerily familiar. Like she'd seen this before. Like she'd *made him* before. She shook her head. That was nuts. Straight-up cuckoo-town nuts. "I take your point about the capitalist—"

"Crapitalist."

"Fine, the *crap*italist—"

Her phone buzzed with a call, interrupting her.

"Ugh, who calls people anymore?" Dafne asked, glancing down dismissively at the device in Maddie's palm.

The phone said RUSTIN SCHOOL.

"Olly's school," Maddie said ominously. "That's who."

She answered it, knowing immediately in that mother's way that something had gone wrong.

4

The Conversation

Oliver listened to his parents talking through the walls of their city apartment. It was midnight, and they likely thought him asleep. He was, after all, exhausted. But his mind raced just the same. His heart, too.

Dad: *You know, I don't know, Mads. He's just—he's just—I dunno.*

Mom: *Doctor Nahid said he was empathetic.*

Dad: *I don't like that word. Sounds too much like* pathetic *and he's not pathetic—*

Mom: *No one's saying he's pathetic, Nate. It's just a word. Go with* empathetic *if you prefer. He has, like, really intense compassion, okay? Other people's pain lights up his brain like an incandescent bulb.*

Oliver wondered: Was he pathetic?

He certainly felt that way. He was in that jangly halfway stage of teenage put-togetherness—limbs a bit gangly, a nose he hated for being too long and too pointed, a chin he hated for being too soft. Unlike his mother's shock of platinum hair or his father's shaggy sandstone locks, his own hair was dark like a crow's wing. He didn't have a girlfriend. He liked girls—liked boys, too, though he'd never told anyone that. Never had sex. Wasn't sure he ever would: The idea felt more frightening than exciting. He did have eyes for Lara Sharp, because she was a nerd, and a total extrovert, and he loved how she didn't take any shit from anybody. Lara reminded him of his mom. He realized how creepy that was, that he wanted to get with someone who reminded him of his mom, but it wasn't like that—he liked his parents. A lot. They were good to him, and he liked to think he was good *for* them.

Whatever. It didn't matter anyway. Not like Lara Sharp would want to get with him anyway. Not after today.

I dunno, Mads. The poor kid—he, he wet himself—

Nate, those ALICE drills are fucking terrifying. They fire off actual guns—

Blanks, they're blanks.

So what if they're blanks! You're used to hearing gunfire—you're a cop. Kids aren't. It's trauma. It's real fucking trauma, and no wonder he can't hack it. I'd probably piss myself, too.

I don't hear that much gunfire, Mads—I know you think being a cop is this dangerous job, but it's mostly not. Besides, it's not just this one thing. Every homeless guy on the street, kid wants to know their names, how they got there, wants to give them money—

That's a nice thing, Nate.

I know. It is. And I'm glad he cares. But he doesn't just care. *He takes it on the chin. It's hard enough being in the world on your own, but he's got no armor. Everybody's pain is his own pain—*

Here, their voices went muffled for a moment. Either talking in a low voice or moving around. He heard his mother say *talked to Doctor Nahid—*

Nahid. His therapist. Been seeing her now for about six months. Oliver liked her. She looked severe—all sharp angles, like a drawer full of knives opened up and dumped out—but she was soft with him, gentle, and always level. He never felt like she was talking down to him or anything, but also like she wasn't judging him. Dad was right, though. Oliver didn't have any armor. He felt people's pain—literally, he could see it, *feel it,* like a dark star pulsating. Sometimes the pain was small and sharp, other times like a geyser of sickness fountaining out of a person. Their fear, their worry, their trauma. They shared it with him. And he couldn't turn it off.

Mom continued: *So, I know this is probably the most fucked-up, su-premely worst day to talk about this, but with your father dying, and that offer of the house . . .*

Wait, Oliver's grandfather died? He didn't know him. Never met him. He didn't think Mom had ever met him, either, and Dad rarely talked about his own father—but he died?

Mads, you can't be serious.

Okay. I know. It's nuts. But bear with me—

I don't wanna think about this. Or talk about it. No. No!

It's Bucks County. Amazing school district. Good jobs, clean air, plus your parents' old house is on a dozen acres.

Thirteen acres. Thirteen is not a lucky number.

It'd be great for my work, too, Nate. I could set up a workshop, have all the room I need. Plus you always said you know people in Fish and Game. That'd be a nicer job than fucking around on the streets of this fucked-up city. You keep saying the cops have changed. They've gotten meaner. Worse. Besides, Nahid said nature could be good for him, and getting out of town—

Jeez, Mads. C'mon. This is nuts.

Honey. Babe. Nate. I know this is hard. Your father was—

Is. He's still alive, and he's the worst, Maddie. A narcissist, a sociopath, an abusive sonofagun—

Yes, of course, but—

And you never met him. You don't know. Not really.

But he'll be dead. Don't you see? He'll be cold and in the fucking ground and that house can be ours, and if maybe you get one good thing out of him—an escape from the city, a pressure release for your son, a new place to work for me (your darling wife), then why not take it? Maybe, just maybe, this is your father's way—

Don't even say it. I know you love to see the bright side of things and, and people, but no. That man had no bright side. It was just darkness.

You could talk about it sometime.

And relive it? Or make you endure it? No thanks. Just trust me when I tell you, there was no good side. The scorpion always stings the frog.

Okay. Okay. But this doesn't have to be like that.

Jesus, Mads! That's what the frog says every time!

He'll be dead. What damage can he do?

I don't know, Mads. Olly won't want to move. He likes his school—

And that was true. Oliver did like his school. The Rustin School was a little private Quaker academy here in the city, but after today, could he even manage to stay there? He didn't want to go back. Didn't want to show his face. So he kicked the covers off himself, threw open his door, and walked to the kitchen in his bare feet. He found his parents, each leaning against an opposing countertop, watching each other guardedly. Before they even noticed him, he said: "I heard you talking. You forget this apartment is small, and it has thin walls."

They turned to look at him in a panic. Then at each other.

Pain bloomed dark in his father. Emanating from his middle like a growing shape. It pulsed there, and did not diminish. Usually it was held back, almost as if by an invisible wall, but tonight it seemed as if it had breached its containment, a bloody black beast escaping its cage. His mother's pain, too, was present—but it seemed contained. Or, at least, *compressed.*

In Oliver's experience, everybody's pain was different; for some it was a compacted ball, others a chaotic fire. One person's pain might be a tidal wave, and another's might look like poison in veins, or a spreading bruise, or shadows on water. He didn't understand it, or what it meant, or why he was cursed with this ability in the first place, but he'd been able to see it as long as he could remember.

He hated it. But it was useful, sometimes, too.

"Hey, Dude," Mom started to say, but Oliver interrupted her.

"I want to move. I heard you talking, and I want to move."

"You're sure?" his father asked.

Olly nodded. "Yeah. The city is . . . hard." It was. The noise. The lights. The uninterrupted hum. But worse than that, the people. They were good people. But that pain he could see? It was *everywhere*. So much pain threatening to crush him. As it had today during the shooter drill. It washed over him like a wave every day. And it was getting worse. He just needed *less* of that. Maybe moving would give him that. Maybe.

Nate forced a smile and then said, "Okay, kiddo. Okay."

And so it was decided.

The Graves family was gonna move.

5

The One Condition

This was the house:

It was a stone colonial farmhouse, its old bones dating back to the late 1700s. It was a tall house with narrow shoulders, and it cast a deep shadow as the sun rose behind it. The door was red. The gable roof above the door was teal. But the paint on both had long faded, peeling away in leprotic strips. The flagstone walkway was cracked and fractured, with weeds widening those gaps. Spiderwebs, some old, some new, hung in the windows. The slate roof was in grave disrepair, many of the tiles broken and shattered. Wisteria hung from the power lines, and ivy—poison ivy and five-finger ivy—crept up from the ground, like fingers looking to grab the house and pull it down into the dirt. Nature wanted this house back.

Just as the trees loomed over the house, the house seemed to loom over Nate. He had a vertiginous moment where it felt like the red front door would whip open, and the house would lean forward and the doorway would become a mouth. Gobbling him up and swallowing him down. This was a house of foul breath and bad dreams.

As Nate regarded his childhood home, not seen by his eyes for decades, he heard an engine, and the pop of stones under tires.

The lawyer, Rickert, drove up the long cracked-asphalt driveway in a decades-old BMW—a welcome interruption. He parked the BMW next to the little Honda Nate suspected belonged to the hospice nurse.

Rickert hopped out of his car and sauntered up, clutching a brown paper envelope with a string-and-button closure.

"Mr. Graves," he said.

"Rickert," Nate said.

"Your one condition has been met."

"He's in there now?"

Rickert nodded, unfazed. *He didn't like Dad, either,* Nate realized. Which was apropos; Dad hated lawyers much as he hated anything.

Nate dug into his pocket and pulled out a ratty, wrinkled dollar. The kind a snack machine would spit out.

The lawyer took it. Then he handed over the envelope. Nate peeked inside, saw a sheaf of papers—ones he'd already signed a few days ago, the day after Oliver told them he wanted to move—plus the deed and a key ring.

The door to the house opened, just then, and the hospice nurse—a broad-shouldered woman with kind eyes, a helmet of brown hair, and a sad look on her face—came out. "Nathan Graves?" she said.

Nate nodded, but sharply corrected: "Nate. Never Nathan."

"Hi, Nate, I'm Mary Bassett," she said, taking his hand and holding it. "I'm the hospice nurse. I'm so sorry for your loss."

"Don't be. I'm here to gloat, not mourn."

A flash in her eye told him she understood. It made him wonder what kind of hell she'd had to put up with from the old man in the last week of his life.

The wreckage that old creep left in his every wake . . .

"He inside?" Nate asked.

"He is. In the master on the second floor."

"Then I'd like to see him."

This, then, was Nate's one condition: He'd told Rickert over the phone three days ago that he would accept the dollar offer if he were allowed a small, private "viewing" at the house, after his father had passed, but before they came to cart the body away.

His father, through Rickert, had agreed to that stipulation.

And now, here Nate was. Looking at his father's corpse.

Nate had seen a handful of bodies in his time as a Philly cop—one time, a heat wave took an elderly woman, leaving her a greasy and swollen mess, blistered and oozing. Another time, a hard winter robbed the life from a homeless man, froze him solid against a dumpster. All the deaths he'd seen were unintentional—overdoses and car accidents and, the worst of the worst, three bodies pulled out of a nightclub fire. What was true in those deaths was true here: A dead body had no soul. Something crucial had gone. A missing piece had turned them from a living thing to a waxen prop.

The old man's skin lay loose on his bent skeleton, wrinkled and sallow, like the pages of a Bible that had gotten wet. The eyes were glassy, the mouth thin, each lip a sickly earthworm spooning the other.

This wasn't his father. Not anymore. It was just a mannequin.

Nate had *expected* that when he saw his father again, he would feel indignation that would give way to rage like some pyroclasm deep within—a rise of lava in his throat, a magma roar of fire that would not, could not, be contained.

He *hoped* he'd feel joy, like a boy told the monster in the closet was gone, that in fact *all* the monsters had been beheaded, that everything from here on out was balloons and carousel rides.

He *feared* that he would feel sad—that seeing his father this one last time would open up something he'd been hiding, a reservoir of sadness at seeing the old man like this. Sad at never getting to have the childhood he thought he'd have. Sad at wondering what made his father become the man that he had become.

Instead, he just felt empty. A chalkboard, wiped clean of all marks and left a gleaming, damp black.

One thing he *did* feel: like he was intruding upon this room. His father had never let him in here. It was off-limits. One time Nate snuck in and poked around and thought he wouldn't get caught, but

Dad knew somehow. He always knew. Something about the way the *molecules in the room* were disturbed.

(That didn't go well for Nate. He had bruises for weeks.)

It made him feel queasy being in here. Like he was gonna get caught again. He didn't give in to that feeling, though. He didn't run, though he wanted to.

The room had changed. It was messier, a hoarder's paradise: stacks of gun magazines on the dresser, piles of dirty clothes, a couple defunct mousetraps in the corner (no mice), a stack of filthy plates on a nightstand next to a knockoff Rolex watch and an old-ass alarm clock, the kind with the two metal bells on top of it. It didn't look like this when Nate had lived here—Mom kept the place immaculate. Those molecules in the room were hers to arrange, and *keep* arranged, all for the pleasure of the old sonofabitch.

Nate expected, too, that his father's guns were still here: a .45 ACP in the sock drawer, a pump-action shotgun under the bed, a two-shot derringer in a shoebox in the closet. And if they were here, they were loaded. Dad was paranoid. Said someone would come one day to steal his shit—the imagined array of racist fears, like a line of Black guys or Mexicans were just lining up in the dark forest outside to rob him of his knockoff watches. *King has to defend his castle,* Dad always said. But he was no king. And this was no castle.

But there was one thing that did surprise Nate.

Dad hadn't offed himself.

That was always his big thing. *I ever get sick, real sick, I'll put a gun under my chin. I go out on my terms.* That was something he told his son when Nate was . . . what? Twelve years old? Who tells a twelve-year-old that kind of thing?

"Coward," Nate said, not expecting any response.

But his father responded anyway.

Dad's body stiffened on the bed, life thrown suddenly back into its bones. The corpse's back arched, the eyes wrenched open, and the jaw opened wide, wider, crackling as it did, the face turning fast into a rictus of raw misery. Dad gasped like wind whistling through a broken window, and then there came a mad flash of light—

"Jesus," Nate said, backpedaling away from the bed.

And then he saw Dad, *another version of his father,* standing in the corner of the room. Impossible, but there it was: one father lying on the bed, one guarding the corner of the room. The one in the corner wore mud-caked jeans, a filthy white T-shirt, carried a boxy army pistol in his left hand, his wrong hand. He was staring right at Nate— staring at him, or staring *through* him, Nate couldn't tell, all while on the bed his father's actual corpse stretched and stiffened tighter and tighter, the high-pitched sucking breath going on louder and longer than seemed possible.

"Nathan?" the version of his father in the corner asked, voice so hoarse it buzzed, buzzed like a wall full of secret wasps.

The door to the bedroom burst open, and the hospice nurse came hurrying in. The body on the bed went slack and slumped. Nate blinked—the presence in the corner, the second Carl Graves, was gone.

"What happened?" the nurse asked.

"I . . ."

But Nate couldn't answer. He marched past her, down the narrow staircase, through the rotten house, and out the front door.

He threw up in the weed-choked flower bed as Rickert stared.

"It's called agonal respiration," Mary Bassett said. Nate sat on the bumper of his old Jeep Cherokee. The taste of sour vomit slicked his tongue, his heart still pounding his breastbone with a kick-drum tumble.

The nurse stood, hands clasped in front of her. "Sometimes after the cessation of life, the body will experience myoclonus—a twitch or spasm—and maybe gasp. It's . . . a terrible sound. I first heard it at

UPenn when I experienced my first coding patient and I've never managed to forget it."

Rickert stood nearby, watching the exchange with detached curiosity.

Nate sniffed. "Dad's been dead, what? How long?"

"An hour."

"Does this respiration happen that late after . . ." He chose to go with her euphemism. " 'The cessation of life'?"

She shrugged. "Not in my experience, but biology is pretty weird."

"There was something else," Nate said. "Saw him, Dad, standing in the corner. Him, but not him. Like a ghost."

Mary made a sad, sympathetic face. "It's not unusual to see things. It's a moment of considerable stress. If it helps you to think that you saw his spirit, that's okay. If you'd rather imagine it was a hallucination, that's okay, too." She tried to smile. "There are no wrong answers here."

"Okay." Nate nodded. *Just a hallucination,* he thought. "Thanks."

She turned to the lawyer. "I've flushed all medications and prepared the death certificate. I can call the funeral home now, if you'd like."

"Please," Rickert said.

She said another small apology and goodbye to Nate, and then Mary Bennett was gone.

"Will you go to the funeral?" Rickert asked.

"This was the funeral for me."

"All right. I'll handle any probate court process. The estate has no executor, if you're wondering."

"I wasn't."

Rickert stood there, silent as the trees on this hot, breezeless day in August. Finally he said, "What will you do with the house? Sell it and take the capital gains hit? Still make you some money."

"I've got an auction company coming in a few days. They'll clean the place out, sell anything that isn't nailed down. Then a week after that . . ." He couldn't believe he was saying the next part. "My family moves in."

"I'm surprised at that."

"Not as surprised as I am, Mr. Rickert. Not as surprised as I am."

Interlude: The Arrival

Animals did not like to go inside the tunnel.

They didn't communicate this to one another, not precisely. They had no shared language from species to species, though certainly they could talk to their own kind—in chirps, clicks and chitters, bleats and grunts. But at no point did any beast need to tell another: *Do not go in there.* They knew. It thrummed in their fur and feathers. They sang the warning in their blood.

The tunnel, they knew, was not merely a tunnel. It was a fearstink place—a dark hollow, a thin spot, a membrane through which darkness, true darkness, could come through, and they could feel it, and they could smell it. They also knew it was not just the tunnel, but the whole of this land—the tunnel, however, was the center of it. And so while they could not avoid all the domain around it, they very wisely went around the tunnel itself.

But today, a person—a human, one of those gangly, rubbery, mostly hairless apes—walked through the tunnel. Jogging. A male of the species. Humans often went through the tunnel. Humans, it turned out, were very stupid. Running despite nothing chasing them.

But the stupidity of humans was sometimes the good fortune of animals. The male, jogging under the deep stone arch and through the long dark, was carrying something, as humans often did:

Food.

Nuts and seeds and dried fruit. He jogged lazily, munching and crunching.

Munch munch.

Crunch crunch.

And then, as humans also often did, he dropped bits of what he was eating. Humans were wasteful creatures. Tremendously indifferent to the world around them, they discarded things with a casual disregard. Food and trash and treasure in equal measure.

The squirrel knew not to go into the tunnel. It was simply truth.

But what was also truth was that autumn was coming.

And with autumn, the cold.

And after the cold grew, it would be winter—the world would become a wasteland of snow and ice and wind. Squirrels survived in winter because the singular drive to acquire, and hide, food overtook them. If they saw food, they were programmed against all odds to go get it, and then to secret it away in trees, and under rocks, and in pockets of dirt dug out by furious little paws.

There, *right there,* in the tunnel, was food.

Prime, desirable food.

So the squirrel did what squirrels do, even when a car is bearing down upon them—the squirrel went for the food.

It crept into the tunnel and into the dark. It moved slowly at first, then in quick bursts. The scattering of seeds, nuts, fruits was ahead. Just ten feet now. Nine. Eight. The squirrel could practically taste them.

But the darkness of the tunnel seemed to become bleaker. And blacker. The squirrel stopped. Its fur bristled suddenly—a warning. A shrill sound arose in the narrow well of the animal's ear. The shadows vibrated and then pressed in like something heavy falling on the squirrel.

And yet, the squirrel was close, *so close,* to the food.

So onward the squirrel crept. Ignoring the sick feeling in its gut that it hoped was just hunger.

Closer now. Closer again.

It reached a paw out to the first nut. It batted it toward its mouth, ready to stuff it in its cheeks—

And then the ringing in its ears became unbearable, like a sharp needle thrust into its brain. The squirrel thrashed, rolling on its back, tail flailing, paws scrabbling as it turned over and over and over again. The animal made a sound in the back of its throat: a desperate squeak that turned into a shrill scream.

Soon it stopped thrashing. All it could do was press flat against its belly, pushing the top of its head down against the hard ground. Hoping to stop the sound that shrieked shrilly in its ear. Its head trembled. Twin jets of blood erupted from its nostrils and a bloody froth foamed past its teeth. Its belly swelled and then split like a cracked egg, all its insides pushing out with such force the animal's body rose up atop of a small hill of its own innards.

It remained alive long enough to see the air warp around it and the shadows cinch tight like a knot. Electricity danced up the tunnel walls, and then from that darkness, a flash of unearthly lightning erupted.

And there, burned into the world like an image seared upon the eye, was a human. A male of the species, too, though different from the one who so casually jogged through minutes before. This one had a face rent with scar tissue, as if he had tussled with a dread beast, some demon. And like a demon himself, the young male human's one strange-colored eye—nested in that ragged slash of scar— glowed and seemed to shift colors, like light bending in a prism.

Then the male human stepped over the squirrel, walking away.

Darkness and death arrived for the animal. The creature expired in a gush of fluids, a sudden shedding of all its fur, and a gassy hiss of steam. It died, but that was not its end. Not really. For soon it found itself slipping between cracks, through darkness, and into mist.

PART TWO

MOVING IN

The truth is simple, so simple a child can understand it. My father was a cold man, a mathematician, who did not love me and did not receive love from me in return, but one thing he told me always made sense: He said the truest language of the universe was not our words, or our body language, or anything that came from us at all. Rather, he said, it was numbers and it was math. Everything was part of an equation and if you understood those equations, if you knew the True Numbers, you knew everything. There was nothing you could not unlock if you knew the combination. For everything there was a variable that would complete the equation. And now I have that number. It is the number of the world, the number of angels, the number of demons. It is the Age of Abraham when God appeared, the age of John of Patmos, it is the number of the 99th Lodge, the Gematria of Amen, the Gold Century, the Unmaker's Number. I had a dream that the Beast of the Tunnel came to me and wrote that number upon my hand, and so that is where I went, to the rocks, to the Tunnel, and it was there I received my mission. My father was right. All things are numbers. True Numbers. True Language. He had eight buttons on his jacket when I killed him.

—from Journal 37 of serial killer Edmund Walker Reese

6

I See a Red Door

Together, the three of them stood staring at the red door.

"We sure about this?" Nate asked.

Maddie laughed, the sound of it nearly lost to the zipper-unzipping buzz of the cicadas. "A little late now. We bought the place."

"Yeah. For a dollar. And for ten grand in taxes a year. And the costs we're probably going to pay in repairs and upgrades over the next year, two years, ten years . . ." He ran a hand along his beard and it rasped like he was running a thumb across an old boot brush. He would have shaved it, had he still been in the city—but out here, somehow, the untamed wildness of the beard felt all too appropriate.

She leaned in close, put her head on his shoulder. "Thanks for doing this, Nate. I think this is going to be a good thing."

"I think so, too," he said, but it was a lie.

"This place is pretty cool," Olly said. It *was* nice to see a smile on his face. Already his son seemed more . . . well, *himself* maybe wasn't a fair way to put it, but that's how Nate scoped it. Oliver seemed lighter and freer. The boy added: "Pretty wild, too. Overgrown and stuff." Olly swatted at his neck. "Ow."

"Mosquito found you," Nate said. He affected a truly awful Dracula impression. *"They vant to suck your blaaaahd."*

"Ew."

"At least it's not ticks."

"Ticks?" Maddie asked, alarmed. "Whaddya mean, ticks?"

"We're in tick territory now. But that's all right. The possums eat the ticks. And bats will eat the mosquitoes."

"Ticks, possums, bats, and mosquitoes." She shook her head. "Fuck it, tell the movers to turn around, let's burn the whoooole shit-show down."

Nate laughed, so did Oliver. They were used to their mother even if they did not quite share her singular *passion* for vulgarities.

"Country living," Nate said, kissing her cheek.

"So this is our new front door," Olly said.

"Two hinges and one knob," Maddie said, making a curious face. "That's all it takes to make a door."

Nate shrugged. "Then let's open the door and get living."

(That phrase. *Two hinges and one knob. That's all it takes to make a door.* It came out of her mouth, but Maddie wasn't sure why. Or where it came from. Had she heard it before? She must have.)

It was getting harder and harder to work in the city, what with all the gentrification going on—why rent space to some artist when you can rent it to some trendy-ass coffee joint or to someone who sells artisanal bespoke Etsy eyepatches to one-eyed hipsters? Out here, they had some real acreage and a pole barn she was going to convert to a workshop. And already her mind was buzzing with lists—*gotta call an HVAC guy to get a split system and an electrician to run power and the cable company to get the internet set up and Trudy Breen to figure out if she can schedule a gallery appearance sometime in spring . . .* and then she started to think, too, about putting a grocery list together because they had no food, and also to make sure that everyone had their new address and—

That was Maddie, too. Lists within lists, plans to make new lists, lists to make new plans. People expected artists to be wifty, fly-by-night motherfuckers, and some *were*—but those artists were either a) starving or b) rich already, and Maddie didn't want to starve, and

Maddie damn sure wasn't rich, so that meant she had to have her fucking shit together, thank you very much.

(Another aspect of Maddie: a mouth fouler than a snake that had drowned itself in a jug of cheap tequila. Men were allowed to speak that way, and women often weren't, which Maddie took as a personal challenge. Fuck them for thinking women couldn't be improper. In her younger years, Mads was fond of saying: *Tell me to smile, and I'll show you my teeth.*)

Right now, her shit *was* together. Things were happening as they needed. Already the movers were coming in and out, stacking boxes, placing furniture. Nate was supervising. Oliver was checking out his room.

That gave her a moment. A moment all her own.

So, she walked out of the kitchen, out the back door onto the raggedy porch, and then off into the woods. Maddie found the overgrown path and followed it to the pole barn. Was only a few minutes' walk until she found it—a pole barn in the truest and oldest sense: constructed from repurposed telephone poles buried deep in the ground, six on each side, with a corrugated metal roof. The poles weren't rotten yet, but rust had long since chewed pits and holes in the roof. The mummy of an old wasp's nest hung from the rafters alongside endless spider hammocks. The structure had no walls, and the dirty, dusty ground bore ragged slashes and divots and box-shaped imprints of equipment long disused and taken away by the auction company they'd hired to get rid of all of the garbage left by Nate's dead father.

This space was hers, and hers alone.

She took a minute to sit with that small epiphany.

She felt like she had room to flex and breathe, room to *make* and *make* and *make some more*. But—

Then, reality came crashing down once more. *I still have to put walls on this thing. I still need to run power, get lights, get an HVAC sys-*

tem, bring all my equipment out, like the welder and the tool cabinet and armatures and and and this on top of all the other chores a freshly-moved-in home required. Normally lists freed her, but suddenly her lists felt like cinder blocks piling on her chest.

But if she could take those cinder blocks off . . .

I don't need the pole barn to make something.

Nate and Oliver don't need the boxes unpacked.

We don't need groceries—we can order fucking takeout.

And at that, all around her, the forest felt alive in a mighty surge—yes, with literal life, squirrels and blue jays and spiders, oh my—but also with the possibilities it presented. These were old woods, and many were the trees lying about like fallen soldiers. If only she could carve into one . . .

A chainsaw would do it.

She didn't have a chainsaw.

"I need a fucking chainsaw," she said to the forest.

Tools mattered. Just as one did not walk into Mordor, one did not sculpt with shitty, improper tools.

One required the right polishing abrasive for glass, a good loop and ribbon to carve clay, an ample vacuum or pressure chamber to create and finish the right molds and resin castings.

And Maddie wanted the right—the *best*—chainsaw for carving wood. Though she'd never dabbled in using a chainsaw for sculpting, she'd been hungry to learn, and so she knew what she needed: a carving chainsaw.

A regular chainsaw was good for butchering trees. But she was no butcher. No, Maddie needed a short-bladed saw, something that would let her do bigger cuts but also gouge the wood in order to make little ditches and dings, trenches and notches, all in the quest for detail. Something lightweight, with low vibration. She had a friend who swore by Stihl, but where the hell would she go? She didn't know this area.

Maybe Nate did.

So, off to find Nate she went.

She found him upstairs, staring balefully at the door to their bedroom. She put a hand on his shoulder—and he reacted like she'd just stuck him with a stun gun.

"Jesus!" he said, startled.

"No, not Jesus, just little old me," Mads said with a wink. He didn't laugh, and she gave him a quizzical look. "Oh, it's Serious Nate. I see, I see."

He shook his head, forced a smile. "I'm good. What's up?"

"I need a chainsaw."

"A what?"

"A chainsaw, like, to carve things."

"A chainsaw cuts things, not carves them."

"Don't mansplain shit to me, buddy. You might be the cop around here, but remember if something needs screwing in, or nailing, then I'm the one who ends up doing it." She smirked. "Oh my. Is all this home improvement getting you hot, too? Think about the things we can get up to in our new master bedroom. Screwing. Nailing. Laying some pipe." She winked cheekily, ran a hand up his arm to feel the firmness of his shoulder.

He pulled away sharply, as if burned.

"*Orrrrr* not."

He winced. "It's not our bedroom."

"It *is* our bedroom. Yours and mine." Disappointment darkened her face. It made sense, suddenly. She was good at seeing through Nate's nonsense. He didn't know it was nonsense, and he didn't mean any of it. But her husband had long tried to hide himself behind a pair of dark curtains, and she was the only one who could easily part them to see who was really standing there. "Oh, I get it. You still feel like it's *theirs*."

"Growing up, Dad was real clear, you didn't go in *his* bedroom. Not *theirs*. Not *Mom's*. He called it his. So I never went in. It feels like . . ." He seemed to struggle to find the right word. "An intrusion. He lived there and died there. It's not ours." He'd told her about Carl Graves being dead in there. And him waking up suddenly, too. One more gasp before going. She'd tried to be empathetic and understand what that was like. (She'd watched her own father die, after all.) But she also needed him to, well—to get his shit together, because this was about more than just him.

"Jesus, Nate. You're really not okay with this. Any of this."

"I'll be fine."

"You won't!" she said loudly, too loudly. She said it again, more quietly. "You won't. God, we shouldn't have moved here. Shouldn't have taken this house." She felt herself snap into default crisis mode. "We can still sell it. The movers haven't put much of our furniture down and, honestly, we don't have enough furniture to fill this place anyway. We'll tell the movers to put our shit in a, whaddyacallit, one of those Pods? We can store it until we find a place—"

But Nate shook his head. "No. I see what you're doing. Stop it. Listen, I'll get through it. We're keeping the house. We left the city. It's safer out here. Olly loves it; god, he's already different, you can feel it. It's quieter and the school is top-shelf, one of the best districts in the state. You need the space, the room, to do your work. Christ, I start a new job *Monday*. Olly starts school soon." He seemed resolute. "We're doing this."

She sized him up. Tried moving those dark curtains again to see if what he was saying, he meant.

Then Maddie put one steadying hand on his shoulder—and at the same time poked one accusing finger into his breastbone. Hard.

"Fine. Just get it together. And *keep* it together. We need this to work. You're not usually like this, and we're counting on you. You're bedrock. So be bedrock. Okay?"

The body language was clear—she'd support him, yes, but she also wouldn't put up with his shit.

He nodded.

"Hey. I get it. This is hard."

"It's fine."

"It's even harder to *admit* that it's hard."

"It . . . is hard. All of it."

She smiled. "There you go. See? Doesn't that feel a little better?"

"It does. Like—" He held up his thumb and forefinger, separated by a few millimeters. "A teeny-tiny itty-bitty little bit."

"I love you. We'll be okay."

"I love you, too."

"Tell you what," she said, turning to head back down the stairs. "You and me, we'll take the back bedroom for now."

"Where will Olly—"

"Sleep? I already told him he can take the attic."

"The attic, Mads, I dunno. It's old and dirty and hot—"

"Funny, that's how I describe you."

"Ha ha."

"Pssh. It'll be good for him. He's fifteen. He could use the space, the separation. It can be his world up there, not ours." She lowered her voice: "Besides, honestly, Dude's already ruining two gym socks a day. We may need to buy stock in Kleenex . . . or at least get a Costco membership to handle the overage."

Nate made a distasteful face, eager to change the subject. "I hope he does okay out here."

"He'll be great. He's already seeming calmer—"

Upstairs, their son screamed.

Oliver crept up the too-cramped staircase—and at the top reached up, found the pull-chain, and *cli-click,* let there be light. The attic was the length of the whole house, equivalent to two really big rooms.

The roof was pitched, so it was easy to walk down the center of the space, but the sides sloped all the way down to where you couldn't stand anymore. But already the movers had put some of his furniture up here, tucking his bed into one of the corners, against the slope of the roof. Oliver liked that. It felt safe, somehow. Hide against the wall, away from the world.

Despite the musty wood smell and the dust and the heat—god, it was an oven up here—Oliver kinda liked it. It was roomier than his bedroom in the city, that was for sure. He felt like he could *breathe* here.

He took a step toward the bed and—

"Oh, *shit*," he said, juggling his feet, backstepping suddenly. Seeing what was on the floor, he screamed for his parents.

The only light in the attic was the light from the one bare bulb, so when Dad came up, he was carrying a lamp from downstairs. He plugged in the lamp, and using it as a kind of flashlight, eased it toward the floor and illuminated what was there.

"See?" Oliver said.

"The hell are we looking at?" Mom asked, squeamish.

"Beats the heck out of me," Dad said.

It wasn't that they didn't *know* what they were looking at.

It's just that—*what* they were seeing didn't make much sense.

A long-dead mouse lay in the dust on the wooden floor. The carcass was desiccated, reduced to leathery skin draped over matchstick bones like a blanket. That wasn't the kicker, though—

Ants marched around the mouse's dead lump body in a nearly perfect circle, rows and rows of them in a mad carousel ride around the rodent's carcass. An endless whirl of insect traffic, going nowhere, but unable to stop. It called to mind a thing they did at the Quaker school—the maypole dance. Kids and teachers holding ribbons connected to a central pole, circling the pole and braiding the ribbons as they wound around and around.

"That is *weird*," Oliver said.

"Possums, ticks, mosquitoes, bats, and now a creepy ant circus? I renew my call to burn the house down," Mom said, but she, too, seemed rapt by the ant spiral.

"Should I kill 'em?" Dad asked.

Mom shrugged. "Maybe they're worshipping the mouse." She raised her voice in a high-pitched insectile whine: *"All hail King Nibbler, glory be to the Dead Rodent King!"*

"I'm sure it's something . . . normal," Dad said. He didn't sound sure.

Oliver, though, was already on his phone, googling *ants in a circle.* In half a second, a gaggle of YouTube videos popped up. "It's called an *ant mill* . . . or, let's see, an *ant vortex.* Looks like a natural phenomenon—they get, like, caught up in their own pheromone trail and it's like a track they can't leave, so they just wind around and around and around until they . . ." He kept reading, and as he did, he frowned. "Die. It's ant suicide."

"It's suicide all right," Dad said, snatching up the dead mouse in his paisley handkerchief. Then he stood up and stomped down a few good times, *whomp, whomp, whomp.* He tilted the lamp again to where the ants were now mashed in a circle. A few more continued to crawl, and Dad put his foot down one last time, twisting the ball like a smoker snuffing out a cigarette.

"We didn't have to kill them," Oliver said. His breath caught in his chest. He knew he shouldn't care about ants, of all things—they didn't have minds, or emotions, and he wasn't even sure they felt pain—but just the same, Dad's stomping felt so brutal. So *final.*

Oliver choked back a ball of stupid feelings. "Maybe with the mouse gone—"

"Olly, I can't save every ant. Like you said, they were on some kinda . . . death spiral."

"But—"

Dad put his hand on his shoulder. "Listen, Dude—" Dude, one of

Oliver's nicknames, along with Olly, Kiddo, Pal. "The movers are finishing up. They'll be bringing the rest of your furniture up soon, then you can start unpacking boxes. Okay? You good?"

"I'm good," Oliver said. He didn't want to say how much the ant thing rattled him. So he forced a smile and hoped they didn't notice. Even though in his mind's eye he saw those ants still turning, and turning, and turning, like a mad, broken wheel.

7

Quality of Soul

I want to talk some more about the ants," Dr. Parveena Nahid said on the screen of his laptop. This was their first official FaceTime video session since he moved. Dad wasn't too happy about paying full price despite only getting a video call, but at the same time he liked not having to drive Oliver back to the city. "They bothered you."

"I—yeah. But, it was like a week ago?" he said, trying to sound dismissive, like he didn't care. The laptop sat on his desk, and he sat on the chair. He planted his chin in the cup of his hands, elbows on the wood.

"Is it still bothering you?"

"Maybe. I dunno." He sighed. *Just be honest.* "A little."

"Why?"

"I don't know." He laughed, but it wasn't a funny laugh. "I know ants aren't like little people or anything, I don't think they have . . . I dunno. Pain or emotions or whatever. But just watching Dad stomp them out?" His palms were wet with sweat and he tried to dry them on his jeans.

"How'd it make you feel?"

"Not great, I guess."

"Are you familiar with Jainism?"

He shook his head.

She continued: "Jain Dharma, an old Indian religion. Little bit Buddhism, little bit Hinduism. There exists a principle among the

Jains called *ahimsa*. Mahavira, one of the earliest teachers of Jainism, wrote something, and it made me think of you: *There is no quality of soul more subtle than non-violence and no virtue of spirit greater than reverence for life.* Maybe that's what you have. A reverence for life."

"Yeah, but, like, that can get pretty crazy, too. If I can't handle someone stomping some ants . . ." His words trailed off.

"Are those your words? *I can't handle it.* Or do they belong to someone else?"

He shrugged.

"Because," she said, "it is quite often that people tell us something—a criticism, or worse, an insult—and it enters our head and—" Here she moved her hands around as if to indicate a butterfly flitting this way and that. The movement sent up a spray of pixels as some pieces froze before resolving. "The thought bounces around and around and around like an echo, and before too long, we begin to hear the echo in our own voice, not the voice of our critic. We adopt the insult as our own and forget it was given."

"You're saying it's from my dad."

"Am I?"

"It is. But it's not like—" He felt suddenly flustered. "I mean, he might not be wrong, okay? Maybe I could use a little toughening up." What was it Dad had said? *Armor.* "I need armor. If I can't hack a bunch of ants getting squashed, the world is going to roll over me like a . . . boulder. So maybe he's right. Like, I love Dad and he loves me, we get along pretty good. He's not an abuser—"

She held up both hands in a kind of *ease-off-the-throttle* surrender. "I suggested no such thing, Oliver."

"No, no, I know."

"Why did you say that? Why did you go there? To abuse, I mean."

"His dad, I think, abused him."

"Do you want to talk about that?"

Oliver shrugged. "Not much to talk about. Dad doesn't really talk about it. I just know I wasn't allowed to meet my grandfather, and then he died and now we live in his house."

"How is that going? Living in that house?"

He thought about it a long time. "It's weird. And kind of lonely. It's nice, too, don't get me wrong, it's like, I dig living in the woods and stuff. Sometimes I just walk and it's calm and quiet. Maybe too quiet, though. Mom's busy getting the house ready and fixing up this pole barn out back. Dad's . . . you know, he's Dad, he's got work and stuff."

"Have you made friends at school?"

"No?" he said, with some hesitation. He didn't want to admit that. "It's only been a week, though."

Dr. Nahid's smile broadened. "That's okay. Friends are good, though. Everybody needs friends, and so, dear Oliver, *we* are going to get you some friends."

8

A Game of Fish

Nate looked at himself in the mirror, in the beige shirt and forest green pants. The ranger's outfit was a far cry from the blues of a cop's uniform. It left him wondering just who he was looking at.

He felt so adrift out here in the sticks. It all added up: quitting the force, leaving the city, leaving their old apartment, moving back into a childhood home that felt like it belonged to a couple of dead people. Oliver seemed better, at least. Not that Nate had much of a chance to really interact with him. *Was* he really doing better? Shit, he didn't know.

He looked down on the sink. A brown fabric holster—well worn, not new—sat there on the corner. A Glock 19 rested inside it.

Nate belted it around his waist, and left the bathroom.

The office wasn't much to look at. One main room with a smaller conference room, a gender-non-specific bathroom off to the side. Two desks sat dead in the middle, facing each other. Walls of wood paneling. Floor of raggedy beige carpet.

His partner, Axel Figueroa—"Fig"—sat at the far desk. Fig was a stocky sonofabitch, thick in the neck, arms, and thighs, but short, too, giving him the look of a tree stump. His head was shorn all the way bald, and every part of him was as tan as a leather belt. He had the littlest damn mustache.

"They finally sent you the outfit," Fig said.

"Yeah, guess they figure I'm in it to win it," Nate said. He gave a halfhearted model twirl. "Think I look all right?"

Fig grunted and frowned.

Nate continued: "Guess you're stuck with me."

Another grunt. Fig went back to some kind of paperwork.

Making friends wherever I go, Nate thought. It had been like this for the last few weeks—most of their interactions were short, clipped, businesslike.

Nate sighed, and wandered by the bulletin board, which had all the expected information: a chart showing dates for hunting and fishing seasons and for hunter safety courses, plus alerts about invasive species. Mostly bugs. He saw one alert for something called a cardinal lanternfly, a red-winged tree sucker that had a real hunger for fruit trees and grape vines.

"You bored?" Fig asked.

"Oh. Just doing some reading."

"Got paperwork needs doing. Permits and the like."

"Sure," Nate said, though in his voice he heard the resignation. He went over and sat at the desk. Fig watched him.

"You come from Philly PD, that right?"

"That's right."

"Bet it was never boring there."

He heard the man's tone—it wasn't friendly. Fig was trying to goad Nate into something. What, exactly, he didn't know. But he saw no other choice but to play along. "Any job has its ups and downs, but sometimes we saw some things, had to deal with some rough business, sure."

"And I bet you had training to deal with all that."

"Of course."

"Well, you must have some real pull out here in the boonies, Nate. Most people who become a game warden—'wildlife conservation officer'—have to first go out to Harrisburg as a cadet, do the whole thing at the Leffler School. It's a yearlong program. Residency and all that. Take classes on wildlife management, agency admin, safety courses, and so on."

Nate suddenly felt a little uncomfortable. The man's stare pinned him to the wall like a cheap movie poster. "I assume you went through that program," Nate said.

"I did." Fig leaned forward. "But you didn't."

"And will that be a problem?"

Fig leaned back and crossed his arms. "No. You did your time in the trenches. Maybe not these trenches, but whatever. Bill Dingel out in Harrisburg said you fly, so you fly."

To Nate's eye, it still looked like a problem. "Listen, I'm not here to pee in your cereal. I'm not some ego guy; I don't think being a cop on the Philly streets gives me some kind of special knowledge or dispensation. I grew up around these parts and I hunted and I fished, but I don't claim to know this job. You do. It's your lead. You want me to do paperwork, I'll do paperwork. You want me to sit and stare at the wall, I'll stare at the wall. I'll collect deer turds for samples, or pick garbage out of ditches. You're the boss, boss."

"And yet, I'm not the boss, am I? Our job descriptions are the same, Nate. Job *titles,* the same. Salary? The same." He laughed, but it wasn't a happy sound. "Shoot, you probably get paid more."

"Why would that be?"

"Don't make me say it."

"Say what?"

Fig leaned forward again, hands flat on the desk. He started to say something, turned away, and then must've thought *fuck it,* because he committed and spoke the words: "You're white."

"So?"

"Really? That's your answer. *So.*"

"It's not an answer—it's a question."

Fig nodded in a way that was frustrated, fed up, and dismissive. "Forget it."

"I don't wanna forget it. I wanna talk about it."

"No, you *don't* wanna talk about it. Shit, *I* don't wanna talk about it. I'd much rather live in a world where I don't have to talk about it, think about it, *experience* it. But I also wish I could eat ice cream every day and that my BO smelled like clean laundry. We're moving past it."

Nate could see he was serious about it, and he held up both hands in surrender. "Okay. You got it."

"You know what?" Fig said with a sniff. "I'm bored, too." With a jangle of metal, he snatched his keys off the desk. "You want something to do? I got something. You got your uniform now, so we can do this for real. Let's head out on patrol."

"Patrol for what?"

"I dunno, Nate, fish and game problems."

"Like a halibut driving a car? Deer running an illegal gambling ring?"

"Great, you're a funny guy." Way he said it, Fig didn't think it was great at all. He pointed to the door with a finger gun. "Just walk out of here and get in the Bronco. I gotta hit the head. I'll meet you out there."

9

The Rattle of Dice

Oliver felt like he was drowning.

His old school was small. One class per grade. But this place, Upper Bucks High—UBH—was three grades, with three classes per grade. Total number of kids: 1,500.

And Oliver didn't know a single one of them.

Obviously he'd met a few. It was almost October. He knew the *names* of his classmates, and had paired up with a few to do chem lab or to read an Emily Dickinson poem or whatever. But that was it. He was a nobody among somebodies. They all knew one another. These people all had *their* people already. He had no one. Worse, sometimes standing in the hallway, it reminded him of those last days at Rustin, when they had the ALICE drill—how he had collapsed in the hallway sobbing like a stupid little baby. How he had pissed himself. Maybe they'd heard that story. Maybe all these kids knew about him already.

Panic rose in him.

But then he heard Dr. Nahid's voice in his head: *We're going to make you some friends, Oliver*. She said to him, it was like encountering a snake in the woods: *It* was more afraid of *you* than *you* were of *it*. The therapist explained that to be "the new kid" felt alienating and isolating, but the truth was, the new kid had a mystique. But that meant he had to take the first step: walk up to someone, introduce himself, and see what happened.

She said, *Pick someone, someone you think you might like. It's okay if you end up not being friends.*

He knew just who he was going to pick.

Lunchtime.

Elbows jostled him as kids pushed past, streaming into the cafeteria. Their voices formed a dull, gabbling roar.

Again, that feeling of being in a crowd, but also alone. Again the gentle black ocean of teenage pain.

He stood with his tray in hand. Food that he probably wouldn't eat, because his stomach was too knotted up.

And there, ahead of him, was the table.

The D&D table.

They played every day while they ate.

Two boys, two girls. Character sheets next to lunch trays. A scattering of dice.

Next to one of the boys sat an empty chair.

Olly found himself standing behind it.

"Can I—" God, did his voice just squeak? He cleared his throat. "Hey, uhh, mind if I sit down?"

All four turned to him.

Baleful stares.

The one right next to him, a roly-poly pill bug of a boy in a gray T-shirt and gray sweatpants, nodded. "We're in the middle of a game."

"Yeah, no, I know, that's why I wanted to sit? To watch?"

The five looked at one another. One of the young women, an Asian girl with a Nyan Cat T-shirt and short-cropped hair, eyed him up like he was a precious mystery. She popped a tater tot in her mouth. "You play?" she asked, chewing.

"Yeah." Then he looked again at the chair with a questioning expression. Again the five looked to one another, and the guy at the end, a thickset Black dude with sleepy eyes and a mop of hair, nodded.

"Sure, sit," he said.

He was the DM, Oliver figured. The Dungeon Master, the guy running the game and telling the story. All he had in front of him was an old beat-ass Garbage Pail Kids folder with a sheaf of papers tucked into it. No character sheet of his own.

Oliver sat.

"I'm Olly," he said.

And then, it was a like a stubborn soap bubble going *pop*. The others introduced themselves—

Pill bug was Steven Rubel.

Nyan Cat shirt was Hina Hirota.

The DM was Caleb Wright.

And the last was Chesapeake Lockwood, aka Chessie. Blond girl with curls, teeth encased in Invisalign braces.

Chessie leaned across and asked him, almost conspiratorially, "What character do you play?"

Olly answered: "Last game I played a Dragonborn Warlock—"

"Ugh," Steven said.

"Why, what's wrong with that?" Olly asked.

"It's—it's just so obvious."

"Says the guy who plays a Tiefling Rogue whose backstory is *orphan looking to get revenge*," Hina said.

"Shut ahhhp," Steven retorted. Of all of them, the pain in him was the darkest: It twitched like a raven with a broken wing.

Caleb shook his head. "Nah, man. Dragonborn Warlock is a legit build. I mean, Devil's Sight and Darkness, you know. That's all right."

"Caleb likes the mechanical side," Hina said, licking tot grease from her fingers. "I care about the story. My character is a Gnome Bard named Esmerelda Sprinklefingers, and she plays the valachord."

"The valachord is from Star Wars," Steven said. "Not that she knew that before she started playi—"

A tot bounced off his head. Hina hissed: "Don't *fake geek girl* me, you fucking turtle."

"Yeah, man," Caleb said. "Not cool. "By the *way,*" Caleb added by way of protest, "I'm the fuckin' DM, okay? I care about story. I made *up* Arduinia. Don't do me dirty like that."

Hina shrugged and continued. "So! Esmerelda is the daughter of a famous Gnome inventor mother—her father is unknown, and *may* be nonexistent, as I think her nativity is, like, magical in origin? Whatever. Point is, I do not care about her stats, I only care that she and her dragoncat, Stinky, have rad adventures and find true love on the high seas of Arduinia—"

They all laughed.

And like that, lickety-quick, they got back into their game. Sheets out, dice rolling, initiative order called, monstrous vampiric merfolk besieging the characters' stolen pirate boat. Olly wasn't sure but—

Maybe, just maybe—

He had found his people.

Dr. Nahid was right, holy shit.

It felt pretty good.

That, until a shadow darkened the table. A tall, broad-shouldered guy in a Ron Jon Surf Shop shirt came up behind Steven, and put both of his big-knuckled hands on the back of the other boy's chair before moving them to Steven's shoulders, gripping them tightly enough to cause the other boy pain.

Oliver knew him, or of him, at least: Graham Lyons. He was on the baseball team—and baseball, here, was pretty big. Much bigger than football or track.

Everyone looked up at Graham as Steven tried—and failed—to squirm out of his grip. Graham wasn't alone, either: coming up behind him was a muscle-bound Italian-looking bro—hair buzzed, his eyebrows like permanent marker lines squeaked onto his too-tan forehead, bulging arms crossed like a couple of ship cannons pointing in opposite directions. Graham Lyons had pain in him, a deep pit in his middle. But the other guy, the meathead? He had pain running through him: a whole circulatory system of anger, misery, and hurt.

"Look at these fucking spergs," Mr. Muscles said. The pain in the meathead reacted like it had an electrical charge run through it.

Graham Lyons said, "What're you nerds up to?"

"C'mon, man," Caleb said. "We're playing a game, fuck off."

"Fuck off? Fuck off." Graham feigned offense and injury. "Wow, that hurts me, Caleb. We used to be friends."

"Yeah, in like, fifth grade. Then you turned into a dick."

"I swear, you're really hurting my feelings."

Then Steven chimed in, under his breath but loud enough: "You don't *have* feelings to hurt, *Graham*—"

It was like a switch flipped. The muscular one rushed forward, thrusting his face into Steven's, only a hair's breadth between their two noses. The darkness in him swelled up. "The fuck did you say? Little cuck bitch piece of shit. You fat fucking turd faggot-ass—"

Graham put an easing hand on Mr. Muscles's shoulder. "Hey, it's fine, Alex. Like Caleb said, they're just playing a game. What game is it? D&D? That's some deep nerd shit, isn't it?"

Olly felt himself speaking.

"It's cool now."

They all looked at him, panicked. The fear in them shimmered. Like light strobing through sickly fog.

As if to say, *Oh no.*

As if to say, *You shouldn't have spoken.*

"What did you say?" Graham asked sharply.

"I said, it's cool now. D&D isn't just . . . nerd shit. It's . . . like, celebrities play it. It's a big thing in L.A. A lot of actors and writers—"

"This isn't L.A. You're new, right? That where you're from, L.A.?"

"Leave him alone, Graham," Chessie said.

"Shut up, Chessie. You shouldn't be hanging with these little shits anyway. Let the new kid answer."

"I'm from Philly," Oliver said.

"Ooh. Philly tough guy." Graham snapped into a bad Philly accent: *"Fullelphia. Wooder ice. Go Iggles."*

"I'm not tough, and I don't have the accent, I just—"

"Uh-huh. Whatever. Let's see what this is—"

Then Graham reached over Oliver's shoulder to snatch up Hina's character sheet—"Hey!" she cried out—but it was too late. He had it.

And when he pulled the sheet away, his elbow jabbed right into Oliver's eye. *Pop.* Olly saw a starburst supernova behind the dark of his lid. He cried out, shoving his chair backward—

But it met some resistance. Not just Graham's middle but—Olly could feel something else. A gentle vibration as something went *crunch.*

Suddenly, Graham was crying out, staggering into the lunch table behind him. He was shaking his hand and hissing a stream of vulgarities like he just got a finger pinched in a door. "Fuck fuck *fuck.* Shit. My fucking finger. This prick fucked up my *finger.*"

That uncorked the bottle.

Suddenly, it was chaos—Alex was on Oliver, pulling him all the way out of his chair and slamming him up against the lunch table. Dice scattered. Alex lifted a fist, a *big* damn fist that threatened to crash into Oliver's face like a meteor, but someone grabbed the meathead, pulling him back—it was Caleb. A whistle blew. Footsteps and yelling. Alex dragged Oliver off the table and someone's sneaker punted into his middle, blasting the air out of him. As he tried not to vomit, teachers swarmed the area, and what had begun had now ended.

Or so he thought.

10

Chainsaw Owls

Maddie bought herself a fucking chainsaw. It was a Stihl 192 carving saw.

Real light. Rear handle. A short black blade. Anti-vibration system in play. And also, oops oh shit, it was four hundred dollars.

Expenses were tight—okay, they paid a buck for the house, but with moving expenses and they needed some new furniture and oh, right, their first tax payment would be due in a week—but this was for art. This was her *work*. And she knew that what the work needed was this saw.

It sang to her, like a metal-toothed angel.

She sang right back to it. "I love you, little chainsaw," she told it in a singsongy voice, and gave it a little kiss before packing it in her Subaru and taking it home. Where it would *feed*.

And oh, *did it feed*.

She found a log, one that wasn't rotten, one that looked like it had just fallen in the spring or summer. Using the saw she cut a hunk of it out—*vvvvt, vvvvt*, like a slice out of a hot dog—and rolled it away from the body. Then she cut the tree's own stump into something approaching a level work surface, and with an old *heave-ho* she shouldered the cut piece up onto its own base. (Which felt suddenly grim—like handing a dead body its own severed hand. "Hi, can you hold this for a second?")

With the log propped, she revved the saw once more. The buzz of it tickled the inside of her arm bones.

And then she cut.

She did not approach with any expectation of what she wanted to make. Sometimes the work emerged out of intent—the desire to make a specific thing. But just as often, what she created was not of her design, but, rather, was like archaeology: It was more of an *uncovering,* as if the artist's job was simply to find what the material was trying to hide. And then wrestle it to the surface, so that all could see.

Or, in her case, cut the trapped spirit free.

Because that's what this felt like, specifically. As if she was *releasing* something. What it was, she didn't know. Didn't *care.* She just kept on and on, a swipe here, a cut there, a twist of the saw, a notch, a tap—and it came faster and faster, her hands feeling numb, her mind doing loops, the blade spraying splinters against her safety glasses as something began to emerge—

Two spire ears—

Dark deep-set eyes under a vengeful frowning brow—

Claws, talons, gripping the base—

Wings, a beak, an *owl,* that's what this was, it was an owl that she found in the wood—chips and dust flying, the saw growling, making its cuts, marking the feathers, shaping wings, and faster and faster she *freed* the owl—

Then she was lost to it. It took her away with the roar of blood in her ears, a roar like floodwaters rushing and rising.

11

Circles, Stovepipes, and the Strange Smell of Funnel Cake

Fig's truck was a hellacious mess. Papers and fast-food wrappers. A toolbox in the second row seat. Couple coffee cups here and there. Soda bottles, too—wait, no, not soda. Kombucha.

"You drink kombucha?" Nate asked, a little surprised.

"I do."

"My wife, Maddie, drinks it sometimes. It always looks like a bottle of mop water with rotten coleslaw floating in it."

"That's the culture. The mother patch, or scoby."

"And you drink that?"

"I do."

"Does it taste good?"

"It's fine, just don't worry about it," Fig snapped. The pickup barreled down a windy back road. Old farms dotted the sprawling hills here. Ahead was Dark Hollow Lane, where the old Dark Hollow covered bridge sat—Fig pulled the truck down that narrow one-lane road. Finally Fig sighed and said, "Honestly, kombucha tastes like electric shit."

"That's descriptive."

"I dunno how else to describe it. It's got this buzzy, vinegar thing. It's fucked up. And the culture . . ." He made a face like he had just licked a cat's asshole. "God in heaven."

"So why the hell do you drink it?"

"My wife, Zoe. She makes me. Wants me to be healthy."

"This truck doesn't make you look too healthy, I gotta tell you."

"Don't be a judgy prick. Most of the time, my truck *is* my office, so you make do however you can." He gestured toward the glove compartment. "I have protein bars, mixed nuts, other stuff in there. And a bottle of raspberry kombucha if you want one."

"I think I'd rather drink pond water. Didn't you just tell me it tastes like shit?"

"Electric shit." Fig shrugged. "Hey, it gives me energy."

"I'll stick to coffee, thanks."

The truck pulled through the old red covered bridge, the paint on it peeling in long curls. Inside, it was a haven for spiders—the upper eaves of the bridge were woven with endless ribbons and bows of web. The uneven boards of the bridge went *whud whud whud* under the tires, and the pickup's shocks didn't do well with the bumps—Nate's teeth clacked together.

They came out the far side of it, and turned north on Lenape Road, taking them past Ramble Rocks park, and the old stone train tunnel. The tunnel hadn't been used since the 1940s, and the tracks that once cut through there had long been pulled up. The tunnel now was part of the park: a lighted jogging path cut right through it. That was fairly recent, though, because for a long time, the tunnel was dark, and the path through it was overgrown. Which only accentuated the stories everyone told about it.

Nate remembered the tales that said the tunnel was haunted, that a conductor in the thirties had heard someone calling his name, and so he looked out the window. What he didn't know, though, was that a piece of stone in the tunnel wall had come loose. A big block of it, still there, still out of place. The conductor looked out just in time for his face to meet the stone—and it decapitated him. Head came off. Train kept rolling.

The tunnel became a place of dares: Kids said that if you walked the tunnel at midnight, you might hear a train whistle, and if you didn't run the half-mile length of darkness at top speed, the conductor would ride along in his ghost train and—

Choo-choo, choppity-chop—

Cut off your head, too.

But as with all things, it wasn't the spooky stories that got to Nate. It was the real-life ones, because, routinely, real-life stories were far worse than the imagined ones. The spooky stories were an escape from the truth.

And that truth was this: Older kids had another name for the tunnel—they called it *the murder tunnel*.

That was thanks to a killer named Edmund Walker Reese. When Nate was a kid, Reese killed four girls in that park. Nailed them to trees (with, as the story went, ninety-nine nails apiece), and then did the final dispatching of them with a pick-ax. Everyone said he killed those girls in the tunnel, which wasn't accurate—apparently, he snatched one of the girls, the first of them, as she took a shortcut through the tunnel on the way home. But stories had a way of getting their teeth into people, true or not, and it became "common knowledge" that he killed all those girls right there in that tunnel.

And so, it became *the murder tunnel*.

Edmund Reese got caught when the fifth girl escaped his capture. The state electrocuted him for it, but even after he was dead and gone, the stories lingered.

And people used those stories. Nate remembered one particular piece of shit, Dave Jacoby, who said he was gonna drag Susan Pulaski, his homecoming date, out to the murder tunnel because she wouldn't "put out." Nate heard the bastard say it to her that day in school. Even now he could still hear that little piggy-squeal voice of Jacoby's. So he took a fist and whopped the sonofagun right in the piggy nose. Blood squirted out like the poor prick had a couple ketchup packets up there.

(He also remembered Susan giving the bastard a good kick to the nuts when he was down on the ground, which was extra satisfying.)

Nate got in deep shit for it. But it was worth it.

"You live around here, don't you?" Fig asked, cutting off Nate's train of thought as he reimagined the satisfying sound of Dave Jacoby's nose under his knuckles. Fig must've looked at his personnel file.

"That's right. Far side of Ramble Rocks here."

"That's only a couple minutes down the road. You lived across from the park growing up?"

"I did." *And, I live there now, again,* he thought grimly.

"You were there when—"

"When the Reese killings went down, yup."

"That's messed up. You heard what they said about him." Fig gave Nate a look. A knowing look, as if to say, *Yeah, you know.*

"About his execution, you mean."

"I didn't even grow up around here and I heard that story."

Story went like this: Edmund Walker Reese sat there in the electric chair, the last person to be electrocuted in the state of Pennsylvania before they switched over to lethal injection. They flipped the switch. He lit up like the Ghostbusters' proton packs, but then—

Poof. He was gone. All that was left were char marks in the chair where he once sat, and the smell of—

"Funnel cake," Fig said, wiggling his fingers up off the steering wheel. "What a strange detail."

"Let me be the one to ruin the story for you," Nate said. "My father was a prison guard at Blackledge, where they sent Reese to Death Row. And I promise you, he died there in that chair."

"Your father said so?"

"Yeah." *Once I got up the balls to ask him,* Nate thought. That was another day that stood out in his memory. It was a year or two after Edmund Reese fried. He saw his father in the den, messing around with fishing lures and flies—not that he ever actually went fishing, but he talked about it a lot. The story about Reese not dying in the chair but rather disappearing had reached the school, and once Nate heard it, he knew he had to ask his father. So he screwed up his courage—you didn't interrupt Carl Graves when he was busy, and it seemed he was always busy (even if "busy" just meant drinking Crown Royal Canadian whiskey). But Nate had a burning need to know, just so he could tell the kids how dumb that story was. So, he asked. And then Carl turned toward him, eyes narrowed, a burned-down cigarette in one hand and a fishing lure caged in the other.

Nate had blurted the question out, but Carl seemed to chew on it. All the old man said was, "That story is nonsense. Reese died there in that chair. And you should know better."

It made Nate feel good for a second because he was right. "I *did* know better," he said, not to talk back or be smart, but because he was proud and he wanted his father to be proud. He was about to say, *I told the other kids it was just a story,* but then his head rocked back as his father slapped him. Felt like he was hit by a dictionary, *whap.* He tasted blood from his split lip.

His father hissed, his breath rotten, "What you know wouldn't fill a baby's shoe. What goes on in that prison, what I see, what I have to *do*—?"

"Dad, I—" Nate said, his eyes filling with tears.

The old man raised his hand again, but before he swung, he told Nate to get out of there. Which he did. He turned tail and hauled ass not just out of the room, but out of the house. Running, blinking back tears, and trying not to acknowledge that his throat was filled with some foul knot of shame, frustration, and sadness. He was twelve years old.

He didn't tell Fig any of that, though. He just said again, nope, didn't happen.

"So it's just horseshit," Fig said.

"That's right."

"I guess that's good to know," Fig said. "Just the same, a little bit of a bummer, you know? Like a little magic is gone from the world."

"World's not magic, Fig. And take some solace that Reese fried, good and crispy, for what he did to those—"

He was about to say *girls,* but just as Fig was rounding the bend onto Butchers Road, he slammed the brakes hard and Nate had to brace himself against the dusty dashboard.

"Fig, what the hell—"

But he didn't need long to figure out why Fig stopped.

There, in the road, staggered a whitetail deer. A buck. Immediately, Nate could see that it wasn't healthy. From a broad six-pointed rack of antlers hung gooey strings of raw, red flesh—that, he knew, wasn't entirely unusual, though. That was just the animal's velvet coming off. Though it was a little late in the season for it, around early September a buck deer worked his antlers against trees to scrape off their soft velvet lining. No, what made the animal look unhealthy was the rheumy gauze over its eyes, and the way its head sagged and drool slicked its long muzzle and thick neck. The animal was thin, too; Nate could see the outline of its ribs under its hide.

It stumbled about in a clumsy circle. From one side of the road to the next, it circled an invisible point, and Nate had a hard time suppressing a chill despite the heat of the day—because sure enough, his mind wandered to those ants in Olly's room. Circling a dead mouse.

He knew one thing had nothing to do with the other.

(And yet.)

Slowly, Fig got out of the truck. Nate followed, unsure if there was some kind of protocol here he wasn't aware of. Already the other officer had unsnapped his holster.

The buck didn't seem to notice them at all. It continued to drool and froth and stagger along its invisible orbit.

"We need to be careful. That deer isn't right," Nate said.

Fig nodded. In a soft voice—softer than what Nate had used—he said, "Probably CWD." Nate gave him a quizzical *WTF* look, and Fig filled in the acronym: "Chronic wasting disease. Zombie deer, they call them. Not really zombies, you know. But sick in the head. Prion disease like mad cow."

"And what's the plan?"

Gently, Fig drew his Glock. "This is the plan."

Nate nodded and unsnapped his holster, but did not yet draw.

"Deer is moving slow. You should be able to line up a clean shot."

"The CDC might want the brain, so I'm going for the lung. Should take the breath out of it and drop it to its knees."

Fig lined up a shot, and already Nate could see that the other man didn't shoot too often. He had a thumb-over-thumb grip, which was better for beginners but, he felt, gave you less control than straight thumbs. His hands even shook a little as Fig drew a few shallow breaths.

"You're all right," Nate said. "Take it easy. Take your time. Here, he's coming around."

Sure enough, the deer stumbled to the side of the road and began doubling back again, still oblivious to their presence.

"He's showing you his broadside—line up your shot and—"

Pop.

The pistol kicked in Fig's hand. The deer staggered sideways by a half step, and stopped walking forward as a hole bloomed in its side. Blood trickled out, darkening its hide. Nate's ears rang from the shot.

The deer turned its head toward Fig.

It bleated, just like any deer making a warning noise, but this was a wet and gurgling sound that blasted ropes of foamy red snot from its nose.

"I don't think it felt that one," Nate said, a little more hurriedly. "Take another shot, Fig."

Fig squeezed the trigger—

But the gun didn't fire. Instead, the slide froze halfway—and now, Nate realized he never saw the spent shell from the first shot eject. Never heard the *tink-tink* as it hit the ground.

The gun was jammed.

Shit.

The deer lowered its head. Another red, frothy bleat from its muzzle. It stomped one black hoof down on the asphalt.

"Nate," Fig said, panic in his voice. He took a step back, toward the car. He tried racking the slide—the wrong thing to do—and it only jammed the gun further. He tried firing once more, but the weapon wouldn't respond.

The buck launched himself forward, and it wouldn't take but three long steps before it had Fig pinned to the side of the Bronco—

Bang.

A shot from Nate's Glock punched through the animal's eye, and out the other. A red mist hung in the air for a second even as the animal hit the ground, skidding forward, leaving a dark crimson streak and a growing pool underneath it. Fig pressed his back to the front bumper of the Bronco, half-poised like he was ready to climb up it to escape the buck.

"Jesus, shit," he said.

Nate lowered the Glock and eased it back into the holster. "You had a stovepipe jam. It can happen in the Glocks. Can't clear it just by racking the slide, either. Sorry I wasn't faster."

"Faster, shit, Nate, I was about to get pinned to that truck like a postcard to a bulletin board. The fact that next time I take a drink I won't turn into a sprinkler tells me you moved plenty fast enough, so thanks."

Nate walked over to his partner and the two of them looked down at the animal. Its tongue thrust unceremoniously out of its mouth.

And then, its muzzle moved.

"Shit!" Fig said, taking a half step back.

The muzzle rippled and bulged—

One of the buck's nostrils swelled up, and something wet and glistening appeared—a fat maggot, damn near the size of Nate's pinky finger, birthed itself from the animal's nose, and plopped onto the ground. But it had friends, too. One by one, maggot after maggot squeezed from the nose of the deer and followed the others as they moved in a single line along the asphalt. "Nasal bots, I think," Fig said, grimacing in disgust. "Fly larvae."

"That's nasty," Nate said. "Maybe that's what was driving the deer nuts? I'd think that many worms up in my head would make me crazy."

"Nah, they don't go into the brain."

And with that, the last one came laboring forth from the black, moist nose hole and got in line with its maggoty cohorts.

The two men watched as the grubs, in their line, moved inch by inch toward the center of the road. The first one began to turn just so—going from a straight line to a circular path. The others followed along. *Like the ants,* Nate thought, horrified. *Like the deer.* Fig didn't seem to notice. He got in the truck, got on the phone.

Nate, meanwhile, just stared until his own phone rang.

It was Olly's school.

12

Fugue State

The darkness pulled away like a curtain from a window, the light coming in bold and bright as Maddie's eyes popped open.

She lurched forward, sitting up, hearing the sounds of the forest around her: cicadas and tree crickets and squabbling catbirds. The chainsaw sat near her on the ground. She felt it. The engine was cold.

How long was I out?

She turned to the sculpture, to the owl she carved and—

And it wasn't there.

Gone. *Poof.* As if it had never existed.

The signs of her efforts were everywhere: triangles of carved-out wood, plus a scattered spray of woodchips, splinters, and sawdust. All around, like a protective circle. She hadn't made it up. Hadn't imagined it. Maddie had made *something* here. Her mind, frantic, tried to recollect the pieces, tried to pore through the darkness to find memories—but none emerged from the shadow and fog except one, and this one was not a full memory but rather just the suggestion of a memory:

This is not the first time this has happened, has it?

She knew it wasn't. Knew it in her heart. But she had no memory of any other blackouts—it was just this mad certainty that no, this was not the first time she'd blacked out making something.

Fuck, fuck, fuck.

Her mouth tasted strange. Like after eating too much pineapple—a mad acid burn, something sour and sweet, but something like metal, too. That stainless-steel blood taste. Somewhere, she heard a sound: a distant buzzing. Not like the chainsaw but like wasps inside walls . . .

My phone, she realized. It was her phone, vibrating on a nearby stone.

She stood, woozily, and snatched it up. Already she spied a whole line of missed texts and calls. Calls from the school. Calls and texts from Nate. The last one from Nate: Olly was in a fight, where the hell r u?

What the fuck happened?

Where the hell was I?

And strangest of all, where did her owl sculpture go?

13

Turtles All the Way Down

Oliver sat outside the principal's office. Cement wall behind him. And Caleb Wright sitting next to him.

"You're gonna wanna put something on that," Caleb said.

Oliver winced. He touched the tender ring of pain around the eye and its socket. "Yeah." He paused. "Thanks for stepping up, by the way."

"Man, fuck those guys. Buncha rich prick assholes."

"I notice they're not here with us."

"Yeah, funny how that works."

They sat there for a little while. It was the gym teacher who broke up the fight—a big, muscular woman, Mrs. Norcross—and next thing Olly knew, they were all being shepherded to the principal's office. The two aforementioned asshole bullies, Graham Lyons and Alex Amati, went in first. When they came out, they sneered and gave Oliver and Caleb side-eye so sharp it could open an artery. Oliver saw that Graham's left hand hung by his side, curled up—like he was trying to pretend it was normal, and that it didn't hurt, but the finger didn't look right. Like it had bent the wrong way and . . . stayed the wrong way.

Oliver felt bad. Despite everything, he felt bad. (*My default emotion,* he thought, dully.) He almost called after them to say he was sorry, but he couldn't quite summon the apology. And then they were gone.

Meanwhile, Caleb and Oliver were told that the school was calling their parents. *Great.*

"I know Graham Lyons," Oliver said. "Who's the other one?"

"Alex Amati. Rich bitch. Baseball players, both of 'em. Central Bucks does football, but here at Upper Bucks, we can't hang with that, so the thing is baseball, and those two are all-stars on the team . . . whiiiich apparently makes them fuckin' royalty."

"Oh."

"Not great enemies to have."

"No, I guess not."

"Making a bang-up impression." Caleb laughed.

Oliver laughed, too. It was funny. A little.

"Ay, man," Caleb said, "you ever want a group to game with, you got one. We meet Saturdays, usually. It's not all D&D—that's just our lunch game. Sometimes we do Star Wars or some indie Evil Hat shit. We play board games, too—Gloomhaven or Betrayal at House on the Hill, maybe Godsforge. Failing all that, we say fuck it and play Magic."

"Thanks. That'd be awesome. I play all those."

"In this fucked-up school, this whole fucked-up world, best thing I can tell you is: We all need some friends."

I have a friend! Oliver thought, over and over again, trying like hell not to wear his excitement on his face lest he somehow look tragically uncool. But the triumph he felt was undeniable. He couldn't wait to tell Dr. Nahid.

Somehow he just nodded when Caleb offered a fist bump and did not vibrate to pieces when returning it.

"Olly."

He turned to see—

His father.

Dad looked at him. Looked *pissed.* Emanating the red of a cape you'd use to summon a bull.

"That your pop?" Caleb asked in a low voice.

"Yeaaaah."

"Shit, kid. You dead."

The two of them sat across the desk from Principal Myers, a stout woman with a tangle of hair best described as "Garfield-colored."

Dad sat silent as a cemetery.

Crap.

He's pissed at me.

"Your son was involved in a fight today, provoking two of the school's best students—" She suddenly corrected herself. "Well, *one* of the school's best students, and two of our best baseball players." Oliver had to guess that Alex was not the best student; though he understood people were not always as they appeared, Alex seemed like he had the intellectual capacity of a backhoe. Graham seemed sharper. She went on: "That is not a good first impression, Oliver Graves. Your first month at a new school, getting into a fight? Is this what we are to expect of you?"

"I didn't get into a fight," Oliver protested, turning to his father. "I didn't. Dad, I swear, I don't start fights. I found a table of kids playing games, and so I went up and they seemed cool, but then these two guys came over calling us all kinds of names—sperg and faggot and—"

"Language," Principal Myers chastened.

"Sorry. That's just what they said—"

"I have no choice but to suspend you for this."

"What!?"

"The rules are clear, if you had read them. We do not condone violence and have a zero-tolerance policy of—"

Wham.

Dad's fist came down on the desk, rattling the picture frames and pen-and-pencil jar. His chest heaved. He thrust a finger at the principal.

"You'll do no such thing," he said.

"Excuse me?" she asked, shocked.

"You heard me. My son isn't suspended. He'll be back tomorrow, bright and early, ready for school, ready to learn. Or else."

"Or else?" She leaned forward, clearly flummoxed. Stammering, she said, "I don't know where you get off, thinking you can threaten me—"

"I was a cop. I know the system. I know how this all works. And I was a kid, too, and I remember this same old bullshit way back when. Bullies mess with some poor kid, and then that victim of those bullies gets it just as bad as—or usually worse than!—the bullies ever do. We're going to chalk this up to a very bad day on everyone's part, and then we move on. Because I know lawyers. I know the best worst lawyers. The kind who know every ugly, slimy trick in the book. Hell, a few of them still owe me favors. You want them crawling up your ass? Then test me. Test my son. Give him suspension, detention, anything less than a smile, and you'll see."

Principal Myers's mouth formed a grim line. "Fine," she said, finally. "We can chalk this up to a bad day."

Oliver wanted to cry out in joy.

"Thank you," Oliver said.

"Mm-hmm," was Myers's response.

"I'm gonna take my son home now. Get him a bag of peas or something for that shiner. Have a very nice day, Principal Myers."

"Yes. Yes. Goodbye."

The two of them sat at a park bench outside an ice cream shop— Sundae School, har har—eating a couple cones. Rocky road for Dad, and for Oliver, rainbow sherbet. Oliver held the cone in one hand, and with the other, he pressed a bag of ice—dutifully provided by an employee in the shop—to his bruised eye.

They hadn't said much since leaving school.

And weren't saying much now.

"Ice cream's good," Dad said.

"I can tell, you've kinda got it—" Oliver made a swirly gesture at his beard.

"Hey, the beard is a flavor saver. I'll be enjoying this ice cream all day." He winked.

"It's kinda hot out."

"It is."

"Climate change, I guess."

Dad shrugged. "I guess." Then he seemed to settle into something, some decision, when he blurted out: "All right, Dude, there are three kinds of people in this world."

"Uh, okay."

"Just—just bear with me. So, let's say you find a turtle crossing the road. One kind of person will just drive past it. They'll try not to hit it, but they won't bother with it. There's another kind of person who will stop the car, get out, help the little shell-head across the road. Maybe they pick it up or maybe they just divert traffic. Then there's the third kind of person. Kind of person who sees that turtle, turns the wheel toward it, and drives over the damn thing. Crushes it like a peanut butter cup. Just to hear it *pop*. Now, most people are the first kind. They won't go out of their way to do good or bad. And some people—like a couple of the cops I worked with—they're definitely the third kind. Might even take a spin in the car specifically to look for turtles to drive over. And you—"

"I'm the second kind." It wasn't a brag. Oliver wasn't even sure if it was a good thing or not.

"You are, kiddo. You are. That's why I stood up for you back there. Because I know the kind of prick who gave you trouble. Graham Lyons, he's the third kind. Coincidentally, I knew his father. Rick. Bully just like his kid."

"I made a friend," Oliver said, changing the subject.

"Good. Me too, maybe." Then Dad checked his phone. "Dang. I dunno why your mother's not answering her texts. Finish up. We better head home."

14

That Nagging Feeling

Once again, bedtime. The house made its creaks and crackles, its arthritic complaints, its small groans of time and fatigue and maybe the pain of some deeper memory.

Maddie was unsettled. She couldn't get into her book. Books were usually a way for her to power her own brain down and borrow someone else's for a while. She had other techniques, too: yoga, meditation, *The Great British Bake Off,* and, of course, *her work.*

Now, though, her work was not a place of solace and succor: It was another burden, one that left her with more questions than answers. So, to the book she returned.

Tonight she settled on *Robbing the Bees,* by Holley Bishop, a nonfic about the history of beekeeping. Last time she picked it up she'd just read a bit about how when a new queen is born in a beehive, that new queen goes on an assassination binge, murdering her as-yet-unborn royal competitors before slaying the old queen—her own mother.

But now, the words just weren't clicking. She looped over a single paragraph again and again, certain each time that she'd really read it, and each time failing to even parse what each word said.

She kept revisiting the events of the day. In particular, that one troubling point: She blacked out. With a *running chainsaw* in her *hand.* And then when she awoke, her creation was gone. The only answer was someone stole it. They must've. Had someone knocked her out? How did that even make any sense at all? She *remembered* the point she blacked out—or, at least, she could recall the last memory she had, which was her carving out feathers, shaping out the wings, and then—

Had she heard a rush of wings?

Damn it, Maddie. Think.

"We gonna talk about it?" Nate asked suddenly.

"What?"

"What? What do you mean, what?" He sat up with a grunt. "Where were you today? School called you, got no answer. Finally got a hold of me. And then when I texted you—"

"I was in the woods. I had the chainsaw running. I couldn't hear," she said. It was a lie. A partial lie, anyway. But what could she say? *Sorry, honey, I fugued the fuck out and the sculpture I was making came to life and flew away.* It bothered her that she not only lost control, but that she missed something—the calls, the texts. She hadn't been present. It was like being lost in a dream, or a coma. Worse was that persistent feeling that this had happened before. "It was fine. You handled it like a champ."

"Olly was in a fight, Mads."

"Oliver was *not* in a fight. He ran afoul of a high school dickhead and the expected dickheadedness ensued. He will face many such dickheads."

At that, Nate grunted. He sat still for a little while, then said, "I had to shoot a deer today."

"Oh. I'm sorry." She tried to imagine what that was like, and couldn't. "What happened?"

He told her the story—sick deer, wandering in circles, came at Fig. He shot it. He told her, too, it was filled with maggots, and he said, "The worms, I guess some kinda bot or warble fly larvae, came out and, like those ants, they were wandering in a circle. Like the deer. That's strange, isn't it?"

"I'm sure it's fine," she insisted with a clenched jaw, even though her brain was screaming over and over again, *It's not fine, it's not fine, something is wrong, something has gone very wrong.*

"I hope Olly's gonna be all right. At school. *In life*—"

"Nate," Maddie said, trying not to bristle (and failing). "Can we just go to sleep? You're not usually this chatty before bed, and I just want to wind down. I have to call Trudy at the gallery tomorrow, I have to keep working on the pole barn, and I just need to *quiet* my mind for a while. Okay?"

He nodded, and rolled over.

Maddie picked up her book. Tried to read, but she'd lost the groove. The words blurred and slid. Gently she shut the book and rested it on her chest and instead tuned her ears to the outside. She didn't hear the clamor and tumble of Philadelphia, of people and vehicles and airliners overhead and trash cans banging. (And sirens. So many sirens.) All she heard was a chorus of night bugs. All the chirruping and *chack-chack-chack*ing and *dee-deet*ing out in the deep dark of the forest. Somehow it felt louder here than there. Both in her head and outside of it.

Nate knew it was a dream even as he dreamt it.

He stood amid the black, broken-teeth rocks of Ramble Rocks park. Fog slid between the stones like sulking ghosts. The air was cold but he wore only a white sleeveless shirt and ratty boxers—a shirt he didn't even own in real life, which was one signal that this was not real.

In this dream, his son, Oliver, stood before him.

The boy's cheeks were wet. As if he'd been crying.

Nate's fist throbbed.

The boy's lip was split. Blood connected his lower lip to his chin like a bright red thread.

This isn't happening, Nate thought. *Just wake up.*

But onward it went. Nate flexed his hurt hand, and to his son, he said, "What did you do?" No. That wasn't right. *He* didn't say it to his son, but rather he *heard* himself say it. *Felt* his mouth moving, and the vibration of the words in his chest. It wasn't something he willed.

It was something he *witnessed*.

"I'm sorry," Oliver stammered.

"Sorry is for sissies," Nate said. And there, in his voice, was the rumble of another voice: his own father's. *No, no, no.* "You screwed everything up. Didn't you? Broke it all real good."

"I—I didn't mean to—"

"I, I didn't mean to," Nate heard himself say, in a singsongy voice. Mocking his own son. He wanted to reach out and grab his own throat, wanted to throw a punch at his own stupid mouth. *Shut up, shut up, shut up.* But still he kept on talking, even as he took another step toward his son. "Listen to you. Cowering like your mother. You fucked up. You need to own that. You're an apple that fell from a perfectly good tree, but sat there and went rotten in the grass. Didn't you? *Didn't you.*"

"Dad, please—"

"Shut up. You invited this in. Made this all happen." He sucked air between his teeth—*tssk.* "Like the world isn't bad enough, Oliver? You just had to push it over the edge, didn't you? Getting into fights at school. Making friends with that . . . that pack of freaks, living in your own heads." He felt the words leaving his face and he tried like hell to clamp them down—and even as he did, he tasted the whiskey vapors on his breath. Cheap shit whiskey, too, with a woody, breathy, acid-piss burn.

"I won't do it again—"

He reached for his son—

Oliver tried batting his hand away—

And then, *wham.*

Nate felt the vibration go from his fist to his elbow to his shoulder. His son's head rocked back with the hit. *Whap.* The boy took one step back, and then looked at his father through a ruined eye. Oliver's left eye had popped like a green grape, leaking ocular jelly. Nate heard himself cry out.

The boy took a few steps backward, bumping into a rock behind him that hadn't been there moments before. Had it? Nate couldn't remember. The rock was long and flat, like a table, though its base made it look like a blacksmith's anvil, too.

A shot rang out, then—a rifle crack dissecting the air like an ax splitting a board, *ka-rack,* and Oliver's head whipped back again, and in the center of his forehead now was a cigar-burn hole that drooled blood, and the egg-salad stink of gunpowder filled the air—

Oliver fell backward against the table—

He landed flat, and the blood from the center of his head found the grooves in the table rock and ran down those stony furrows toward the edges, where it dripped against thistle and grass, and as it did, the sky grew dark, and a clotted red rain began to fall, one spattering drop at a time—

Pat, pat, splat, pat—

Nate gasped awake.

Time passed. The night deepened. He was slick with sweat. The dream clung to him like a bad smell. *Just a dream,* he thought. *Olly is okay. It was just a dream.* The house, he told himself, had unsettled him.

Nate tried to fall back asleep. He rolled over onto his right side. Then his left side.

Then onto his back.

He sighed and stared up at the dark ceiling.

Maddie snored lightly, a gentle sawing of wood.

He focused on her soft breathing. Here he thought she'd be the one who couldn't hack living in the country. But maybe it was him. Because this was his every night since moving into this house. He'd get to sleep eventually for three or four hours. Bad dreams would stitch his night together. And then it'd be morning.

While not sleeping, he'd lay feeling like the house was somehow *awake,* and agitated. It wasn't just that the house unsettled him—it felt *unsettled.*

Nate looked into the dark. He half expected to see his father there, staring from the corner. Or worse, from the end of the bed. *Gun in the wrong hand,* he thought. What a strange vision that was. Hallucination due to stress, he had to figure.

But no one was there.

He sat up with a groan and slid out of bed, his feet bare on the uneven wooden floor. Their room was the same one he'd slept in as a boy—his muscle memory kicked in and he didn't even need to think about the house's layout. He left the room, wandered down the hall, the floorboards squeaking and complaining.

Nate checked in on Olly, creeping up the attic steps and peering in at his boy—

He's not there. He's not in bed. He's gone.

But then his eyes adjusted, and he saw Olly's long body tangled up in the sheets. Head half under a pillow, limbs splayed out.

Nate breathed a relieved sigh, then headed downstairs into the kitchen and poured himself a glass of tap water. The water tasted strange—bitter and with a strong mineral tang. He reminded himself to get it tested.

Then, in the quiet of night, in the dark of the house, a sound met his ears. Distant and small, but persistent.

Tic.

Tic.

Tac.

What the hell was that? Didn't sound like the normal sounds of a house settling, but it scratched something familiar into the wood of his memory. He couldn't quite figure out what yet.

He listened closer. Nothing. He shrugged, set down the glass, and—

Tac.

Tic.

His mouth went dry. His palms, gone sweaty. An absurd reaction to small, quiet sounds—wasn't anything to worry about, wasn't a burglar coming in. A little voice put the image in his head again of his father, dead but suddenly awake on the bed, gasping as some other version of him stood in the corner, gun in hand . . . the *tic-tic-tac* of him messing with the gun's safety, thumbing it on and off, on and off . . .

This wasn't that. *That,* in fact, Nate decided, didn't even happen. It was just a trick of the eye, a jarring moment brought on by the surprise of his father's . . . what was it called?

Agonal respiration.

He heard the sound again—*tic, tac, tic*—somewhere toward the front of the house, so he made no effort to be quiet, and he marched out of the kitchen, past the cellar door, past the entrance into the dining room on the left, the living room on the right, and—

There.

The answer.

A handful of fireflies were gathered at the square window in the front door. He watched one pull away before flying back toward, and into, the glass.

Tic, tac, tic.

The bug, lightly tapping before settling back down.

A few more fireflies joined, clustering around one another—each glowing an ethereal green. Ghost lights squirming against the black.

Nate was surprised. He didn't remember fireflies being out this late in the season. Summer had just ended. But it was still hot out. Maybe their season had changed—climate change had gone and borked everything up, hadn't it? The seasons weren't really the seasons anymore.

He took a few steps closer until he was right at the door. This close, the firefly glow illuminated the actual insects themselves—their little long bodies crawling this way and that.

Nate put a finger on this side of the glass. He wasn't sure why he did it, but something compelled him to. Pressing his finger pad against the window, he watched as they began to line up—

No.

And slowly spiral around it in a winding carousel of glowing insects. Around and around they went. Some would take momentary flight, as if trying to escape the vortex of their brethren—but then they'd settle right back down in line, orbiting the tip of Nate's finger pressed on the other side of the door.

Ants and deer and maggots.

And now, lightning bugs.

Something's wrong.

He yanked his finger away, and that seemed to break their pattern. The spiral dissolved and they scattered. Nate watched them fly away, drifting into the dark, their green starshine flicker over the grass. The moon through the trees cast long arms of light—and the trees in return cast long legs of shadow. His eyes passed over the forest—

And found one tree. A strange tree he didn't remember. Small. Closer to the house, in the front yard, than it should've been.

The tree moved.

He blinked to make sure that what he was seeing was what he was truly seeing—

It wasn't a tree at all.

A figure stood out at the edge of the yard. Just inside the woods.

He couldn't make out much, but Nate could see the moonlight shining around a too-tall figure. He blinked, knew he was seeing things again. This was just his mind gone wonky from too little sleep. Or maybe it was another dream. He stared at the image, certain as anything that the silhouette would slowly resolve and reveal itself to be a tree, but then—

The figure's head moved.

Tilting like an animal that didn't understand.

An animal. *Just a deer,* Nate thought, but his gut clenched like a closing fist, and even as he told himself that again and again, *just a deer, just a deer,* he found himself darting back up the steps, quiet as he could. *Just a deer, gotta be that,* he thought as he eased back into their bedroom and, from under the bed, withdrew the small safe. He pressed a finger down on the lock, and he heard the locking pins disengage with a *whirr-click.*

Just a deer. But just in case.

He snatched up the pistol inside—an old Browning Hi-Power 9mm—and snapped the magazine into the underside of the grip before he hurried downstairs again on the balls of his feet.

Nate eased open the front door, pistol in hand.

He walked out onto the cracked stone steps.

The figure was still there.

As if waiting for him.

Just a deer. Just a deer.

He scanned the margins of the yard, looking for antlers, or for the rest of the animal to manifest—four legs, not two, maybe the flash of a tail—but he found no such thing. He swallowed hard and called out: "Hey!"

A moment passed.

Then the figure turned to run.

Nate's heart was fast out of the gate, urging him to move, move, move—so he bounded across the leaf-strewn lawn, snapping back the action of the pistol. He saw the shadow crashing through the trees, deeper into the woods, and he, in bare feet, followed. Nate leapt down off a shelf of earth, tearing through a tangle of dry thorn. His eyes adjusted as he strode the paths of moonlight, chasing after the presence, who loped ahead of him in long-limbed strides. Branches cut across Nate's cheeks and forehead. He nearly stumbled across a leaf-covered ditch between trees—a place where a log once lay, but was now rotted into mulch. Pain tweaked through his ankle, up his calf, but he kept going.

It occurred to him: *We're heading toward the park.*

Toward Ramble Rocks.

Toward the place in his dream.

Suddenly he was crashing through a tree line, and onto soft grass.

Ahead, in a shaft of moonlight, stood a man. As if trapped there, pinned by the spear of light.

The figure was scarecrow tall and prisoner thin. A long, raggedy rat's nest beard hung down his bare chest. A pouch of belly hung over the hem of his rotten jeans, and Nate saw sores marking the man's skin—sores like little bite marks, like welts.

Nate skidded to a halt, and brought the gun up, pointing it at him.

"You. Who are you. You were outside my house—"

It was then he saw the stranger's face.

It was *crawling.*

Something moved over it, black dots, squirming in the light. Shiny and twitching. Twitch, twitch.

He heard the fly-wing buzz—

Flies, he realized. Horseflies, maybe, or deer flies. Then they lit up in a ghoulish glow: *fireflies.*

"Who. Are. You."

The man's mouth opened wide, too wide, showing a set of bony teeth and a pale, wriggling tongue. Then the mouth kept going, *crack, crackle, snap*—and it suddenly cracked hard as if something inside had broken, though the skin had not, leaving the jaw hanging there loose in the thatch of beard like a broken porch swing. The man began to keen, a long, mournful wail—and then all the world lit up, lights blinding out the darkness, a silent thunderclap of air slamming Nate in the chest. The light ripped through the stranger, washing it all out, erasing him.

15

The Writer

Nate gasped.

He blinked, shielding himself from the sudden light with a forearm.

The figure, the long man with the ratty beard, was gone.

He heard himself panting. Like a dog in pain. His own ragged gasps were everything, filling the world, expanding the void.

Then: A voice called out. "Howdy, fella. You okay?" From the direction of that voice, a shadow emerged—another person, a man, though this one was not like the bone-thin stranger, but rather appeared average in every way: average height, weight, everything. The voice had an almost avuncular amiability to it—the tenor of a friend you haven't yet met.

"I—" Nate looked to the pistol dead-ending his own arm, and he let it dangle at his side, realizing he had been pointing it in the direction of the other shadow. "I'm all right, thanks."

The man came closer. He was older. Late fifties, early sixties. Still hard to make out his features, given the bright lights behind him—which weren't from the moon, but rather from floodlights that Nate could see came from a house. The realization struck him:

He was at his neighbor's house, wasn't he?

Uh-oh.

The other man must've reached a similar conclusion about who was standing on his lawn. He said, "You're the fellow from next door, am I right about that? We're neighbors, I believe."

"I . . ." Nate winced, flush with embarrassment. "That's right."

Embarrassment gave way to worry. He didn't want to lose his job, and wandering onto his neighbor's lawn just past midnight with a loaded 9mm was . . . *not* a great way to ensure local government of your stability.

But the man said, with a wave of his arm, "You wanna come inside? I tend to be a real night owl. Happy to offer you a drink if you partake."

"I don't want to bother you."

The man laughed. "I'd say we're already well past that, friend."

"I suppose so. Sure. Just for one drink."

"All righty, then." The man clapped his hands together. "Come on in."

The house was an A-frame. Deck out the back, balcony overhanging the front. Inside, the house was airy, open—too open, creating a vacancy almost suggestive of abandonment. Everywhere Nate looked was wood—wooden floor, wood beams, butcher-block counters, trees outside. It hovered somewhere between minimalist modern and log cabin ski chalet. The only real feature of note was a pair of tall bookshelves against the far wall—it was not the kind of bookshelf one kept for purposes of decoration, no. It was full of sloppy, messy books shoved in at all angles, well used, well worn. Well *loved.*

The man grabbed a stool by what looked to be a breakfast bar, plonked it down for Nate to sit on, and then went around the other side.

"What do you want? Oh hell, my name's Jed, by the way, Jed Homackie. Pick your poison, as the saying goes—got wine and beer, cider and mead, and of course a whole cabinet of the hard stuff. If you're a whiskey man, we can take a tour of the Scottish Isles—"

"Oh, sure, that sounds fine. I'm Nate Graves, by the way."

"Graves, hm. You the son of Carl?"

He hesitated. "I am."

"I'm sorry for your loss," the neighbor said. Then, in a lower, sly voice, added: "Your father, if you don't mind my saying, could be a real bite in the ass."

Nate felt a whoop of laughter come up out of him, unbidden. "You'll find we are in total agreement on that one, Mr. Homackie."

"Jed, call me Jed, c'mon."

Nate got a good look at Jed Homackie now—his avuncular vibe translated over to the way he looked, too: Sure enough, he seemed like someone's, or maybe *everyone's,* uncle. He had a big smile and a ruffle of eyebrows that looked like exotic caterpillars, but also dark eyes that seemed like they were studying everything carefully— scrutinizing the world with the pick-apart strategy of a champion chess player.

He plunked down a bottle between them:

The Balvenie, twelve-year.

Then, two glasses, *clink, clink.* Jed poured a couple fingers in each.

Nate looked down awkwardly at the pistol in his hand. "Ahh."

Jed put up his hands as if to surrender. "Don't shoot." Then he chuckled and waved it off. "Put that on the counter, no worries."

Nate sprang the chambered round, then dropped the magazine out and set it all down next to him. The single bullet he sat on its flat end, so it stood up, a little golden watchman.

With a wink and a nod, Jed offered the glass up. "There are many toasts and many cheers," he said, "but my favorite is this: *Nie mój cyrk, nie moje małpy.*"

Nate gave him a quizzical look. Jed translated the toast in a faux-Polish accent: "Not my circus, not my monkeys."

They clinked glasses, and drank.

A warm caramel hit filled him up like the heat from a fresh-out-of-the-oven apple pie. "This is something," Nate said.

"It's a Speyside. Real nice. *Real* nice. Like butter on pancakes."

"Well, thank you for sharing it, Jed."

"My pleasure, Nate."

They sat there for a few moments. Finally, Nate said:

"About the gun—"

"Bah. You don't have any explaining to do if you don't want. I'm a man who favors privacy."

"I think you have a right to know. Honestly, I considered just lying about it, telling you there was a . . . black bear or something."

Jed nodded, smacked his lips after taking another whiskey sip. "There are bears around here—once in the bluest moon, at least. Coyotes, too."

"That's right. But the truth is . . . I thought I saw someone."

"Do tell."

"On my lawn. A . . . figure, a man, just standing there."

Jed leaned forward, almost conspiratorially. "Hnh. That *is* troubling."

"So I grabbed my gun and went after him."

"Sensible. I'd have done the same damn thing—er, were I not a bleeding-heart liberal. Not that I have a problem with commonsense gun ownership, friend, not at all! I just don't think I could *do* it. Point it. Pull the trigger. Turns my blood to water, the thought of it. I am a peace-loving man, raised a Quaker, though not practicing these days."

Nate sighed. "I'm not bleeding-heart, not really, but I vote Democrat eight times out of ten. And last thing I want is a gun. But I had to train to use this—I was on the force in the city."

"Police officer, you mean?"

"That's right."

Jed smiled even bigger, then poured another whiskey for himself, and added another hefty splash to Nate's glass, too. "Then let me thank you for your service. Blue lives matter, and all that."

"I appreciate that, but turns out, people on the street had a lot more to fear from us than we did from them." He felt himself relaxing a little. Shaking off the yoke of stress. Something about Jed was easygoing, affable—like the man was a happy sponge, just soaking up all the bad vibes and learning all about you. "How well'd you know my father?"

"Not well. We had 'encounters,' as neighbors do. We each have some acreage, as you know, so there wasn't much cause to really interact, but he'd complain from time to time—I have a smoker, and I smoke meats, and that made him sour. Sometimes I'd play music off the speakers I have out back—nothing crazy, not like I was playing, you know, heavy metal or loud *rap* music or something, but that ticked him off, too." Jed leaned forward, looking down his own nose like he was about to confess a state secret. "I get the sense he was not a very *happy* man."

"*Unhappy* would be an understatement. I would go with *miserable*. Usually followed by *asshole*."

"Again, I'm sorry for your loss, just the same."

"I'm not. I'm glad he's gone."

Jed's somber face turned the other way—his frown fishhooked into a cheeky smirk. "I felt the same way about my own father. Real sonofabitch. Meaner than a kicked copperhead." He *hmph*ed and stared for a moment into the middle distance. "On to better things. Better *people*."

"Cheers to that," Nate said.

Again they clinked glasses.

"Do you . . ." Nate started, but the words died in his mouth.

"Do I what?"

"It's stupid."

"No, no, please. Proceed."

"You ever see anybody out here? People, I mean. In the woods."

"People in the woods, oh, sure, sure. Usually around hunting season. One time I had some ding-dong come bumbling through the woods. It had snowed and he was dressed in all manner of snowy camouflage—he looked like an extra out of *Ice Station Zebra*! Armed to the teeth, too, had one of them . . . what do you call 'em, those military rifles."

"A black rifle. Like an AR-15 or the like."

"Right, the kind they always use to shoot up a workplace or school. Anyway, he comes through the trees and onto the lawn like he just doesn't give a care. I went out to yell at him. Didn't have a gun so I took a chef's knife and a pot and I was banging the knife on the pot like a lunatic—I find that if people think you're crazier than an out-house owl, they act more *warily* around you—and he held up his hands and let his gun hang, said he didn't know this was private property. I said to him, well, what gave it away? Was it the mailbox? The freshly plowed driveway? The big *house*? Or me waving around a knife and some cookware! He stammered an apology, said he'd . . . gone and shot a buck but he only grazed it, and he thought the buck had gone through my yard—not that he knew it was a yard." He chuckled softly. "But that's not the kind of person you mean."

"Ah. No. Not so much—though, I am now a Fish and Game officer, so anything like that ever happens again, give me a ring." He sighed. "I just . . . the man I saw, a tall, lanky, bearded figure. He looks, I don't know. Homeless? Sick, maybe. Maybe my eyes are just playing tricks on me. Maybe I'm the crazy one."

"Might be, rabbit. Might be. But—" Jed waggled a finger, not in a chiding manner but in a *Well, hold on now* gesture. "These are strange times, and we live in a curious area. We're still rural, but close enough to the turnpike to bring all sorts up around here. And there's an opiate epidemic out there, plus meth toward the west, out past Kutztown, into Pennsyltucky proper. You get more than the steady stable of oddballs and freak shows. And . . ." He lowered his voice. "We *are* near Ramble Rocks."

Nate felt an uninvited chill grapple up his neck.

"Ramble Rocks."

"The park, sure."

"What's that got to do with anything?"

"Well." Jed leaned back again, as if entering pontification mode. "Even beyond the stories of the rocks themselves, you've heard the tales of the tunnel, of course."

"I have."

"Whether you believe that sort of thing or not, there are those who *do* believe it. Devil worshippers and the like."

"I think Satanism is a scare best left to my childhood." Back when Nate was a kid, everyone blamed Satanism for everything from kidnapping to sexual molestation. People went to jail for being Satan worshippers, without a shred of evidence, often exonerated later— *years* later. Wasn't a single proven case, but hysteria's a helluva drug.

"Don't be so fast to discount it. They find animals dead in that tunnel sometimes. Sacrificed, perhaps."

"Or just run over by some ding-dong on his four-wheeler."

"Fair enough. Maybe ghosts, then."

Nate laughed, then saw Jed was serious. "Ghosts."

"You're not a believer?"

"In ghosts? I used to be—when I was ten years old."

"Nate, come now. We live in an area famed for its spectral entanglements. The Revolutionary War, and not far south of here, the Civil War, caused a great many brutal, untoward deaths. Not to mention the more common, smaller deaths—the ones caused by human calculus, jealous murders and grief-struck suicides and mysterious accidents."

"You sound like you have a pretty deep interest in this."

Jed's eyes lit up. "In the weird and fantastic? I do. A *professional* interest."

"You're not some kind of ghostbuster, are you?"

Jed snapped his fingers, gave a wink, and then tottered over to the bookshelf. He got halfway there and then waved Nate over. "Come on, come on, I'm not taking this trip by myself."

"Oh." Nate hopped off the stool, surprised at the faint wobble on the inside of his skull, his brain seesawing one way, then the other. *The whiskey,* he thought. He reasserted his balance, and walked over.

Jed did a game-show hostess reveal.

In the middle of the bookcase was one whole shelf devoted to what looked like paperback true crime novels—which Maddie read from time to time. Except these were less *true crime* and more *haunting historical* nonfiction. Books like *The Haunting of Sibley Manor, The Ghost Engine (and other Haunted Conveyances),* and *Lost Legends of LBI: True Tales of Mysterious Long Beach Island.*

The name of the author on the spine of each was JOHN EDWARD HOMACKIE.

"John Edward," Nate said. Then he got it. "Jed."

"Winner, winner, turkey dinner."

"You wrote all those?"

"All by my lonesome. It's how I made my nut, so to speak." He gestured broadly, as if to behold his home and its many things. "Well, before that I wrote a lot of smut and sports journalism under a pseudonym, but once I found my groove writing this stuff, it took off for me. A couple bestsellers, but the royalties from each form a nice long tail." He looked sad, for a moment, almost lost. "I haven't written anything new for a while."

"Why not?"

"Life gets in the way," he said, still smiling, but there was a stiffness to his words. Like he was holding something back.

Nate decided it was not his place to probe. His gaze trailed over the books, and one caught his eye: *Sacrifice at Ramble Rocks: The Satanic Murders of Edmund Walker Reese.* The killer's face leered on the cover in black and white, high contrast. Little eyes and a lean, hungry mouth trapped by an uneven fence of dark facial hair.

At that, he raised an eye. "Satanic murders?"

Jed feigned a bit of bashfulness. "Well. You know how it is, Nate. The more lurid you can make it, the more people buy it." A mask of seriousness fell over his face. "There is some truth to it, though. The walls of his home had all kinds of numbers and equations written on them, though hard to see anything cogent there, anything more than just the nonsensical ravings of a broken mind. More of the same in his journals, of which there were quite a few—more than fifty books, all scrawled with his gibberish. Some guards on death row said he spoke of 'the demon,' a creature he obeyed that 'would save him.' And then there's the fact that Walker disappeared the day he was to be killed. Not just the day of—the *moment* they flipped the switch on that chair, he went away. Rode the lightning in a big way, I guess."

"My father was a guard there. He said that story was horseshit."

"Oh, I know." Jed's eyes twinkled. "I got him drunk one time. Your father."

"Smart money says he was already drunk when he got here."

Something passed over Jed's face then. A coldness. Something steely, something hard. Like a shadow from a cloud, it moved fast and then was gone. "Your father told me that it was true. That they never had a body. That they marched Walker in, sat him down, and soon as they ran the juice through him—" Jed snapped his fingers on both his hands. "Gone."

"He said that?"

"He said that."

Nate chewed on this new information. "He liked to tell stories." That was a lie. His father didn't give in to embellishment or fantasy. In that regard, he was buckled tighter than a straitjacket.

"Maybe that fella you're seeing out in the woods is him."

"My father?"

"Edmund Reese."

"Sure, Jed." Nate faked a smirk and gave a half nod.

"Aw, I'm just playing around. It's probably nothing."

It's definitely something, Nate thought. He just didn't know what, yet. "Anyway, I've taken up enough of your time—and too much of your very fine Scotch. It's late. I should head back, in case my wife wonders after me."

"Wife, you say."

"Wife and son, yep. Teenager. Not yet driving age, thankfully."

"That's nice, that's very nice." There it was again: that faraway stare, that tension tugging at his words like a doctor stitching a wound shut. Did his eyes glisten a little? Nate could read people okay—

Was Jed suddenly struck by grief?

Nate decided to poke that bear a little.

"You have a family, Jed?"

"Ohh. Well, sure I do." Back to the bookcase, he lifted up something that had been put facedown. A picture frame, Nate realized.

When it was tilted up, it showed Jed—younger, maybe when he was Nate's age, in his forties—standing there with what looked to be a wife and a teenage daughter. The daughter looked especially like him—the same warm-but-wild eyes, the same quirky smile. She had the mother's button nose.

"That's, ahhh, that's my wife, Mitzi, my daughter, Zelda."

Nate hazarded another quick look around—more a reflex than anything else—and noted again how sparsely this place was decorated. It wasn't very *lived in.* Certainly not the home of a family.

Nate had no intention of asking about it, but Jed must've sensed what was going through his head, so he offered an awkward smile and said, "They're gone. If that's what you're wondering. My wife left me a few years ago, and Zelda went with her."

"I'm sorry. Divorce?"

Jed hesitated. He shrugged and smiled a sad smile. "Afraid so. I was not a good man, Nate. Not a good man at all."

"You seem all right to me."

Jed held out a hand. Nate took it, gave it a good shake.

"Good to meet you, Nate Graves."

"Back atcha, Jed."

He turned to leave then—and then, halfway through the door, back out into the darkness, he stopped. A little voice inside him told him, no, don't do this, don't make the offer, but there was no denying it: He got a good vibe off this guy. He just *liked* Jed. Liked the hell out of him.

So out came the offer:

"Halloween's coming up," Nate said, "and our son is too old to go out, you know, dressing up and begging folks for candy, so we're doing a thing at the house this year. My wife's idea—I'd be content not to see another soul—but ennh, you know, maybe she's right. Good to have people over, since we're new to the area. So, it starts at seven and—"

The smile that went across Jed's face was so big and so deep it looked like his head would go full-on Pac-Man, *chomp chomp chomp*.

"My word, I'd love to come," Jed said. Then he barked a sharp laugh. "What a peculiar night! A man shows up half-naked on my lawn with a gun—ooh, don't forget that, by the way—and it ends with an invite to a Halloween party. I always say, Nate, to trust your intestinal flora." He poked at his gut with a finger before winking and adding, "That means go with your gut. Listen to your *instincts*."

"I agree with that, and thanks," he said, juggling himself back over to the counter where he—with no small embarrassment—picked the pistol back up. They said their goodbyes.

And out into the darkness Nate went once more.

On the way back through the woods, through the chill of the forest, Nate found the path easy—once his eyes adjusted, he could see the black cutout of his house through the trees, and he made his way slowly but surely home.

And on the way, he saw something up in a tree—

It was a massive owl, bigger than any he'd ever seen. A great horned owl, by the look of the points on its head. It seemed almost to blend into the tree at first, as if it was part of it. And then it took flight with the sound of creaking, crackling wood. Probably just the sound of the branch, Nate thought, as the raptor disappeared off into the dark.

16

The Fragile

October.

Olly stood at his locker, trading books from BioSci to Geometry. Behind him, the hall was thick with kids going from one class to the next. They bumped and jostled him, like usual.

A dark feeling came over him—not something internal, but an external wave of emotion. It rose up and crashed down on him, just as something—no, some*one*—shoved hard into the middle of his back. He slammed into the locker door, and someone tried closing it on him as they passed. It happened fast, and the guffaws were already fading, Doppler-like, as he quick pulled away and spun around.

He saw two familiar people wading back into the crowd. Graham Lyons and Alex Amati. Darkness pulsed within them. Anger and pain.

Lyons still had two fingers in a splint. All taped up.

"You all right?" Caleb asked, coming up.

Olly blinked back tears. "I'm—I'm fine."

"It's just some bullshit, man. Don't sweat it."

"Yeah—I—yeah." He had to take a minute not to be pinned down by what he was feeling. He felt suddenly, woefully fragile. He didn't want to feel that way. It wasn't as bad as that day back at his old school. He didn't feel quite so alone. (And at least he didn't piss himself.) But somehow he still felt *off*. And it didn't help that someone like

Graham Lyons hated him. People *loved* Graham Lyons. So if Graham hated him, maybe everyone else did, too.

But Caleb didn't seem to. And that wasn't nothing.

"Fuck that guy," Caleb said. "Glad he busted that finger."

"How busted is it?"

"Busted good. I dunno if it's broken but the tendon got fucked up, so they had to slice into the finger and, I dunno, move the tendon or some shit. It means he probably can't do fall practice for baseball, and if he can't do *fall* practice, means they might not let him play in spring. Then again—" Caleb shrugged. "Who knows. Rules don't seem to apply to dudes like him."

"Why's he such a dick?"

"Dunno. His dad's a big swinging dick, too, so maybe the dick doesn't fall too far from the dick tree."

"Ew."

"Haha, yeah. Hey, after school, I gotta do a thing—babysit my little dumb cousin, Reg. But that's for an hour. I'll drop you off and then an hour later, maybe bike on over to my place? We'll play some Fortnite or do some Magic trades or whatever."

"I don't really *do* Fortnite." The guns in it bothered him. "I could come over, help you babysit."

"I asked my auntie about that and she's paranoid about having 'strange teenagers' around Cousin Reg." He lowered his voice. "Especially white kids. You white boys are all school shooters and shit."

Oliver knew it was a joke and he simulated something like a laugh, but it knocked him off his axis. Fear unspooled within him—*there could be a shooter in here right now, coming through the front door of the school, gun in his coat, and he'll start shooting and we'll start screaming and blood on the walls and brains on the blackboard and*—and then his mind went to abusers and serial killers and bad cops and, and, and—

"You in there, man?" Caleb asked.

"Oh. Yeah." Olly swallowed a hard lump in his throat. He felt the pulse in his neck fluttering like a trapped bug. "No, yeah, I'll come over, it'll be great. All right, I, uhh, I gotta get to class."

"Me too, man. Have fun in Geometry, said no one ever."

Oliver rode his bike down Church View Lane. Caleb lived about five miles from Olly, as it turned out—Caleb's family on the north side of Ramble Rocks park, Oliver's family on the south side—and so it was an easy enough ride from one to the other. The two of them had been hanging out a lot. Sometimes with the game group of Steven, Chessie, and Hina, but a lot of times, just the two of them. It made him feel less alone. Less fragile.

It was closing in on six o'clock. The sun was setting through the trees, pushing bands of crepuscular light across the road ahead, capturing motes of dust and spore. It was warm, too—though October by this point should've been crisper than a newly circulated dollar bill, it wasn't. It was damp and humid, the air froggy and groggy and so thick it felt like pedaling his way through oatmeal.

Now and then, a car would pass. Not a lot of traffic on this back road, but there was enough he had to keep wary.

He blinked sweat out of his eyes, passing Ramble Rocks on his left. All along he saw the slate-gray and blue-black boulders that gave the park its name. The trees would give away and open up into scraggly fields of just those boulders, one after the next, some huge, some smaller, some bulging, some flat, like an audience of earthen creatures frozen in geologic time.

He heard a car coming—a deeper rumble, like a truck. He slowed his pace and eased farther over to the side of the road as he pedaled closer to the drainage ditch. To make it easier for them to pass.

His brain flashed back again to today: He felt so damn *screwed up*. He felt worried. All! The! Time! People's pain felt *smothering* to him. It made it so he couldn't catch his breath—like their pain was his pain and it filled him up while pushing him down.

(Now he felt the vibration of the coming truck behind him in his tailbone, his elbows, his teeth. A diesel-engine growl grew louder.)

And Dr. Nahid wanted him to feel like, oh, he was just really empathic, and maybe that was a good thing, because, as she put it, "There's not nearly enough empathy to go around, Oliver." But he didn't *want* this. He didn't want to feel what he felt about other people. Even someone like Graham Lyons, he wondered, *What made him that way?* Maybe it was hard to have the pressure of being a huge baseball star. Maybe he didn't have much academic background to lean on, so it was a sports scholarship or nothing—and maybe his father really was a dick, and maybe Graham's ego was like a big inflated balloon: all puffed up but ultimately hollow. And Oliver felt guilt, *genuine guilt,* over injuring Graham's finger and—

The truck, growling like an earthquake, barreled up alongside Oliver. He spied a flash of red paint, and a shadow fell—something whipped toward him, something that only later would he realize was a hand. That hand caught him at the elbow, giving his own arm a hard hit—*whap!* Before he knew what was happening, he jerked the handles of his bike hard to the right without meaning to, and the front wheel bounded down into the ditch.

He cried out as he lost control—

The wheel bent—

He felt the world go up over his head—

And then he crashed back down, hard, into the ditch. Mucky, muddy water splashed. Got into his mouth. He blinked it away and choked, and as he tried clumsily to stand, Oliver felt a screwdriver turn of pain behind his shoulder blade. Somehow he managed to get to his feet, dripping.

Behind him, his bike lay there, twisted up. The front wheel was bent in half like a ruined pizza. The chain was off the gear teeth, too.

"Shit," he said, tasting the mineral, clay-slick tang of mudwater. He spit, *ptoo.* Tried hard not to gag. Wiped his chin.

Then he turned, saw that the red pickup truck was parked about fifty yards ahead. Engine idling, *chug-chug-chug*. He spied an American flag sticker on the back window, and one of Calvin pissing, too.

He stood there. Chest rising and falling.

He wondered: *Who did this?* Was it an accident?

Or was it on purpose?

Do I run?

The truck idled.

(*Chug-chug-chug.*)

The passenger-side door opened. Then the driver's side.

Alex Amati stepped out from behind the wheel. And Graham Lyons from the passenger side. The pain in both was dark—and it seemed to move between them, a kind of liquid darkness moving from one to the other and back again. Oliver wasn't sure he'd ever seen that before.

He didn't know what to do. He was pissed that they'd done this to him—now he knew it wasn't some accident. But he was afraid, too. Oliver wasn't exactly a tough piece of rope. He never had to be.

Just run, he told himself. Turn tail and bolt.

But his bike . . . Dad would kill him if he just left it.

He stood his ground, stepping up out of the ditch.

"You almost killed me," he called out. His voice cracked in the middle like he was going through puberty. Embarrassment bloomed in his cheeks as the other two came closer. "I could've been hurt."

I may be *hurt.*

Alex had a cruel smirk stitched between his cheeks. Graham, by contrast, looked all the more serious.

"Hurt?" Graham asked, arms wide, as if demanding that Oliver behold the world and Lyons's dominance over it. He held up his busted paw. "*You* hurt *me*, dickhead. I'm officially out of fall league. *They benched me.*" Those last three words he said with such ill-contained grief and rage, Oliver again felt sorry for him—and then cursed himself for feeling that way. It made him feel weak and stupid and gullible. And even with that, Oliver said:

"I'm sorry. Okay! I'm sorry." He held up both hands in supplication. "You—but you came over to *our* table, though, and—"

"We're gonna *fuck* you up, sperg," Alex said. His hands formed into fists and swung by his side like a pair of sledgehammers. The anger in Alex was profound now: a pulsing heart of fire and black blood.

And that's when Oliver knew:

He had to *run.*

He spun on the front of his foot and bolted. But already, he felt a new twang of pain snap like a broken guitar string up his left shinbone—pain from the fall, maybe, pain that was just catching up to him. He cried out but kept going, *go go go—*

Even as he heard heavy footsteps pounding asphalt behind him.

Run, run, fucking run!

But he was too slow. Something slammed into him sideways: Alex's arm, crashing into his neck like a baseball bat. He gurgled and fell, not forward, but to his left, once more tumbling into the wet ditch to the sound of yawping laughter and applause. But even that didn't last long. As Oliver flailed in the ditch, trying to crawl back to standing, Alex fell on him like a downed tree—*whoom.*

A fist hammered into his kidneys, once, twice, three times. *Boom, boom, boom.* Agony flooded out from that singular point, filling his body, making his limbs slack. He gritted his teeth and hauled back with a clumsy elbow, and to his surprise, it connected. Alex grunted, a nasal whine, before redoubling his assault.

Oliver felt a rough hand grab the back of his head—cinching up a wad of his hair between knuckles—before plunging his face forward.

Into the muck and the water.

Everything was a gray-brown wash. Oliver held his breath as his head sank deeper into the brackish water, then the greasy mud. He tried to extract himself, tried to get leverage, but he had none. His pulse crashed in his neck and his temples like a pair of cymbals. Alarm raced through his veins. He felt shadow circling him, encroaching like a pack of wolves, and panic came along with nauseated wooziness—

He realized then:

They're going to kill me.

I'm going to die.

17

Rescuing Oneself

W*ub-wub.*
     Wub-wub.

That sound, pulsing in the dark. Oliver's lips pressed shut, and in the deep well of his ear, he heard his own heartbeat, *wub-wub, wub-wub,* even as hands of shadow threatened to pull him down. And then another sound, too, like voices heard behind a half-dozen walls, under a blanket, behind a rubber curtain, *womp womp, tamp tomp,* all while the heartbeat kept on:

Wub-wub.

Wub-wub.

The hand holding his head was suddenly gone. With it, the pressure. He was free.

Oliver wrenched his head back out of the mud and the mess. He drew a hard, wind-shear gasp. He pushed himself up on his arms, propping himself there, sucking in massive gulps of breath even as he again tried very hard not to puke, and even harder not to cry. He turned over, crab-walking up out of the ditch—and the voices once behind the wall of water were now loud and clear. Graham and Alex were talking. No. *Arguing.*

"—almost killed him," Graham said, gesturing like, *What the fuck.*

"So fucking what," Alex bit back.

"So fucking what? You dumbass! We're just roughing him up, not putting him in a casket. You think it sucks for me being benched for the season? What about jail, you fucking shit?"

Alex stood there, mouth agape. Like he was processing it all—slowly, too slowly, like his mouth was connected to his brain on a bad Wi-Fi signal. "Man, shut up, I'm sorry, but . . ." He pinballed between looking mad and confused and sorry. *Alex Amati,* Oliver realized distantly, *is an idiot.*

Then, Graham's gaze flicked not toward Oliver, but past him.

At something.

No—some*one.*

"Who's this?" Graham asked in a low register.

Alex turned to look.

And then, before Oliver could look, too, Alex flinched and yelped as a little flower of blood blossomed in the middle of his forehead.

18

Jake

Alex Amati cried out, pawing at his head like he was trying to smack a bee. His palms came away slick with red.

Graham launched forward, saying, "What the fuck, man—" and then there came a little pneumatic *pop* and he yowled, jerking the side of his head down toward his shoulder. He clutched at his ear, juggling his footsteps backward. And it was now that Oliver crawled his way out of the ditch, to see exactly who was coming—

Some guy, a young dude, maybe a few years older than him, casually strode down the road. Black T-shirt with an electric chair on it. Ragged, vent-slash jeans. Ratty, unruly mop of hair. And his face came with the mother of all scars. His left eye, tucked in a nest of scar tissue, was a different color than the right one: It seemed not to be one color, but many, depending on how you looked at it. From blue to green to ochre and back again.

But all that faded quickly to the background when Oliver saw what the strange kid held in his hand:

A long, boxy pistol.

The blood in Oliver's ears was a river. This was it. It was happening right in front of him: a young man with a gun. It wasn't in school, or in a Walmart, or at a concert, but right here, on the road. He tried to remember something, *anything,* from the ALICE drills—where to go, what to do—but all of that was lost to the murk and mire in his own head.

The one-eyed dude pulled the trigger again.

It didn't go *bang*.

It went *piff*.

Not just once. But again and again as he tugged the trigger.

What the—?

Graham and Alex each looked like they were being stung by wasps—they flailed, crying out, swatting at themselves. Little red beads of blood blew up and tumbled down their skin—arms, collarbones, even bleeding through Alex's white T-shirt. Graham still clutched at his ear, too.

The two of them, defeated, turned tail and bolted for the truck. The attacker kept firing—now not at them, but at the truck. Something ricocheted off the back gate, *tink, tink*. Then the back tires spun on the asphalt and gravel, spinning until they caught—and then the pickup lurched forward, gunning it down the road, making an escape.

Oliver stood up. Dripping. His neck and head throbbing.

The dude stood there, long and rangy like an overcoat on a coat rack. He lifted his chin in a *'sup* kind of greeting.

Oliver had no idea what to say. Thank you? Please don't shoot me? What the fuck is wrong with you? That was awesome?

"Hey, man," the dude said.

"Hey," Oliver answered in a small, bewildered voice. Still dripping, he began wringing muddy water out of his shirtsleeves.

"Your bike's pretty fucked up," the dude said.

"Yeah."

The dude offered a fox-faced grin. The one strange eye fixed on Oliver like a laser. It seemed to evade definition—was it blue? Green? Was it hazel, and what even was hazel, anyway?

"It's okay," the guy said. "I can see fine out of it." He laughed. "Actually, I have better vision in *that* eye than the other one."

"Oh," Oliver said.

And it was then he noticed something else:

This new dude—

He was a blank slate. Empty of the pain so common in everyone else. No misery, no fear, no worry. None of that darkness coiling up, bleeding out, or pulsing like a black hole.

Oliver had never met anyone, *not anyone,* who was devoid of pain.

"You could say thank you," the guy said.

"You shot them."

The dude held up the pistol. Looked like something out of WWII, or, like, *Call of Duty* or something. Real boxy and industrial. "What, this? Relax, it's just a pellet gun. They'll be fine."

"Oh." Oliver blinked. "Thanks." *I think.*

"That one motherfucker was going to drown you."

Oliver finally snapped out of his numb state. The memory of that came rushing back, and a paroxysm of shuddering shivers came over him, like he'd just come up out of a frozen lake. Even in the hot day he felt suddenly cold and dizzy—

And fucking *pissed.*

"Yeah. Alex Amati." Oliver quaked. "What a prick."

The dude tucked the pistol into the waist of his jeans, pulled his shirt over it. "Why'd those guys have such a boner for beating your ass, anyway? I mean, besides the usual answer of bullies gonna bully. This seemed pretty personal."

Oliver didn't feel like getting into the whole thing—so instead he just said, "Because they're the kind of guys who would go out of their way to run over a turtle."

"That who you are? A turtle?"

"I—no, I dunno. I just mean they're fucking assholes."

"Fucking assholes, indeed." The dude took a step forward, offered a fist to bump. "I'm Jake, by the way."

"Oliver. Olly."

They bumped fists.

"Hey, I was just headed to the park, planning on, I dunno. Smok-

ing some weed maybe. Though I got pills, too—I got vikes, oxy, xan-
nies—"

"What? No. No, I uhhh," He felt super uncool saying this, but: "I
don't, like, do any of that. I mean, I've had a drink before. Drinks.
Multiple drinks." That wasn't a lie, not entirely. Once when they were
at a Phillies game, his parents ordered him a Shirley Temple, but
some numbnuts bartender put actual booze in it. Vodka, probably.
Oliver got drunk at the game—he was six at the time. Apparently it
was a real thing to see, a six-year-old getting sauced. Lots of pointing
fingers and dramatic gestures. His mother said he acted like a little
crabby stevedore, slurrily complaining about his job after a long
workday down at the docks.

"Cool, cool," Jake said. "You live around here?"

"Like—yeah, couple miles that way."

"Right. I'm the other direction. You know Emerald Acres? The
trailer park?"

"Sure," Oliver lied. He didn't know why he lied about that. It was
like laughing at a joke you didn't understand—just a thing people
did.

"Yeah, I live there with my aunt."

"Oh, cool."

Jake laughed. "It isn't cool. It's shit. Our one neighbor is a tweaker,
and the other is a Nazi furry, which . . . well, it's pretty fucking extra."

Oliver made a face, but he laughed, too, because that *was* pretty
fucking extra. "What's his fursona?"

"He dresses up like they all do—a fucking fox or wolf or something. But like, with the Nazi armband and shit, too. I'm pretty sure
they have orgies there. Buncha furries show up every other week,
and the double-wide rocks back and forth like it's a boat on the
ocean. Whole lotta, *Fuck me, der Schutzstaffel.*"

And now Oliver was *really* laughing, and it felt really good to
just . . . let that out. It didn't erase what had happened, but it felt like

it picked him back up, dusted him off, and put him back to standing again. It was like wind and sun pushing the fog away from shore.

"That's crazy," Olly said, his laugh slowly winding down.

"This is a fucked-up world, man," Jake said, smirking.

"Yeah."

"Hey, you seem pretty dope."

"Oh. Uh. Thanks."

"I'm new here—"

"What? I'm new, too!" He heard the eagerness in his voice—he felt like a dumb puppy, so he tempered it by throwing a little *who-gives-a-shit* into his voice. "I mean, cool, yeah."

"We should hang out sometime."

"Yeah." Oliver wasn't sure. This guy wasn't at all like him; they had nothing in common. Oliver sure as hell wouldn't go pop pills in the park, and he wouldn't wander around with a pellet gun. Still, he liked Jake. *And* he'd saved his ass from Amati and Lyons, which was no small thing. "I'd dig that. I don't think I've seen you at school—"

Jake laughed. "I'm eighteen. Got my GED, got the fuck up out of there. No more school for me."

"That's awesome."

"Awesome as long as you don't mind nobody wanting to hire you because there's no jobs."

"Oh."

"Like I said, what a world. Enh. Whatever. Hey, plug my number into your phone."

"Right, okay." Oliver fished his phone out of his pocket and—

The screen glitched. Pixels and color bleed.

Because, of course, *he'd just dunked it in water.*

"Shit!" he said. "No, no, no, c'mon." First the bike, and now his phone? He was dead. Double dead. He tried to tap the screen but it just went even glitchier, like some 8-bit video game gone buggy.

"Here, let me." Jake took the phone out of Oliver's hands, pressed the buttons on the side, up, down, then both at once—and after five seconds, the phone went totally dark.

"Hey—"

"Hold on, hold on." He powered the phone back on again and—

Bingo. It looked as good as new.

"What did you do?"

"Sometimes, when shit is really broken, you need a hard reset. Reboot, unplug, whatever. Shut it all down to bring it back."

Oliver let out an exasperated sigh of relief. This day had been one weird-ass roller coaster. "Thank you."

"When you get it home, don't put the phone in rice like they say. That's bullshit. Get some DampRid—it's a thing you put in, like, a wet basement to dry it out. Put the DampRid and the phone in a Ziploc bag, leave it for twenty-four hours. Be good as new."

"Thanks." Oliver smiled. "I'm glad I met you."

What a mystery this new person was.

He was a question mark, and not a period.

How amazing was that?

"Glad I met you, too, Olly." Jake grinned, and plugged his number into the phone. "I think we're going to be good friends, you and me. Maybe even best friends, who knows? Let's get you and your bike home."

19

Seizure

I t's because you're not working," Trudy Breen said to her. The two sat on the patio of Watercolors, a small vegetarian place—Breen's suggestion. (Maddie knew vegetarianism was the ethical decision for the world. She also knew how good a hamburger tasted. It was an ongoing war.) Trudy—*Gertrude* to anybody who didn't know her—owned a gallery about a half hour south, right on the Delaware River, in New Hope. "That's your problem."

"I'm working," Maddie objected.

"Mm-hmm." Trudy leaned forward and stared through cartoonishly large bug-eyed spectacles. Her mouth formed a flat line, and all up and down from her lips radiated sharp wrinkles, like the creases in a cupcake wrapper—the telltale signs of a former smoker. Her throaty voice was part and parcel of that old habit, too. "Maddie, you just told me you haven't worked on anything since you moved in."

Since the owl . . .

"And I *also* just told you that I was busy getting the workshop situated. If I'm going to work, I need a *space* to work." She laughed, if a little mirthlessly. "That was kinda the whole point of me moving out here."

"I thought it was to get your son and husband away from the city."

"Well—"

"Maybe it's not really about you. Maybe it's never about you."

"Trudy," Maddie warned.

"Is your art even yours?"

At that, Maddie shuddered. She couldn't help it. In her head, she heard—and *felt*—that rush of wings past her head.

Worry dropped into her stomach like a dumbbell. Now she wondered: Was it good they moved out here? Nate wasn't acting right. He was up at weird hours, looking out the windows. Just this morning, she saw that the gun safe had been pulled out—it was closed and locked, thankfully. She asked him about it and he said it was nothing. But in the morning, his bare feet were muddy. And she found muddy footprints downstairs, too, after he headed to work and Oliver was off to school.

And Oliver . . .

He was cagier than when they'd first moved in. She told herself that was normal; he was adjusting to a new school and new routine, plus he was right at that *moody-as-hell mopey-ass teen-tornado* age of fifteen . . . still, it was jarring. He'd always been open with them and touchy-feely, too—never shirking a hug offered, and never failing to ask for one when he needed it. But now, it was like some door had closed between them. They could still talk past the hinges and the frame, but it wasn't the same.

"Never mind all that," Trudy said suddenly. "You need to work, that's the problem here."

"I know, and I will."

"Will you?"

"I will! I will."

"This is why you invited me to lunch."

"And why is that?"

Trudy dipped her chin and tilted her big-ass glasses far enough down her finchbeak nose so she could properly stare over them.

"Mads, I am like a horse whisperer for artists. And you know that. I am a Sherpa, a spirit guide, and you need me to unblock you. A psycho-artistic colonic, mm? Whatever this is, it isn't just, *Oh I'm too busy.* That's not you. Something's up." Trudy's gaze was like a pair of screws boring deeper. She gave a curt little nod, like she had it all figured out. "There. There it is. You're scared."

"Scared? What? Of what?"

Trudy narrowed her eyes to suspicious slits. "The art."

Outside, Maddie laughed and scoffed.

Inside, she thought: *How the hell does she know?*

Because it was true. Maddie had approached the work time and time again, telling herself, *I'll just work for ten minutes, maybe thirty, just enough to get a taste, to put my hands on something and make a change, any change at all, to the material.* But every time, she'd seized up like an engine in winter. Almost felt like she couldn't breathe. Like the blood was pooling hot behind her ears. It was absurd. It was *insane.*

Every time, she remembered losing control. Going dark. The owl she made, *gone.* And again that sneaking suspicion it had happened before.

Scared of the art. Or scared of the artist?

"Something about it scares you," Trudy said, her left hand gesturing in the air like an erratic butterfly. "I can't say why. I'm not *psychic.* Maybe you tapped into something other than everyone else's pain. Maybe you found something inside you." She *hmm*ed before leaning in to say, almost conspiratorially: "I do know a psychic if you wanna talk to her. Nice lady. I mean, *nuts,* but nice as cookies."

"You're weird. And wrong." And she added: "And *no,* I don't need to talk to your psychic friend. Jesus."

"Fine. Then what you need is a dunk."

"A dunk?"

"Mm. Isolation tank. Next best thing to LSD."

"Ahh, hah, yeah, no, I'm not gonna—"

She didn't get to finish her thought, as they were interrupted by the waitress, asking if they knew what they wanted. "Sorry," Mads said to her, "I can't—I don't know, didn't look at the menu. Can I have another minute?" The waitress nodded, wandered off. Maddie looked at the menu, saw words, didn't read them. With some hesitation she asked Trudy:

"Were you ever an artist?"

"Psssh." Trudy waved her hand. "Gods, *no*. I know art when I see it, but I don't make it. Some people are makers, others are vampires— that's me. We grow fat on *your* ideas and imagination. I'm just a *beautiful* tapeworm, darling . . ."

"But you know a lot of artists."

"Obviously."

"Do they ever . . ." How even to ask this? "Do they ever have episodes?"

"Episodes."

"Like, a mental breakdown."

Trudy barked a sharp, way-too-loud laugh. "Mental breakdowns? Artists? That's like asking if a man has ever scratched himself in public. It's so common amongst you creative types it's practically chocolate and peanut butter, sweetheart." She lowered her voice. "You know, two great tastes. But you. You never seem to have them. You're always so . . . *put together*. Which makes me think that when you fall apart, it's *quite* spectacular."

"Don't flirt."

(Trudy was a lesbian and could in fact be an incorrigible flirt.)

"Not flirting. You're bread and I'm low-carb. I just mean— someone so zipped tight would probably go *pop* if they strained too hard. Mind telling me what happened?"

"No, it's nothing—"

"It's something, please, stop the foolishness. Tell me."

"I . . . made something."

"Something. What something?"

"An owl."

"An owl?" Trudy made a face. "Pedestrian."

"No, I mean—yes, but it felt right and—"

"And then what?"

"I bought a chainsaw, I carved this owl—and then, somewhere along the way, I just . . ." She whispered, even though no one else was out here on the patio with them. *"I just fucking blacked out."*

"Blacked out, like—one too many pills, and poof?"

"No. No pills. I fugued. I lost consciousness but *still kept on making the owl.*"

"With a running chainsaw."

"With a running chainsaw, yeah."

Trudy's eyes went wide. "Oh, honey, you're lucky you didn't lose your damn hand. Chainsaws are thirsty for blood. I have a tree guy—now that you live in the woods, you need a tree guy—he's a botanist, see, his name's Pete. And he had an assistant, a little fella, funny mustache, thought he could handle a chainsaw and—boy, woof, it hit a knot in an old oak and popped back like a spooked horse, got him right here." She tapped the middle of her forehead. "Missed his nose, but it went right to the bone. Blood everywhere. Like something out of a horror movie, I tell you. Grisly business, those chainsaws."

"I didn't even think of that." She neglected to mention the last part of the story: *And when I awoke, the thing I had created was gone.*

Trudy shrugged.

"So," Maddie asked, "what the fuck do I do?"

"What do you do? You do what you have to do."

"Go to the doctor," Maddie said, anticipating the answer.

"What?" Trudy barked. "No. Honey, you're fit as a fiddle, look at you. The problem isn't your body. It's your mind."

"So, therapy."

"No, no, no. Art is therapy. Go back to work, Maddie. *You go back to work.*"

20

The Killer Is Revealed

So that was what Maddie did.

She pushed back the fear, and she got to work.

Before her sat a rickety, half-rotten wooden crate. Its contents? Junk. Literally junkyard junk, the purest form of junk. Metal scrap and car parts and so forth: the frame and bulb of an old brake light, a rusted coffee can of nuts and bolts and de-threaded screws, the handle off a washing machine door, and more. She'd picked it up on the way home from lunch with Trudy. Stopped in an old junkyard, fished around there for a few hours, bought a box of curated junk, and now, here she was, back at her workshop, ready to make something.

She tugged the welding mask down over her face. As she was cast into the dim shadow of the helmet, she felt a sudden bout of vertigo. The world tried to slide away from her, spinning leftward, but she planted her feet and bore down like a woman giving birth and then . . .

It stopped.

And she worked. Sparks rained down around her, leaving searing streaks burnt into the air. Then the mask was off again and she was hammering metal. And twisting wire with pliers. And sparking up the soldering iron, *tzzt, tzzt*. Maddie didn't even know what she was making—she simply turned her brain off and let her hands work and wander.

It was long, too long, before she realized she was creating a face. Not just a mask, but rather—

A whole damn head. Replete with neck, shoulders, and a single arm outstretched—an arm with bone made of rebar, with arteries of insulated wire, with skin formed of broken shards of dashboard. She didn't know why this was where the work took her; she allowed it to be a river that pulled her along in its current, regardless of the rapids ahead.

Maddie stepped back from what she was making. A quick glance at the little LED alarm clock on the workbench showed her it would soon be time for her family to come home.

I should make dinner, she thought.

She took one last look at what she had wrought. It remained unfinished, she knew, though sometimes an unfinished thing was finished, just the same. There she beheld a head, a neck, an outstretched arm—and, of course, its face. It was like staring at one of those Magic Eye paintings, where visual noise and static suddenly bled together, blurry, allowing the true picture (a dolphin, a unicorn, whatever) to emerge—

I recognize that face.

Maddie knew it.

A surge of nausea rocked her like a storm-tossed sea.

And then the face of plastic and metal blinked. It turned toward her, its neck creaking and crackling as it did, and as its dead gaze fell upon her, the outstretched arm of her creation reached for her throat.

Maddie screamed.

21

The Man Who Fell Between the Cracks

Maddie pulled away as the hand flailed for her. It missed her throat but caught the collar of her shirt, yanking her hard toward it. Her creation was anchored to the worktable in a fat, flat vise—even as she tried to pull out of its grip, she couldn't. She grabbed the thing's arm and wrenched it toward her in a twisting grip, and *still* it didn't budge. Meanwhile, thoughts raced through her head, and with each came a sharp twist of panic:

I know this person.

I've seen him before.

I know his name.

What the fuck is happening.

This isn't real.

This cannot *be real.*

The head craned toward her on a neck that was long, too long, longer than she had made it—one red taillight eye regarded her with mad, wild-eyed scrutiny. The metal lips twisted in a wretched sneer, the whole face cinching up into a rough-hewn rictus, its plastic dashboard skin cracking like the top of burnt crème brûlée—*kkkktt*—as its face bore a visage of rawboned rage.

"*Lit-tle gggirl,*" the thing hissed in a broken stutter. "*I know yyyyyou! You st-tt-tt-stole my Num-ber Ffffiiiive, you b-b-bitch—*"

Her arm outstretched, catching the lip of her workbench—

And her fingers, like spider legs capturing prey, snatched the handle of a bushhammer—a hammer whose end was studded in pyramidal tips in order to texturize stone, wood, or concrete.

She brought the hammer down on the thing's head.

The taillight eye shattered. Red plastic shards clattered to the floor.

"Where am-am-am I? Wh-what world is this? WHAT NUMBER WORLD ISSSS THISSsssss."

Again she brought the tool down, *whack, whack, whonggg,* and the head jerked hard under the assault. Metal crumpled. The mouth fell away. The bent metal fingers—made of screwdriver tips and coils of braided wire—went slack, and she pulled her shirt, now ripped, out of its dead grip.

The thing was dead. Head slumped forward, like a deactivated robot.

But it wasn't fair to call it *a thing,* was it?

No, it wasn't. It was someone. A face she knew, but didn't know that she knew. Didn't make *sense* that she knew.

"Edmund Reese," she said, half-expecting, half-*fearing* the name would summon life into this creation once more. But it didn't even twitch.

Maddie had no idea what had just happened. Only that this was now the second time—two for two—where she had made something and lost control of what she had made.

Worse was that *this* time the art tried to *kill* the artist.

22

Brood Parasites and Egyptian Rivers

The day felt long. Work was work in the truest sense, a slog through the mire of paperwork. But even so, Nate took a bit of small pride that he was finally settling into the job. Even Fig no longer treated Nate like he had somehow stolen a desk. He even said, "You're not a cowbird, after all."

"Cowbird?" Nate asked, not following.

"Yeah. Cowbird. They're brood parasites." He meant that it laid its own eggs in the nest of another bird, forcing the owner of that nest to raise the cowbird chick on its own. But it wasn't so simple as a forced adoption; the cowbird, before laying its own eggs, often pecked the other eggs into ruin . . . or just rolled them out of the nest in order to make room for its own.

"That what I was?"

"Well, you know. Someone dropping you into a nest you don't belong . . . I'm not saying, but I'm just saying."

"So I belong now?"

"Maybe." Fig laughed. *"Maybe."*

"You're too sweet."

"Sweet like strawberries, and don't you forget it."

"Hey, lemme ask you: If you find a cowbird egg in a nest, do you remove it? Or do you leave it?"

Fig stared thoughtfully out over a logbook, a look of consternation on his face. "Law is pretty clear on that one. As is the science. It's a natural phenomenon, way a cowbird does its thing, and so, what you're supposed to do is just let it be." But now his eyes narrowed as he said, "Just the same, the cowbird outcompetes for resources. And there's no shortage of them. If that were my nest, I'd be pissed. So you ask me, and this is me, not the law of the great Commonwealth of Pennsylvania, but I say you smash the fuckin' egg."

"Fair enough. Thanks for pondering this ethical conundrum with me."

"Yeah, yeah. Go home, Nate."

They said their goodbyes, and Nate headed out. It felt good that he and Fig were warming up their relationship—especially since the other man was coming to their Halloween shindig. Still, those warm-and-fuzzies faded into the rearview the closer he got to home. Nate couldn't help but feel more and more agitated. Like the scrape of a dentist's hook against a cavity, it worried at him.

He became aware of a sensation—an odd, alien sensation, a feeling of displacement, uncertainty, and panic.

Like something was *off*.

Off-kilter. Off-putting. *Off.*

He couldn't say what. Like the bird that knew one of its eggs was wrong, he just felt like something had changed. Like it had broken, or slipped out of joint. Gone wrong. *Gone sour.* It was a jarring sensation, and it had no real *anything* behind it. He couldn't point to any one thing—okay, sure, being in Fish and Game meant they got a lot of news about climate change, and that was bad news. And North Korea was banging a sword against their nuclear missiles again. Then you had Russian hackers, mass shootings, flu epidemics, and on and on. Turn on the news, you got a fire hose instead of a water fountain, and it shot pure sewage into your face with the expectation you'd guzzle as much of it down before you had to puke it all back up again. It was why they had to keep Olly away from the news, *any* news—if it was on, the kid fell into it like it was a hole. A bottomless hole, at that, just falling and falling and falling.

But he also told himself that's how the world always was. Not like the news was ever good. When he was a kid, you had fear of a nuclear winter, and acid rain, and satanic kidnappers. And even that was better than they'd had it in the generations that had preceded his own: Vietnam, both world wars, the Spanish flu. Christ, there were periods in American history where they locked Japanese people in camps; where, prior to WWII, Nazis were on the rise here in the United States; where women couldn't vote; where being Black meant you not only couldn't own anything, but were yourself owned like livestock or furniture. Long before that you had Pompeii, and the black plague, and the Crusades. And onward down the spiral.

Things were better now. The whole *world* was better. It had to be.

Certainly he was better than what had come before him. His own father was—how even to qualify it? Probably bipolar. Definitely an alcoholic. Beat on Nate on the regular. Beat on Nate's mother less often, but when it happened, it was a whole lot worse.

But Nate wasn't like that. All of what fell to him, he kept it contained. He often thought of it as a seawall: All *that* shit, all the abuse and the history and whatever was inside him thanks to nature or nurture? It formed a dark, turbulent, turbid sea. And he held it all back. Kept it at bay, a big emotional wall, a seawall, making sure none of that ever drowned his family.

He was good, he told himself. The world was *fine*. Both things better now than what had come before.

And yet.

And yet.

Why did it feel like something was broken? Like a gear had slipped somewhere deep in the machinery, and they wouldn't realize it until it was far, far too late? Was the world broken? Or was he?

In the driveway, as Nate stepped out, gathering his lunch thermos and his sweatshirt—unnecessary today given the rare October heat—his wife stalked past him, the collar of her shirt torn.

"Hey, Mads," he said, "you okay?"

But she kept walking, clearly frazzled, barely even seeing him. "Fine, yeah, fine. Just gotta get dinner started."

"Something happen?" he said, trailing after.

"An accident in the workshop." Before he could ask, she called over her shoulder, "Not a big deal, don't worry about it."

Then he heard a sound behind him—a scrape and a clatter. He turned to see his son coming up the driveway, dragging his bike. The front wheel looked bent to hell.

He wasn't alone.

Another kid walked alongside him. A little longer, and rangier, like a coyote in human form. Most remarkable was the one strange eye, trapped in a rumple of scar tissue.

Nate dropped his stuff and hurried to meet Oliver halfway.

"What happened?" Nate asked. "The bike—your clothes—"

"I'm fine," Oliver said, snapping. "I know you're going to give me grief because I wasn't wearing a helmet, and yes, I'll make sure to wear it next time, and I *know* I have to be more careful—"

"Hey, *hey*," Nate said. He reached out and touched his son's shoulder. They both stopped. "I'm just glad you're all right."

Oliver blinked. He seemed to relax a little.

"Thanks, Dad. This is Jake. Jake . . . helped me."

"Hiya, Jake," Nate said to the other boy. Calling him a boy wasn't right, though—he was a couple-few years older than Olly, easy. The real mystery was, why did this kid seem so damn familiar? Nate was sure he'd met him somewhere before. Or seen him around town, maybe? Maybe he knew his parents from when he grew up. It needled at him.

"'Sup," Jake said. Kid looked Nate up and down. His jaw clenched, like he was mad. "Wasn't your son's fault, by the way. Couple guys ran him off the road and then—"

"And then kept on going," Olly said, jumping in. "Pickup truck.

They didn't stop. And no, I didn't get plates or anything. I landed in the ditch."

"All right. Okay. Don't worry about the bike. Just pop it in the garage and I'll take a look this weekend."

"All right."

The two boys moved past him, heading back up the driveway. Jake gave him one last dark look before turning away.

"Hey," Nate called after. "Jake can stay for dinner if he wants."

Olly gave a thumbs-up, and they kept going.

And as they did, Nate caught movement in the upper attic window. He saw a figure standing there, and he knew without question that it was his own father, gun in hand. When Nate blinked, the old man had gone, and the window was empty once more.

Dinner with Jake

"So, where you from, Jake?" Nate asked.

The raggedy young man looked up with a squid's beard of lo mein noodles. He slurped them up messily, and gave a curious smirk. "I dunno. All over."

"Military family?"

"Nope, just a shitty one."

In the doorway leading from the dining room to the kitchen, Maddie paced. She was on the phone with someone—Trudy, Nate thought. He tried to signal her, *Hey, why don't you sit down, pay attention to your son and his new friend,* but she seemed lost to some conversation. Agitated, too.

"Why were they shitty?" Oliver asked.

"Who knows." Jake shrugged, tapping the tines of the fork against his teeth. He poked then at a lump of too-orange General Tso's. Nate had hoped Maddie would've cooked something but things were still in chaos since they moved. He kinda wished that the chaos, too, would've been remediated, but it wasn't like he'd been around to help much, what with work and all. "If you wanna know *how* they were shitty, well, that's a whole different question."

"Olly," Nate jumped in. "Jake doesn't need to answer those kinda questions—"

"It's all right, he can ask. You don't need to police your kid's words, let him ask what he wants to ask, and if I don't like it, I'll be the one to tell him." Jake's mouth formed a hard line, but his eyes—there was a smile in his eyes. Like he liked talking back to Nate.

Nate told himself to let it go, this was Olly's new friend, and Jake had helped the kid haul a busted bike for a couple miles. So that meant he got the benefit of the doubt. (For now.)

"Fair enough," Nate said, forcing a smile.

Olly said, "No, seriously, it's okay if you don't wanna—"

"One time, my *father*," Jake began, not blinking as he fixed his gaze on Nate, "handcuffed me to a radiator while he slapped my mother around. Sometimes it went the other way—he'd make her sit in a chair or he'd hold her down while he knocked the snot out of me. And if anyone tried to talk back, he'd make their lives hell. He'd hide food or lock the bathroom door so you couldn't go. Or he'd tear up your pillows and blankets so you had to sleep on a cold-ass bare-ass mattress. He'd hurt me to punish her, hurt her to punish me. That was just one fun part of my wonderful life."

"I can see why you live with your aunt," Olly said. Nate could see the shine in his eyes of tears threatening to spill. He couldn't much hide it. His hand trembled on the table like a nervous spider.

"Hey, it's all right," Jake said, patting Oliver on the shoulder. "Not your fault. You didn't know." Again he threw a poisonous side-eye to Nate. *Why is he pissed at me?* Nate wondered. Then he got it: *He doesn't trust me, doesn't trust anybody's parents.* That made sense.

Oliver stood up suddenly. He gestured with his shaking hand and proffered a small smile. "I have to use the bathroom."

He hurried away.

In the background, Nate searched for Maddie—who had gone from the kitchen and was somewhere else in the house. He could still hear the murmurs of a conversation through the ceiling and the floorboards creaking with her footsteps. *Maddie, goddamnit, please come downstairs so I'm not alone with this—*

"He's a good kid, huh?" Jake asked. The question felt pointed in a way Nate did not yet—but would soon—understand.

"The best. He just—he takes it all on the chin sometimes. Emotionally, I mean. I think his therapist calls it 'empathic,' I dunno. It's hard on him, even looking at the news—whatever bad news is going on that day. It's a burden. Wears him down. At his last school they did shooter drills and the last one really affected him." Nate flinched. He shouldn't be telling this kid any of that. It was Oliver's to tell. Guilt arose in him. He tried changing the subject. "So, hearing your story, I think it upset him—"

"So he goes to therapy."

"Sure, yes. Sure he does." Nate felt himself overcompensating, as if he felt somewhere down deep that he needed to defend his son going to therapy. Or worse, that he distrusted the therapy himself. Did he? Was he that kind of parent? He supported it, but wasn't there some little part of him that worried about his son needing therapy at all?

"That's weird."

"I don't think therapy is weird, Jake."

"Not the existence of therapy, just that—your son seems pretty fragile, and as a result, he has to go to therapy." Jake paused, and licked a bead of Chinese brown sauce off the fork. "What do you do to him?"

"Excuse me?"

"You hit him? Garden variety ass-whuppings? Or is it like, you wouldn't do *that,* but you'll *say* mean shit. Maybe you neg him, cutting away at his self-worth and his identity, a knife whittling a stick down to toothpicks?"

"You're outside the fence on this one."

"Are you touching him? Maybe you're hiding something—"

Nate pounded a fist against the table. The whole room shook. He hated that Jake got to him. He tried to take a lesson from his own son, and be a little more empathic. Like, why was Jake asking him these questions? Just to get under his skin? Maybe. But maybe it was something else.

"Your father hit you, and so you look at parental figures as if they're all the same," Nate said, nodding slowly, and leaning forward now on the bridge of his hands as he rested his elbows on the table. (Trying to project a calm veneer, to regain some of his center.) "I get that. You have no idea how plainly and personally I get that. And I'm sorry all that happened to you. But I'm not like that. We'd never be like that."

Just then, footsteps from upstairs as Oliver came back to the room. Maddie poked her head in behind Nate. "Everything okay?" she asked. Oliver echoed the question.

"Everything is cool," Jake said, holding up his arm and rubbing it. He made a fakey *ow* face. "I banged my elbow on the table."

Nate gave him a small nod. Jake didn't return it.

On the way out, the whole Graves family walked Jake to the door. The older boy seemed to be a bit awkward about that, but Nate didn't intend to back down. Something about this kid was strange.

And again, he looked damn familiar.

"Your parents—" Nate started.

"*Dad,*" Oliver chastised.

"No, I just mean, not about them, but you seem familiar. Did you grow up around here originally? Did they?"

Jake shrugged. "Nope. We were from upstate. Sorry."

"Just a brain glitch, then. Have a good one, Jake. Sure you don't need a ride or anything?"

"Aces and eights over here." He shrugged again. Didn't thank them for dinner or anything—he just said bye to Olly, that he'd call him. And then he was off.

"Dad, I can't *believe* you asked him about his parents. Again!" Oliver erupted. "You don't like it when people talk about *your* dad."

Oliver growled in frustration and stormed off. Nate called after him—"Hey!"—but Maddie put a gentle hand on his chest.

"Let him go, it'll be all right," she said.

He puffed out his cheeks, popped his lips. "What a dinner."

"I guess I missed something?"

"Yeah, you sure did." He spun to face her. "I guess his new friend had a rough life. His parents used to beat him and—" He saw her face twist into a wince so deep it was like she'd just licked a battery. "Hey, way to be on the phone the whole time, by the way. You know, I coulda used you down here. It got . . . weird, Maddie. Real weird."

"I'm not here to fix everything you two break," Maddie snapped suddenly. He recoiled, speechless.

"I . . . I didn't mean you had to fix . . . and wait, what do you mean, what we break?"

"I just mean—I don't know what I mean. I'm tired."

"No, I think you know what you mean."

She hesitated. "I'm saying that sometimes I feel like I have to care for the both of you like you're my kids instead of two supposedly responsible people. I was on the phone with Trudy, talking about work. I *do* work, remember? I can't always be around to babysit the two of you."

"Mads, that's not fair."

"It's perfectly fair and you know it. I don't want to always have to fix everyone else's shit. Maybe you can save yourselves once in a while?"

His hackles rose. He bristled at that—not because he knew she was wrong, but because a not-so-little part of him feared she was right. But instead of acknowledging that part of him, he went the other way. "Great. The Dude is mad at me, and now you are, too."

He felt how cheap that was of him. It was a low road move—instead of acknowledging her complaint, he just moped. But moping felt better.

"I'm not mad. He's not mad. It'll be fine."

He rubbed his eyes so hard he saw star lines. Nate decided to change the subject. "I don't like that Jake kid."

"Nate. That's just an Overprotective Dad thing. Push past it. Jake seemed all right."

"You weren't down here."

"And yet, my *Spider-Sense* did not tingle just the same."

"Fine, fine."

"Maybe tell Olly he can invite Jake to the Halloween party."

"He's already bringing Caleb and some of those other nerd kids. They seem nice. Can't he just hang with nice kids?"

"Don't be like that. Did *you* always hang with the nice kids?"

After some hesitation, he grumbled, "My friend Petey Porter once set his room on fire because his parents wouldn't let him go to a Slayer concert. And my first girlfriend sold weed out of a stolen camper."

"So, that's a no, then."

He sighed. "All right. I'll tell him." At that, he looked his wife up and down. Her posture was still . . . *tight*. Like she remained on defense. Against him? Against Olly? Maybe. But there was something more to it, too. Something deeper. "You okay?"

"Peachy," she said, her smile strained.

It was a lie. He knew his wife well enough to know that.

But he also knew well enough not to poke that bear. She'd tell him in time. She always did. Didn't she?

24

The Boy Who Talks to Books

Walking home in the deepening dark, Jake gave a twist to his wrist and a snap of his fingers, and with that flourish, a book appeared in his hand. The book was ratty and old, with a fabric cover and time-stained pages that fluttered as it appeared in his grip. On the cover of that book was a title, hand-stamped with erratic, drunken kerning:

A BOOK OF ACCIDENTS

And beneath that:

An accounting of accidents at Ramble Rocks Number Eight

Even though it was dark, he flipped to a page somewhere in the middle. His hand traced over the weathered pages, pages that had endured water and wind, even fire, but that still remained as they were. They were not soft, they were not smooth, but rather hard and raspy. Stiff like the skin of a dead animal, if not as rigid, or as thick.

He couldn't read the pages. What meager light shone down from the moon did so from behind a veil of muddy clouds, affording him little to read by. He could *feel* the letters, though, the texture of hand-writing having dented the pages, and his fingers traced along these soft ink-dipped ditches, and he took a deep breath and—

And they began to move underneath him. Like worms, squirming as they dug tunnels.

The pages gave a gentle glow. They throbbed beneath his fingers. Hurt, even. Not a burn but a deep ache, up through the tips of his fingers and into the knuckles before corkscrewing to his elbow. A good pain, he told himself. A *necessary* pain to keep him clear and remind him of his mission.

The book reminded him as well that he was close, so close. This was the 99th, it told him, and with no small agitation it demanded he not screw this up. Everything relied upon it. He'd done so much, and to fail now . . .

"I won't fail," he told the book. "I've met the boy. He's weak."

But the family is strong, the book said with some anger.

"This family is never strong. There's always something." Jake had to admit it gave him some pause that this family—*this* Nate, *this* Maddie—seemed so *together*. But Oliver really was thin as tissue paper. Maybe the family was strong, but that boy was soft—gentle as a butterfly. He just had to catch him. And then, crush him.

25

We All Float Down Here

This is what the nice young woman with the vacuous stare and the smell of cheap, candy-like perfume told Maddie:

Tay (the girl's name, maybe short for Taylor) said the tank was sealed up and lightless, and within waited one foot of water, heated to body temperature and treated with Epsom salts.

They did not, the young woman explained, permit first-timers to use the tank for more than a sixty-minute session, but the average session should Maddie return was usually ninety minutes long.

"You will enter the tank nude but it will be totally private and safe. You may experience a sense of weightlessness, but first-time users do not always dissociate."

"Good. I don't . . . want to dissociate. I just want to relax."

"Of course." She added in a softer voice: "There is a thousand-dollar contamination fee."

"Contamination fee?"

"Yes," the woman whispered, her voice going even softer. "Any accidental release of any kind of bodily fluids or solids will incur that fee."

"What if it's intentional?"

"I. Um." The girl's cheeks went dark and she struggled to find words.

"Relax, honey, I'm not going to shit in the tank. On purpose or accident."

"Oh. Hah. Right." She cleared her throat. "You said you have a gift certificate?"

Maddie produced the printed-out email, sent to her by Trudy just that morning. "Ta-da."

"Great. I'll just need you to sign our waiver."

"Can't wait."

I'm in a fucking casket, Maddie thought.

No, she added, correcting herself, *I'm in a wet casket. A watery grave. This is a place for dead people.*

Maybe dead pirates, she thought a few moments later.

It didn't look like a casket on the outside. It looked like a big futuristic blob of semen, designed by Apple. Underneath it glowed a precious aquamarine, but inside the tank, after it closed, it was as black as the Devil's mouth and quiet as death.

In other words: a casket. This was how she expected to spend her eternity after death. Except, at present, she was not dead at all, but very much alive, and very much hating Trudy for putting her here. Last night on the phone she told Trudy . . . well, she didn't tell her exactly what happened, only that she was having "difficulty" making new things (*The last thing I made tried to kill me,* she thought, but did not say). And Trudy said, "Sweetheart, I'm telling you: You need a dunk in an isolation tank. It's fabulous. Opens up all the wonderful alpha and theta waves in a way basic-bitch meditation does not. LSD without the chemicals. I'll buy you an hour at a float joint I like to go to, it's down in New Hope, not far from the gallery. It'll unlock your potential."

But what Maddie sought was not an unlocking of her potential, or her creativity, or her art. Her art had attempted to *murder* her. And it had a face that she recognized, a face she didn't know *how* she recognized:

It was the face of Edmund Walker Reese.

The Ramble Rocks killer.

What she wanted to unlock was the answer to the question, *why did she recognize him?* She's sure at some point she'd seen his picture: She didn't grow up around here, rather in Philadelphia, but she remembered the news at the time. All that talk of a serial killer up in Bucks County, killing girls—girls that were a little older than her at the time. Prepubescent, preteen girls. But she couldn't have picked him out of a lineup.

And yet, something in her reached deep into the back of her mind, and pulled out *that* face, of *that* man, and put it on a sculpture.

A sculpture that promptly spoke, and tried to choke her.

So, *that* was her purpose here in this briny casket. She needed answers, and she hoped this would give them to her.

But so far—

She floated.

Float float floaty float float.

In the moist darkness, in the dark moistness. Her mind wandered uselessly through the labyrinth of anxiety that was both part and parcel of having moved into a new house and also containing those special twists and turns and dead ends unique to her own uniquely fucked-up brain. It was a jumble of checklists and contingencies, a worthless hastily scrawled scroll of what boxes they hadn't unpacked yet and what new furniture they'd need (because though the farmhouse was small, it was still bigger than what they'd had in the city) and ugh, had she really been there for her family, and fuck, was it a mistake to move to the middle of the woods, and oh hey by the way *you lost an owl and a sculpture tried to crush your trachea.*

"Fuck!" she called out inside the saltwater coffin. She slapped at the water and it fruitlessly slapped back.

Deep breaths, she told herself.

In, out. In, out. Meditative breathing. That whole fucking thing where you imagine a balloon blowing up, up, up, and then slowly deflating down, down, down. *Don't pop the balloon,* she thought. *Don't pop the balloon.* Christ, she almost popped the balloon. An imaginary balloon and she almost popped it. Shit. She tried to clear her mind, and just let it be a formative space: a blank, black canvas into which she released something raw, something generative. A creative place. Maybe Trudy was right. Maybe this could unlock something for her in *that* direction—if it wouldn't help her dig into her memories, perhaps it would help inspire her.

She imagined a shape. No specific shape, just a shifting, changing shape there in the void. Quote-unquote "real" artists mocked someone like Bob Ross for his public-access, lowest-common-denominator approach to painting, but she had always found inspiration there— the way he just seemed to follow where the art took him, and that's what she did here, in her mind. She just let the shape be what it was going to be. A happy little cloud, a happy little tree, a—

A happy little doorknob.

The fuck? A *doorknob*?

That's what it was. There in the dark of her mind—or were her eyes open?—a doorknob. Golden. Then silver. Then made of wood. Its material shifted and so did its look, from a basic office doorknob to a primitive knob that seemed to just be a stone against the wall to an ornate black pewter plate with a crystalline knob. It was a doorknob that she made, that she willed into existence. A doorknob that she *knew* was connected to a doorway beyond, a portal, and she knew her certainty in this regard was strange as hell, but it was also *damn interesting*, so she reached out—and here she didn't know if she was reaching out with her *real* hand or just the hand inside her head—to grasp it, giving it a gentle half turn—

She felt the click of a door opening. But it did not open only ahead of her. It opened all around her. It opened beneath her. Then she was falling, falling down through dark water, then through open space. She cried out and

"Oh, oh, *no,* please tell me you didn't vomit in there."

Maddie was half in the tank, half out of the tank. Her lower half was in it, her knees still in the saltwater. Her arms were out in front of her, propping her up as water dripped from her hair and chin. It occurred to her, too: *I'm naked as a baby.* But Maddie was not one for shame, so she remained as she was, all her bits hanging out.

The girl, Tay-Maybe-Taylor, held her hands up in front of her like a cartoon housewife watching a mouse in her kitchen.

"I didn't—" Maddie half gargled before coughing, "I didn't puke in there." At least, she didn't *think* she did. "What happened?"

"You started screaming."

"I did?" *I did.*

"You were. You were screaming words."

"What—what words?"

"Um. You were saying, *I remember, I remember.* Like, loud. Really loud."

"I remember?"

"Yeah."

"I remember."

"Yeah, I said yes, yeah."

And then she did. She remembered.

Edmund Walker Reese. Standing at a door. Hearing a sound behind him. Looking to see what made the noise and—

Something. Maybe not everything. But something.

26

Staring at It Isn't Gonna Fix It

Nate poked his head up the set of steps leading into Oliver's attic bedroom. The boy had truly made it his own—bookshelves and movie posters and a desk whose chaos looked artful and designed rather than like the shitshow Nate's work desk had become—and he regretted ever thinking it was a bad idea to give the kid his own space. In the corner was Olly's guitar case, sitting there like a tomb, its mummified inhabitant long sealed away from the world of the living.

"You should play again," Nate said.

"Huh?" Oliver asked, looking up from his bed, an iPad propped up on his chest. He plucked a pair of earphones out of his ears.

"The guitar. You should play again, I was saying."

"Oh. I dunno. It's not really my thing anymore."

"You could sell it. It's a nice guitar."

Oliver scowled over his iPad. "I don't *want* to sell it."

Both hands up in surrender, Nate said, "Okay, just thought you might want some spending money. It's your guitar. You like it as decoration in the corner, no problem."

The boy said nothing. Just sat there, simmering.

Finally, Olly broke. "Do you still need something?"

"I'm just saying good night."

"So say good night already."

So, Olly was still mad. A day later, still mad. Ah, hell.

"All right. Good night, kiddo."

"Uh-huh."

Oliver clutched the iPad, white-knuckled. His eyes scanned the screen furiously. His face made a twitch, like a twinge of deep pain.

"What is it?" Nate asked.

"Just watching YouTube."

"Whaddya watching on YouTube?"

"Nothing. Just—like a game streamer. Spohn Zone. He's playing—I dunno. *Cuphead.*"

Spohn Zone was one of his favorite game streamer accounts. *Cuphead* was . . . Nate guessed some kind of game? Olly didn't really play many games outside what he had on his iPad, but he watched the hell out of other people playing games. Nate always joked that thirty years ago, dads always said things like, *When I was your age, I had to walk to school through snow, uphill, and fight off bear attacks!* These days it was, *When I was your age, we had to play our own damn video games! And we liked it, too!*

But here, something wasn't right. Olly looked too tense, too upset. Nate hated to do it, but he went over, put his hand on the iPad, and spun it around—much to Oliver's protestations. "Hey!"

On the screen, it was a live news feed. CNN.

Earthquake. A 7.0 on the Richter scale. Peru.

"Olly."

"I know."

"Olly."

"I know! Okay. I know I'm not supposed to be looking at the news." Olly's ears were red. The iPad shook in his hand. "There are people hurting, I saw a girl covered in dust and, and, and blood just wailing for her parents, there are people trapped under collapsed buildings just *screaming,* and can you imagine being in there, how scary that would be, and what if nobody finds them, Dad, what if—"

"Okay. I know. I know."

Gently, Nate put his hand on the iPad screen and pulled the tablet away from his son. He didn't force it, and Oliver let it go.

"Those people."

"Kiddo, staring at it isn't going to fix it. You can't help the situation now. You don't have to be a sponge, soaking it all up."

He was sure that would earn him a rebuke—but the fight seemed to go out of Olly, as if the boy were relieved to be told that he didn't have to bear witness to it as it happened.

"Maybe in the morning, we can throw a couple bucks to charity? Save the Children or UNICEF but not Red Cross."

"Sure, Olly. Sure."

Nate kissed his son's forehead, and headed back down the creaky attic steps. As he rounded the bend to head back down the hall, he heard something—the muffed twang of guitar strings above him.

Oliver was playing again.

A small, but essential victory, Nate decided.

He went into his and Maddie's bedroom, and there he found his wife standing over a small carry-on suitcase, putting clothes in it. And like that, any sense of victory went away like the pop of a soap bubble.

"Maddie," he said, his voice low.

He knew what this was.

He didn't understand it, but he knew what it was.

A wife. Packing her suitcase. She was leaving him.

"I'm not leaving you," she said. "I see the look on your face, and that's not what this is, so you can just ease off the throttle, okay?"

"All right," he said, trying to take this slow. "But you *are* packing a suitcase. Out of nowhere. I mean, we haven't been fighting—"

"I told you already, I'm not leaving you. Besides, the suitcase is a small one, you'll note. If I were leaving you, I'd take the big motherfucker out of the walk-in and throw *everything* in it." She stopped to give him a hard stare. "And all *your* shit would be on the lawn. Soaked in urine."

"I'm glad that hasn't happened. For all kinds of reasons."

"Same. I don't think I have that much rage pee in my body, anyway." She paused. "In the morning I have to go somewhere."

"You know our Halloween . . . party, or whatever it is, is this weekend. Three days away, Mads." She said nothing. So instead he asked, "All right. Does this *somewhere* have a name or maybe at least a latitude and longitude?"

She stopped for a moment, her arms stiff, her hands framing the outside of the suitcase—as if she were afraid she'd fall into it.

"I just need a day."

"That wasn't an answer. Where you going, Maddie?" Still, she hesitated. "I need to know how to reach you. Or where you are."

"I'll have my phone."

"Maddie—"

"I can't tell you. I can't talk about it. I don't—" She swallowed hard, her eyes pinched shut, her nostrils flaring. Like she was trying hard to center herself. "I don't even know what this is, but please just bear with me." She was sure to remind him of an unspoken debt: "I've stuck with you through things. Including your strange behavior lately. Now it's your turn to stick with me. To trust me."

He wanted to protest.

He wanted to say, *That's not fair.*

But it was fair.

One hundred percent.

So, he did what he did. He nodded and smiled and said, "Whatever you need." And he meant it, too, as much as it pained him to say it. She told him he was a good husband, and then explained she'd leave in the morning after they got Oliver off to school. Then she'd be back the next day.

And that, it seemed, was that.

27

A Day Without Maddie

The morning Maddie left, Oliver seemed worried by her sudden escape, and both parents went into overdrive to reassure him—which, as they realized, only made him worry more, because all the divorced parents did the same song and dance, put up the same smoke and mirrors, didn't they? *Oh it'll be fine, this is just us needing a break, here, have a pony, pay no attention to the man behind the curtain, that's just your mother's new, ahh, yoga instructor, Julian, have a great day at school, kiddo.*

Oliver left for school, and then off Maddie went, too.

Hitting the road to who-knew-where.

Without him.

That was what killed Nate.

They were a team. Up until now. Up until the house.

It was absurd to blame the house. Better to blame his-own-dang-self, really—he'd been sleepless and moody and downright *weird*. Maybe he drove her away. Maybe she just needed one precious night without him. She could've told him that. Anger suddenly lanced through him. *She could have told him.* He would've understood.

Right?

Suddenly, he wasn't so sure.

But it would've been better than whatever this was. Her just going off, without nearly any information at all.

He felt like he was spinning. Angry and sad and confused, and he didn't even know if he deserved to be. Olly being mad at him. Maddie being gone. And him, here, in *this place.* Everywhere he turned it still felt like *their* house, like it belonged to someone else.

Man the seawall, he told himself. *Get your shit straight.*

He manned the seawall. Went to work. Fig sussed out that something was off but Nate wouldn't let on what. Then home he went. Oliver texted Nate to say he was going to hang with his friends, and they were getting pizza if that was okay. Nate said it was.

At home, Nate sat at the kitchen table, alone. His stomach reminded him he hadn't had lunch, in that over-hungry, little-bit-queasy way. An acid surge moved him to the fridge, where he poked around until he went with a dinner that required only a caveman's skills to prepare: lunch meat ham and sliced Cooper cheese. On the cutting board he plopped down a slice of ham, then cheese, then ham again. Like a sandwich, except screw you, bread. He made one, then another, then a third. Poor man's charcuterie.

By the time he finished that last one, an odor reached his nose.

Cigarette smoke.

His guts churned. He had to choke back the ham and cheese. He tried to will the scent away, concentrating on making it dissipate— and it did, only to be replaced by an unholy host of new smells— *familiar* smells, at that.

The stink of sweat.

The heady aroma of gun oil.

The sour reek of an old man dying—the rot of his skin, the pickled brine in his clothes, the specter of piss and shit and puke, all carrying the telltale traces of cancer in every ruinous molecule.

Nate closed his eyes as his heartbeat drummed in his chest like the hoofbeats of a wild horse. A waterfall of blood rushed through his temples, wrists, and neck.

Then the strange odors, the odors of his father both alive and dying, were gone.

With that, he thought, *I need a drink.* And he didn't want to drink alone.

Jed stood at his own doorway, gave Nate one good lookover, and declared, with a screwed-on smile, "If you don't mind a little bit of brutal honesty, Nate, you look like you've been run through the intestinal tract of an angry elephant." He lowered his voice to a comedic register: "And the elephant has a raging case of irritable bowel syndrome."

"Yeah, well." He gestured to see if he could come in. "Mind if I—?"

"Oh, sure, sure. Come on inside, fella."

And again Nate found himself in Jed's all-too-put-together cabin. And again he found himself with a glass of something whiskey-scented in his hand. It happened so fast he barely saw the man pour it.

"Scotch?" Nate asked.

"Single malt, yes, but American. Colorado single malt, actually. Stranahan's whiskey. Snowflake, they call this one—available only one day a year, every December, just before the long, true dark of winter. Had a buddy, a real estate guy, out west in Grand Junction procure me a bottle."

Nate took a sip. It nearly floored him—not because it was strong, though it was. But because it had all these peculiar flavors.

Jed must've seen his face light up. His eyebrows waggled in a salacious, dirty-old-man way. "Isn't it something?"

"It is."

"But I assume the fruit of my whiskeyed labors isn't why you're here, though you're always welcome to partake. What's on your mind, neighbor?"

"That's the problem. I have no idea what's on my mind."

"Hm," Jed said, as if he actually understood. He pulled over a stool and sat next to Nate. "Go on."

"I think I'm losing it, Jed."

"The mind is less precarious than we think it is, Nate. Often, I believe it is our *fear* of losing it that's more dangerous than actually losing it, if you'll follow my logic. The fear of a thing is quite often worse than the thing we fear, whether it's terrorism or immigrants or what-have-you."

Nate shook his head. "No, this is a real thing. I'm . . ."

"You're seeing things."

"How'd you know?"

Jed grinned like the cat that got the canary. "Because I see the look on your face, dear Nate, and I *recognize it*. It's like looking into a mirror, but a mirror from my past. As that bit of Shakespeare goes, 'There are more things in heaven and earth, Horatio, than are dreamt of in your philosophy.'"

"I don't believe in ghosts, Jed."

"Doesn't matter, because they believe in you."

A chill rappelled down Nate's spine at that.

"I'm seeing my father, Jed. My dead father."

Then he took the rest of his whiskey and downed it in one gulp.

"Attaboy," Jed said, finishing his own glass, too. He poured another two rounds and said, "Now we can have a real conversation."

Hours later, Nate was drunker than a songbird on fermented berries.

Jed had leaned in close, almost too close, when he said, "Thing is, Nate, we live across the street from—"

"Ramble Rocks," Nate said, and the words slurred. *Rambah Rahhcks.* His mouth felt tacky. Tasted like butterscotch and campfires.

"It's a *thin* place. The Lenape thought so. Early Quakers did, too. *Thin* meaning, the barrier between worlds there isn't like it is in other places. For years people have seen strange things there. An early Quaker account had them seeing 'strangers in the woods.' Others saw *themselves*—versions of themselves, like doppelgängers. Lotta ghost sightings out there among the boulders. It's why a serial killer like Edmund Reese did his killing there of those girls. He said it was a special place."

"You're drunk," Nate said.

"*You're* drunk," Jed said. "*J'accuse!*"

Seemed they were both drunk.

"So whaddya telling me, Jed? The weirdo beardo I've seen, or my father, they're because of Ramble Rocks? I heard tales growing up but . . . none of that shit is real. I'm just losing my mind is all."

"I don't think you are, son."

"Then what? What do I do? Hire an exorcist? A, a dang shaman?"

Deadly serious then, Jed said, "No. You just watch yourself. Careful with what you're seeing. Careful with who you trust. Maybe something or someone out there is playing tricks on you."

"Maybe *you're* playing tricks on me," Nate said with a wink.

Jed licked his lips and eased back. "Nate, I think you ought to get back home. Get some rest."

"Yeah." He *urped* up a charcoal burn in his throat. "Probably right, Jed. I'll see you. Thanks for the drink and the crazy stories."

"The stories may be crazy, Nate, but you aren't. Remember that."

"Uh-huh." With that, Nate stumbled out into the forest. Found his way to the house through the trees, trying not to trip on sticks and underbrush—be embarrassing to bust his ass this way. Jed was a bad influence on him. Once home, he found Oliver wasn't home yet—so he pulled up a bit of couch, told himself he was just giving his eyes a rest. When next he opened them, he'd find sunlight burning the bottoms of the curtains.

28

Into the Woods

You good, man?" Jake asked. He passed Olly the bottle. It was whiskey—some whiskey he'd never heard of. Jack Kenny American Single Malt. "You seem restless."

The two of them sat outside on a fallen log. They'd wandered down past Mom's half-finished pole barn, and that's where Jake decided he wanted to smoke. The October night was unseasonably warm. A few flies buzzed around them, excited that the warmth afforded them the privilege of, well, not yet dying. "I'm all right," Olly said, taking a plug from the bottle. The whiskey was like a caramel blowtorch in his mouth and throat. "My dad would fucking kill me if he knew I was out here drinking."

Jake laughed. "Your dad is, *at this very moment,* passed out drunk. He'd be a mighty fuckin' hypocrite to give you shit for it."

"He was a cop, you know."

"Like a detective?"

"No, a—I think a sergeant or something."

"Then you don't gotta worry. He's not Sherlock Holmes, kid." Jake snatched the bottle out of Olly's grip and screwed it to his lips and chugged it. "So, you're pretty fragile, huh?"

Oliver felt embarrassed suddenly and looked off into the darkening forest. Jake put up both hands—the bottle still in one, whiskey sloshing about—and added: "I don't mean any disrespect. I just mean, shit really gets to you."

"Yeah." Oliver didn't really want to be talking about this, but at the same time, *really wanted to talk about it.* "It's fine. I have a therapist."

"Fuck therapists, man."

"What?"

"I've done therapy. They don't tell you the truth."

"But I like my therapist."

Jake scoffed. "I didn't say you didn't or shouldn't *like* your therapist. I'm just saying, they're liars. They don't know they're liars. They just are. It's been coded into them, the lie."

"And what lie is that?"

"That you're broken, and that the way you are is on you to fix."

"I don't get what you mean."

Jake leaned forward, passing the bottle back. "I mean this: You being fucked up? It's normal. It's because you're keyed into something most people aren't. You're like an antenna, and you're always receiving the frequency. Other people are just lumps of nothing, man. They aren't receiving shit. But you? You're always getting the transmission."

"What transmission?" Oliver asked, taking the bottle but hesitating before taking a drink. "This sounds like conspiracy talk."

"No, it's not—it's not a literal transmission, Oliver. You just see what other people don't. Which is that the world is broken."

"No, I don't know about that—"

"Really? Looked around recently?"

"Yeah. It's screwed up out there. But . . ." The words died in his mouth. Jake echoed exactly his next thought:

"But what?"

"I don't know."

"You *do* know. But nothing, that's what. Look at school shootings."

At that, Oliver tensed up. He felt his pulse quicken. His hand began to shake. His mouth went dry even as his palms began to sweat.

Jake continued, putting a finger gun to his head and rocking his skull to the side: "Boom. Kids get popped. Little kids. Older kids. And who does what? Does anybody do anything? No. Thoughts and prayers, right?" His eye for a moment seemed to shine a moonsilver glow—Oliver was sure that had to be just his imagination, because when he looked again, it had stopped. "I'm just saying, nobody does anything. And the shootings keep coming. Malls, movie theaters, churches, synagogues, fuckin' everywhere. If the needle didn't move for a bunch of dead elementary schoolkids, it's never gonna move. It's broken. Unfixable because it's too big, too complex, too, I dunno. Too *much*. And you feel that. In your gut. In your head. In your—" And here Jake reached out and thrust a hard finger against Oliver's chest, making Oliver flinch. "In your fuckin' *heart,* kid. You're not crazy. You're the sanest one in the whole damn world. Sane as me, because I get it, too."

Oliver wasn't sure. Was the world broken? Could he even tell that? That didn't feel right. He couldn't think about big sprawling systems. Only about the people caught in them. Trapped, chewed up, crushed.

"What do you mean, you get it, too?" Oliver asked.

"I used to be like you. Upset all the time. Scared like a constantly pissing Chihuahua."

Now, *now,* Oliver took the bottle to his lips. No little sip this time; he took a big gulp. It lit him up like a city at night. He leaned forward and asked:

"So how did you stop being that way?"

"Oh, man, we don't have nearly enough time to answer that question, but we'll get there. For now, just know this: First and foremost I had to quit dicking around with therapy. I stopped listening to strangers, and I started listening to myself. And to the words of good friends. Friends who had my back. Friends who *got me.* You feel me?"

Oliver nodded. Because *that* he understood.

29

Aaaaaand We're Back

Morning progressed in fits and starts. Like being half in and half out of time. Nate sat at the table, cradling a glass of water, a quartet of Advil still feeling stuck in his throat. Olly was cooking breakfast for himself: oatmeal. Which Nate absolutely did not want because right now eating oatmeal would make him feel like a dog eating his own yack out of a bowl instead of off the floor. He did want coffee, though, and Olly was good enough to get that going for him.

And then, just like that, the front door opened and in popped Maddie.

Soon as she stepped into the kitchen, Olly leapt up out of his chair and met her with a monster hug, one that lingered a long time. She kissed the top of his head. He looked like a little kid again. Their boy had always been freewheeling with affection: giving a lot of it and demanding a lot of it, too. Which was nice, and never unwelcome, even if Nate sometimes wondered if it spoke to something needy about the boy. Just the same, it was very nice to see that affection again.

Nate looked at his watch, told Oliver to take his oatmeal upstairs and finish getting ready for school, because they'd have to leave soon. He skulked past Nate, giving his father a dubious look.

For a moment, an icy distance spanned the space between Nate and Maddie. The rolling carry-on sat at her side.

"You look like shit on sandpaper," she said.

He barked a laugh. "I maybe tied one on with Jed."

"I guess I need to meet Jed."

"He's coming to the party, so."

Silence widened the chasm between them. But then she stepped over to him without reservation. She melted into him and kissed his cheek.

"I'm sorry I had to go," she said.

"It's okay," he said, and he meant it. "I missed you."

"I missed you. I'm back now."

"Will you tell me where you went?"

She didn't answer. The absence of a response dug its teeth into him. *Where'd you go, Maddie?*

"We'll be okay," is all she said, finally.

"Okay."

But the fact she had to say it at all made him worry it was a lie.

Interlude: The Coal Mine at Ramble Rocks

The boy, twelve years old, ran through purple-top grass. He could not see very well, for he had been crying—crying so hard that his nostrils hurt from being snotty and wiping the snot on his sleeves again and again until his nose chafed and the skin went raw. His body felt sore, too, like it had been crunched up like an old soda can. This was not the first time he'd felt this way. It was, he also knew, not the last. It would go on and on like this forever. Wouldn't it?

Though why, then, did he run away? He ran and ran, ran for what felt like miles, dozens, *hundreds* of miles (even though it was not so far as that), and running away felt like a grasp at freedom. Like maybe there was a chance of keeping going. He told himself that he didn't have to turn around, didn't have to go back home again.

But what about Mom, he thought.

You can't leave her alone.

Not with him.

A new pain found him: a hard stitch in his side. A cramp that felt like someone was pulling on one of his rib bones with a pair of pliers.

So, the boy slowed to a walk, and then stopped.

Ahead, a shape loomed.

He'd seen it before, but never this close. The Ramble Rocks coal mine. The pale white logs framing the entrance were wrapped in poison ivy and creeper vine. The ivy had started to turn colors already in advance of autumn. The mine had long been shuttered; it was a dead place now, just a hole in the world, a void.

Behind the entrance, the trees were mostly dead, only a few meager leaves on bone-finger branches. The light of the late day coming through those trees seemed strange—weak and thin, like the glow of a lamp through an old, filthy bedsheet.

The boy stood, chest rising and falling. He put a hand to his side to massage the cramp between his ribs.

He blinked and, for a moment, the entrance to the mine seemed to . . . change. One blink and it became a hungry, gaping mouth. A black maw with a train-track tongue emerging from it. A blink and it was back to what it was: the mine entrance, with a big number 8 painted at the top in fading, cracking black.

A small part of him thought, *I can go in there. I can live there.* A faint breeze stirred in his direction, moving against him, as if coming from within the mine entrance. As if it were breathing. And that breath carried a whisper:

Come to me.

He gasped and forced the whisper from his mind. But it came again and again, *Come to me, come to me,* then in song like a howl through broken window glass: *Cooooome to meeeee.* The boy squeezed his whole body until it went away. But it did not go away, and wouldn't, he realized. The boy knew he had to get away from this place.

So he turned and ran the other direction, not quite toward home—he wasn't ready for that commitment, no, not yet—but away from the mine.

And then, something sprang up in front of him out of the falling thatch of purple-topped grass—a dark shape summoned by the stirring of the boy's feet, and it bolted into the air, *flut-flut-flut-flut,* and even as he pinballed the other direction and ran even harder, he knew it was a bird, just a stupid, stupid bird. Some kind of pheasant or dove. It didn't even matter. But he was scared and so he ran harder, his string-bean legs carrying him forward hard and fast—until he took a step onto ground that was no longer solid. It was soft and wet. His leg sank in and he pitched forward, crying out. His hands tried to catch his fall, but ahead the ground was soft, too.

Black ooze gleamed underneath a carpet of leaves and sticks. The black morass licked at his chin, and he realized what this was: coal silt. Wet like quicksand. His heart trembled in his chest, an anxious spasm. He tried to reach out and find solid ground, but the goop turned into a viselike grip when he tried to pull out of it. And working to crawl out of it only seemed to sink him deeper. He said, "Please, no," to himself, and then screamed, but as he did, the silt mire glommed onto his lip, dripping across his mouth like a clot of crawling slugs, and it sputtered as he yelled into it.

The boy then tried to spin himself around—certainly he had *come* from solid ground, he just had to find it again. But it was like screwing a screw deeper, and he only sank even farther down. Now both legs were under the ooze, and then most of his arms. His elbows were in the slurry, but his hands were still stretched out, though they could stretch no farther. His fingers scrabbled fruitlessly against the muck, even as the mire pulled him down.

He began to cry. Because this was how it would end for him, he realized. And a little part of him wondered if maybe that wasn't for the best. Maybe what he was running away from was worse. Maybe this was what he was running to. But then as the silt bubbled up over his mouth, covering it, pressing against his nostrils and stifling his breath, panic swarmed through him and he thought, *No no no this isn't better I don't want to die here I don't want to die,* and he couldn't breathe and he knew that suffocating in this silt scum would be a terrible way to die—at least drowning in water would feel somehow cool, somehow peaceful, but this was holding him fast like a tightening fist.

He imagined suddenly that he'd never see his mother again. That his father was the one pushing him down, holding him here, urging him beneath the morass of coal silt. That this was just part of the end-less cycle—or maybe one that would end right here and now.

He disappeared underneath the surface.

The silt drew him down into the true dark. Even under the bub-bling black skin of silt, his stifled scream could still be heard.

Until, of course, it couldn't.

PART THREE

TOO LITTLE SKIN FOR TOO MUCH SKULL

June 6 1907 Alfred Kaschak, dead by inhalation of gasses

June 8 1907 Anatol Sekelsky, legs crushed between cars

June 8 1907 Ten men ded by explosion & rooffall at breakline 112 feet from Cold Spring breast [Randall Aherne, Mickey Hart, Stacker Wiznewski, Jerry Munroe, etc]

June 10 1907 Stefan Schwarzhugel, kicked by cantankarus mule

June 13 1907 Miners say Liam O'Neill blugeoned Rodolf Kasternak with handl of pick ax while Kasternak was using breast auger to drill into wall for explosives

O'Neill gone missing

June 14 1907 Liam O'Neill found deceaced near Pipersville bed, tunnel 7, with breast auger drill in fore head and chest bone broken in half

something had aten his leg above him on wall someone had chiseled in rock

KA REISKIA SAPNUOTI PASAULIO PABAIGA

—page 42 of 176, Ramble Rocks coal mine Book of Accidents

30

This Is Halloween

Worries chased worries around Maddie's head. Worries about art, about murderers, about her family, about her place in all of this. Even days after her time in the sensory deprivation tank and her drive out to State College, she was only more off-kilter than before. She felt like, *I don't know who I am anymore, and I'm afraid of what I can do.* But all that had to be shoved in a drawer, slammed shut and fucking locked, because at this very moment the doorbell was ringing, *ding-dong, ding-dong,* because now their Halloween shindig was in full swing.

Maddie stapled a smile onto her face as she answered the door—

And there stood *two* people, not one.

One, she recognized: Trudy Breen. The other was a man roughly Trudy's age. He had a muss of white hair, a set of frizzle-fried eyebrows, and a look that was both somehow mischievous and comforting in equal measure. He wore a dark cardigan sweater over a lavender button-down, accentuated by a pair of shiny new Nike sneakers on his feet. Sneakers that matched the outfit, of course; this was a well-put-together fellow.

A cold wind swept in. Just yesterday it had gone up to the nineties, and today it was in the fifties, with the mercury dropping fast.

"Trudy," Maddie said, welcoming her friend. And to the man she said, "And you must be Jed?"

He nodded, and she invited them inside just as a light rain began to fall.

"Nate said you were beautiful, but he did not remark on your cunning intellect. Indeed, I'm your neighbor." A comment like that could be coded as snarky, but Maddie felt that he meant it, and so when he went in for a half hug and a kiss on the cheek, she went with it. Anybody else and she might've given them a stiff shove. But something about him put her defenses at rest, like he was an old friend, or a member of the family she just hadn't seen in a good many years.

With his unhugging hand, he offered Maddie a bottle of something.

"Oh, thank you," Maddie said. It was Cognac.

Trudy jumped in to appraise the bottle and said, "Your neighbor here drinks the good stuff." She tapped the bottle with a long fake nail. *Tink tink.*

"Well," Jed said with some combination of humility and embarrassment, "I simply cannot abide anyone drinking inferior adult beverages; it would pain me and bring shame to my doorstep. That, my dear, is De Luze XO, a Champagne Cognac—it's won awards. It's fascinating to me," he went on, "that alcohol is the product of ruination. As many of the best things are! It's perfectly good grape juice gone past sour into something sublime. Art is like that, too, and I know you're an artist—a blank canvas is white before anyone touches it, white and pure and perfect, like a yard coated in a carpet of freshly fallen snow. But if you want to get out there and experience it— maybe build a snowman or two—you have to ruin it, don't you? Have to muck it all up. So it is with all things, I believe."

Maddie attempted a loose mimicry of Jed's voice: "Nate said you were beautiful, Jed, but he did not remark on your cunning intellect."

Jed's eyes lit up. "Oh, I like you already." He whooped with laughter.

Outside, the wind met it with laughter of its own.

*   *   *

"So who's this dude again?" Caleb asked.

Caleb and Hina were hanging out in the garage with Oliver. They sat around eating candy and drinking soda and playing Magic. Chessie couldn't make it, and Steven rolled his eyes at the idea of a Halloween party at Oliver's house.

"I told you," Oliver said, "I crashed my bike one day and he helped me bring it home. He's new to the area."

He hadn't yet told them about Graham and Alex running him off the road. And how Alex had tried to drown him. *And* how Jake had appeared, as if out of nowhere, with a pellet pistol in his hand. Why he hadn't told them, he couldn't be sure.

"You sure he's coming?" Hina asked. She was the only one of them in costume: She came as Link, from *Legend of Zelda,* but, specifically, *Breath of the Wild*—her blue, almost Mediterranean-style tunic matched the anime-slash-Greek-myth vibe of her shield, bow, and Master Sword. She'd handcrafted all of it. She cosplayed a lot at Comic-Cons, made her own outfits from scratch. Sewing, 3D printer, foam-core stuff.

"Because your man is late," Caleb said.

"He's not—" Oliver shook his head. "He's not my man."

"Ay, it's just a saying, Olly. Relax."

And then came a *rap-rap-rapp*ing on the garage door.

They all looked at one another.

"Maybe that's him," Hina said.

"He does know there's a front door, right?" Caleb asked, eyebrow up. Oliver shrugged and hurried over, hitting the button that elevated the garage bay door. It growled open, and when it did—

It revealed Jake standing there on the other side. Dead leaves whirled around him in a little cyclone as a spitting rain started to fall. He smirked from underneath his black hoodie. "'Sup, Olly."

Once Jake was inside, Oliver made introductions. Hina was super-friendly, but Caleb offered him little more than a cursory nod.

"You not know there's a front door, man?" Caleb asked.

"Caleb, c'mon—" Olly said.

But Jake waved him off. "Nah, it's cool. I just figured, you guys are out here, so I'll come out here. I don't wanna fuckin' deal with adults and shit. They gotta ask you twenty questions and I don't feel like getting my leg caught in that particular bear trap."

"What, you don't like questions?" Caleb asked.

"Not as much as you do, apparently," Jake said, bristling.

Hina twirled in between them. "Hey. Ignore Caleb. He's dressed up tonight as Rude Motherfucker-Man, the worst Marvel superhero."

"I'm like Spider-Man," Caleb said, "but instead of slinging webs, I just throw shade."

And that did it. Whatever ice wall had started to build up between them, cracked and shattered with one good round of laughter. Olly felt suddenly relieved. He hated it when people didn't get along.

Nate had been watching his wife. Since she went away, she'd been guarded. Cagey in a way he didn't understand. He gave her whatever space she needed, but something was off. Just like, he thought, things felt off all around him. Always in ways he couldn't quite *grasp*.

Maddie, who had seemed tense around Fig and his wife, Zoe, seemed to instantly relax around Jed. And Nate suspected he knew why: Jed was a writer. A fellow artist of a sort—didn't hurt, too, that it turned out Maddie had not only read some of his books, but was a big fan.

She was saying to him as the others listened in, "I could never be a writer. I think you have to live too much inside your head. Art for me is about getting *out* of my head. It's like a doorway to somewhere else."

"Well," Jed said, laughing a little. "Sure, sometimes writing can mean lingering too long in your skull, so to speak, but when it really hits you, it's like a wave carrying you out to sea. I know that the muse is—" And on this word he lowered his voice like he was sharing some salacious secret. "*Horseshit,* and I know we are in full control of what goes on the page, but sometimes . . ." He sucked air through his teeth. "Sometimes it feels like there's *some* kind of magic going on, not just the kind with rabbits and hats. Sorcery! Bona fide sorcery. You open yourself to it, then you capture it. Or maybe *it* captures *you.*"

At that, Nate saw Maddie nod. But her demeanor shifted once more—she crossed her arms defensively. Had Jed just pissed her off? He couldn't see how. But her lips were pursed and she was going *mm, mmm,* like she was faking agreement.

"Are we just vessels for the art?" she asked. "Doorways?"

Jed seemed to ponder this. "Could be, could be. But like I said, I think we control it. I don't think it controls us. The question is, do you really see it as *the art,* or *your art*? That deserves an answer. Or an attempt to find that answer, at least."

"That means we have to ask if we do it for other people? Or is it just for ourselves?"

He smiled, almost viciously. "We pretend we do it for others, but I think we make art for ourselves. The selfish masquerading as the selfless."

Worry darkened Maddie's face like a shadow.

Trudy said suddenly and bluntly, "So you write ghost books."

"Ah. Ha ha. No, not really," Jed said. "Ghosts are certainly a part of it. I like to say I write about haunted spaces and haunted things, but that is not always—or even often—purely about specters and wraiths. Folklore is really my thing, and this area, I must say, is positively *bloody* with it. The cannibal albinos of Buckingham Hill, or the Hansell Road ghost lights, or the Devil's Church of Ghost Mountain."

"So tell us a story," Fig said. It didn't come across as hostile, exactly, but Nate could detect a bit of ball busting in there—a whiff of dubiousness.

"Fig," Nate cautioned. "C'mon."

But Jed, his eyes—hell, his whole posture—lit up like Frankenstein's monster coming alive on the mad doctor's table. "I can tell you about the rocks of Ramble Rocks. And why the stories say that they *move*."

Everyone shared a look of curiosity. Jed grinned, eyebrows waggling—the look of a fisherman who had just got a big bite on the line.

Nate, for his part, tensed up. This again?

"Let's hear it," Zoe said.

"They call them the Ramble Rocks," Jed began, "because they have been proven to move. Six instances, in fact, throughout recorded local history, where the rocks have moved. Shifted. Every last rock in the *felsenmeer*—that's fancy talk for a boulder field—moved just a little. Sometimes less than an inch, sometimes as much as three or four inches. When they do this, they leave gentle tracks behind in the dirt, as if *slowly migrating* like glacially slow turtles. But these are no turtles, no—they're rocks, subvolcanic rocks. Basalt and diabase."

"There's gotta be a scientific reason," Fig said.

Jed snapped his fingers. "The scientific theory is this: The rocks move because of earthquakes and sound frequencies. The rocks themselves are said to emit, when struck with a mallet, a ringing sound. A frequency. Barely detectable by the human ear. Sound waves have considerable power in concert—one need only to consider how different tones could vibrate a scattering of sand into almost mystical patterns to see this in action. So, were there to be even an insignificant tectonic movement on one of the micro-fault lines beneath the park, that might in turn cause the rocks to ring their frequency, humming in just such a way that they would literally move. Like a phone on vibrate as it rang, juddering its way across a nightstand before eventually dropping to the carpet below. *Vbbt, vbbt, thud.* And of course, below Ramble Rocks *is* in fact a fault line—the Aquetong-Lahaska fault. Starts in central Bucks and runs all the way up here."

"See?" Fig said, looking around like, duh.

Jed grinned big and broad. "But there are *other* theories."

"Oooh," Zoe said.

"Do tell," Trudy said dryly, feigning disinterest, but it was easy enough to see she, too, was a fish on Jed's line.

Nate leaned over to Maddie, who seemed only half-listening. He asked in a low voice: "You okay?"

She nodded and said, half-distracted, "Sure."

Jed went on.

"The Lenape, who once claimed this territory as their own—you know, before we took it from them—had their tales. Most agreed the rocks moved as the result of some manner of spirit or god—perhaps Kupahweese, the trickster. Or maybe it was an act performed by the mischievous little Wemategunis—these spirits of the forest were known for moving things about, sometimes a misplaced tool, sometimes a landmark so that it became difficult to find your way home. Others in the tribe believed a figure of darkness and death was responsible. Mahtantu was its name"—and here Jed gave a look to Nate—"and they said he slept beneath the boulder field, and when he turned over in his troubled dreams, the boulders moved.

"Some said the Devil himself fell there from Heaven, and he moved the boulders from time to time as a way to confound early settlers to the area. And there's always the more modern spin on the tale, chalking it up to a government conspiracy, magnetic fields, or aliens—given that UFO sightings are considerably higher here than in most parts of the country."

Fig waved it all off. "C'mon. Aliens and the Devil and spooky spirits. That's fun and everything, but it's all made up."

"Axel Figueroa," Zoe chided him, using his full name like a bludgeon. "You are being rude."

"He's right, of course," Jed said. "It is all made up. But you know what isn't? History. The history of this area may give you some pause."

Just like that, he had them. And he started reeling them in.

"The Lenape sold this area to the Penn family (yes, the family of

William Penn, Penn as in *Penn*sylvania) as part of the 1737 Walking
Purchase, and records show that in 1850 the Penn family in turn sold
it to a man named Tiberius Goode, though no other records would
ever confirm the existence of this Mr. Goode. All that was known was
that this supposed benefactor was very clear on one point: He'd left a
mandate in place to ensure that the land could never be developed,
nor could the boulders be mined or used for any purpose—they
would remain utterly undisturbed. Later, a man named Benjamin
Caine Smithard—a supposed 'friend' of the mysterious Tiberius
Goode—purchased a 128-acre zone around the seven-acre boulder
field.

"It was also around this time that a pair of bank robbers—the
Doal brothers, Leviticus and Lemuel—came to Ramble Rocks after
robbing a bank with the intent of hiding their plundered bank loot in
one of the caves around the area. One problem, though: Ramble
Rocks had no caves. They were under the mistaken belief that the
area was rife with caves, but it was not. (Many speculated that they
had gotten it confused with an area known as Wolf Rocks, which
exists about twenty miles to the south, on Buckingham Mountain.)
Finding no caves, they sought to leave the area—but found themselves confounded how to escape. Though seven acres is not a particularly large space, the journals of the one brother, Leviticus, indicate
that they were trapped there for days, unable to flee. They lost their
loot. And eventually they lost one another. Their bodies were discovered only ten feet apart, even though Leviticus's journal indicated
that, at the end of their lives, they had separated and could not find
each other.

"Then there are the tales of the train tunnel—and what happened
there. A conductor, *literally* losing his head. The serial killer, Edmund
Walker Reese, snatching up his first victim from within that tunnel—
and other girls from around the area. He even killed one of them on
one of the rocks in the felsenmeer. He was fascinated with them. He
had detailed maps and drawings. He said he counted *ninety-nine 'spe-*

cial' rocks, and felt that number was somehow . . . sacred or special in a numerological way. He called the boulder field a 'place of sacrifice.' Which of course only deepened and darkened the urban legends around the area. The satanic panic spun up stories about other acts of ritualized human sacrifice, though none were ever discovered."

"Jesus," Fig said.

Nate, for his part, was still listening—but he'd stopped paying *attention* to Jed as much. Instead, he watched his wife.

As Jed had rounded the bend on the last leg of his story—talking about Reese—Nate saw Maddie visibly flinch. She gripped the counter behind her as if the whole floor were about to fall out from underneath her.

Just then, the wind really kicked up outside. And with it, a pounding rain. The whole house creaked and groaned under the sudden assault. A chill seemed to move through the room; they all felt it, and reacted to it.

Jed, meanwhile, wore a cheeky face, as if this surge in bad weather was all part of the plan. Special effects, maybe. Pleased as peaches, he said, "I dare say we've angered the spirits of Ramble Rocks."

"I say we've angered the Earth," Zoe said. "It's climate change."

"Zo," Fig said. "Not again."

"Oh, gods," Trudy said, "let's talk about something a little less of a bummer, please."

Just then: *Bang!*

The loud sound came from the front of the house.

They all froze and stared.

"A branch, maybe—" Maddie started to say.

"Or ghosts," Jed added, grinning with cheeky ghoulishness.

The room grew cold.

"It's just the front door," Nate said. "Feel the temperature drop in here? Wind must've blown it open. Maybe it wasn't closed. I'll go get it." On the way, he passed his wife, and he asked her: "You okay?"

"Great," she said, stiffly.

I wish you'd tell me what's bothering you, he thought. But then he thought of his own emotional seawall—and maybe Maddie had her own.

He gave her a quick, cursory peck on the cheek before heading out of the room to close the door.

31

Of Masks and Magic

The garage bay doors rattled and banged as the wind shouldered against them, as if eager to gain entry. Something in the house went *bang*, too, and Oliver and the others looked to each other. They shrugged and then laughed it off, but a tiny flash of Halloween-tinged fear went through them like a shared electrical spark.

A chill crept into the garage. The garage was far newer than the rest of the house, and it had vents that blew fuel-oil heat into the space, but the insulation was terrible. The walls felt paper-thin against the growing storm.

"We could go inside," Olly said.

"No way," Jake said, hands stuffed down deep in his jean pockets. "It's fine. It's just weather."

"I'm with him," Hina said, staring at Jake, moon-eyed.

Caleb spun a chair and sat in it. "I'm cool with that. Let's game. Jake, you in? We can start over—we didn't get far in our first thing, so we can do something else."

But Jake just looked confused. Oliver smiled and said, "Wanna play Magic? I can get you one of my decks since I'm assuming you didn't bring your own. I have a cool blue-black deck—pirates and assassins. It's a tempo-deathtouch strategy and—"

"I don't know what the fuck you're talking about. What's Magic?"

"Magic," Caleb said. "You know. *Magic: The Gathering*. MTG. Card game."

"Like magic tricks."

"No, what? Not like magic tricks, man. Boy over here says he doesn't know Magic, all right, okay. Ay, come on over, sit down, Jake, it's cool. We'll teach you. It'll be fun. You pretend to be a wizard and shit, and you bring out these creatures and then battle them and stuff. It's like, I dunno, if Pokémon and D&D got teleported together like Goldblum and the fly."

Jake wore an acid look. "You're still speaking total gibberish."

"You know, *The Fly*. Jeff Goldblum?"

Still nothing.

"Pokémon? D&D? Ringing a bell?"

"Sure," he said, but it didn't look like he got it. Jake waved it off. "I'm just not a huge nerd about it." When everyone gave him salty looks, he rolled his eyes. "Okay, don't get sand in your assholes about it." Then he leaned forward, grinned so big his mouth was like a boomerang. "Hey, you guys wanna see some *real* magic?"

Outside, thunder tumbled in time to Jake cracking his knuckles.

Nate headed to the front door and found that, sure enough, it was wide open. The wind juggled it open and closed in front of him. Outside, the rain had gone from spitting to a steady pour, and as Nate shielded his face from the cold wind, thunder growled in the night.

Helluva little storm rolling in here, he thought.

He stepped outside, the porch roof shielding him from most of the rain—though the roof was in such dreadful shape it had already begun to drip—and as he reached for the doorknob—

Nate felt someone step behind him. He heard the creak of floorboards, but even more, he felt a heavy presence. It closed off the sound of the storm behind him, like a wall built suddenly.

He felt breath on the back of his neck. Smelled cigarettes and sour beer and gun oil.

Lightning lit up the Halloween dark, and Nate saw someone

standing out there on the front lawn—he spied the familiar raw-boned body, the raggedy beard, the mouth stretched wide.

And then the dark resumed and the thunder rolled.

Another breath fell upon the back of his neck. Once more he wheeled around—careful this time because *what if it's my son,* but it wasn't Olly, not at all. Nate's father stood there, meeting him nose to nose. The skin of the old man's face shifted and rippled as if the bones of his skull were breaking down and re-forming, popping and crunching. The man hissed, a gassy mush-mouth, and backhanded Nate with the pistol. Nate's head rocked back; he tasted blood as his lip split. He staggered backward, falling off the porch and onto his ass. And the realization hit him once again that his father held the gun in his left hand—

But the old man had always been right-handed.

Everyone waited as Jake tugged back the sleeves of his hoodie, as if to demonstrate that nothing was up them.

He did a little spin, too, hands up, palms out.

When he returned again to face the three of them, he tickled his fingertips against one another and said, "Abracadabra, alakazam, something-something . . . goddamn flim-flam."

And then, in a flamenco pose, he held his left hand against his stomach while raising his right hand in the air—

He snapped the fingers on the raised hand.

And a gun appeared there in his grip.

"Voi-fuckin'-la," he said, cackling.

Blood and rain ran into Nate's eyes. He was flat on his back, off the porch, the air kicked out of his lungs. He struggled to get a breath. More blood in his mouth. He spat, then tried sitting up, certain that the specter of his father would once again be gone, vanished into nothing as it had so many times before—

But Nate was wrong.

The old man was walking toward Nate. Slowly. Erratically. Like he was a science-class skeleton being puppeted by the kids. Tics and twitches cascaded through Carl Graves's body: the jerk of a shoulder, the twist of his head, the sharp *clack* of his teeth—that sound, loud enough to be heard over the wind and the rain. And all the while, the gun swung in his left hand.

"Gone rotten," the old man said. A saying Nate knew all too well: Whenever the drink was in him, that's what he said to express his disappointment in Nate, or his mother, or the whole world. *It's all gone rotten. You're rotten. She's rotten.* Then he'd grab her by the throat, or throw a punch into his son's stomach, or slam one of them into a wall. It's what he said, too, before he killed their dog, a little rat terrier Nate had named Cookie. Carl came at Nate one time, and Cookie bit him on the hand. He hissed at her, *You rotten goddamn dog,* and then grabbed her by the throat and gave her head a hard, sharp twist like he was trying to open a stubborn pickle jar. One yelp and she went limp. It saved Nate a beating that day, though.

So he knew that phrase well.

Rotten. Gone rotten. You're rotten, she's rotten, rotten, rotten, rotten.

And with those memories came rage. He leapt up, catching the wrist of the old man's gun arm. It was real. Flesh and blood. He twisted it. Felt it snap. The old man cried out, blinking against the rain—

Can ghosts feel the rain? Can you break one's arm?

"You sonofabitch," Nate hissed.

"That you, Nathan?"

Carl's voice was weak and pleading. Blubbering as rain sputtered on his sickly gray lips. And then the bones under his face shifted once more, and suddenly the old man was younger, young like Nate remembered him.

Nate forced the broken arm toward his father, moving the gun barrel toward the old man's skull.

"Gonna kill you now like I wish I had so many times," Nate growled through grinding teeth.

"*Rotten. Rotten. Ruined. And now it's here. You need answers, Nathan. You need to see.*"

The gun barrel pressed hard against his father's cheek. Nate forced his finger into the trigger guard, over the man's finger—a finger that didn't feel like a finger, but mushier, softer, like a gummy worm.

And then, as he went to pull it—

His father cried out, his whole body seizing up—

The air flashed bright. Nate heard a crisp electric sizzle, and the stink of ozone filled his nose and blinded him.

Then the old man was gone once again.

And as the flash of lightning receded, he saw Jed standing there in the doorway. Eyes wide. Mouth agape.

Moments passed between them. They stared at each other.

"You saw that," Nate said. "You saw my father, too. Did you? Jed?"

"I . . ." Jed said.

Which was all the answer Nate required.

Jake sneered and raised the pistol.

Hina cried out. Caleb stood up so fast he nearly fell over his own chair—the chair toppled backward. Olly hurried forward, stepping in front of his friends as fear pulsed in them, bright as a full moon.

"Put it down," Oliver said, hearing the tremor in his own voice.

Jake, looking incredulous, held up the gun and looked at it like he was holding something absurd: a cucumber, a snow globe, a rubber dick. "Jesus, you guys are wound tight. Olly, this is the *same* pellet pistol you saw the day I met you. The day I saved your ass from those dickheads?"

"What?" Caleb asked. "Olly. What's he talking about?"

"He didn't tell you?" Jake asked.

Caleb wheeled on Jake. "Shut up, dude. Did it sound like I was talking to you? And put that gun away. Pellet pistol or not, that shit

right there looks like a real-deal army pistol, man. You can't be fuckin'
waving that around and pointing it at people."

"Here I thought you all might appreciate a little magic," Jake said.

"I can't do this," Hina said. "I can't handle this energy. I'm gonna
go?" That last bit, asked like she wasn't yet sure. "Yeah. I'm gonna go."

"I'll go with you," Caleb said.

"It's all right," Olly said, stepping in front of Caleb. "He'll say sorry.
Jake. Right? Jake, say sorry."

Jake, indignant, shook his head and sneered. "I'm not apologizing.
I saved your ass with this pistol, Olly. Put some steel in your back-
bone."

Please don't make me do this, Olly thought. His pulse throbbed in
his neck, his temple, his wrists. He felt sick and sweaty. He could see
the anger and fear now in Hina and Caleb. It was real. Jake, on the
other hand, was a blank slate. Or worse: an empty hole. But just the
same, he *did* save Oliver. And Oliver owed him. Didn't he?

Caleb said to him in a low voice: "Tell him he's gotta go, Olly. Tell
him to get his ass out of here."

"I—I can't. He did help me out and—maybe we can all talk. Or
just forget about it. Plus the weather is—" As if on cue, the wind
shoved hard against the garage doors, and they rattled so hard he
thought they were gonna crash inward.

The look of disappointment was plain on Caleb's face.

"All right, man. I'll see you." Then to Hina: "C'mon, Hina. Let's
bounce. I'll drive you home before the weather gets serious."

"Please," Olly said. "Guys."

"Hit the button, man," Caleb said.

For a moment, Oliver thought to be truly indignant—he wanted
to act like a baby and stomp his feet and say *no,* and refuse to hit
that button, but what was the point? They wanted to go. He didn't
blame them. He'd want to get away, too. He'd screwed up. No fixing
it now.

He hit the button. The garage door lifted. Caleb and Hina walked out.

"I was just messing around," Jake said, finally.

"Shut up," Olly answered.

And that's when the lights went out.

32

Precipitation

*J*ed *saw my father.*

Nate knew it. He could see it in the man's faraway stare. Nate eased his neighbor in through the front door and he said, "You saw him."

"I—Nate—"

"Don't stonewall me. You said you've seen things. Don't tell me I didn't see what I saw. Don't tell me *you* didn't see it."

"I saw. I saw Carl." Then his eyes refocused and looked to Nate's brow. "Nate. Your mouth. You're bleeding."

And that's when the power went out. A *click*, a *pop*, followed by darkness. The usual electronic hum of modern life left them, and they were alone in the black with the sounds of the weather—the wind that shifted from whistling to sounding like a black train blasting past, then sounds of the scattering, seething rain, and after came a rattle-hiss noise like someone casting driveway gravel against the roof and side of the house.

"Is that hail?" came a voice from the other end of the hallway.

Fig.

"Sounds like," Jed said, putting a little bit of that avuncular charm back into his voice. It wavered—Nate knew it was a false chumminess.

"We'll talk about this," Nate said to his neighbor on the sly. "Later."

And then, still half-dizzy, his head throbbing, Nate snapped into storm prep mode. He felt his way down the hallway, zeroing in on a square of light there in the dark: the light of Fig's phone.

In the kitchen, Maddie asked: "What's wrong?"

Nate said that it was . . . it was fine, just some bad weather. "Accident maybe knocked down a pole somewhere or a transformer blew. Mads, can you dig out some candles or flashlights or something?"

Maddie said they were probably still in boxes, but she knew where. She headed off to collect them.

Nate fumbled for his own phone, turned on its native flashlight.

"Anything we can do?" Fig asked, standing next to Zoe.

"Nah," Nate said, trying not to seem rattled. He'd just been choked by his dead father as a bearded freak stood in the woods and watched. And Jed *saw it happen,* or so it seemed, at least. And if that was the case . . . then that meant this wasn't in his head. It was real. How real, though?

Idly, he reached for his head. His palm came away wet. The light from Fig's phone hit him, and Zoe said: "Nate. Oh my god. You're bleeding."

How real?

That real. Real as blood.

Ghosts weren't known to hit you with a gun, were they?

"I'm all right," Nate said, pretending it wasn't anything. "Wind caught the door and clocked me in the noggin. Everybody all right in here?" They nodded that they were. But was *he* all right?

No, he decided. He was not.

But at least he wasn't crazy.

Just then, Nate's phone buzzed.

So, too, did Fig's.

"Oh, damn it, baby," Zoe said.

Nate didn't understand, until he did. Their phones were buzzing with a text alert that the security system at the office was down. He said to Fig, "It's just because of the weather, I'm sure."

"Yeah," Fig said, but in his voice Nate could tell what was coming next. "Still, policy is, we gotta check it out. We're not exactly a police station there, but we have guns and evidence samples in lockup, can't have someone taking advantage of the storm. That'd be on us."

"All right, then," Nate said. The job was the job. "I'll get my jacket."

On the way to the hall closet, he ran into Maddie—physically ran into her—and had to juggle the box of flashlights between them. "Whoa," he said. "Sorry about that."

Her face in the flashlight glow was frozen in fear. She was trying not to let it show, but it was strong enough she couldn't hide it. *Her seawall is breaking,* he thought. He held her close. "What is it?"

"Nothing." She bared her teeth. "Everything. Something? I don't know. We have to talk."

"Yeah. I figure we do. But I gotta go to the office. The security system is down and—"

"Nate, the weather is awful. Wind sounds like a beast." Not usually one to be overly concerned, it was jarring to him when she said: "Don't go."

"I have to. But I'll be all right. I'll have Fig with me."

She closed her eyes and sighed. "Okay."

"We'll talk after."

"You be safe."

"I will," he said, a corkscrew of worry turning tightly in his middle. Then he kissed her cheek and told her to say goodbye to Oliver for him. And he reiterated again that he'd be okay.

Because what could possibly go wrong?

33

The Spiral

Anxiety trapped Oliver like a ring of spears.

In one direction: the storm. It was bad. He knew it was bad. Wind shook the house. Hail scattered against the walls like shotgun pellets. This wasn't a normal storm. The specter of climate change rose in his head: a great hot shadow that would burn up the earth and boil the seas. But there, the fear in him was not about its effects on him, but the effects on everyone he loved. On people he didn't even know. On *birds* and *fish* and—for a moment, his mind spiraled and he thought of people screaming as wildfires burned their houses down, or someone as they drowned in rising floodwaters, on refugees forced from their homes and thrown into camps . . .

Or his own father. Who, right now, was out in the storm. A few minutes ago, Mom popped her head into the garage, told Olly that Dad had to go check on the office, but did he *really* have to go? Oliver had always worried about his father being a cop and getting killed in the line of duty. That worry was supposed to be over and done with. But now, here he was, worrying his dad wouldn't ever come back. Again. An absurd fear, but his mind played it out: *We'll find the truck crashed, slammed into a tree, Dad's body in a ditch, the corpse frozen,* and then he imagined how his mother would be ruined by it, and her pain would only multiply Oliver's own pain, and in this imaginary multiplicative pain, growing ever bigger, reaching eternity, Oliver now dwelled.

And then, *and then,* there was the fact he now felt like a social pariah: He'd just sent two of his only friends in school packing. Was it the right choice to defend Jake? He felt like he *knew* Jake, like, knew him *deep down,* like the two of them had this strange, almost primal connection. But Jake's pain was a mystery to him. He could see it in others. But Jake showed him nothing. It made him a fascinating question mark.

Why had he chosen Jake over the others?

Stupid, stupid, stupid.

Oliver sat in one place, the flashlight shaking in his grip, making its beam tremble.

"Hey, fuck those guys," Jake said.

"Don't," Oliver cautioned. He pointed the beam right at Jake's eyes. In the moment before the older boy shielded his face with a forearm, Oliver saw that left eye shift and shudder—going from one color to the next like a too-fast slideshow. Then Olly saw the bottle of whiskey in Jake's hand. "What the hell?" he hissed. "If my parents see that—wait." He stood up suddenly. "Where did you even get that? And where's the pistol?" Oliver looked around, moving the beam this way and that, and he didn't see the pellet gun anywhere.

"It's gone. I put it away."

"Put it away where?"

Jake offered a vulpine grin. "Same place I got the bottle from."

"Quit talking in riddles."

"It's magic, Olly. Real magic."

"There is no such thing."

"Wanna bet?"

"And now it's snowing?" Fig said. "Christ, what a mess."

"Happy Halloween, I guess," Nate said, easing the pickup down the road. He figured slower was better; it was good to be cautious. Wind could knock down a tree, hail and snow could mean unexpected slippery spots, and not that he expected any wayward trick-or-treaters out here, but one never knew.

Fig said, looking at his phone: "Thought I'd call Zoe, let her know about the snow, but . . . no signal."

"Hm." Nate grunted. "Maybe towers are down. Or just . . . weather."

"Could be."

They sat quietly for a little while as Nate took it slow.

"You still having trouble sleeping?" Fig asked, finally.

"Sometimes."

"Explains why you're such an asshole at the office."

In the dashboard lights, Nate spied Fig's *gotcha* grin.

"You're funny."

"A real chuckle factory. No, but for real, you could try chamomile or, like, melatonin to counterbalance your cortisol levels. Maybe take a look at your potassium and magnesium intake, too—worse comes to worst, CBD oil. Weed isn't legal yet, but that's okay to take."

"First kombucha and now this. You're a regular Doctor Oz."

"That guy's a fuckin' hack. He's no different than Alex Jones or Gwyneth Paltrow. They're all selling the same shit. No, no, these days Zo and me, we gotta pay attention to real doctors."

"Oh?" Nate turned the truck up Lenape, past the old wooden bridge. Lightning flashed and wind pushed the side of the truck so hard he thought they'd land in a ditch—he had to pull hard at the wheel just to stay on the damn road.

"Bumpy out here."

"Yeah."

"Zo's pregnant."

That, just blurted out.

"What?" Nate blinked and offered a big celebratory laugh. "That's amazing, Fig. I had no idea. Congratulations to the both of you."

"Yeah."

"You don't sound so happy."

"I'm happy. I'm just . . ." Fig paused. He gestured like he was trying to be careful with his words—or like he was trying to conjure them from thin air. "You ever think with the way the world is, it's irresponsible to bring a kid into it? It's like, this fucking president and climate change and god, what else? Antibiotics are failing and they say all the bugs are dying and the coral reefs, too. Countries are building up their nuclear arsenals instead of paring them down. I just . . . shit, a new kid might be a burden on this world, and this world will sure as hell end up a burden on our kid."

As Fig spoke, Nate saw the turnoff for the office ahead through a spitting curtain of snow and ice. He pulled the truck into the parking lot, then let the engine idle for a minute, since the heat had just finally kicked on enough to warm up the truck some. "I worry. I worry about the kind of world I've left for Oliver. But this is the thing that gets me past that, most times: I think maybe Olly is a kid who will help to fix it all. Maybe he'll see what's wrong and he'll take a chance and make a change—a big change or even a little one—that works to make this world better instead of worse. Best I can do is raise him right and not . . ." He was about to say, *not pass down all the bad stuff that's in me,* but as lightning flashed, he saw something gleaming by the side of the office.

Fig saw it, too.

"Window's broke," he said.

"Looks like," Nate answered.

"We'll put a pin in this conversation for now, but seriously: thanks."

"You got it, partner. Let's get our asses to work."

"Follow me," Jake said. "Can't open the garage door because the power's out, so—come on." With that, he left the garage, sneaking into the dark house. Oliver hissed at him to stop, but Jake kept going, and so Oliver followed. He heard voices mumbling somewhere in the kitchen: Mom, Jed, and Fig's wife, Zoe. Oliver recognized the low tones of a worried conversation, and even that triggered his gut to go sour—if the adults were worried, then he should damn sure be worried, too.

But he didn't have time to think about it, because Jake was at his elbow, grabbing him and pulling him. Hard. "Come on, come on."

"Wait, ow, I—"

Already they were at the front door. The wind howled behind it. Jake went to open it, and Oliver freed himself and stepped backward.

"Hey, we can't go out there. It's hailing."

"I don't hear any hail. That part is over."

Sure enough, Oliver tilted his ear to the outside—

And heard no hail.

Jake opened the door while Oliver was distracted. Together they headed out to the front porch and saw no rain, no hail—but rather snow. White streaks slashing sideways across the dark.

"Snow," Olly said.

"Good work, detective."

"Shut up."

"Come on," Jake said, stepping off the porch and into the storm. Jake had to steady his footing even as his hair formed a wind-whipped mess. "I don't want anyone to see what I'm going to show you."

"Jake, I don't know about this."

And then came the question:

"Do you trust me?"

It hung there in the air, that question. Unmoved by the wind, untouched by the snow, a question so loud it drowned out the storm.

Do you trust me?

Did he? Did Oliver trust Jake?

Jake was rough and raw. Bit of a punk, bit of a prick. But he was also unafraid. He seemed to move through the world without a single care to slow him down. And that, Oliver found fascinating, though it did little to answer the question of trust. It was hard to deny that he found the other boy captivating in a way he couldn't describe.

Not in a romantic way—he didn't love him, wasn't attracted to him, and some part of even considering that felt strange, as if he were asking himself if he was attracted to a cousin or brother. Because that's how Jake felt: like a brother. More than a friend, or different, at least. A brother. One who'd saved Oliver when Alex Amati wanted to kill him, and one who told him what seemed like the unvarnished, if unpleasant, truth about things.

And that answered the question.

Oliver stepped off the porch, following Jake across the front yard, through the storm, and into the woods beyond.

"Check this out," Fig said, shining his own beam on a smear of red: Blood gleamed on one of the jagged peaks of broken glass still in the frame. Already the blood had started to gather ice crystals.

Nate shivered. "I don't know what happened here, Fig.".

"Me neither, partner."

"Partner. Listen to you. That's sweet."

"I'm sweet as peaches, Nate."

"Thought it was strawberries."

"I'm just sweet is the fuckin' point."

"Fair enough." Nate sighed. "Guess we can't just forget about this and head home? Pretend we didn't see anything, go have a beer, and eat some Halloween candy? Just until this all blows over?"

"I won't lie, that sounds pretty all right."

"I guess we gotta do the job, though."

"That's why they pay us the big bucks."

They both laughed at that because, yeah right, big bucks.

Together, they headed for the door to check out the office.

Oliver moved in a straight line, forging ahead through the forest, through the storm, surprised by how everything seemed to take on an eerie glow in the snow. The wind and snow sometimes whipped like a blizzard and other times went still, the air filled with nothing but gently falling flakes. Oliver shuddered as the cold took its bite. The weather had gone mad. The temperature was plunging. He, too, felt like he was falling.

Ahead, Jake moved just nearly out of sight. "Jake!" Oliver called after. He heard laughter ahead. The other boy was a shadow in the glow. There, then gone again. Oliver struggled to catch up, jogging through the trees, through the brittle understory—

But he couldn't see him. Couldn't see Jake at all.

"Jake!" he called again.

Something rushed at him from the side—a black, fast-moving shape. A reaper's cloak spread wide.

He cried out—

And Jake laughed. It was just the other boy, his hoodie sweatshirt lifted up and spread out behind him like a pair of bat wings.

"You are easy to spook," Jake said.

Oliver, his heart going wild in his chest, leaned against a tree, wincing against the stinging wind and the biting snow. "You're a dick."

"Maybe. Here. Just ahead, a little clearing."

They took ten steps, and ahead the trees and understory cleared out a little—in part because a tree had fallen here, probably many years before by the look of it. It had collapsed across a big turtle-backed rock, its trunk broken like a rotten bone. Already snow had begun to gather atop it.

"This'll do," Jake said. "Ready to see some magic?"

Oliver wasn't sure. He had the vertiginous feeling of a roller-coaster drop. "What are you going to show me?"

"Everything," Jake said. "*Everything.*"

The power was out inside the office. (Even still, Nate did the all-too-human and yet-so-useless thing of flipping the light switches three or four times just to see.) The alarm, silent, was set on a battery backup, and hence was still able to contact them. Fig turned it off, punching in the code.

After which, Nate and Fig together moved their flashlight beams around the office. Everything looked pretty much in order.

Except, of course, for the broken window.

That was a puzzle.

Glass dotted the carpet by the window. And a little more blood. Nate's flashlight highlighted a small trail of it.

Nate flagged Fig over silently, pointing the beam. He put a finger to his lips, the message clear: *Be quiet. We might have company.*

An animal, he hoped.

Gingerly, he moved the beam along the dots of blood. No fur. Just the blood. The trail wound through the office, straight down the middle, and around the far side of Fig's desk. He shared a look with Fig to make sure they both saw the same thing.

They did.

Nate unsnapped his holster. Fig followed his lead.

He flagged Fig to go around the left side, and he tapped his own chest and signaled he'd head to the right. They split up, each going their way.

Slowly, Nate crept down the middle of the office, stepping around, but not on, the blood. He pointed the flashlight beam at the leg of the desk, and then called out: "This is Fish and Game. Is someone there?"

Silence.

But then: movement. He thought he saw the top of someone's head—slick and wet. And a pale limb, maybe a knee, around the side of the desk. Then both were gone as whoever it was tried to hide.

His guts turned to slush. Something was wrong here, and not wrong in the way that was obvious: Yes, a broken window and blood on the carpet were both indicators that something wasn't right. But again came the feeling that something was really, truly wrong, wrong in a way that went beyond this moment and into something deeper. The fundamental machinery of things was starting to break down in a way he couldn't understand or even see—but rather just something he felt. A coldness in his bones, a subtle tinnitus in his ear. Fear struck him then: an icy wave of it. It rooted his feet to the ground, and he felt like he might piss his pants. A question haunted him then: *Is this what Oliver feels all the time?*

And then, a stranger question:

Does Oliver know something the rest of us don't?

Fig, now, spoke firmly, his gun up and out.

"We see you there. Stand up. Slowly. We are armed."

A shudder from behind the desk. A murmur, a whimper.

And then, someone stood up. Pale. No clothes. A young girl, younger than Oliver but not by much, her shivering, bleeding arms crossed over her nakedness. Her legs bled, too—scratched up, probably from where she came through the broken window. Stringy blond hair framed her face like wet curtains, but it failed to obscure what was on—or rather *in*—her cheek:

A number was carved there. Scabbed over, but fresh enough, was the number 37.

"Tell me about Edmund Reese," Maddie said to Jed in the kitchen of the house. "I want to know who he was."

"Can't we talk about something nice?" Zoe pleaded.

"I'm always fine to talk about nicer things," Jed said. "But I also tend to skew to darker narratives. And I am curious, Maddie—why the renewed interest? Just because I had mentioned him in the tale of Ramble Rocks?"

"No. I—I don't know. I'm just curious." She offered an awkward smile. "At least we're not talking about the weather."

Jed nodded. "Sure, sure. What do you want to know?"

"He killed girls."

"I feel like that's a statement, not a question, but it's true. Young girls. Girls who hadn't come of age yet, so to speak."

"And he . . . did he cut numbers into them?"

"He did, at that. He was quite obsessed with numbers and numerology. Demonology, too. Eschatology. Lots of occult business, but numbers were the focus of it. Had a thing about the number 99 in particular, and some of the guards on death row said that he had planned—now how's this for an overachiever?—to kill ninety-nine girls. And that the culmination of those killings would unlock something, not a power in him necessarily, but something, some event, some *eschatological* consequence—'the summation of an equation,' he said."

Zoe moved closer to one of the candles, as if to be comforted by its glow and its warmth. "You said a word I don't know. Eschata . . . what?"

"Eschatology. It's the study of the end times: the final events of mankind—er, sorry, *human*kind, I don't mean to be patriarchal. You know, your apocalypses, your armageddons, the ragnaroks and raptures."

"That's what Reese wanted? The end of the world?"

"It's hard to know for sure. He wasn't precisely chatty. But between his conversations with guards and his notebooks and the things he scrawled on the walls of his house—that is not an unreasonable conclusion."

"Why?"

"Why try to end the world?"

"Yes."

Jed didn't hesitate when he said: "Maybe it's some combination of megalomania and PTSD. Maybe he was a sociopath. Or maybe, just maybe, he got it into his head that he was doing something good. Something righteous. Some of the worst things are done under righteous pretense."

"Is that what you think? That his mission was righteous?"

"Oh, my dear, no. Of course not. But it's also not my job to judge. It's just my job to record what I find. To teach and to entertain." He hesitated a little. "To find some truth in the clamor of the storm."

*　*　*

In Jake's hand was a book: a ratty, fabric-covered book. Old and weathered, its cover the color of mud-churned water. It took a moment for Oliver to realize that the wind did not stir the pages. And the snow didn't touch them, either. They seemed to move around it in a way that defied his understanding of physical reality. *Magic,* Jake had said.

He opened the book to the middle, and Oliver got closer, huddling near to the book. It was a logbook, by the look of it—longer than it was tall; landscape, not portrait. And it was definitely old—not made to look old, but truly *old*-old. Decades old. Maybe a hundred years old, even.

The open page showed a log of what looked to be accidents. Mining accidents. A lost finger. A broken arm. A rock fall. A collapsed tunnel.

A fatality.

All inked on weathered pages the color of cigarette smoke. The ink itself, a powdery denim blue. Fading, as if the book was trying to forget the tragedies it had catalogued.

It occurred to Oliver, *How can I even see this?* It was night. They were in a storm in the woods. But the pages, he realized, glowed softly. An eerie light emanated from the book, like light through a pool of water.

"What is this?" he asked.

"The Book of Accidents," Jake said. He smiled at Oliver. That one strange eye of his seemed to gleam. His voice took on a soft, deep timbre—the sounds of the storm were now gone. "A logbook of accidents from a coal mine. Accidents that aren't accidents. Because accidents are never just random, Olly. They're the end result of some kind of breakdown. Things falling apart. But it's not just a logbook."

"What do you mean?"

"In terms you'll understand, think of it as a . . . spellbook of sorts. My spellbook."

Jake's fingers traced the pages, and the words seemed to shift and squirm—like ants after you knocked over their hill. Then he lifted his fingers from the page and began moving them in a spiral, starting from the center and moving outward. And as he did—

The air began to shimmer and shift. Snowflakes hit the space inside that gestured circumference and sizzled, hissing into little coughs of steam. *Tsssst.* At first, looking at the shimmer was like looking at the air above a hot road, but then, as Jake's widening gesture went faster, the air in front of them grew even more distorted—

Until it looked like the spiral was opening the world, opening reality. Like Doctor Strange opening a portal to somewhere else.

Was it a door? Or was it a window?

Whatever it was, what waited there was—

Nothing. A blank space. Deep. Maybe endless. But then, no—not empty at all. *Something* was in there. Something darker than nothing. And something shining there, too, lots of little somethings. Like stars.

Oliver stared into the void. And the void stared back.

The girl stood shivering.

"Nate," Fig said. No other words came with it—it was just an exhortation of horror, shock, and with it, the implicit question, *Are you seeing what I'm seeing, and if so, what the hell is going on?*

Outside, thundersnow boomed. It rattled Nate all the way into the teeth, but it seemed to rattle the girl more. She yelped and clenched her eyes shut, all of her body tensing up into a tight ball.

"It's all right," Nate said, trying to be gentle. He eased his pistol down and back into its holster. Fig followed suit. "Fig, you got any blankets in here?"

"In the other room," Fig said, and hurried out of the office. Leaving Nate alone with the bleeding girl.

"Why don't you come out from around the desk?" Nate asked.

The girl stayed put.

"Can you speak?"

She nodded, though that was the sum total of her answer.

"What's your name?"

"I . . . don't remember."

Shit. Okay. "Where do you come from? Do you have parents? Do you live nearby?"

No response except a gentle shake of the head.

Nate eased a little closer. "Can I at least pull out that chair for you? Give you a place to sit so you don't need to sit on the floor?"

Here, now, came Fig with the blanket. He handed it to Nate, who in turn eased a little closer to her. The girl flinched and a fearful animal sound arose from the back of her throat. *What the hell has this girl been through?* He tried changing his tack, set the blanket down on the edge of the desk before taking a step back. And there was that number on her cheek . . .

Nate knew who was fond of carving numbers into girls' faces.

But Edmund Reese was dead. So, a copycat, then.

The girl reached for the blanket, took it off the desk slowly, and bundled herself up in it.

"Nate," Fig said, pulling him aside. "We should get her to a hospital. She's injured from that window glass—and her face, Christ. Someone did that to her. Or she did it to herself. Either way, she needs treatment. Maybe a psych eval. Doctors, cops—we're not trained for this kind of thing."

Nate nodded. "Miss. We think what's best is taking you to the hospital. St. Agnes isn't far—a ten-minute drive." That was a lie. The weather would make that trip three times as long, but it seemed easier to goad her into a shorter trip than a longer one. She seemed fragile, like a stack of teacups that would clatter and shatter if you applied just a little too much pressure. "We'll walk out of here—"

Her head spun. Her eyes were wide with panic. "No. No! *He's* out there. He'll find me. *He'll find me.*" She scrunched up into herself again and pulled the blanket all the way around.

"You're safe with us," Fig said. He gave Nate a wild look and mouthed the words, *What the fuck.*

Nate eased around to the front of her. She flinched, but did not panic, did not flee. He held his hands out. "Miss, I'm an ex–Philadelphia cop. And me and my partner here are local Fish and Game officers. We're capable of protecting you from whoever it is that hurt you." Her head poked back out from the blanket bundle. Mostly just her eyes. They regarded him warily, but he thought they had softened. "I have a son. Roughly your age. I keep him safe, too. That's what I do. I keep people safe. All right?"

He didn't take his eyes off her.

And she didn't take hers off him.

Finally, she nodded.

"Okay."

The girl stood up.

Here we go, Nate thought.

Thinking about Edmund Walker Reese and his victims only made Maddie worried for her own son—the thought of children, on whatever part of the gender spectrum, in danger, twisted her guts up like a washrag. She headed out to the garage, flashlight in hand, to check on Oliver.

"Olly?" she called, flashing the beam this way and that. "Dude. *Dude.*" But there was no one here. She pressed deeper into the garage, looking between the cars, then on the far side of them.

No Oliver, no Jake, no Caleb, no Hina.

The garage was closed. Nobody had opened it. Power was out.

Shit.

Back inside, she whipped through the house calling her son's name. Panic drove at her heels like snapping wolves.

Jake slowed his gesture, but the spiraling space remained open. There remained the calm and endless void. A place so deep and so dark it was almost purple, like a bruise beneath the skin of reality itself. Somewhere beyond it all he focused on those glittering lights twinkling in the deep. Like stars, but also not. They didn't look like eyes, and yet, he felt like they were watching him just the same. The lights seemed prismatic, too. Fractured beams from a broken lighthouse— spears of cracked light, pulsing, flickering, dying out before glowing bright once more. The quiet of this other place bled into him. An emptiness inside him spoke to the emptiness there in the void, and even as something there slithered in the bruise-black he felt something in himself answer in kind.

Maddie rushed out of the house, into the storm, and a gust of wind hit her so hard she thought she might be picked up and thrown into the trees. Thunder boomed all around as snow and ice bit into her cheeks. Somewhere in the woods, off in the dark, she heard the crackle of a branch breaking off its tree, and crashing through other trees until it slammed into the ground. She called Oliver's name again and again, "Olly! *Olly*, are you out here!" and her mind raced through a series of increasingly insane possibilities: that he had stowed away in the truck as they headed to Fish and Game, that he had wandered into the woods and was now trapped under a fallen tree, that Nate was right about Jake and the strange-eyed boy had led her son to his death, that Edmund Walker Reese's spirit was out there somewhere right now with the intent to carve a number into her son's cheek before disemboweling him on a rock—

Her eyes scanned the yard, and the forest beyond—

Please, Olly, please—

A glow. Out there in the woods.

Maddie shouldered her way into the storm, running toward it.

Outside they headed back into the keening, cutting storm. Nate walked the girl as gently as he could out the door of the Fish and Game offices. His mind attempted to calculate the fastest way to the hospital while simultaneously making calming sounds and statements to the girl. Fig was on the other side of her, and together they took steps against the wind and snow, one by one, toward Nate's truck.

"It'll be all right," Nate was saying, as much for himself and Fig as for her. "Everything's going to be—" *Fine,* he was going to say. But he felt a buzz in his back teeth. His eyes began watering and he smelled something strange, like burning electronics.

Lightning pulsed ahead of him, lashing the earth just ten feet in front of the pickup—the world closed behind a curtain of white light, and he saw that this lightning strike was not like any other he'd seen. It formed a pillar of electricity, whips of stark blue voltage crackling off it in flicks and curls, and in that space *stood a person.* Or just the shape of one: a man, silhouetted by the light. With something in his hand. *A knife,* Nate thought.

Thunder boomed, slamming into them like a sonic wave.

Then the lightning was gone, and so was the person.

"Nate," Fig said.

"You saw it, too," Nate said.

"It was *him,*" the girl said. She tried backpedaling now, twisting out of their grip to run back toward the office—

Nate cried out for her—

She screamed in a howl of terror—

The sky ripped open again with lightning. This time, the pillar of light and electricity hit the girl—

And it hit Nate, too.

The void flickered. A flash of static like on an old broken TV rippled across it. In it, Oliver thought he saw a face. Something in that space, watching him. A white mouth and black eyes. It hummed and murmured and sang a song, discordant and strange. The sound of its song had weight, it had *heft,* and it began to fill the void with shapes—a literal act of creation, like God or *a* god (or the opposite of one) summoning things into being with naught but its own grave utterances.

But what it summoned was not anything new, but rather what already existed: It showed Oliver a high-school hallway, not one he recognized, but one he knew by the lockers and the gray class bell on the wall and the bulletin board just beneath it. The hallway was teeming with high school kids just like him, students moving to and from class, bags over shoulders, books in hand, some laughing, some looking upset, all with a little core of dark pain nestled somewhere within—a girl with a *Star Wars* backpack laughed, a boy with an eighties popped collar gave two middle fingers to a friend, a teacher stepped into the hall and ushered the kids past him with a tired wave of his hand—

And then *bang*. Like a gunshot in Oliver's ear. The halls were cleared. No one remained there—

At least, no one alive.

Seven bodies lay on the floor. Blood pooling. A shot in the center of one boy's back. A girl slumped against the locker, two holes in her chest, drooling red. Another kid, in a Captain America T-shirt, lay faceup, his jaw gone, the wet dark tunnel of his throat exposed as blood slicked the sides of his neck, the floor, his blue shirt, making it purple. Somewhere in the distance, a person wept. Another screamed.

Bang.

The scene in the void changed once more. Now a young man, not much older than Oliver, sat in a chair, facing a bank of monitors. He wore some kind of uniform. Army, navy, it was hard to tell; the glow from the screen washed him out. He had headphones on. In one hand, a flight stick; the other fumbled to unwrap a stick of gum before popping it into his mouth. He chewed and chawed it like a horse. Pain flashed in his dead eyes, pain only Oliver could see, pain like a breeding ball of snakes winding together and rolling around, making more of itself. On the screen, a wedding: the bride in white, with henna on her hands; the groom in a red kaffiyeh; toasting and cheering and laughing; dancing then in circles and circles and circles; the young man's hand clenched on the flight stick, pulling a trigger; a few more moments of marital bliss before *voosh,* the sound of something unzipping the sky and then all of it is erased in fire; the young man at the console pops another stick of gum; the pain in him did not diminish, but only grew darker as it swelled.

Bang.

Kids knelt in dog kennel cages, fingers thrust through the little metal gaps in the mesh, all of them weeping, snot hanging from their noses in swinging ropes—

Bang.

Someone delivered a hard boot into the ribs of a man sleeping on a huge cardboard pallet. The ribs crunched like stones under a boot—

Bang.

Elementary school kids circled another smaller, weaker boy. It was winter. Snow on the ground. Sky the color of pencil shading. They rubbed ice on his head and in his eyes. They pressed stones against his forehead so hard they left marks, raw red marks. One of them had a frozen piece of dog shit on a long-forgotten Frisbee and moved it toward his mouth. The boy clamped his mouth shut, but he was crying and his nose was stuffed up and soon his mouth would open and these vicious kids would get their chance—

Bang.

A boy knelt handcuffed to a radiator. His lip was split. A fresh line of bright red gleamed down the middle. *That's me,* Oliver thought. That didn't make any sense. How could it? It was him. Younger, yes. And a little different, too—his hair was more blond than it was brown, and shorter, too, like a buzz cut. Some freckles on his cheek but he thought, *That really, really looks like me.* Like looking in a distorted mirror. Then someone stepped into frame, and at this Oliver flinched and tightened his jaw and a hand came out of nowhere, slapping him against the old iron radiator with a *clong*—and a voice said, "That's what you get for trying to run away." And Oliver thought, *I know that voice,* it was his father's voice—it was the voice of Nate Graves. Growlier, rougher, throatier, like he'd been smoking cigarettes or had a bad acid reflux burn, but it was definitely him, and this Oliver, the real Oliver, tried to look away, tried to yell out, but he found his tongue thick, his throat dry, and he could neither pull away nor make a sound and—

"Oliver."

Was that his voice? Or

"Oliver."

Was it someone else's or

"Oliver!"

He gasped, blinking. Snow whirled around him. He spun. Jake was gone. Dark trees rose above him. They seemed to grow larger, arching above his head as if threatening to swat him down to the ground, holding up there. He felt dizzy. Oliver spun one way as his brain and guts seemed to spin the other. Then, footsteps. Coming fast. Someone rushed up on him—

His mother.

Mom.

She was the one calling his name.

Maddie found him, hugged him, and Oliver collapsed against her, gagging and weeping.

In the lightning, the girl screamed. Her face shuddered and eroded, as if the white light were swallowing her one inch at a time—Nate reached for her and grabbed her hand tight. He shouted for Fig, but no one answered, and he couldn't see his partner in the blinding light. All he had was the girl's hand in his own, and he tried to draw her closer to him—he had to save her from whatever this was.

But he met resistance. Something pulled at her from the other side. He saw the girl's face—almost all the way gone now. But her eyes met his. They were wide with terror. Her voice was a loud, hissed whisper:

"Help. Me."

A hand closed around her throat. She choked—"Grrk!"

And a second face roamed into view above her shoulder. A man's face. Nate knew it. He knew it *instantly*—he'd seen it recently enough.

Where? On the cover of Jed's book: *Sacrifice at Ramble Rocks: The Satanic Murders of Edmund Walker Reese.*

"Reese," Nate said, his voice swallowed by the lightning.

The other man roared, and something swiped out in a broad, flashing arc—Nate saw the knife just a half second before he felt it slice across his face. His vision became blood. Pain fired across the top of his head like a line of match tips burning. He cried out, and felt his grip loosen just long enough to lose the girl.

The man hissed, "She's *mine*, robberfly."

The stranger again lunged toward him with the blade, but something swooped down—Nate could barely see what. A winged thing. The rush of feathers came between him and the killer as the lightning dissipated with a crackle.

The girl vanished. The lightning was gone. Nate tumbled to the ground.

34

The Line Between

After.

Nate sat outside. The storm had gone. The wind fled, and the snow stopped. Now the forest was quiet. And white, like the world was piles of soft, marshmallow bones.

Fig had put some snow in a bucket and told Nate to scoop it out and press it to the injury across his head as he went off to find some gauze. Nate did as he suggested; the snow burned the wound like salt.

Now, Fig emerged with gauze, medical tape, and a wad of paper towels. "Dry off, then we'll get this on you."

"Thank you, Nurse Ratched." He winced as he dried off the wound. It came away black with blood. "How's it look?"

"Like something tried to take the top of your head off. You're gonna need some stitches. Make you look a little like Frankenstein."

"Frankenstein was the doctor, not the monster."

Fig shrugged. "The doctor *was* the monster, Nate, and that's not the point. We gonna talk about what we both saw?"

Nate stared off at nothing. "I dunno, Fig. I dunno."

Heated now, panicked, Fig said with a wild gesticulation, "Because *I* saw a girl with a number cut into her face. And I saw a man standing in lightning—lightning that then came for her, and made her disappear like, like, *like she wasn't ever there.* Then she was gone, and you were bleeding."

"I can't explain any of it."

"Me neither, partner. Me neither." Fig wound the gauze clumsily around Nate's head with all the delicacy of a pit bull high on yard mushrooms. Nate pulled his head away and did the work himself. "You're gonna need to head to the hospital, you know."

"I know, I know."

"I'm gonna go find some cardboard and tape up the window. You good out here? We'll head to St. Agnes after."

Nate nodded, awkwardly using his thumb and forefinger to pinch and tear the tape around his head. Fresh blood soaked it. *Shit.* "Yeah, I'm good, you go ahead."

Fig went back inside the office.

Help. Me.

The girl's last plea intruded on Nate's mind once more. He sat on the back bumper of the truck for a while, replaying that moment over and over again. Her face. Her plea. Then: Reese. With a knife. How was that even possible? How was *any* of this possible? His forehead throbbed like his heart had climbed up from his chest and planted itself right underneath the wound.

As he was replaying all this, a gentle shadow passed in front of the exposed moon and drifted over Nate. He flinched, looking up—

There was an owl.

No, he thought. Not *an* owl.

The owl. Same one he saw outside Jed's that first night.

It sat on the branch in a beam of moonlight, rotating its head sideways in a look of quizzical amusement, or bemusement.

"Was it you?" Nate asked it. "He was going to kill me. The man in the lightning. Reese. And then I know I felt the rush of wings on me."

The owl hooted, a gentle *oo oo.*

And then it was gone again, taking wing silently.

Except he was sure this time that the bird he just saw was not a bird at all, but rather only a wooden carving of one. Which he knew was also not possible, but did the line between possible and impossible even matter anymore?

35

Glitches Get Stitches

Nate put on his coat. He'd been at the hospital for hours, but finally they'd got his forehead stitched up and filled him a prescription for antibiotics. Seven stitches.

Maddie wasn't here. She said Oliver had had an "episode" and that she had to stay with him. Said too that Jed was nice enough to hang around for a while and help out. Zoe, as well. He of course tried to ask just what she meant by an *episode,* but she wasn't really sure what had happened, just that he'd wandered out into the woods and had something of a meltdown. She told Nate not to worry, which was like asking somebody not to scratch a bug bite—soon as you heard it, all you felt was that damnable itch.

Now, he could finally go home.

Except his exit was halted by a man standing in the doorway to his ER room.

It was a cop. Bald guy, kind of a meathead. Wrinkles above his eyes and on the back of his neck like a stack of knockwurst.

Statie, by the look of it. Not local. "Nate Graves?" the guy asked.

"Uh-huh."

"John Contrino, Jr., deputy chief, state police."

"Sure, how you doing?" Nate offered a hand and the other man shook it.

"Not too good, Nate. Not. Too. Good. I'm out here, for one. On a bad night. We got accidents out the ass. Power's out in half the county. The other half's still got trees on houses and basements full of water."

"Didn't know it was your job to pump out wet basements."

Contrino paused for a moment, licked his lips. "That's a good one, Nate. That's real good."

"What I'm trying to ask is, what brings you out here? Because I was just on my way home."

"I think you can spare a moment to confirm—or, I hope, deny—your partner's story."

"My partner's story."

Fig, what did you do?

"Sure, Axel Figueroa gave my office a call, reported an *incident*. Said you and he went to check on an alarm malfunction at the Fish and Game office, but instead of a malfunction, you found a girl there. Naked and injured." All of Nate tensed up at hearing that. *Why'd you have to call the police, Fig?* Nate had been police. They weren't equipped to deal with reports that didn't add up. They mostly treated those kinds of stories with disdain and mockery—or worse, roughed their tellers up, maybe shot them if they weren't white.

"What'd he say happened then?"

"He said the girl ran away."

Whew. At least Fig didn't say anything about *lightning* and *creepy ex–serial killers hiding inside that lightning,* and then the girl up and disappearing. This put him in a tricky situation. He either confirmed Fig's story, which made him sound nuts, too. Or he denied Fig's tale, which put Fig even further on the outs. Maybe even cost him his job.

Which was not an option. Nate knew: You stood by your partner.

"That's accurate. Fig tells it true. You need an official statement from me about it?"

"No, just wondering why you didn't report it. I mean, you used to be a cop, yeah? You know the importance of this sorta thing, I'd think." He sniffed. "This incident how you got the cut across your melon there?"

"Oh, that." He quickly summoned a lie. "The girl, she pushed past me. I slipped on a patch of ice. Must've hit a . . . rock or a branch or something."

"Uh-huh. Nurse said your injury was consistent with a blade."

Goddamn cops, Nate thought. Contrino didn't seem like a good guy, but he seemed like a good cop, at least. Doing his due diligence.

"Well, maybe I fell on a piece of scrap metal or something—it was pretty wild in that storm," Nate said. "And I didn't report it because I knew Fig would handle it while I got my, ah, 'melon' stapled up."

"Uh-huh. Okay. Okay." Contrino forced a smile. "Good to meet you, Nate. We'll keep an eye out for that girl. And you keep doing . . ." His hand gesticulated dismissively toward Nate. "Whatever it is Fish and Game does. Find some jaywalking trout or some shit."

"You got it, Deputy Chief Contrino."

He watched the other man go. And it was then, only then, that the tiredness hit his bones like a sack of rocks. It weighed him down. He just wanted to go home. See his wife. Check on his son. Christ, what a day.

36

Sharing Is Caring

It was three A.M. by the time Nate sat down across from his wife at the dinner table. He poked at a slice of reheated pizza.

"That was a pretty fucked-up night," Maddie said, finally.

"Halloween earning its reputation, I suppose."

"Jesus, you aren't wrong about that."

"I'm just glad Dude is okay." He leaned in. "Olly *is* okay, right?"

Maddie gave him an exasperated look. "I really don't know, Nate. I mean, he's okay in the sense he's not hurt. But his heart hurts, and I don't even know why. I think maybe he was worried about you."

"I'm sorry."

"Not your fault. Job is the job." She reached out and took his hand while eyeing up the bandage across his head. "I'm just glad you're all right. When I couldn't reach you . . . fucking hell."

"Sorry. Cell service was down, I guess."

She nodded. Her smile felt begrudging in some way. Not exactly insincere, but hiding pain, or fear, or something else.

"So—" she said.

"So—" he answered.

"I—we—"

"Yeah. Yes. We—"

"We need to talk," they said in unison.

And then they talked.

Interlude: Where Maddie Went

Then.

The so-called Happy Valley encompassed State College, Pennsylvania, but also several of its outlying municipalities, like Harris, Patton, and Ferguson. The story went that the area earned its chipper, cheerful name during the Great Depression, for while the rest of the country plunged into economic darkness, this area's economy remained relatively sound due to the presence of both Penn State University and local farms, meaning everyone could dwell in a fairly insulated bubble where they were well fed and educated. Everyone was happy—

Hence: the Happy Valley.

Maddie, however, was in a valley, but she damn sure wasn't happy. She felt lonely. Scared. Uncertain. She packed a carry-on and just . . . left. She was four hours from home. She missed her son and her husband. It killed her that she kept any of this from them. She knew she had to tell Nate. But how? He wouldn't believe a lick of this.

She barely believed it. Her own memories felt like a lie.

It was those memories that brought her here, standing on a doorstep of a townhouse a few blocks down from the sorority houses. It was noon. She knocked, waited, and knocked again.

The door opened, and Sissy Kalbacher finally answered.

Sissy had blond ringlets and cherub cheeks, the only sign of a plumpness she had in youth that had since gone to the rearview. The rest of her looked taut and fit—a yoga mom and an MMA fighter all in one go. Time had been kind to her. Or maybe she had been kind to herself.

Which, considering everything, was probably deserved.

Sissy looked to Maddie with the glimmer of something close to recognition—which wouldn't make much sense. They'd never met.

"Sissy?" Maddie asked.

"That's right."

"My name is Maddie Graves. I'm the one who emailed you?"

Sissy nodded. Again that look of recognition. She must've looked up Maddie online. It was easy enough to find photos of her, mostly from gallery appearances over the past ten years, some that landed in the paper.

"Sure, of course."

"Can I come in?"

"Yes. Yes, please, come on in," the woman said, warily. And then, as Sissy turned, Maddie saw it: the ghost of a scar on her cheek.

A scar in the shape of the number 5.

The house was well lit, and damn near everything was white or gray or silver. Very modern. A stark contrast to Nate and Maddie's farmhouse. It bore a few sorority house–style touches: pink pillows on the white leather couch, a bowl of lime-green Christmas ornaments (out way too fucking early, if you asked Maddie), Phi Mu sorority paraphernalia framed on the foyer walls. And photos of children, too. At Maddie's count: three. All girls.

Good for you, Maddie thought.

Sissy, in a comfy tee and yoga pants, sat across from Maddie.

"You want something to drink?" Sissy asked. "I have dandelion tea. It's really very good, very vanilla, though—" She faked lowering her voice in a conspiratorial tone. "It really makes you have to pee, ha ha."

"Oh, yeah, no, this won't take long."

"Oh. Okay. I confess, I didn't—I didn't know if I wanted to meet you. Given the subject matter. I don't talk much about it. About what happened."

"I get that. Do you . . . even remember it?"

"In fits and starts. Mostly it's not a thing I think about."

"That's a gift." At that, Sissy flinched a little, and Maddie tried to pave over it: "I just mean, not everybody's mind is so capable of self-defense. My son, he's like a bear that lost his coat in a snowstorm. He's hanging out in the wind, you know?"

"I'm sorry to hear that."

"No—I mean, no, I'm not trying to solicit sympathy for me or my kid. I'm really fucking this up. Let's try again: I just wanted to ask a question. And I know I could've done this over email, but I needed to see you. I needed to *meet* you. In part to see that you were okay, but also to . . . I don't know. Watch your face as you answered this because, Sissy, I gotta tell ya, I'm going through some things right now. Some things I do *not* understand and I'm really hoping like hell you can help me figure this out. Even if it's just to tell me I'm nuts. Honestly—honestly!—that'd be the nicest gift you could give me. So, I just wanted to know . . ." She swallowed a hard knot as she got to the question. "How did you get away from Edmund Reese?"

Sissy stared down in her lap for a while before saying, "I know I offered you dandelion tea, but do you drink hard liquor? Because I'm suddenly craving something like that."

Maddie nodded. "I do, when the mood strikes me."

"Well, the mood has struck the shit out of me," Sissy said, standing up. "I'll bring two glasses."

The hard liquor was Maker's Mark. Dark as cold brew coffee—and with that same rich, complicated odor.

"My husband, Parker, he oddly prefers girlier drinks—and I mean, no knock, he's very proud of tying on what he calls his 'girl-drink drunk.' But he can't stand real whiskey. I love the stuff. Loved it maybe a little too much when I was younger, and then—" Here came a vaguely regretful sigh. "Clean living got in the way after I had kids and, well." She took a heavy swallow of it. "I'm delaying answering your question and I realize that, so I should just get to it."

"Please," Maddie said with a sympathetic smile.

Sissy said: "The day I got free. Yeah." Her eyes unfocused, but Maddie could see that though she wasn't looking at anything here, in this room, she *was* looking somewhere. In her own head. At her own memories. Her eyes shined with what might've been the threat of tears. "The monster, I can't say his name, so I just call him that, not the killer, not the serial killer, just that: the monster. The monster kept me for several days. He said he had to . . . prepare the way. I didn't know what that meant then and I don't know now—I only know that he saw the murders he committed as part of some larger cosmological plan, some sacrifice or, or, some grand purpose. I don't know, I really don't. I just know I was going to die. I knew it then, too. After the first day trapped in his cellar, I knew. I knew because he basically told me. He said I had to eat and drink the food and water he gave me because I couldn't die on him 'too early.' It had to be the right time. Under the right 'stars.' No—under the right 'number of stars.'"

"Did he have a thing for numbers?"

"He did. Yes. The day he took me up out of the cellar he . . ." She blinked a few times like she was trying to remember the details. "He went on and on about counting, or an accounting of things. How many keys he had on his key ring. How many hinges and doorknobs were in his house. How many places the paint was peeling on the cellar door, that sort of thing. One of them stuck with me, really stuck with me. He said, traditionally, a coffin needed only ten nails to be closed. 'Ten nails to close a coffin,' he said again and again, and then he added, 'But it takes ninety-nine to kill the world.'"

It takes ninety-nine to kill the world.

"Is that when you got away?"

"Soon after. He took me upstairs, bound my hands with tape—my mouth, too—and marched me toward the door. It was nighttime. He said he had a quota to fill and I was part of that quota—Number Five, he called me. Never my name. I don't even know if he knew my name. Just that, Number Five. And he marched me to the front door. It was an old ratty screen door. Filthy, with holes in the screen. Spiderwebs filling those holes. And before it, before you got to the door to go out, was another doorway—this one leading into, I think, the kitchen."

As Sissy spoke, Maddie felt like she could see this place in her mind's eye. Vivid and clear. *It smells like mold and dust,* she thought.

"He had me ahead of him. Like he was marching me. Little shoves and pushes to get me to go. And I kept looking for places to run. So I saw this doorway, and I thought, that's where I'm going to run."

"And did you?"

"I didn't have to."

A chill grappled through Maddie's blood. "Why not?"

"Because as I got close—and I know this sounds cuckoo, but as I walked up to the doorway, I saw something standing in the kitchen. Standing there on this garish orange, dirty 1970s linoleum floor."

"Something standing. Like what?" Even though Maddie feared she already knew, she had to ask. Because it *couldn't* be true.

"A little . . . creature."

Maddie laughed, and quickly stifled it as it came out. "Sorry?"

"That's . . . what it was. This little creature. Made of cardboard."

Maddie's laugh died in her throat. She felt dizzy. "Cardboard."

"Like, a little box creature. Something cut out of cardboard into the shape of a little . . . fellow. No higher than two feet tall. Little bent legs. Little bent arms. And a box head. Too big for its body, in a way."

Maddie closed her eyes. "And on its face was a smiley face. Like drawn in—"

"Marker," Sissy said, nodding. "Like permanent marker."

"And it was holding something, too." *Not a knife, but a—*

"A pair of scissors."

"The very same pair of scissors that made it," Maddie corrected her.

"Okay. Sure, if you say so. What I know is, it lifted its one hand, if you can call it that, to its smiley mouth, as if to say *shhh*. And I did. I did shush, because even though I was *sure* I was losing my mind, I thought better to listen than to not. So I nodded and kept walking. And so did Reese. When that monster moved me to the front door, he reached past me to open it—and that's when he screamed. A terrible scream. Right in my ear, and of all the things I remember, I remember that sound the most, and—" Here she was heated, red in the cheeks, like she was *mad* but also *triumphant*. "And I remember it because it makes me feel joy. His pain gave me *joy*."

"Why was he in pain?"

"Maybe you already know this. Maybe you don't. But when he passed that doorway, our little friend, the Box Man, came out and stuck those scissors in the meat of his calf. Sank them real deep, too. Then the Box Man ran away, bop bop bop, and the monster hobbled after it, howling."

"And that's when you got away. You . . . went out the door."

"Yes. But not without help."

Maddie leaned forward. "What do you mean?"

"This is where it gets a little weird."

"It's already pretty weird, Sissy."

"Yeah. Well. Just you wait. Because I remember seeing someone, a face in the window. A strange man with a long, haggard face—big beard, wide eyes. And then I remember . . . someone else being there. I remember someone who helped me. A little girl."

"A little girl? What little girl? One of his victims?"

"No. Someone new." Sissy drank the rest of her whiskey in one go, shuddering after she did. "I'm pretty sure it was you."

PART FOUR

THE MANY KINDS OF MAGIC

And in talking about the stories that surround the Owls Head Lighthouse, we must reckon with a perhaps more ancient question: What is the owl? Or, rather, what does the owl mean? In symbology, the owl is many things. The Sioux favored the owl as a messenger. The Lakota considered it both a fierce protector and a creature given over to preternatural sight—the ability to see things that were hidden, even to see through the worlds themselves. The Greeks, of course, saw the owl as a symbol of that same sight, which translated to wisdom more than anything in battle—though the owl was one of Athena's animals, and therein you see too that the owl served for them as an idol of mystical femininity—the feminine spirit given form, silent and powerful, wise and overarching. Watching us from the trees. Some saw the owl as evil, some as good, others as an independent spirit, separate from our ideas of what is right, wrong, good, or bad, a creature in judgment like Egypt's jackal. Which one of these is true? Who can say? Maybe all of them. Thanks for joining us this week. I'm Elon Mankey, and you've been listening to *Fable*, the podcast of folklore and legend.

—Elon Mankey, *Fable* podcast, Episode 29, "The Lighthouse," March 13, 2019

And Then They Talked

It came pouring out of her, the story. Maddie fixed Nate with the most intense gaze she'd ever given him—like a pair of lasers designed to melt steel beams—and she told him how she went to meet Sissy Kalbacher, Edmund Walker Reese's fifth abductee, the one who'd escaped. She explained to him what Sissy told her. And now she told him *her* side of the story, too, about how while in a sensory deprivation tank she started to remember things.

"I lived in the city at the time with my father." Her father, Denny, was a cop. He's the one who got Nate to join the force. (Nate thought, *Rest in peace, Denny.* Poor bastard died of prostate cancer five years ago.) "And because Dad was a cop, I had something of a *mature palate* when it came to crimes and stuff. I just knew about it. I knew about carjackings and the Rittenhouse Rapist and local gang activity. He tried to keep it from me, but c'mon. I was intellectually curious. And a pain in the ass. I knew. I knew about all of it. And I knew about Edmund Reese. I knew about the four dead girls and the fifth—who had gone missing, but hadn't turned up dead."

Nate sat, quiet as a stone. In him was the creeping dread of how their stories were going to intersect—but beyond the dread, too, was a mad, wild kind of excitement. The sheer internal suspense of *oh just wait till you hear what I have to say* was about to burn him up, turn him to a pillar of ash.

Maddie, who hadn't blinked yet, continued:

"I remember dreaming about that girl. Being out there somewhere, lost and alone, afraid and certain she was going to die. You
know, my dad, helping people was his thing. Maybe at the cost of
himself, a little. Maybe even at the cost of his family. I dunno. But I
wanted to be like him. So I woke up that night, and I started to make
something. I was already a little artist by then. My grades were terrible except for Art and English. And I got up, creeping through our
dark townhouse, trying not to wake my father—who had fallen
asleep on the recliner downstairs in front of the news, like he did
every night—and I found scissors and tape and cardboard boxes."

"And that's when you made the Box Man," Nate said.

"That's when I made the little Box Man. And I remember now
how in making him, I . . . lost time. I remember gathering the materials. I remember sitting down to start. And then—next thing I remember, it was already done. I remember someone being there with
me. Not my father, but someone else. I don't know. The rest is still—"
And here her brow furrowed into deep, frustrated ditches, as she
struggled with whatever was going on inside her head. "*Hard to access.* But Sissy said that the Box Man was there in Reese's house, and
that he, or it, or whatever the fuck, saved her by sticking a pair of scissors, *my* scissors, into his leg."

Nate raised his hand. "I have questions."

"Lay them on me, Big Poppa."

"I will, as long as you never call me Big Poppa again."

She shrugged. He asked anyway.

"I want to be sure I understand this—you're saying the Box Man
was alive. Or animated somehow."

"Correct."

"And you did that?"

"Two for two."

"And the Box Man was there. In Reese's house."

"For the trifecta, the hat trick, a threefer."

"How? How did he get there?"

Maddie leaned in, and now her stare was positively *manic*. "I don't know. But Sissy said something else. She said . . . she saw some bearded freak staring in through the window. And then she saw *me*. And . . . I helped her out somehow."

A bearded freak.

All the hairs on Nate's neck and arms stood up like sentinels. He didn't even know where to begin, or how to organize his response to this. "All right. The bearded guy, we'll get back to that, and honestly real soon, Maddie, I'm going to say some things that are going to make this all a helluva lot weirder, okay? But you're saying you were there. In Reese's *house*, with the Kalbacher girl."

"I think so. Or something like that. Here's the corker, Nate: I sat in her driveway and pulled up my phone and found news stories from back then. Sissy got back to her parents when a cop drove her there."

"Okay. So?"

"It was a city cop, not a local, not state police."

He blinked. "A city cop?"

"I *think* it was my father," she said. "I . . . have a memory of it. It's fuzzy as fuck, but I remember him dropping me off at my Mom-Mom's house—my grandmother lived a block away—and he said he had to take a little girl home. I think it was her, Nate. I think it was Sissy. In our house."

"In Philly."

"Yeah. In Philly."

"Jesus, Maddie."

"And it wasn't the last time something like that happened." She hesitated. "It's been happening again."

"Happening again? What's been happening again?"

"I've made things. And they've come . . . alive." She told him first about the Box Man she'd made recently—without really even realizing she'd done it. Then about the owl that flew away, and how she seems to have made some crass facsimile of the killer, Edmund Reese.

Nate took a moment. Just to take it all in. He needed that time to sponge it up, pickle in it. "You okay?" she asked him.

And that's when he told her everything *he* knew.

He told her about all the times he'd seen his father—and about how the old man had a gun, but held it in the wrong hand. He described the tall man in the woods, the one with the rat's nest of a beard and the sores on his skin, the one whose jaw broke as he screamed and who simply . . . disappeared. Also in a bolt of lightning. He talked about how the injury across his head wasn't from falling, but because there was a girl there who appeared in the lightning, and was stolen by the same lightning—lightning that seemed to carry an all-too-familiar face: Edmund Walker Reese.

Maddie shook her head, slumping back in the chair. She half covered her face with her hand, as if she couldn't believe what she was about to say. "He's it. He's the nexus of all this. Everything intersects with Reese. There are more victims. Somehow. More victims people don't even know about."

And then he said, "There's something else."

"The way you're looking at me," she said, "I have a bad feeling about whatever it is."

"I don't know if it's a bad thing . . ."

"Okayyyy."

"The owl you carved."

"Out of the log."

"I think I saw it."

She looked astonished, not upset. "Where?"

"Well . . ." He hesitated. "Twice now. I saw it once in the tree. And then . . . again after the girl."

The look of astonishment became one of concern—the color in her cheeks thinned. She thought he meant he saw it as if it were an object—something someone stole, a thing just lying about. But that wasn't how he meant it at all. She said, "I don't know what that means. And you're sure?"

"It wasn't . . . a regular owl, Maddie. It looked *carved*."

"Carved."

"Like out of wood, carved."

"Well. Shit."

"Yeah."

The two of them sat there for a while, each chewing over *all* of this in silence. Sometimes one of them looked like they intended to say something—a rumpled brow, a tightened jaw, a whispered incredulous hiss presaging words that never came. And then they'd lapse once more again into silence. It was, of course, Maddie who eventually broke that silence:

"So," she said abruptly.

"So."

"Way I see it is, either we are both crazier than a wasp's nest before winter—and crazy in a way where we are somehow sharing in the same delusion? That's the nice option. Being crazy is the easy way out, honestly, because the alternative . . ."

"Is that this is all real."

"All too fucking real."

"I think it's real," Nate said, finally. Up until now he hadn't been sure—honestly, he'd been leaning more and more toward the idea that his brain had slipped a couple vital gears. Now, though, he was going the other way with it. In part because of what he said next: "I think Jed saw, too."

"Saw what?"

"When I was out there—you know, when I suffered my *first* head injury of the night—and I saw my father again? Jed came outside. I think he saw me fighting with the old man."

"That was a weird fucking storm."

"Pretty weird, yeah. Climate change ain't got nothing on whatever that was."

"So Jed may have seen. He didn't visit you in the hospital?"

Nate shook his head.

"Then you have to visit him," she said.

"I guess so. It's going to be a weird conversation."

"No weirder than the one we just had. It'll be good, though. He knows about this kind of stuff. *And,*" she added, "he's an expert on Reese. Maybe he can help us sort through it all. I don't know. I know I love you, though." At that, they both stood up then and came together in a crashing hug. It was like some massive barrier between them had fallen, like they'd each been in prison without the other until right now. She said in his ear, "I'm glad you don't hate me. I'm glad you're not judging me."

"I'd never hate you. If anything, I'm even prouder of you now."

She kissed his cheek. Then his lips. Then his jawline. And next thing they knew, they were ripping each other out of their clothes, and they were doing something that people only seemed to do in movies—they fucked on the dining room table, him on top of her, then flipped, stirring up the kind of energy they hadn't summoned since before Oliver was born, the kind of energy that could power a mountain village for the better part of a year, the kind of energy that reminded them both that their love was vigorous and eternal, lust-slick and heart-strong, as bright as starlight, as loud as thunder, and dirtier than a gas station bathroom.

38

Post-Coital Reality Check

Came a point that they had to retire to the bedroom, because a dining room table was one of the least comfortable places for lovemaking. Especially the kind of lovemaking that they just did; Maddie
was a gleefully foul-mouthed lover, and their energy matched the
vim and vigor of her directive profanity. Already Maddie knew she'd
have bruises. Nate, too. Banging was both metaphor and truth here,
the way they knocked into the corners of the table a half-dozen times.

Now, they lay sprawled across the bed, limbs akimbo, bodies
slicked by sweat. Maddie basked in the glow. "That was amazing."

Nate didn't even say words to agree with her—his accord came in
grunted utterances. Kind of a *nngh* and a *mmm*.

"The way you did the thing, with the finger and the thumb—"

"Nn-hm."

"You're a gifted man, Nathan Graves."

Finally he mustered some actual words: "I figure a queen such as
yourself is worthy of the best I can give."

She barked a laugh.

For a weird moment, she felt happy. Sure, she also felt totally
deranged—like a child's top spinning toward the edge of a countertop. But she also felt weirdly free, having told him everything, and
having come together (literally and figuratively) as they just had.

But reality encroached upon her haze of body-mind joy, and she figured it was best to rip the Band-Aid off instead of peeling it so it plucked one hair at a time.

"We need to talk about Oliver," she said.

"I don't think he needs to ever know what we did here today. You think therapy is expensive now? He'd be in therapy for the better part of his adult life. And Dr. Nahid is too nice for such filth."

She laughed. "No, not *to* him, I mean about—"

Gently, he said, reaching out and touching her shoulder, "I know what you mean, Mads. You mean . . . everything else. All of this."

"Do we tell him?"

"About Reese? The owl? The girl with the number on her cheek?" For a time all Maddie heard was the soft inhale and exhale. If the topic at hand weren't so important, she might've found that sound so meditative that it would lull her to sleep. Now, she awaited his answer, which he gave in time: "No, I don't think we tell him."

"I agree," she said.

"It's just—this is all pretty gonzo. He's a kid. He doesn't need this kind of stuff. It's not our job to protect him from reality, but it's also not our job to fashion it into a bat and beat him over the head with it. And he's got friends now. Caleb is a good kid. Jake—okay, Jake I don't trust, really, but we can't control all aspects of our son's life, and he's got a good enough head on his shoulders. I just don't want to rattle him."

A twinge in Maddie's gut made her worry that it was the wrong choice. They were a team, the three of them. And to keep Olly at arm's length had already caused them problems. At the same time . . . this *was* all super-duper fucked up. Maddie couldn't even imagine how they'd broach the subject to him. *Hey, honey, how was school today? I'm making chili for dinner. By the way, my art comes alive and also there's a supposedly dead serial killer who is somehow back—Oh! And also your father has been literally fighting the ghost of your grandfather. Do you have any homework?*

This was the right thing to do.

In part because it was the *only* thing they could do.

"That's that, then," she said.

"So what now?" he asked.

"I don't know. We need answers. You go to Jed. I definitely don't sculpt or build a single fucking thing. I might do some research—hit the library, see what I can see about any of this. Worse comes to worst, we call an old priest and a young priest and get this exorcism party started."

"We could move," he said. "Pack our things and go."

"No," she said. "We don't give up. We don't give in. This is our home. So we fight to keep it that way."

39

Broken Stars

When Oliver closed his eyes to drift off to sleep, he saw the void. He saw all its broken stars. And he heard the sounds of gunshots, or ribs breaking, or something exploding as people screamed. And then he'd jolt awake and have to try it all over again.

And it was happening now, too, in school. If he took too long at blinking, he could feel the vertigo of falling into that void. In AP Bio he started to drift off a little bit and there it was again—the bang of a gun. He gasped awake, and it was loud enough that everyone heard, which earned him a stern admonishment from the teacher.

That, and the laughter of the other kids.

Because of course.

Afterward, he was in the hallway, filling up his water bottle at the fountain, and he felt a presence behind him. He smelled the sharp tang of frat-boy cologne. When he turned around, he knew who he would see.

Graham looked rough. A bit of stubble decorated the space under his jawline and the real estate riding up his cheeks. His fingers remained bandaged and splinted. And in him, that twisting core of pain. Blacker than black. A consumptive serpent, eating him up, and growing to fill his spaces.

"You look like shit," Graham said.

"So do you," Oliver said, and what rocked through him were the warring emotions of *You shouldn't have said that* and then, *Holy shit, did you really just say that?* He wobbled between two feelings: first, being afraid that Graham was going to punch him, and second, feeling empowered.

Because fuck you, Graham Lyons.

Graham looked struck. As if slapped.

"You little turd. You hurt my finger. And you talk to me like that?" Graham got closer to him.

Oliver rode this feeling of empowerment. He knew it was probably temporary, and it was further gonna get him into trouble, but here he heard his mother's words in the back of his mind: *Fuck it.*

"And what are you going to do about it?"

At that, Graham grabbed him by the arm—

"Yo," came a voice.

Caleb.

He stood there, phone up, like he was filming. "Smile for the camera, man. You wanna beat on my boy here, you wanna put on that show, I figure why can't the world see it?" And at this point, other students stopped in the hall and gathered around Caleb to watch what was going on.

"Just talking to my friend Oliver," Graham said.

"Keep walking," Caleb said.

"You sure you wanna do this?" Graham asked.

"You sure *you* wanna do this? You're already booted from fall practice, man. You need a one-way ticket off the team forever, keep pushing."

At that, Graham let go. He grinned a big Cheshire Cat grin before melting back into the flow of hallway traffic.

Oliver let out a breath.

"Caleb," he said.

"Hey, Olly."

"You're not mad at me?"

Caleb arched an eyebrow. "Nah, man. I'm good. You *did* kinda play me at your house, though. Your boy, Jake? I don't trust that cat."

"I don't know if I can trust him. I'm sorry I didn't tell you about Alex and Graham. But . . . Jake did save me from them. I just figured I'd give him the benefit of the doubt."

Caleb rolled his eyes. "Look, man. I'm not your dad, I'm not your boss, you're in this life, not me. So I won't tell you how to act. But I think that guy is shady, and he doesn't have any length of leash with me. You're a nicer dude than I am, though, so you wanna give him that shot, by all means. Just don't ask me to go with you on that journey."

"Does that mean you and I won't hang anymore?"

"Pssh, c'mon, Olly. I'm not like that. People can be friends with other people I'm not friends with. That's called *life*."

"Because I still need to see him. Jake. I feel like I'm not done with him yet. Does that make sense?"

"Nope. But it doesn't have to."

"I'm gonna try to head over there after school. To his house. I think he lives in that trailer park? Emerald Lakes?"

Caleb shrugged. "Cool. I'll drive you."

"You don't have to."

"Shut up, man, and just lemme do it. Maybe you buy me a Five Guys burger later on or something, toss me a couple bucks for gas."

Oliver grinned. "Deal."

The school sat east of town, and when school ended that day, Oliver texted his mother, told her he had some extracurricular work to do, that he'd either catch a ride with someone or call her later. She texted back kk.

Then he and Caleb headed to the trailer park where Jake supposedly lived.

Emerald Acres was on the south side of Quaker Bridge, miles from Ramble Rocks park. Caleb drove a real beat-ass car, a pine-green Saturn two-door that had so many dents and dings in it, it looked like a crinkled-up beer can. It had 247,000 miles on it and smelled like vinegar—that, Caleb explained, because mice had gotten into the car and his mother made him clean out all the mouse shit using vinegar instead of bleach.

The car eased into the Emerald Acres trailer park. The paved driveway and parking lot were pitted with potholes that could better be described as volcanic craters—some big enough to lose a small car in. The trailers themselves were a blend of single-wides and double-wides, their meager front lawns a slapdash canvas of random shit: birdbaths and children's toys and lawn chairs, plus a scattering of decrepit old charcoal grills, cars on cinder blocks, time-worn and weather-scourged patio furniture. Not to mention the occasional pink flamingo.

"This place looks like the end of the fuckin' world," Caleb said. "Man, I thought *my* house was shitty."

"Yeah, it's sad, actually."

Oliver felt suddenly bad for thinking it was sad. It made him feel judgmental in a way that didn't sit right with him—at the same time, it *was* sad, wasn't it? That people had to live here? Like this? While ten minutes north other people lived in old stone colonials and new-construction mansions and had acres and acres of heritage conservancy land instead of three postage stamps of dead grass? Poverty was pain, he realized, and for a moment that revelation felt like a fist about to grind him to a stump. He had to take a few deep breaths not to succumb to it.

They passed by a trailer with a rickety front porch cobbled onto it. A big woman in an Eagles hoodie stood outside it, smoking a pipe.

"That bitch smoking a pipe?" Caleb asked.

"I think so." It wasn't a glass pipe for weed, either—but, like, a proper wooden pipe with a swan-neck bend. She puffed on it, watching the Saturn balefully as it passed.

"She must think she's Sherlock Holmes, look at her." Caleb lowered his voice. "Trailer parks attract some strange ducks, man."

"Yeah."

Somewhere down the way, they heard the dull *foom foom foom* of cranked-up bass coming from inside one of the trailers.

"Ay, the hell are we doing here, Olly? For real. You seriously want to find this dude again?"

Oliver shrugged. "Kinda." He hadn't told Caleb all of it. He hadn't told *anybody* all of what he saw out there. "I want to make sure he's okay. He kinda bailed on the party that night and . . ." *And I have questions.*

"Man, it's nice and all to care about the dude, but it's also a-o-fuckin'-kay to care about him from a distance. Like, *Oh, I'll care about that guy from over here, where it's safe and warm,* and even better, it's also okay *not* to care about some people, because fuck some people, man, just fuck 'em. You don't owe anybody anything. Okay? Listen, I got an older brother, and you know why I don't talk to him? Because he's a real piece of shit. Stole from us, crashed my dad's work truck, even threw a punch at my dad one time. I don't owe him anything just because he's my brother. Yeah, we share blood. Yeah, we're 'connected.'" At that, he made vigorous air quotes and then turned that gesture into a vigorous air-jerking-off motion. "But he hasn't earned my love and attention, so he doesn't get it."

"I didn't know that. About your brother."

"Yeah. James. Like I said, real piece of shit." Caleb pleaded once more: "Anyway. C'mon. What say we just give this shit up—not like you even know which trailer is Jake's—and we go get the group together, play some D-and-fuckin'-D."

Because, Oliver thought, but did not say, *something weird happened out in the woods and I don't understand it.*

The book. The void. Those *visions.*

Still, though, Caleb had a point. Maybe this was all too crazy and he shouldn't get too close to Jake. Whatever had happened out there, maybe it was best left to history. Someday he'd take it to Reddit, post it on one of those weird *Glitches in the Matrix* boards, and enjoy the upvotes it gave him, and everyone would be like *Whoa that story is crazy* and some people would tell him he was lying and maybe he'd convince himself he *was* making it all up. Even now, only days from it, he wasn't sure if it had been real, or was some nutball delusion his brain had conjured in the storm.

But before he could tell Caleb okay, they'd go play D&D, Caleb said, "Don't you know that dude?"

Oliver followed his finger, and saw a familiar face across the street. Leaving one of the trailers, heading toward a black Lexus SUV.

"Your neighbor, right?" Caleb said. "He was at the party."

"I think so." But Olly *knew* so. What was his name? Mom had his books. Ned. No. *Jed*. Jed Homackie.

He looked rough. Same way Graham Lyons looked rough, though maybe worse. Mussed-up hair, days of unshaven face. Jowly and tired looking—the circles around his eyes so plain and so visible they were a stone's throw from looking like shiners.

"Wonder what *he's* doing *here*," Oliver said.

"Yo, look."

As Jed got into the SUV and started to pull away, someone opened the door of a dingy double-wide to watch him go.

"That's your boy," Caleb said.

"He's *not* my—" Olly didn't even bother finishing. Because Caleb was right. It was Jake. Framed by the door, hand out, leaning against one of the crooked posts propping a rough, half-ruined awning. Jake watched Jed's car leave.

"That's him. You can see it from here. My dude looks like he wrestled with a weed whacker—and the weed whacker won. I mean, sometimes you try to fuck the bear, and sometimes the bear fucks you—"

"*Okay*, Caleb. He's got a fucked-up face. It's not his fault." Under his breath, he added: "I think it makes him look kinda cool. Like Zuko in *Airbender*."

"Zuko was evil, dude."

"No, Zuko was *bad*, but he turned *good*."

"Okay, okay, whatever. Sorry. I shouldn't make fun, it's just—the fuck happened to him?"

"I dunno." *But I want to find out.*

"Welp. You wanna talk to him, there he is."

"I do." He did, it was true. But now, he was afraid. Afraid in part that Caleb would come along, and would hear what he asked Jake—or that Jake wouldn't tell him *because* Caleb was along. He didn't want to mess this up. This felt important. Like he was standing on one tiptoe atop a mountain's peak—one wrong move would send him tumbling back down.

Again came the vertiginous rush of falling . . .

But where was he falling? *Into that void.*

"You all right?" Caleb asked.

Olly snapped to it with a sharp gasp. "Yeah. Uh. Yeah."

"Good, because your boy is walking over here."

"What?" *Shit!*

Sure enough, here came Jake. Looking quizzically at them as he approached, his head ducked low so he could glance past the glare on the windows and see who sat inside. When he finally saw, he smirked as he rapped on the glass.

Olly buzzed the window down.

"Hey, Jake," Olly said, faking a voice like, *Oh, I didn't see you there,* or *Yeah, this is totally normal.* Like that meme of the cartoon dog sitting in the burning house. *This is fine.*

"Olly. Caleb."

"'Sup," Caleb said.

"What're you guys doing here?"

"I was just, ahh," Olly said, swallowing hard. "I thought I'd check in with you. See if you were good."

"I'm great." Jake showed his teeth—big and white—in a shark-mouth smile. "Caleb, how are you?"

"Ay, you know me, man. I'm vertical."

"Vertical. Yeah. Right." Jake looked hard at Olly. "You wanna come in?"

"Okay, sure."

Olly and Caleb both started to get out of the car, but Jake interjected. To Caleb he said:

"Hey, not you, though."

"What?" Caleb asked.

"Olly and me, we have a connection. And we have something important to talk about. And it doesn't include you."

Olly gave a pleading look to Caleb. "I'm sorry, I . . ."

"I'm not your fuckin' taxi, man. I won't wait around."

"I know. I'll . . . get a ride somehow. Or I'll walk—"

Caleb leaned across the middle of the car and in a low voice said, "Olly, dude, don't go with him. Just like you shouldn't have followed his ass out there in the woods? *Don't follow him now.* I don't like him. I don't trust him. I don't think this goes anywhere good."

"I can *hear* you," Jake said, still standing outside the car.

"I *know* you fucking can, dude, I'm good with that, now step off."

Olly put a steadying hand on Caleb's shoulder. "I'll be all right."

"Shit. Don't say I didn't warn you, Olly."

"Thanks, Caleb."

"Uh-huh."

Olly gave a reassuring smile to his friend, though it was a lie. He was far from reassured, and worry pulled at him like an ogre sucking a bone. But he got out of the car anyway, and followed Jake to the house. Caleb took off, the tires peeling on the Saturn, sending up a spray of shattered asphalt. Then he was gone.

40

The Wizard's Castle

The inside of the trailer was a shitty mess. Ratty carpet, wood paneling on the walls. Pizza boxes and fast food containers lay scattered throughout, even on the mauve couch that looked like it had been through a war. A flat-screen TV with a spiderweb crack in the corner hung on the wall, a last-generation PlayStation hooked up to it. On the coffee table between couch and screen sat an opened-up fishing tackle box, except it did not contain things like lures and hooks and rubber worms. It was full of *pills*. Blue, purple, and pink in triangle shapes and circle shapes and capsules. Like Lucky Charms marshmallows, except made of drugs.

Jake was saying as they walked in, "Hey, I'm sorry your friend couldn't come in, but I figure this is between you and me. Though what is *up* with Caleb, anyway? He's like, a cool Black guy on the outside, all . . . whatever, but then on the inside he's . . . gooey nerd nougat, those stupid fucking cards and games and shit."

"Caleb's my friend. What are you, racist? Because he's Black he can't play D&D?"

"Nah. I mean—I guess structurally, we're all racist, right? Me and you, all part of a system of privilege and oppression—"

Ugh, shut up. An answer that felt like just hot air. "Whatever. And I play those games, too, you know," Oliver said defensively.

Jake paused then. Looked him up and down. Sucked on a tooth as he scrutinized Oliver with that one shifting eye.

"Yeah. You do. That's interesting."

"Why is it interesting?"

"It just is. Here, come on, sit down." Jake took a couple stacked pizza boxes on the couch and frisbeed them into the corner of the room.

Oliver eyed up the pills. "You don't live here with your aunt."

Jake shrugged. "Nope."

"I should go."

"Relax, I'm not going to try to peer pressure you into popping pills." Another odd pick-apart glance from Jake. "I think you're too good for that."

"Yeah. Well." Indignantly: "I am."

"I'm starting to see that. So, sit. You want answers, don't you?"

"You bailed on me. Left me alone in the storm."

"Your mom was coming. I couldn't have her see me there. You wanna know more or not?"

Reluctantly, Oliver sat. The couch had so little support he felt like it was a soft mouth about to swallow him up. It made him feel more anxious—like if he needed to, he wouldn't be able to jump up quickly and run out of here. It would be like sprinting in mud, like trying to outrun a nightmare.

Falling, falling into that void . . .

He forced the memory, and that feeling, from his mind.

"Why was my neighbor here?" Oliver asked. "I saw him walking out."

"Jed. Yeah. He's my landlord." His eyes flashed like moonlight on dark water. "But that's not what you want to talk about. No. You want to talk about what happened in the woods."

Oliver's voice nearly broke when he said: "That book. The things it showed me. It was . . . it was crazy."

"You're welcome, by the way."

"Why would I thank you?"

What looked like anger flashed across Jake's face. "Really? I show you something private, something that is *literal goddamn magic,* and you're not sure you should be gracious?" But then the anger seemed to subside. Jake smiled with his mouth, though not the rest of his face. "I'm a wizard, Olly. That book is my *spellbook.*"

Oliver almost laughed, it was so dumb. "I know, you said that, but like, what does that even mean?"

"You saw. I can do magic."

"Magic. This is like in the garage. And the woods."

"Yeah. Sorta." He pulled out the Book of Accidents from underneath the coffee table and flipped it open. "With this I can—" He snapped his fingers, and a hooked hunting knife appeared in his hand. The book glowed a little with dark-edged light. "Make things appear."

He gave the knife a twirl.

Oliver pressed his back into the couch.

He's going to kill me.

It was like Jake sensed that thought, because he said, "Jesus, man, I'm not going to kill you, relax."

He pivoted his wrist again with a flourish and—

Whoosh. The knife disappeared.

Then another snap—

Now it was the *pistol* that returned. The pellet gun.

Jake moved to clap his hands—with the gun still in one—and the weapon literally disappeared between his palms.

"Magic," Jake said, with performative panache.

"It's just a magic *trick.* Not real magic. I've seen magicians on Netflix do way weirder shit."

"What about what I showed you?" He put his hand out, fingers splayed, as if to conjure the memory. "Or was *that* just a magic trick, too?"

"Maybe it was just, I dunno. A hallucination." He gestured toward the pills. "Maybe you drugged me."

"Or maybe I showed you something important. A glimpse into

more than just our world, kid." He winked. "Did you know I can not only see into other worlds? I can travel between them, too."

"Travel between worlds."

"That's right."

"What does that even mean? Like, you can go screw around on Mars or something?"

Jake took a knee, like a coach about to tell his team some intimate truth about the game they were about to play. "No, Oliver. It's not like that. I can move between worlds like I'm flipping pages of a book. *This* book. But only one direction. Only forward to the next one, never back to the last one."

"And why would you do that?"

Jake's mad eye gleamed. "That's the real question, isn't it."

"Fine. Prove it."

"Prove it."

"Yeah." Oliver puffed his chest out, trying to look tough even though inside he felt like a soap bubble quivering, ready to pop. "Prove it. Make something appear. I'll say a thing and you can snap your fingers and make it come out of nowhere. Like . . ." He tried to think of something really odd, really rare. *A Magic card,* he thought. "A Black Lotus card from the black-bordered alpha *Magic: The Gathering* set. Probably the rarest card. I think one went at auction recently for a hundred grand or something. So: Pull one of those rabbits out of your hat."

"It doesn't work like that."

"Of course it doesn't. How convenient."

Jake licked his lips, and flexed his fingers into fists and then back again, like he was trying very hard to manage frustration and anger. "Seriously, that's not how it works."

"Explain it to me then."

"I am, if you'd shut the fuck up and listen."

"Whatever. Fine. I'm *listening*."

"It's like this. I can take a thing, and I can put it in . . . a place. A faraway nowhere place. I call it the In-Between because that's where it is—it's like, the space behind a couch, or underneath it, where you can hide stuff. It's not useful for anything *but* hiding stuff."

"So just some big Bag of Holding."

"I don't know what that is."

"It's a D&D thing—" Now it was Oliver's turn to mitigate frustration. "You don't know what D&D is. It doesn't matter, never mind."

"I hide things there. Things I might want. Things I might need."

"Like what?"

"Like this."

Jake twisted his wrist. His fingers danced. And something appeared in his hand: a candy bar in a shiny wrapper. Bold purple and almost-glowing green.

Oliver didn't recognize it.

With a flip of his hand, Jake tossed him the candy bar.

"Flix Bar," Oliver said, reading what was on the package. Next to the fifties-era font like you might see outside a diner or on an old jukebox, he saw a little cartoon character: almost like one of the aliens from that movie *Toy Story*. Little green alien with antennae and multiple eyes. Plus a mouth of white, circular teeth. Teeth like white pebbles. Underneath it was printed a tagline: FLIXY SAYS IT'S OUTTA THIS WORLD! Oliver turned it over in his hand, saw that it was made by some company called Perigee, Inc. "I've never heard of one of these. Is it new?"

"Nope."

"Canadian? New Zealand?" Oliver watched YouTube videos on BuzzFeed, where the rotating cast of temporary internet celebrities ate weird snack foods from around the world: Pineapple Lumps and Vegemite and Chicken Twisties. But even as he asked the question, he saw the phrase MADE IN THE USA next to the Perigee logo. "Wait, this was made here."

"Here. But also, not here."

"I don't understand—"

"Made in the USA. Sure. But it wasn't made in *this* USA."

"I don't—" *Follow,* he was about to say, but then, suddenly, he did follow. Other worlds. Alternate dimensions. Quantum reality. Not *this* United States of America, but another one. From another dimension. Again that feeling of tumbling down, down, down. *The void.*

"Try it."

"The candy?"

"Yeah."

"No, I . . ." *I shouldn't be eating candy from another dimension.* That was easily the weirdest, stupidest thought that had ever occurred to him, but there it was, lingering in his mouth, unspoken, but also undying. *Another dimension.* It wasn't possible. Jake was just fucking around with him. Playing a prank. As soon as he bought into it, Jake'd make fun of him. This was probably going on YouTube, wasn't it? Anger rose in him. He tossed the candy bar back at him like a throwing knife. "I don't want it. Probably poison. Or full of ants or something dumb."

Oliver stood up as Jake twirled the candy bar like a drummer's drumstick—and with that, the object helicoptered into nonexistence once more. "It's not poison. But fine, don't eat it. But you can't leave yet."

"I am leaving. I'm going home."

"I have one more thing to show you."

Just go, Oliver thought.

Don't wait.

Don't ask.

Just go.

But—

Question marks were shaped like a hook for a reason . . .

"Oh yeah? What's that?"

"I want to show you who I really am. And who you really are, too."

41

The Book of Accidents

Jake handed Oliver the book. It felt surprisingly heavy in Oliver's hands. From it arose a smell: an earthy, mineral tang.

Again he saw the title:

A BOOK OF ACCIDENTS
An accounting of accidents at Ramble Rocks Number Eight

"Ramble Rocks," Oliver said. "That's the park. Why is it accounting a series of . . . park accidents?"

But Jake didn't say anything. He just let Oliver take the book, and he watched carefully. Eagerly, even, with a kind of desperate interest. Like someone who had cooked a dinner and was waiting for the jury's decision: *Did they like the food? Did they make a face or utter a satisfied sound?*

Oliver tried to be gentle with the book, for it felt so old and so abused that it seemed as if it would go to dust in his hands were he to turn a page too fast, or even give it a stiff little shake. The pages themselves were the gray of death, colorless as a rain-soaked corpse. But they felt dry, too dry, like as soon as Oliver's fingers touched them, they sucked away the moisture—pages like vampires, hungry to drink him dry, and in his mind he saw himself momentarily like a desiccated bug husk upturned on the ground.

The pages themselves were as the cover promised: mostly just a handwritten (and sometimes misspelled) accounting of many accidents, big and small, inside what appeared to be a mine. A coal mine.

> *Charlie Tompkins' hand crushed tween two rocks . . .*
> *. . . explosion of gasses left three dead: Eddie Uhl, Issac Streznewski,*
> *Jonesy Steven-Graeme . . .*
> *. . . footbones shattered with tamping rod . . .*
> *. . . took a cat's head mallet to the hed held by fella miner, John*
> *Gold . . .*
> *. . . lost finger to a fuse-cutter . . .*
> *. . . impaled by a iron candle stick . . .*

Then there were the pages detailing those who suffered from, or even died from, various diseases: gangrenous limbs and men coughing up black phlegm and red chunks of lung tissue, plus discussions about those who lost their minds down in the dark. His eyes drifted over a sentence—*Frederick said we were being watched down here, so certain of it was he that he began to carry a revolver with him into the tunnels*—and he looked up from his reading.

"These are mining accidents. Ramble Rocks isn't a coal mine."

"Not in your world."

A rough, raw vibration ran through Oliver. "What?"

"In your world, it's a park. In other worlds, it's an amusement park, or a cemetery, or a quarry, or a Superfund site. In my world, it was a coal mine."

"You're . . . saying you're from another world."

"One just like this one, yeah. But different, too."

"I don't understand. This is crazy." He scowled at the book, which suddenly gave off a surge of colors—a sickly bloom of algal green, shot through with threads of foamy orange bile. Olly gasped and held it at arm's length. "You're saying you're not from here? You're from somewhere else."

"That's right."

"And this—" Oliver held up the book. "Came with you."

"Didn't just come with me. Helped me come here. Helped me escape those other worlds. The boundaries became thin, and my spellbook showed me the way through. It helped me find a thin spot. A doorway."

"This isn't even a spellbook. It's just a logbook of tragedy. A spell is . . . is . . . like, *Mix toadstools with salamander eyes in a cauldron full of widow tears* or something. This is just some creepy historical artifact."

"Maybe tragedy is the spell. Or maybe it's magic in the truth behind the tragedy. It's called the Book of Accidents. Are they accidents, Olly?"

"They seem to be."

"When is an accident an accident? Say someone loses a finger or a foot down there in the dark. Think about it. *Imagine it.*"

"It's just an—" *Accident*, he thinks, but then he pushes past it. He imagines being someone down there. A coal miner. Headlamp illuminating the dark. A half-broken, filthy headlamp. The place filthy and poorly lit. *They put you down here. To dig up coal. They don't pay you anything, they give you subpar tools, they work you for hours and hours down in the nowhere of the mine, and what does it get you? A lost finger. A shattered foot. Maybe a crushed head.* He could feel their pain, their anguish, rising up off the page like heat from a stove. It made him sick. "It's not an accident. None of them are. These people suffered down there in the dark."

"Now look at the book again," Jake said, pushing the book back toward Oliver. He didn't want to look at it, though. He shook his head almost petulantly—he felt like a child refusing to eat his peas, which in turn made him feel small and embarrassed.

So, in turn, Jake held up the book, open to a random page.

"You have to stare at it. Stare *through* it. Like one of those, whaddyacallits, a Magic Eye painting." Jake's smirk tightened. "See, there it is. More magic. Magic cards, magic book, magic eye." He winked.

Oliver looked to the book. He didn't want to. He thought about just walking out of here, nope-ing right the hell out of this entire experience. But he had to know. Something about all this compelled him to follow through.

Again, the pages looked as they did before: gray, worn, the dark charcoal scratches marking the horrific accidents of miners in the coal tunnels. And then, as Oliver stared at them, *through them,* those dark pencil scratches started to move, just as they had that night in the storm-wracked forest. It was like they fell just a little, just a half an inch, before they came alive and started to twitch and squirm like ants. Then they *were* ants, he was sure of it, and he felt his feet fixed to the floor (*can't run*) and his eyes fixed to the book (*can't look away*) and those ants crawled over one another into new words, new sentences, and the insects seemed to sink into the page like blobs of ink blotted by a paper towel. Present on the page now were not the accountings of dead and injured men, but rather a language Oliver did not know, *could not have known,* because it wasn't real, it was something out of a fantasy book, something out of Lovecraft, or inscribed on some forbidden dungeon tomb in D&D, some mad jabber of letters he knew and many he didn't—twistings of ink pressed into tails and whirls and intricate knots. In the center of his forehead he felt a sudden, intense pressure, like someone's thumb pushing there harder and harder and harder, almost hard enough to *pop* through his skull bone like a carpentry nail tapped gently through an eggshell, *tap, tap, crack*—

Beyond it?

The void.

It called to him, sang him a song of invitation—a song sung in the screams of men dying in the mine, of children dead in school hallways, of homeless men and women freezing to death on a city grate with a whispered plea on their lips to a god that won't hear them.

He cried out and looked away.

"Intense, right?" Jake asked.

"I don't know what that was," Oliver stammered. He looked to the coffee table to see—to see what exactly? If Jake had somehow slipped him the pills? Maybe the pills were ground up into dust and left on the couch. He wondered, could this have all just been some hallucination?

"It called to you. It showed you the truth."

"What truth?"

"The world is fucking broken, man. Everything is falling apart. You've felt it. I know you have. You know what entropy is?"

"Of course I do." He'd always loved the idea of entropy. All the world and all its systems were constantly drifting toward chaos. A descent. But life, as Goldblum said in *Jurassic Park,* found a way— and it responded by fighting entropy with birth and growth. Even when something did decay—a tree falls, let's say—an animal might find shelter in it, or use it to hide, or mushrooms would grow on its surface, and that tree would eventually yield all its nutrients back to the soil where other trees would gain from it. This gave him a lot of hope. Entropy was persistent. But so was the natural world's efforts to counter it.

"Welp. Entropy's winning. School shootings, terrorism, serial killers. Bigotry and abuse. Sex trafficking, human slavery, cop killings. Do things seem normal to you?"

"I don't know. I don't know!" His pulse quickened. *Keep it together, Olly.* "They're not normal, but my dad always says that every generation has its challenges, from Hitler to Nixon to the Dust Bowl and the Great Depression and—"

"Your dad *was* a cop, wasn't he? Like he knows anything about anything. Why you gotta see a therapist? I bet it's his fault. I bet his father beat his ass, and now he beats your ass. Or diddles you, or puts you in a dress, or—"

"Shut *up,*" Oliver seethed. He shoved Jake backward, hard. "You don't know fuck all. I don't know exactly how bad my father had it, but I know *his* father used to beat him on the regular. My grandfather was a drunk, a bully, a *snake.* And none of that came down through my father. Not one bit of it. Abuse doesn't make abuse." He pushed past Jake and called over his shoulder, "And if I wanna wear a dress, I'll *wear a dress.*"

"Olly. Listen. You need to understand, what's happening here is what happened to the other worlds I came from. They're all gone now. They're fallen worlds, collapsed into one another—there, entropy won. I'm here now like a . . . a prophet. A prophet nobody has listened to so far. This world, your world, it's going the way of the others. It's collapsing, and it'll fall soon. But I think we can fix it, you and I. I think we can save the world. We can stop entropy—"

"You can't *stop* entropy."

"But what if you could?"

"This is insane. *You're* insane."

And with that, Oliver stormed out the door.

42

A Mirror, Slowly Cracking

The book trembled on the coffee table, pages fluttering as if by a stirring breeze. The book roared inside Jake's mind.

You LOST him.

"He's not *gone* gone," Jake seethed, pacing the trailer.

This one is willful. You call him weak? Perhaps he is the strong one.

"No. No! I have to give him the chance. The chance to get on the right side of things. To see the way forward. They *all* get the chance. You understand? That's the deal. *They all get the chance.*" *This is the process,* he reminded himself. "He just needs a nudge."

He needs more than a nudge. Push him. Drag him. Force him.

But Jake wouldn't have it. The process was the process. The way was the way. He needed something. A lever. A vulnerability.

A weak spot.

My dad always says that every generation has its challenges, from Hitler to Nixon to the Dust Bowl and the Great Depression.

Optimism. Hope. A way forward. All weaknesses. And it all came from the same place—a wellspring of faith in a better world.

"His weak spot—it's the father, isn't it? It's fucking *Nate.*"

A sharp rebuke from the book: *No! The father is a bolstering influence, boy. A source of strength, not a vulnerability. You should've told him who you really were. You should've shown him your true self.*

"He'd never believe me. And you're wrong. The source of his

strength *is* his vulnerability." Jake cackled. "You know, for a demon, you're pretty fuckin' worthle—"

His throat closed. His one normal eye bulged, and the other one, the one of many colors, threatened to pop from his skull like a wine cork.

APOLOGIZE.

"Y-you n-need me."

I did not need Reese, and I do not need you, boy. I can be patient. I can find another way. I have all the time. But your time can end now.

"Pl-*please.*"

Do what needs to be done.

The invisible hand relinquished its grip. The book on the table fluttered shut. Jake gasped and made a sound somewhere between a strangled cry and a barked laugh. *Strength as vulnerability.*

A plan formed. He had a call to make.

43

Expert in the Ways of Weird, Weird Shit

Nate walked into the office earlier that morning and found Fig sitting at his desk, staring at a computer screen with bloodshot eyes.

"Morning," Nate said.

Fig looked up, blinking. He rubbed his face. "Yeah. I guess it is."

"You look like . . . well, me."

"I seem to have caught your insomnia bug."

"I don't think that's why you have insomnia, Fig."

Fig made a guttural sound: a grumble of frustration. "No shit. You know, I can't find anything about any missing girls who matched that description. And then that storm—that storm wasn't normal, Nate. Wasn't natural. It was some weird, weird shit."

"Well, you might be right about all that. Good news is, we got an expert in those matters."

"Jed Homackie?"

"Jed Homackie."

After work, he headed straight for Jed's. And he did so possessed by that roller-coaster feeling—the rush and roar and *clackity-clack* toward something bad, toward some strange, mad end. He was haunted by the feeling sure as he'd been haunted by his father, by the man in the woods, by the burning sensation across his skull where the madman's knife had cut him.

He knocked at the door.

Nothing.

More knocking. More nothing.

He looked behind him and saw that Jed's car was in the drive-way—a Lexus SUV. The front door didn't have a window, or he'd peek in. He offered his knuckles to the door once more—

The sound of a lock disengaging came from the other side.

The door opened on a haggard Jed. Like a man who had been run through a gauntlet of insomnia. Maybe also a couple mountain lion attacks.

"Nate, Nate, come on in," Jed said. His voice was grumbled and growly, like he'd been gargling a broken coffee mug. He quickly smoothed back some of his whitening hair as he gave an awkward, nervous smile before disappearing into his own home.

Nate trailed after. "Jed, you seem a little on edge, you doing okay?"

He wasn't doing okay.

The house, pristine the last time Nate saw it, was the opposite. Food containers sat strewn about, opened, half-eaten—a tentacle monster of old lo mein crawled out of one Chinese food container and across a counter. A stool was knocked over. Books were off the shelves, scattered around. A paper towel roll sat half unspooled in the middle of the floor, a purple spot soaking through—as if the man had spilled something there and instead of using one or two rectangles of towel, he just kicked the whole roll over it like a steam-roller. Nate half expected that Jed was going to say someone broke in here, stole a bunch of shit—but then amid the trash, Nate saw something else: the distant, erratic towers of liquor bottles. Whiskey, gin, brandy.

All of them, empty.

"I'm fine now," Jed said, as if to explain. "I had a . . . few rough days, Nate, a few truly tough days—" His eyes as wide as a radio host con-spiracy theorist: "What I saw there, that night, with you? It challenged me, Nate. Challenged my beliefs in all things heaven and earth, so to speak. Rattled me to the *core*."

"But why? You . . . you dabble in this kind of thing. Your books, your stories, what you've seen."

A soft cackle babbled up out of him. "Nate, I've never really seen anything. Not like that. A feeling here or there, but nothing really real."

So, Jed was just telling tales, Nate thought. Maybe that's how writers really were—they were just entertaining liars.

"Well, you saw something real this time, didn't you?"

A kind of happy madness gleamed in Jed's eyes. "Yes. That's right."

"You, ahhh." Nate pointed to the bottles. "You were single-handedly keeping the liquor stores in business, I see."

"Well. Nate. If we're being honest, I once tussled with the old *demon*. The demon of drink, as it were."

"Nothing to be ashamed of."

To that, Jed had no comment. He only looked at his feet. The rise and fall of his back as he stood there and simply *breathed* told Nate that the man's fight with that demon, as he put it, had been long and dark.

And given the situation, not entirely won.

"You want me to help clean up?" Nate asked.

"No, no, put that thought out of your fool head, Nate. I'm a grown man, I can clean up my messes." He spun around, and again that glimmer shone in his eyes. "In my drink, I did some research."

"Research."

"Sure. On what I saw, with your father—he wasn't a spirit, not exactly. He was able to touch you, to *hurt* you, and, ahh—" Now Jed squinted as he looked at Nate. "He hit you in the lip, didn't he?"

"He did."

"So where'd those stitches come from?"

Right, of course. He doesn't know.

So, Nate figured, to heck with it. He told him everything about what happened that night. The girl, the number on her cheek, the man in the lightning, the knife. With every word, Jed's eyes went wider.

"It's all real. All of it," Jed said, breathlessly.

"Whaddya mean? Spill it, Jed, I don't have time for games."

Jed nodded. "I . . . I'm coming to terms with the reality that something well beyond just a mere *haunting* is going on here. This is something bigger, stranger. I spoke metaphorically of a demon, but this may be the real thing. I've long held at bay the idea that there was a *good* or *evil* dimension to spirits and the supernatural, much as I eschew the idea that people are purely good or purely evil—we're a blend, all of us, a cocktail peanut mix of niceness and badness, all bound up in a bundle of inexcusable indolence and ignorance punctuated by unanticipated moments of genuine heroism—but maybe, maybe, there's something out there, something truly evil. Something that's *broken through*."

"No games, Jed, no fancy talk, just cut to it."

"What you're seeing—your father, that diseased fellow with the raggedy beard, and Edmund Reese? They're intruders. Trespassers. An invasive species, of a sort. *Invaders,* if you'll allow me the luxury of such poetry. And you and me, we can go get some answers. If you're willing."

Nate nodded. "I need answers."

"Let's find them. Together."

"Sooner the better."

"I suspect I know where we can look first." Jed grinned.

"You're going to say Ramble Rocks park, aren't you?"

"I am indeed, my boy. I am indeed."

44

Nate and Maddie

ighteen years ago:

Vamp Records, South Street, Philadelphia. Used to sell records—like, *records* records, proper vinyl, but now it sold only CDs. Half of them new, half of them used, all of them encased in those giant plastic contraptions that required a special key and an ancient Egyptian blessing to open. Maddie liked working here. It wasn't the music—yeah, sure, music was great and whatever—but the *organization,* oh, wow, chef's kiss, fuck yeah. The tactile sensation of arranging albums and CDs was Maddie's porn. But today she was on counter-monkey duty, and she hated it, but this was her first job out of college and she didn't want to fuck it all up.

Guy came up to the counter, hair a little too long, a mustache over his lip and all the way to his chin like a horseshoe turned down, and he said, "Do you have the new Radiohead?" He meant *Kid A,* and she said, "Do you not know how the alphabet works?" Meaning, *All the CDs are arranged by alphabet, dumbass.* And he rolled his eyes and said, "Yeah, I just don't see it."

She went over and, sure enough, it was gone, so she told him she could special order it. He said not to bother—it was for his girlfriend, but then he said, "I shouldn't even get it for her, she never gets me anything. She kinda sucks." To which Maddie replied: "You shouldn't do her dirty like that. Don't be a fucking asshole. Don't like her?

Dump her." And that seemed to bother him. "Maybe you could help me to not be an asshole," he said. But she answered, "That's not my job." Just the same, she smiled at him. He smiled back. That was the start of it.

Seventeen years ago:

They kinda orbited each other for a while, but when they finally came together on a date, it was like two meteors hitting each other on the way down to earth. The first time they fucked was on the hood of her car, a white '97 Camaro, parked in a cornfield on an unseasonably warm day in late October. They'd come from a show in Philly at the Theatre of Living Arts—Sleater-Kinney. She had tickets through the store. Their lovemaking was fumble-clumsy and artless, but the two of them were ratcheted up from the music and the crowds at the club, and what they lacked in sexual elegance they made up for in sheer young dumb animal passion—not to mention, the both of them found the whole experience fucking hilarious, and together they decided that people who couldn't laugh during sex were joyless lumps resigned to, in her words, "a banal motherfucker of an existence." He said he didn't know what that meant, but he liked it.

Sixteen years ago:

They were married at a firehouse wedding in Bensalem, Pennsylvania, in the south end of Bucks County. Neither of them was religious, so they were married by a local judge friend of Maddie's father, Denny. It wasn't a big wedding, and it wasn't a small wedding—it was a "just right" wedding. Afterward, Denny and Nate had a long heart-to-heart about Nate's future, and that's when her dad said Nate should come down to Philly, join the force. Nate said he'd think about it. That night, he and Maddie consummated their nuptials, as it were, and a month later, the pregnancy pee test came up positive. Oliver, manifesting first as a tiny little plus sign.

* * *

Thirteen years ago:

Together, Nate and Maddie collectively decided that she had been emotionally cheating on him with a man she knew from the Fishtown art collective where she'd been sculpting. The guy was named Bryce, and she and Bryce found each other at a time when everything was just heinously fucking difficult for her: Olly was two, and not just two, but a *tempest* of two, a smart little hell-baby who didn't meet a table corner his soft toddler skull didn't like, and to make it all harder, Nate had taken on extra shifts at the station to cover some budget deficits. Bryce and she had never kissed, had definitely never fucked, but they spent more and more time together and were hugging and rubbing backs and crying it out and one day she just knew, she *had* to tell Nate. She confessed.

Nate lit up like a Christmas tree catching fire from a glitchy strand of lights. He raged fast, coiled his hand in a fist, and punched a hole in the drywall of her apartment. She told him that what he did was abuse-adjacent and he explained that he wasn't mad at her, but mad at himself, and embarrassed, and he wanted to hit himself, hurt his hand, not her. She said, either way, if he ever did that again? She'd take Oliver and be in California by morning and he could fuck off into the sea. She patched the wall. He never did it again.

Ten years ago:

Nate's father, Carl, came to their door. Nate didn't know how the old man had found the place. Looked it up online, maybe, or tricked someone down at the station. They never found out. He came to the door, drunk as a skunk in a bucket of his own piss (as Maddie's own father used to say). Maddie had never met Nate's old man, and wasn't about to meet him now—Nate said he'd handle it. Then he put on his holster, dropped his service pistol into it, and started to head out the door. Maddie, incredulous at the time, asked him if all that was really necessary. All Nate said was, "Yes." And then he went out. She heard them yelling. Nate, mostly. Then someone crying: Carl, the old man. A bottle broke. Nate came in, slammed the door. She saw the pistol was out of its holster, and in his hand. Oliver was upstairs, thankfully, and didn't see anything. She asked him if everything was okay, and he said that it was, and not to worry, they'd never hear from the old man again.

Five years ago:

Oliver, age ten, had taken on the practice of giving money or food to the homeless people he saw on the street—which, in Philadelphia, was a considerable number. Half a dozen on the way to school, same half a dozen back, plus all the others whenever they walked any-where. Most of them were nice, some of them didn't seem *all there*, exactly, and a small number of them were people who had been bro-ken in some way—a man who, for instance, routinely removed his pants, and either defecated or masturbated (though never both), often falling over in his own leavings. Oliver never left money for him, but he always tried to leave food—an unopened snack pack of Oreos or potato chips from school.

One day Oliver saw someone new, a white homeless man in a sweat-soaked white T-shirt and fatigue sweatpants, unshorn, greasy. Oliver didn't want to give him money or even get close, and when Maddie asked why, he said, "I dunno. He's too angry. Angry like I haven't seen in anyone." Maddie didn't understand—the man mostly sat there, staring into his own lap. But later that night, Nate came home and said there had been a stabbing—someone had tried to give a homeless man money, and ended up getting stabbed thirty-seven times before an officer showed and shot him. It was the same man. Maddie told Nate that night, "Oliver's special, you know that?" Nate said he did. And she said, "No, *really* special." They never really figured out how, or why. It was what it was, and though it had no evidence behind it, they always just took it as fact their son wasn't like everyone else. Maddie never told Oliver about the shooting.

Now:

Once again, Nate tugged on his holster. Maddie gave him a look.

"You sure you need that?" she asked, suddenly worried.

But his smile was a true one—and it gave her some comfort. "No," he answered. "I don't suspect I do. But after everything, I'm not interested in going out there unarmed."

"Fair enough."

"Hear from Olly?"

"Yeah. Dude's still out with Caleb. Said he'll be back soon."

"Sounds good."

Nate tugged on his coat and a pair of gloves, too. The cold from the night of the storm had never really gone away—it was a deeper, more bitter chill than they were used to at this time of the year, weeks before Thanksgiving. He tucked the gun into the holster, snapped it shut.

For a moment, she simply stood there and admired him. He looked good. Shoulders back. Beard a little long, hair, too, but it gave him a rough-hewn edge—the beauty of a tree rather than the clean-sawn board. All those nooks and crannies, the texture and topography of the bark, the knots, the lines of imperfect grain. Raw, unmachined, and blissfully uneven. That was Nate. *Her* Nate.

"You're gonna be okay?" she asked.

"Of course."

"You trust Jed, right?"

"Well." Nate laughed. "I don't know that I trust him to be right about all this, but I trust that he thinks so." He seemed for a moment to be lost in thought. "I like him. He's been through some shit, I think, though I don't much know the depth or the breadth of it. I think he's conquered some of his demons, and not others."

"We all go through some shit," she said. But then she wondered:

Was her shit just other people's shit? Was her burden the burden of everyone else? Maybe that's just who she was. And she didn't know if that was a good thing or a bad thing or what.

"I guess. All I know is, there's just something about him."

"He's damn likable."

"*So* damn likable." Nate waggled his eyebrows. "Don't get any ideas. You can't sex up Jed, Mads. I know he's a fancy *writer* and all—"

"It's okay, it's part of my personal code of honor to never fuck someone named Jed. Or any name that rhymes with Jed. Ned, Ed."

"Ted."

"Oh, god." She faked a shudder. *"Ted."*

"That guy from *Pulp Fiction*? Zed?"

"Definitely not a Zed. Although . . ."

"Uh-oh, here it comes."

"Red. I could fuck a guy named Red."

He smirked. "You asshole."

"*You're* the asshole." She helped zip up his coat, then tugged on the collar to pull him into a kiss. A hard, long, soul-trading kiss. "Be good. Get answers. I love you."

"I love you, too."

Nate went out the door, *this* door, for the last time.

45

Ramble Rocks

The boulder field of Ramble Rocks did not comprise the entire park but rather the acreage at its center. Hundreds of them here, Nate saw. Maybe thousands. Some gray like flint. Others, the blued-black of gunmetal. They were broken at odd angles and edges, like a mouthful of bad teeth.

As Nate regarded the boulder field ahead of them, he tried to imagine Reese here. Snatching girls from the tunnel, or the woods, or from the school nearby. Taking them first to his house, where he cut a number into their cheeks. Then bringing them here, eventually, to this place.

Where he gutted them on a rock.

His mind wandered to the girl with the 37 carved into her cheek.

Who was that girl?

Where did she come from—

And where the hell did she *go*?

Was she still alive? Or had Reese—if that even was Reese, impossibly—already killed her?

"Here, ahead—" Jed waved the beam across the rocks. "The tree line has ended. We'll enter the boulder field, though I think our best bet is to go around the outside edge of it—"

"It'll be quicker to cut through."

"It's rougher going. Sharp boulders in the dark, Nate."

"We have flashlights. We'll be all right."

Jed nodded. "You're the Fish and Game man. I trust your judgment."

"I'm more a city boy than a nature man. This is more about expedience and impatience than anything else. But I gotta ask you, Jed. What the hell are we doing here? What are we looking for?"

The other man hesitated. He stammered a little when he answered, "I don't rightly know. Like I said before, this is a thin place. If we're gonna see anything or sense anything, well, it's at Ramble Rocks. We'll head to the tunnel, I figure—always some strange stories about what people see there. But this whole area, the felsenmeer in particular, this was Reese's hunting ground *and* killing field. The girl you saw, if she's dead, she's dead here. And if Reese is back..." He sighed. "Then he's here, too."

"All right," Nate said. "Onward we go."

Into the ramblin' rocks they went.

The moon was big and bright over the broken-tooth rocks. It hung full in the sky, pregnant with light. It lit their way.

Didn't make it any easier to get through the boulders, though.

Nate had been here as a kid, but not since then. He'd forgotten just how densely packed this area *was* with all these hard, craggy rocks. Some barely had any space between them, and so that meant you couldn't wind your way through them so much as go up over them.

So, that's what they did. Up and over. Feet planted on angled rocks, carrying them forward over every asymmetrical, irregular boulder.

It was, as Jed feared, rough going.

"Sorry," Nate said. "We should've gone around."

Behind, Jed grunted. "We're in it now."

"That we are. I think we're about halfway through and—"

His foot landed on one rock that was slick with moss. The foot skidded, the ankle twisted, and he felt a *pop* go down through his heel and up through his calf like a twist of lightning. Then the moon was going one way and he was going the other as he tumbled into the boulders, the flashlight spiraling away in the darkness. He knew, even as he was falling, that landing wasn't going to be any good—not out here. Not in the rocks.

But then, before he hit—

He stopped.

Poised at a forty-five-degree angle.

His arms and shoulders strained at his barn jacket—the end of which was held fast in Jed's grip.

"I gotcha," Jed said, grunting. "You okay?"

"You saved me from breaking my face," Nate answered, but when he tried to step off the rock, a sharp screw of pain dug its way into his heel anew. His Achilles tendon felt on fire. "Ah, hell."

Gently, he sat down, nursing the foot.

"Uh-oh," Jed said. "That doesn't sound good."

As Nate massaged his ankle underneath his boot, Jed shined the light there. "I think I'm all right. Not broken, at least. Just gimme a second."

"Sure, of course, sure."

There, in the dark, under the moon, Jed paced in the small space afforded to him. Up over the rocks, back down again, back up, and around again. Nate watched him under a furrowed brow.

"You seem nervous," Nate said.

"No, I'm okay."

"No, you're not. I can tell something's up."

Jed seemed cagey about it, chewing a lip until he finally folded like a beach chair. "I'm just anxious about what we're going to find. I . . . I had a worldview, Nate. An idea of how things worked, and now I'm not so sure."

"That's all it is?"

"That's all it is."

Nate had to be satisfied with that. He didn't know his neighbor well enough to tell if he was lying. He liked Jed, and the man seemed to put a lot of stock in that *worldview* he was talking about. Made sense it would knock him off-kilter a little bit.

But, a small voice inside Nate wondered, *shouldn't it make him excited, too?* He feared there was more digging to do in the strange dark earth that was his neighbor, but now was not a good time.

"Gonna just grab my flashlight," Nate said, gingerly nursing his foot with every step. He winced and limped his way through the boulder field, wishing like hell they'd gone around like Jed had said—or even better, that he'd just stayed home, in a chair, beer in hand. As he moved, he saw the flashlight about ten feet away—the beam blessedly still on, meaning he hadn't broken it despite the thing tumbling into the rocks.

His eyes followed that beam of light.

And then Nate stopped. What the light illuminated robbed him of breath. A small sound came out of him, a sound of strange horror and imagined grief. Jed asked if he was all right.

"I know that rock," Nate said, his voice quiet. "I've seen it before."

46

The Table Rock

The dream came rushing back with the force of a flash flood: him striking his son, the gunshot, the boy falling back onto the rock.

The rock shaped like a table.

A rock he saw here, now, in life.

That dream he realized was set here, in the felsenmeer of Ramble Rocks—though in that dream there were differences, too. In his dream, the rocks were round, not jagged. But this one stone shaped like a table? It was the same here as it was in the dream. Nate took up the flashlight and swept the beam over its elevated surface—he found the smooth grooves in it, winding out from the center. Grooves that, in the dream, had carried rivulets of his son's blood.

He must've remembered it in his subconscious somewhere, and the dream drew it out the way that dreams did—blotting up old memories like a dish towel, soaking them up, wringing them back out into his slumbering mind. Surely it was from some earlier memory. Wasn't it?

Was this where Edmund Reese killed the girls?

He thought that maybe it was. Deep down, was that a thing he'd already known, and so his dream took him here?

Or was that dream something else? A portent? A warning?

"You okay?" Jed asked.

"Sure," Nate said. His turn to lie. Ah, to hell with it. He was tired of lying. He said, "You know, Jed, no, I'm not okay. Everything feels like it's gone a little sideways, and this . . . this stone here, the one that looks like a table? I had a dream with it, weeks ago. A dream of my son dying."

Jed, at that, was quiet.

"I'm sure it's nothing," Nate finally added.

"I don't know what's nothing and what's something," Jed said, and his voice had changed. He said it very softly, and sadly, a hoarseness to his words, too, like he was trying to hold something back. Tears, maybe. Tears making a tide of some deeper wellspring of sorrow that Nate did not, or could not, understand. "What I know, Nate, is that life is strange. It's full of mistakes and regrets, and our minds are very good at bringing those out at the worst times, the times when we're most vulnerable. Like dreams. The best we can do, I think, is to figure out how to move forward. How we correct the errors that we made to give some peace to ourselves. And to those we may have hurt. Or so I like to hope."

"Sounds right to me."

"Glad you feel that way. Means we should get moving—if, of course, you're okay to walk."

"I am."

"Then let's keep on."

And on they went.

47

True Dark

Took a while for them to limp their way out of the boulder field, but once they did, they found a hiking trail on its far side—and that brought them through a copse of paper birches that in turn opened up onto a paved path.

Ahead awaited the old train tunnel. In the silver scattering of moonlight, the tunnel looked as if it went on forever—a portal not to the other side of the park, but to somewhere else. An endless walk through the dark to nowhere.

A shrill scream cut the air from off in the trees. Like a woman's scream, but something in it was inhuman, too, a howl of rawboned pain. It was short and sharp, barked out into the black night. Jed startled, and Nate felt his own blood jump.

Nate held out a hand. "It's okay," he said. "Think it's just a fox."

"The hell you say."

"Yeah. Horrible sound, I know. A lot of animals make terrible sounds at night. Foxes, rabbits, fishers."

"The majesty of nature," Jed said, grousing behind a scowl.

Nate almost laughed. It was a moment of levity—much needed before they plunged into the dark of the tunnel. Because here it stood, looming before them. Again the mouth: this time, ready to swallow them whole.

"Jonah and the whale," Jed said, obviously thinking the same thing.

Nate stared down into its singular blackness. He half expected to see a glimmer of light—a ghost train ushered forth by its headless conductor.

But no such light pierced the dark.

"You sure we can't do this during the day?" Nate asked.

"Night is when they say the veil between worlds is thinnest, Nate. Besides, you don't want people seeing you poking around the tunnel looking for boogeymen and boojums, do you? Being Fish and Game and all."

"I suppose not."

"Then so, here we are, Nate." Jed suddenly waved his hands, as if trying to warn a driver away from a collapsed bridge. "We should leave. Yup. That's it. We should turn around, Nate, and head on home. I—I don't like this. I'm having second thoughts. Come on."

He tried tugging Nate back down the path.

"Whoa, hold up. No, we're here. We walked all this way."

"Nate . . ."

"No. If you're saying this tunnel is a, I dunno, a place of some significance, supernaturally—god, I can't even believe I'm saying these words—then it falls to us to go in there and see what we can see."

Jed nodded, a sad smile on his face. "Okay, Nate. Okay. If you say so. Just know that I'm sorry."

"Sorry. Sorry for what?"

For a moment, Jed was silent. Like he was considering his next words. "I'm just sorry that all this is happening. You came here, moving your very nice family, and now . . . this. I'm just sorry is all."

"Hey. Not your fault, Jed. Come on. Let's walk the tunnel."

The dark felt total and true—less an open space where no light reached and more a physical object with weight and presence.

It was not sufficient to simply walk through the tunnel, but rather it felt necessary to *push* through it, into the dark, for Nate to *urge* himself forward every step of the way. The dark was so oppressive, it seemed to swallow the beam of his flashlight. It reminded Nate in a way of pushing through that storm—it felt like it was working against him.

With every step, his worry deepened. Anxiety scrabbled around his head like a box of starving rats emptied into his skull. *Turn around,* he thought. *Go home. Jed was right. We don't have to do this.*

Nausea curdled his stomach.

His skin felt hot, cold, and pricked with pins-and-needles numbness.

He wasn't sure he could breathe right, and then he was thinking about breathing, which made breathing even harder.

A smell hit him: the rank, ruinous odor of something dead. He flashed the beam around, tried to find what was making that smell.

Nothing.

He kept going. Deeper, deeper.

All the while he was trying to imagine, what would they see here? What even was this? Something was off. That much he could tell. This *was* a weak spot; he could feel its thinness, as if reality here had all the tension and toughness of off-brand Kleenex. Like he could reach out and peel away the skin and watch the world bleed.

The ground, too, though asphalt, felt oddly . . . soft. Almost spongy underneath his feet.

"Jed?" he asked. "You feeling that?"

But no answer came.

"Buddy," he said again, swinging the flashlight beam behind him—

Only to find that Jed wasn't with him.

But back at the entrance, framed by the moonlight and faced by the dark, stood a silhouette. Shoulders slumped. Chin dipped.

The hackles on Nate's neck bristled. Something *was* wrong.

"Jed," he called, more commandingly this time. He turned all the way around and started walking back toward the entrance.

The figure at the mouth of the tunnel raised an arm—

Nate heard the telltale click of a revolver's hammer drawing back. It echoed through the tunnel, along the stones.

Cla-click.

"I need you to stay there, Nate," Jed croaked. His voice trembled with fear, or regret, or maybe both in concert. "Don't come any farther, now. Or I'll shoot. I will, I swear."

"Jed, I need you to put the gun down."

"Can't, Nate. Can't."

Nate held up both hands in surrender, and he turned off the flashlight beam. (Best not to make himself a target.) "You wanna tell me what's going on? I know things have been a little strange recently—but I'm here if you wanna talk." Nate was sincere about this. But he was also formulating a plan. He had his own gun in his holster. He wasn't fast enough to win some kind of cowboy battle—*Draw, pardner,* his brain said, as if trying to be funny—but if he juked right, into the dark, hunkering down? Jed wouldn't be able to track him well. Maybe. *Maybe.* Christ, it was a risk, though. Maybe it gave him enough time to draw his own pistol. Maybe he took a bullet. Maybe he hit Jed before he got hit himself.

"Again, I'll say I'm sorry. I'm sorry, so sorry, Nate," Jed said.

"No need to be *sorry,*" Nate answered, trying to bite back his anger. "Just put that damn gun down."

"Mitzi and Zelda need me." Those were the names of Jed's wife and daughter, weren't they? What was he talking about? "They need me, Nate, and . . . and I want them back. This is the only way."

Slowly, Nate eased his hand down to his holster. Thumb out, ready to unsnap it. As his hand moved, he talked, hoping to distract Jed. "That doesn't make any sense, Jed. Pretty sure you getting them back doesn't mean pointing a *gun* at someone. That's not how they come back to you."

A cold, brutal bark of a laugh came from Jed.

"You have no idea, Nate. No idea. My wife and my girl, they're both dead. I killed them. Not like *that*—wasn't murder, I'm not that kind of man despite what you may think of me right now. But they were in the car with me one night. And I'd had . . . I'd had quite a few to drink, you see, and . . . I turned onto a road that wasn't there, and I—" He made an animalistic sound—a bear's chuff of pain in its struggle against a trap closed upon its paw. "We crashed. A tree, a— a branch, it came through the windshield glass. Killed my wife instantly. Snapped her neck. Then the branch broke and we rolled down an embankment and my daughter . . . the injuries she sustained put her into a coma. Took weeks for her to die, Nate. *Weeks.*"

"Jed, I'm sorry. But I don't know how any of this—"

"And me?" Jed continued. "I folded up under the dashboard of the car like a piece of trash. I was drunk enough I didn't even know we'd been in an accident until it was over. I killed them, Nate. I did that."

"You didn't. It was an accident." To cover the sound, Nate forcibly cleared his throat as his thumb unsnapped the holster, finding the cold steel of the pistol hanging heavy there. "Nothing you do here can bring them back, Jed. You know that."

Another laugh. "*Au contraire, mon frère.* That's exactly what this is, Nate. This is my way back. This is part of the reset."

Reset?

The man had suffered a break with reality. That's what this was. Something inside him tweaked, then snapped.

Nate tensed his muscles, each a coil ready to spring.

"Nate, you're awful quiet—"

Move.

He ducked low, moving right. His hand came up with his pistol in it, safety off, hammer back—

Something struck him from behind, knocking him forward. Embers and sparks lit up the darkness behind his eyeballs. The front of his skull cracked against the asphalt. The gun spun out of his hand, clattering away. The bandages across his head were hanging loose, and everything hurt. He lifted his head up, blood drooling down the bridge of his nose—*split my dang stitches*—and the back of his skull throbbed with whatever had hit him.

"Hnnh," he said, trying to form words, and failing. Nate rolled over.

Someone stood over him. Not Jed, no.

Someone else.

Someone he recognized.

"You," he managed to say.

"Hey, *Nate*," Jake said. In the dark, his left eye seemed almost to glow with opalescent light. He had a wooden baseball bat in his hand, and he gave it a performative twirl. "Sorry for all this. Ah, who am I kidding? I'm not sorry. Not even one little bit, you piece of shit."

He reared back with the bat again—

Nate held up his arm to protect his face, and the bat connected with it. Pain shot through his arm. He cried out and tried to scramble away, but Jake grabbed the heel of his foot and dragged him back. Nate kicked the boy in the gut, and Jake staggered, giving him some room.

"The fuck is this?" Nate seethed. "What do you want with me?"

"I *want* you out of my way. I need it. I have work to do."

"Work. Fuck you, work. Who are you? *Who are you.* I know you," Nate said, pointing a finger in the dark at that gleaming eye, now shining with milky white light. The voice, something so familiar about it. "Who the hell are you?"

Again, that eye gleamed. Teeth, too: white, shining.

"Don't you recognize me, *Dad*?"

Jake put out both arms in cruciform display, as if to say, *Behold.* Though there was little to behold here in the dark but shape and shadow and the glow of that mad eye.

"You're not my son," Nate said, but then it settled into him. The realization: *This* is why Jake looked familiar. He looked like Oliver. Some rangy, rough-hewn coyote version of him—a starved version, a sour and foul version, but a version of him just the same. Older. Put through the wringer.

But still undeniably Oliver.

"I'm one version of him. And he's a version of me."

"He's nothing like you. He's a good kid."

Jake shook his head. "I know. That's the *problem,* Dad. You're the one good father out of the ninety-nine. The one who got it right, who raised a good kid in a good family and—" Jake roared in rage, banging the bat against the ground again and again. "And I can't have that. The boy believes in you. You're a *wellspring* to him, and from you, I fear he can drink, and drink, and drink. You give him strength. And I can't—"

Nate lurched forward, trying to grab for the bat—

But his arm felt heavy. Too heavy, *impossibly* heavy.

He could barely lift it. He grunted, tears straining at his eyes as he tried to move his arm—but it wouldn't budge. His leg wouldn't move, either, and he strained and pulled at his own body. He was stuck. The ground had gone soft again. And now it was drawing him down into it. Like heavy, thick mud.

This doesn't make any sense.

This is a nightmare—this is all just a bad dream.

"It's thin here, like Jed says," Jake said. "Thin enough for me to push you through to the other side. To where I came from. To what I left behind."

Nate cried out for Jed.

Jake said, "Aw, Jed won't save you. He's on my team, Nate. I got a deep bench. People who can see what's at stake, who have nothing left to lose. And now Olly will have lost someone very important to him. And he'll be willing to do anything, *anything at all,* to bring you back."

Nate wept, his one arm sunken now up to the elbow. His legs were down past the knees. And sinking still farther, down, down, down.

"I'll kill you," he raged. "I'll find you and I'll kill you. You leave my son alone. Leave my family alone—"

"Can't do that, *Dad*." As Nate sank, Jake knelt by him. He gave a flashy pivot to his wrist, and the baseball bat held there suddenly *disappeared,* poof, like it had never existed in the first place.

The boy reached out and cupped Nate's face even as the wet, hungry asphalt crawled up his chest, to his shoulders, sucking him down like a gluttonous man siphoning a piece of soft meat off the bone.

Kneeling there, Jake said, "I'd kill you, old man, but then that would leave a body for them to find. Besides, where you're going, you won't last long. Enjoy the fallen worlds, Nate. Enjoy the wreckage I've left for you."

Interlude: The Boy Who Lived

The boy gasped as he awakened.

He opened his eyes into a dark so perfect that he could not see any difference between closing his eyes, and opening them.

He called out. For someone. For anyone.

(Anyone, of course, but his father. Being alone in the dark was better than being with him, always and forever, amen.)

The ground beneath him was hard and dry, though his hands themselves felt . . . damp. Gooey, gummy, even gritty, like sea-soaked sand. He moved his knuckles together, rasp and crunch, crispy-wet like cereal popping in milk. Then the memory came back to him: He had fallen into coal silt. Like quicksand, it drew him down. Gripped him like a vise and closed him off from light and air.

How he was *so* sure he was going to die . . .

But it took him here. He reached for his face, and found his cheeks messy with the silt—he rubbed it from his arms, out of his hair, shook it out of his clothes.

The boy stood up and—

The only light he could see erupted behind his eyes as his head struck rock. He cried out and shrank, hugging himself as a line of blood crawled its way from the top of his head, across the tract of his forehead, down to the cliff's edge of his nose.

Again the boy wept. How could he not? He knew now where he

must be: deep in the coal mines, a place where light would not and could not go. A place of tunnels. A pitch-black *maze*.

Would've been better if I died, he thought.

But then, defiance:

No.

He was alive! He'd run away from the monster, got gobbled up by the hungry earth, and he'd *survived.* That had to mean something. The boy was a reader, you see, a reader of fantasy and horror, and he knew from those books that characters had destinies. They *endured* great and terrible things, things that did not kill them, but marked them and changed them. A hero, a chosen one, surviving to conquer destiny.

Slaying villains, along the way.

Now: The villain was no longer his monstrous father, but rather the unabiding dark and the endless maze. But he told himself that was just fear talking. The mine tunnels could not go on forever. Perhaps he was already close to the surface. In fact, he *had* to be, right? He had sunk into the silt, okay, but he wasn't in there long enough for it to suffocate him completely. Which meant he was only, what, ten feet below the ground at most? He could find his way out. He would slay this dragon. He knew it.

He tried to remember: When you solved a maze, how was it that you did it? There was a trick, wasn't there? *Follow the right wall.* Right meaning the direction—pick the wall to the right of you and keep following it, and if it dead-ends, you stay on the right and turn around. Ultimately in this way, a maze would stretch out like a line—or was it a circle?—and you would find your way to its end.

That was what the boy resolved to do.

Follow the right wall.

Again, he stood, feeling his way up the wall with one hand and with the other feeling for the rocky mine tunnel ceiling so he didn't crack his skull into it again. Hand on the cold, wet stone, he began to move slowly, but with purpose and hope in his heart.

He stepped forward—

His foot caught the lip of something—

The air clapped out of his lungs as he fell hard against that same something. It struck him in the ribs, and pain pistoned into his side. He wondered, could his rib be broken? He touched it and new pain forked out like fresh lightning.

Trying very hard not to cry again, he reached out and felt for the thing that he had fallen onto—and there he discovered something long and cold and unbroken. He kept feeling and it did not end—it just kept going. Metal, he thought, but the way it flaked suggested rust . . .

Oh. *Oh.*

He reached out and found another metal protrusion, running parallel. A rail. *Two* rails. And between them, as he swept away the dust and dirt, wooden boards. Tracks, like railroad tracks. Except, not for a train.

For a mine cart.

Mine carts! New hope lit up his mind as he thought, this was the way out, *this* was the way to freedom—and again he stood, and again he continued on through the dark, using the rail as his guide.

Oh, but the dark was a terrible thing. It was hungry, and it swallowed time like a greedy pig eating slop from a trough. It slurped up any sense the boy had of hours passing, or where he was. Woe and despair threatened to drag him down. He was lost in the dark and he would never find his way out.

He felt unpinned from the world, almost like he was floating through space. It was harder than it seemed, to follow the rails in the dark. The boy had to keep pausing and stopping, bending over—an act that caused him considerable pain, and stole the breath from his chest—to feel for the track with his hands.

As he continued through the impenetrable darkness, his mind kept returning to why he'd run away in the first place. And every time it did, he gritted his teeth and bore down, focusing instead on the pain in his side. He let that pain bloom big and bright, a sun gone supernova to wash out the shadows darkening his memory. *No,* he said to the specter of his father there in the back of his skull, *I won't think of you. I won't think of you at all. You're dead to me. I will burn you out of my head.* A house fire destroying all the photos and heirlooms inside of it.

But concentrating on the pain had its downside, and the boy had to stop. His breath came out in trilled wheezes.

He gasped, and took a knee.

How long he sat there, he didn't know.

There was no wind, no sound but the occasional dripping of water somewhere off down the tunnels. The silence was all encompassing. Enrobed him like a black cloak.

But then, a sound.

Down in the direction from where he came, he was sure he heard footsteps. They were slow yet persistent, as if someone else was feeling their way through the darkness, too.

The sound was followed closely by an odor . . .

He hadn't even realized it before, but the tunnels had a strong mineral stink, and the dank, musty odor of unstirred air. The air of tombs. Now, though, a new aroma punctured the mineral stink: cologne. One that was familiar to him. He didn't remember what it was called, but it came in that white bottle with the red boat on it.

It was the same cologne his father wore.

Old Sailor. That's what it was.

The old man would say, *My father used it, and I use it, and now you'll use it, too.* He liked to pat a little on the boy's cheeks, an act that once upon a time felt like a nice shared moment between son and father, but as their relationship darkened, so too did that simple act. His father demanded it—no matter where the boy was in the morning, if Dad was putting on some cologne, the boy had to receive his blessing from the old man, pat-pat-pat. Worse and crueler, if the boy ever suffered a cut on his hands or his face—from playing, as boys were wont to do—then the old man would summon him, and splash a little of the cologne on the injury. It burned like hell and his father would laugh. *Toughen up,* he'd say. *Besides, it's mostly alcohol. Antiseptic.* And the smell of the cologne would almost, *almost* push away the stink of liquor on his father's breath . . .

A voice called out from down the tunnel, echoing—

"Boy? You down here?"

His father.

His father was *here.*

The old man laughed.

The boy, without meaning to, made a low, mewling sound. He did the calculus. He knew he could go to his father. Maybe the mean bastard would help him out, and then he could run away again, and not be down here in the dark any longer. Everything in him sang with panic and pain.

I won't go back, he decided, and then he stood up and took off running in the same direction he'd been going, away from his father, away from his voice and his *stink*—

And then, *wham.* He slammed into something. He reached out, feeling a wall ahead of him. No, not a wall—a pile of rocks. The tracks disappeared underneath it.

A cave-in.

A collapsed ceiling.

It closed off the tunnel.

"No, no, god no," he whimpered, his words dissolving like paper in a wet mouth. He sobbed, still feeling around, hoping there was a way through, a cubbyhole or a little tunnel punched through the collapsed rock, but he could find nothing. And so he leaned against it, crying into the stone, sure now that his father would find him and take him away, and again he'd be beaten, and his mother would be, too, and his father would drink and call him names and lock him in his room with the rats in the walls and in the ceiling above, rats he had to scare off by throwing marbles at them, and books, and as he wept, he heard something nearby.

The scrape of something against the stone—

And then hands came out of the darkness, pawing at him, pressing him against the ground, and he cried out in rage, in pain, in sorrow, knowing that he'd been found and even though he was saved, it would be his end.

Someone said:

"Who are you? Are you real? Are you really here?"

Hands groped at him—feeling his face and dancing atop the cut on his head, and he cried out. The hands suddenly disappeared as fast as they had come.

But the boy knew he was no longer alone.

He could *sense* the person near to him. Only a few feet away. Their breathing came in loud and eager huffs.

The boy, sniffling, speaking through the hitching stammer, said: "Who-who are y-you?"

"You are real! You're really really real, oh my god, thank god. I'm found. *I'm found.*"

The voice was a man's voice, but not his father's—no, it was younger than that, younger, but haggard, too. Like he was gargling loose scree in a dry throat.

"I . . . I don't . . . I . . ."

The person came closer. The boy knew not because he could see, but because he could hear the way the man scuttled closer. "I've been trapped down here for . . . god knows how long. Jesus. I didn't think I'd ever get to be near another person again." The boy could hear that the man seemed on the verge of tears, his voice ragged, lilting higher. "I thought I was going to die down here. Alone."

The boy had no response.

The man continued:

"But we can get out now. We can just go back the way you came and—and we'll be free. Thank you. Are you a kid? You sound like a kid."

"Y-yeah."

"What's your name?"

"O . . . Oliver."

"Hi, Oliver. My name is Eli, Eli Vassago."

"Hi."

The man, Eli, scrabbled closer. "Now, c'mon. Let's go."

"I . . ."

"What is it?"

"I thought this was the way out."

Eli laughed darkly. "This isn't the way out, Oliver. This tunnel collapsed after I came through and—I mean, we just go back. We go back the way *you* came, that should work, I don't see why—"

"I fell down here."

A pause. "You . . . fell?"

"I g-got here through a—um, a pool of silt, c-coal silt."

"That's not possible. Those are just urban legends—I'm a researcher, I've never heard of that here in Pennsylvania. Indiana, okay, yes, Indiana—but that's not a real thing, Oliver."

That's not a real thing.

The boy began to cry once more because it was simply all too much. The man stayed near, quiet, finally reaching out and offering his hand—which made the boy gasp and flinch and pull away.

The tears came and went like a passing storm, and when that storm had gone, the man said, with grim cheer: "I think we can do this, Oliver. I say we go back the way you came and we find our way out of here. There are two of us now. Two great minds like ours? Nothing we can't accomplish. How about it?"

Oliver swallowed hard. He nodded, but then when the man said, "Whaddya say?" he remembered that Eli could not *see* his nod. So he answered in a small voice (what his father called his "little mouse" voice):

"Okay."

Together, they wandered the dark.

Eli talked a lot. What Oliver learned about the man was this:

He was thirty-two years old. He wasn't married, though he had an on-again off-again relationship with a woman who was a nurse and a volunteer firefighter. ("She's a lot tougher than me, I'll tell you what," he said.) He lived about an hour from here and grew up just outside Scranton.

These days, Eli worked for a local museum in a town called Jim Thorpe, Pennsylvania. Eli worked for a coal museum as its curator and archivist, which he said sounded more important than it was and that, ultimately, he ran the place. He had a degree in history and it was his job at the museum to understand the history of coal and coal mining, particularly in this region of Pennsylvania. He had a special interest and focus on, according to him, mining *accidents*—dust and gas explosions, mine collapses, or lesser mishaps such as men losing their fingers or breaking their feet under the wheels of rolling carts, or injuries from bad tools and improper use. (One man, he said, struck the wall with a pick-ax whose handle was rotten, and the ax head rebounded as the handle broke, and struck the man in the eye. The man did not die, but lost the eye, and was back to work in the mine three days later. "Grisly, huh?" Eli said with what was clearly ghoulish delight.)

And so it was "ironic," Eli said, that he'd come here to explore a previously unstudied mine—the Ramble Rocks Number Eight—and found himself the subject of just such a mining accident. "I wasn't right there when the ceiling collapsed," he explained. "I was following the mine cart tracks, and as I rounded the bend—I felt the rumble, like a little earthquake, and then, *whoom*. It shook the ground. Dust in my hair and eyes. And then darkness. Total darkness."

Darkness.

Surely the man knew he'd be exploring in at least partial darkness, right?

"You had to have some kind of light," Oliver said, suddenly. "A lantern, a flashlight—right?"

"Oh." The man paused for a little while. "I did. But I dropped it when the ceiling collapsed. Broke the bulb in the flashlight."

"We should turn around—see if we can find it. Fix it."

"It's unfixable, Oliver, trust me. Anyway—"

"What about your phone?"

Eli ignored him. "The thing about accidents like the ceiling collapse is, they're so often the result of so many *little errors*. It's a cascade. Do you know what a cascade is? All systems are complex—the architecture of earth and rock is an interlocking system of molecules and crystals all pushing and pulling on one another, but little failures build up. You dig these tunnels, you *intrude* upon the earth, and you create all these points of potential failure. You introduce weakness. And with weakness, things break. Do you know anything about entropy, Oliver?"

"No," Oliver answered mopishly—because he did not want to be discussing any of this. He didn't *care* about whatever the man was saying; he only cared about escaping this place. The man went on and on about entropy—how all things are constantly trying to break down or *whatever*—and all Oliver could think about was if the man still had his phone, and if there was any chance at all that the voice of his father he'd heard down here was real, and if they'd run into him somewhere. Surely his father had gotten down here somehow. Couldn't they find the way out? He thought to call out for him, but then he thought better of it. They could find escape on their own. He didn't need his dad. Didn't want him. So Oliver stayed silent as they walked, looking for their egress.

*   *   *

Once more, time unspooled. Physical reality seemed both to collapse in on itself, sometimes leaving Oliver feeling crushingly claustrophobic, and other times the mine became just an endless nowhere place of the deepest, thickest shadow. Everything hurt. His ribs ached, and his wounds had crusted over, though sometimes they reopened as he walked. They found a dead man in a mine cart, just skull and bones wrapped in threadbare clothing. A hole in his head, as if from a sharp object. Oliver wept at their discovery and Eli just chuckled, as if it were some kind of joke, but Oliver didn't think it was funny, not at all. And it wasn't funny when just past the mine cart they found that the tracks stopped dead. Eli laughed at that, too. He knocked on the rock wall and said, "Knock knock?" But when Oliver wept harder and wouldn't play along, Eli pretended to be his voice. "*Who's there? Colby. Colby who?* Colby the stuff you find in a coal mine!" And with that, he bellowed with laughter and wandered off into the dark. Oliver didn't want to be with this man anymore, but he wanted to be alone even less. So he chased after. Because what choice did he have?

They roamed the tunnels. In one direction and then the next. Panic crashed over Oliver in high tides. He'd think, *We forgot to follow the right wall,* and it would leave him feeling lost and hopeless. And then the panic would drift back out to sea again, leaving him feeling like a doll washed up on shore. Eli wanted to talk again, wanted to ask him who he was, where he came from, what his family was like, but Oliver wouldn't say. Was afraid to say. So, Oliver kept quiet. Said nothing. Kept on. And on. And on.

Oliver was hungry but there was no food. Eli said they could drink the water that wet the walls, water from aboveground, and that's what they did. The water was bitter and chalky, and it was hard to get enough to quench his thirst, but it helped. Oliver was so tired, though. The fatigue hung on his limbs like anchors, and he asked if

they could stop for a while. Eli, sounding impatient, said "Fine, *fine*"
and stood in a huff as Oliver sank down against the wall and curled
up like a pile of old clothes. As he faded out, he heard Eli's footsteps
retreating and he wanted to wake up and yell for the man to come
back, but tiredness dragged him into the long faraway reaches of
sleep.

Oliver startled awake, crying out as he did so. His cry echoed down
the tunnel and spiraled into the dark.

He knew instantly: *I'm alone.*

He sat up. His body protested, wracking him with little pains. He
grunted. Tried again not to cry.

"Eli?" He tried again. *"Eli!"*

No footsteps. No response. No nothing.

His stomach tightened in a one-two punch of nausea and hunger.

And despite how hard he tried not to, he cried again. This time it
was not the body-throttling sobs that had found him earlier. This was
quieter, softer, the tears tickling his face like the legs of little spiders.

A sharp whisper hissed in his ear:

"Oliver."

He cried out, pulling reflexively away—

It was Eli's voice. But how? He hadn't heard him come up. No
sounds, no movement, no shifting of the silence to accommodate the
man's return—but here he was, in Oliver's ear.

"Eli?" Oliver asked.

"It's me. I found some things."

"Where—where were you, where did you go? How did you . . ."

"Look look look," Eli said, hurriedly. And suddenly—

Light.

Oliver had to wince at the sudden illumination—though the light
wasn't bright, it still felt like staring into the sun. He had to close his
eyes to slits just to accommodate the light, and even then, the bright-
ness seemed to consume everything.

But slowly, his eyes adjusted. And when they did, he saw the shape of the thing that made the light: a little old-timey lantern. Like a little teakettle with the front of a flashlight hanging from the side of it— and the bulb inside the flashlight glass was no bulb at all, but rather a tiny flame. Dancing like a trapped fairy.

When he was done regarding the thing that made the light, he saw *who* was making it. For the first time, he saw Eli Vassago.

Small dark eyes nestled in a white face. Too white. *Bone white.* A little pair of round eyeglasses sat on his bent hammer-claw nose, so far down they looked like they were trying to jump off and commit suicide. His hair was dark, and around his mouth was what looked to be a hasty sketch of facial hair—soft, dark, thin. He looked disheveled and pallid, and he said, "I'm sorry for the way I look. I borrowed my face from someone else." Then he laughed, and Oliver didn't understand the joke, not at all. "It's a carbide lamp," Eli continued, as if moving past the strange joke as fast as he could. "Water drips onto a pellet of calcium carbide at a slow rate, which releases acetylene gas, which burns at this wick here. This one is from the 1950s, if I had to guess."

"How does it still work?"

Eli's eyes twinkled. "Magic, I guess."

"I don't believe in magic."

But to that, Eli had no response. Instead he turned to Oliver, and seemed to take him in. Staring. Sadly, almost. "Look at you," Eli said. "Poor little guy. You are just a kid. How old are you, Oliver? You can tell me."

"I'm twelve."

"Twelve." Eli smiled. "I remember being twelve. That was a good age. I'm thirty-two now, long way from being a kid. It's hard being an adult. But I guess it's harder being a kid, isn't it?"

Oliver wanted to scream: *I don't want to talk about that! I just want to use that light and leave this awful place!*

"Are we going to get out of here?" Oliver asked. He heard the impatience in his own voice, like a starving dog scratching at the door. "Can we use the light? To find a way out now?"

Again, Eli didn't respond. Instead, his eyes lit up as he pulled something out of the back of his pants and under his shirt. "Oh! Look at this. I found something *else.*"

He waved it around—it looked, to Oliver's eyes, like an old notebook. Like the blue books teachers at school sometimes made them write essays in. But much older: beaten to hell, weathered, water stained.

He saw text stamped on the cover, and Eli read it aloud:

"A Book of Accidents."

"So what? It's just a stupid book. *I want to leave.*"

"Shh. Listen. It's a logbook. A mine foreman would log every accident big and small that happened down here. I guess for accountability's sake—accountability is important, Oliver, very important—you wouldn't want to go through life unaccountable, would you?"

"I just want to get out of here." Oliver blinked back tears.

"I know. I know. We will. We're close. I found a way. A sign that told us how to get out. But first I want to keep looking. We might find some more things, Oliver. Maybe we'll find *treasure* down here." He giggled a strange schoolboy laugh that seemed out-of-sorts.

Now Oliver could not contain his frustration. "What?" he asked. "We can't stay down here. We're going to *die.* If you know the way you gotta tell me, please, Eli, please just lead the way and get us *out* of here." He reached for the man's hands to clasp them in a prayer of shared despair.

"I will, I will, we'll head in that direction, I promise. Soon."

"No. *Now.*"

"I need to turn the lamp off now, Oliver."

"Wait, no. Take the light. Let's use it."

"I don't want it to run out. Those little pellets don't last forever, and the gods only know how much of it has already been worn down by time and use. We'll use it again."

Oliver grasped for it, greedy, desperate, but already Eli was taking it away and blowing out the flame. *Foosh.* The light was gone, and darkness rushed in like a tidal wave, and all that was left of the lamp was a ghostly halo in the memory of Oliver's eye.

It became almost a routine:

Eli would wander off. Sometimes with the lamp lit.

Oliver would wait for the man to come back with whatever he found in the darkness: a coal cap, like a helmet; empty blasting tins; a nickel-plated lunch pail that had the shit kicked out of it; something that looked like a little pocket watch but that Eli said was an "anemometer," a device used to measure drafts and the movement of gases down here in the coal mines. (And to that last one, Oliver said, "We can use it to find a way out. Find a draft, maybe it'll lead us to an exit." And Eli said, "That's so smart—you're really a smart kid, Oliver," but then he said the anemometer was broken, and then he was off again, scurrying into the dark.)

But after a while Oliver started following Eli, trailing after the glowing lamp when it was lit, other times just following after the receding footsteps. He lost the strange man time and time again, and he found himself wandering the tunnels in the dark, talking to himself, sure that he was lost and had seen Eli for the last time.

He often lost Eli. But somehow, Eli always found him.

He slept again. He fell asleep wondering how long he had been down here: To him, it felt like weeks, but that couldn't be possible, was it? He hadn't eaten anything. Weeks without food and he'd be dead, right? So, days, maybe. Or maybe even only one day. He just didn't know. Eli didn't seem to have a watch. Any time Oliver asked about a phone, Eli snapped, "It doesn't work down here." Or, "The battery is dead, stop asking."

Oliver grew weak. And numb. Even the pain slowed, became less the bright shock of hurt and more an ebbing, distant presence. Like it was happening to someone else, like it lived in another body.

There came a moment when he heard a scuttling sound. Not fast, either, not at first: but a gentle *tack tack* against the stone, like a crab walking. It was somewhere to his right, down the tunnel. Its slow movement became suddenly quicker, a flurry of clicks as it approached him—*tacka tacka tacka tacka*. Oliver recoiled, tensing his whole body up, wondering what horrible thing lived down here, what mad monster, some blind thing that had smelled his sweat, his blood, or the piss he'd left in the bend of the tunnel to his left.

Then the carbide lamp flared to life once more.

It was Eli.

Eli, who was not some crazy crab monster, but who simply crouched there in the flickering lamplight. His smiling teeth shone yellow, like the jaundice from a bad liver.

"I've been thinking about what you told me," Eli said.

"Okay," Oliver said quietly, unsure what that meant, or what he'd even told Eli that was worthy of thought.

"You really hate your father."

"Wh . . . what?"

"Your father. To be fair, he sounds like a real monster. The things he did to you? And your mother? Don't get me wrong, abuse is never okay, Oliver—but there's a big difference between calling your kid a bad name here and there, or maybe giving him a slap or a spank, versus what *he* did to you and your mother. Like that time you broke the microwave when you accidentally microwaved a spoon in the soup? He didn't take it out on you, no—he lay that hurt into your mother. Hurt her to hurt you. Broke her ribs, didn't he? Just like your soft little tender ribs now."

Oliver reeled. Had he told Eli these things? When? Maybe when he was unconscious, maybe he talked in his sleep . . .

Eli went on. "And how long did you spend in the hospital when he kicked you down the stairs? You were, what, seven years old at the time? Seven. Can you imagine? Being a little kid and your dad just . . . kicks you in the gut, and you tumble backwards down old wooden

stairs. All those bruises, sure, and a few cuts, but the fall also broke
your ankle like a broomstick, snap. And because he was mad at your
mother, your *whore* mother—sorry, his words, not mine—and made
you pay for her sins. Again, *his* words! I don't believe in sin, Oliver,
not at all. It's just a concept we made up, sin. Some . . . transgression
against God or the gods? Something that endangers our relationship
with the fucking prick bastard *Skyfather* who lays down all these rules
so we have to live life *His* way?"

"I . . . don't want to talk about this anymore."

"*I* don't want to talk about it either, Oliver, but . . . Here. We. Are.
You and me. Down in the dark, talking like two old friends. Old
friends with bad fathers." Eli placed both his hands hard on Oliver's
knees, pinning him there. "That's right. My father was horrible, too.
Used to beat the snot out of me on the regular. You know what it was?
I figured it out. Early on, when you're little, you like what your father
likes: football or fishing or fixing cars. But then you get a little older,
you start becoming your own man, you know? You like what you
like. I liked books and computers. And *history.* And he wasn't a book
learner, not that troglodyte *fuck,* oh no—gods, one time he whaled
on me with one of my books, this Time-Life book called *Our Universe,* and I don't think there was ever a crueler beating—oh, not because others weren't more painful, no, they were, they *definitely* were,
but because not only did it hurt me but it hurt the book, too, just
busted it out of its binding. Pages everywhere. He burned it. Do you
believe that? *Burned it.* And he did it because I grew into something
that wasn't him, and when he regarded the thing that I had become it
infuriated him. Instead of him seeing pride in that, it made him vengeful. It was like . . . I got away. I learned more than he'd ever learn, and
escaped who he was, and *wow,* how he hated that. I was a better monster than he was, though, oh ho, so I did what I had to do, boy, *I did
what I had to do.*"

Oliver didn't want to ask, but also, he did. Curiosity gnawed at his
brainstem like a starving animal.

"Wh . . . what did you do?"

"I moved out of the house, Oliver. Got a life of my own."

"Oh."

Eli snorted and then bust out laughing. "I'm just kidding. I fucking *killed* him, Oliver. I stuck a steak knife in his belly as he slept, and when he lurched upright, I zipped it side to side, opening him up like a sack of fish. His guts spilled out and he thrashed around the room, tangled in his own literally shitty intestines, and then he slipped—*whoopsy-doodle!*—and fell against the dresser in the corner of the room. Corner of that old dresser embedded in his forehead, and he didn't even fall all the way to the ground, nope! His body sat propped up there by the corner of that dresser, and then he shit himself and *died.* People shit themselves when they die, Oliver. Because they're finally at peace. They can relax for once in their gods*damn* lives."

And again he laughed. A big belly laugh, this one.

"Please leave me alone," Oliver whimpered.

"You should've killed your old monster man," Eli said, his teeth gleaming, his eyes flickering. "Still a chance, if we ever get out of here. But that remains to be seen, doesn't it?"

Then he blew out the flame, plunging them both into darkness.

Oliver cried out: "No!" But it was too late.

As Eli hurried off, Oliver once again heard the scuttling of a crab, its claws and pincers *clacka-clack*ing on the hard ground.

Eli came back sometimes and deposited more garbage he'd found in the mines. Most of it just incomprehensible piles of metal: rivets and scraps of tin and splintery, half-rotten boards. Then he'd douse the light and scurry off again. On the last trip, he brought something new: a short-handled coal pick. The kind you'd use in one hand to chip away rock.

I'm so hungry.

Oliver felt like his body was eating itself. Like his middle was that awful thing from that movie *Revenge of the Jedi*—the wet mouth and probing tentacles in the desert, sitting inside his body, slowly eating him from the inside out.

Eli was nearby. He could feel him in the dark. Roaming. Oliver couldn't move. He was too weak. He wanted to die.

Eli whispered, as if on the verge of tears: "I've made mistakes, Oliver. I've trapped us down here. All because of my *curiosity,* my desire to know more. A mistake, an error. An experiment. An *accident.* But accidents are never really accidents, are they? No no no, no they are not."

"We could go," Oliver said, his words hoarse, pushed up through a brittle, dry throat. The words sounded more like wind than a human sound.

But Eli kept on.

"I, I, I feel like this, all of this, like I've been here before, like *we've* been here before, you and I, in this place, in this deepest dark. A turning of the gear. You know, Oliver, in cyclical cosmology, that's a pattern, the turning of the ages, one after the next after the next. At the human level there's what, there's reincarnation—you live a life, you die, you come back. But at the cosmic level, it's the same, too: An age goes, the wheel turns, and it all starts to break down. The machine starts to fall the fuck apart, Oliver, just shaking itself to godsdamn *pieces,* and only then do you get to start the new age. That's it. That's how you move on. But you *can't* move on until you end the one cycle. And how true is that? You really wanna fix something, you gotta break it first, Oliver. You can't fix a fucked-up floor. You just rip it up. Down to the struts. A house goes too bad, lost to termites and mold, you gotta bring out the old wrecking ball—*whoosh, crash,* knock it down to the ankle bones and build something better in its place."

In a small voice, Oliver asked: "Is that why you killed your father?"

On this, Eli seemed to think.

As if discovering the truth of this, he answered, almost brightly: "I think that it is, Oliver. I think that it is."

"I want to get out of here. If this has all happened before, then maybe we can do the right thing this time and we can leave. You said you thought you knew the way."

Eli chuckled. "I do know the way. Maybe you do, too. Do you wonder, Oliver: Will death let you escape this? Does it start all over? Do you get a second chance? If you die, do you get out of the mine?"

Oliver thought, but did not say:

Not if I die.

But maybe if you *do.*

The smell of warm, cooked meat slithered into Oliver's nostrils and stirred him from sleep. It was the smell of a pot roast—juicy and salty, a little greasy as you pulled the soft muscle apart with your fingers.

Eli said: "I found food."

"How?" Oliver asked, because it didn't make any sense.

"Just eat. I'll explain."

And the smell was right beneath him now, and he sat up as straight as he could, struggling past the weakness and the pain, and he could *taste* the steam rising underneath his chin. Eli urged him to take a bite, so that's what he did: He bent down, mouth open, and his teeth and tongue found that roast meat and it flooded his senses with pure joy. He greedily ate, getting his hands underneath the meat so he could pull it closer to his mouth. Juices dripped down his chin. The meat was pillowy and tender. Tasted more like pork than beef, though, despite the smell, but that was okay. It filled his belly and gave him strength and hope, and he pushed his face so far into it the meat squashed against his cheeks like the loving pressing hands of an old grandmother. *What a good boy you are*, she'd say, *eat up, eat right up—*

The carbide lamp flared to life.

Beneath him, on his lap, was blood. So much of it. It streaked his forearms. It dripped from his chin. The roast of meat in his lap was a leg, a human leg, the skin chewed open (*oh no,* I *chewed it open*) exposing the wet red gristle of flesh beneath it, blood oozing up, not pumping, but *squeezing* out like water from a gently compressed sponge. Nearby sat Eli, on his ass, one leg out, the other missing all the way to the hip. In his hand he held a round, rusted, circular saw blade, the teeth all gnarled and bent, and he cackled and said, "I found a saw, Oliver, look. *I found a saw.*"

The light went out as Oliver vomited.

As he pressed himself up against the wall, away from his puke, Oliver drifted once more into unconsciousness. When he awoke anew, the metal tang of rotten blood in his mouth was gone. His skin was no longer tacky with it, either. Everything felt dry again.

(Even though his stomach felt curiously full.)

A dream, he thought, *all just a dream,* but then he heard a soft chuckle ten or twenty feet away. It was Eli, who said, "Don't tell me you're hungry again, little mouse. I need one leg, at least."

But then he walked off—and there, Oliver heard his footsteps distinctly, one after the next, the walk of a two-legged man, not the hop of one who'd removed one with a rusty saw.

Oliver didn't know what was happening. He suspected his mind was breaking down, but even so, he also knew deep inside that something was wrong with Eli. He was messing with Oliver. Toying with him. *Torturing him.* And Oliver knew then that he had to get that light, had to steal it away from the man, and so later, when Eli came back, Oliver had already found what he needed: the coal pick. He was weak, but the desire for life and escape were stronger, and he clutched the handle until his knuckles were bloodless. As Eli toddled about, humming quietly to himself, Oliver crept closer, trying very hard to zero in on where the man was in the wide-open darkness. But he couldn't get a fix on him. He seemed *here,* and then he seemed *there*—and Oliver knew he had only so much strength before he was out, before he was collapsing, before the pick tumbled from his hands.

Eli was mumbling: "World's gone bad, Oliver. World's gone rotten. Chewed up by the worms, by Those Who Eat, like a bad apple, *chomp*. Better to stay down here than to go back up there, yessir. It's safe down here. It's all falling apart, but the wheel turns and the wheel breaks and—"

There.

He was right in front of Oliver.

His head low.

The words soft and murmured.

Now, Oliver. Now!

Oliver grunted, hefted the tool, and swung the coal pick—

Thuckkk! It was like sticking a knife into a fat pumpkin. The sharp tip sank deep. He felt the skull give.

"—is remaaaade," Eli groaned—

Before collapsing.

Oliver gasped as he let go of the pick. It fell with the body, still stuck in it. He recoiled from what he had done. Though he could see no part of his crime, he could smell the greasy stench of blood, and now, as Eli had promised, the sudden efflorescence of shit-stink. Then he felt an alien feeling, an *insane* feeling, rise up in him like soda bubbles: He laughed. Because *Fuck you, Eli*. Because *You're a batshit piece-of-shit shitty-pantsed monster,* just like Oliver's father, just like Eli's own dad—a monster down in the dark, keeping the light away, measuring it out only in tantalizing, torturous doses. Oliver laughed, and crawled his way over to the dead man. He shoulder-bumped the handle of the coal pick by accident, and Eli's dead chin scuffed against the hardscrabble ground.

"Oops," Oliver said, and giggled again.

He felt around for the treasure—felt down to the right arm, nope, then down to the left, and still not there. *No no no, where is the light?*

And now the fear surged within him that he'd done this wrong. He should've gotten a fix on the *lamp* first, now it could be anywhere. Eli might've been keeping it somewhere else, down in the tunnel, or behind a rock, or—

Or underneath him.

Moving Eli was easy—the man was lighter than a bundle of sticks—and he rolled him over and *there it was.* He hurriedly rescued the lamp—

And what?

A new realization struck him, cold as the plunge into a frozen lake. *I don't know how to light it.*

He found no button, no auto-lighting mechanism. He found a key like the kind you'd use to wind up an old toy, but he turned it left and right and it didn't do a damn thing.

Somehow, Eli had been lighting this, right? It needed fire. But had he ever seen Eli strike a match? Or use a . . . a flint or any kind of spark? He would've seen that, wouldn't he? Even still he went through the man's pockets, finding nothing but lint and coins. *Coins.* That could do it. Oliver didn't pay much attention in class, but he knew metal against stone could create sparks, and so he took one of the coins—a nickel by the feel of it—and dragged it against the ground, *kkt, kkkt, kkkkkt,* but it didn't do anything so he went to the *wall* instead and tried again, dragging it back and forth, faster and faster. And still? No sparks.

Oliver cried out in rage and despair.

He'd done it. He'd ruined it. He took his shot and screwed it up. His father was always telling him he was a fuckup, and sure enough, the old monster was right. He'd fucked up. *Big-time.*

You were right, Dad.

You were right.

Oliver fell to his knees. He couldn't even cry. He just knelt, penitent to the darkness, forehead against the ground, waiting for nothing.

*　*　*

It became too much.

The smell of death. The stink of feces. The darkness. The loneliness. Oliver almost preferred being tormented by Eli to this.

I need to end this.

Oliver struggled to unbury the coal pick from Eli's skull, rocking it back and forth. It gave way, eventually. Then he moved it back toward the wall, and he felt along the rocks until he found a crevice. Using his last ounce of strength, he gave a heave-ho and wedged the pick into that slit. He jostled it, and it held. Again he knelt.

He lined his head up to the curve of the pick, which faced him.

The softest part of him was, he thought, his eye.

So he closed his left eye and pressed it gently against the one end of the pick, the end sticking up.

Then he slowly reared his head back.

He knew that when he launched his head forward, the pick would go into his eye. Into his brain. And he would die.

And maybe, just maybe, there would be a blessing in that—the blessing that Eli, in his torment, in his madness, had figured out some essential truth, that sure enough, death was the way free. With it, Oliver would reawaken somewhere else. Somewhere new.

Somewhere *better.*

"The wheel breaks," Oliver said, as if a prayer. "And it is remade."

"Oliiiiiver," Eli groaned, the voice stretching out, a bleated echo.

Oliver gasped.

Behind him came a rasping shuffle sound. And then came the gentle *ticka-tack* of carapace on stone.

Oliver spun, pressing his back against the wall, steadying himself alongside the pick. There in the darkness he *saw* a shadow: a human-like shape, but too long, too lean, too tall. It rose from where Eli had been. It shined not with its own light but like moonsilver on an oil slick. Ribbons of white light flashing with rainbow iridescence.

"Who . . . what . . ."

"Oliver," said the voice again. It was Eli's voice, but it wasn't. It was only Eli's voice *at the top,* but beneath it were hundreds of other voices, layered there, each on top of the last.

"You *died.*"

"And yet, I stand."

"I'm sorry, *I'm sorry,* I'm so sorry I killed you."

A wet chuckle. "Don't be. It's time, Oliver."

"Time . . . ? For what?"

"Time to see your purpose. To learn magic. To break the world."

PART FIVE

THE 99TH

The four Kings:
Lucifer. Leviathan. Satan. Belial.
Their eight Dukes:
Ashtaroth. Morquin. Asmodai. Baalzebub.
Uthuthma. Mathokor. Abigor. Baal-Berith.
And twelve Knights:
Moloch, Malus, Pelsinade
Lith-Lyru, Hyor-Ka, Dantalion
Vissra, Orcobas, Vollrath
Nycon, Mymon, Candlefly

And beneath them are the 74 Revelators who oversee the architecture of the cosmos. Call upon their numbers and their sorcery shall be yours. All but the Archfiend's. Only one is above and below, the one who fell out of time, the one who escaped Hell and will raze the pillars of Heaven and that is the Archfiend, whose magic you do not call upon. That magic calls upon you.

—a page from the *Compendium Singularis,* translated from Latin, written in 1776, but passed off by its creator as an artifact from 1047

48

Broken Fingernails

I t occurred to her on the third day of Nate being gone that she had lost it. Maddie had long prided herself on being someone who, in the face of chaos, *kept her shit together*. She had brain weasels, she knew that: anxiety and, though not diagnosed, something approaching an attention deficit disorder. Maybe even a little OCD. But she knew how to self-medicate. With lists. With books. With her art. And, most of all—and this was a part she hadn't quite realized until now—her family. Now, her family was broken. A vital third of them, chopped out and gone missing.

Though sometimes, intrusive thoughts warned her of a different feeling lurking beneath the surface: *Don't you feel a little good, too? Now he's gone. No more of his pain. No more of his strange moods. You can be you, now. You don't have to be selfless. Now you can be selfish.*

She didn't believe that. Didn't agree with it. But intrusive thoughts were trespassers. You didn't invite them in. But they broke in, anyway, whether they were true or false.

Now, eight days in, she wandered the woods. She'd stop sometimes and just stand there and stare. Like the ghost of a tree that had been chopped down and was just looking for the stump of its old body to sit on, and rest, and reflect. When she did this, her mind wandered—not by choice, but almost like it was trying to find something. Some idea, some memory, something she couldn't quite hold. A dream evading its pursuers.

The forest around her house was quiet and cold. The trees looked dead, thanks to the coming of winter. The once-colorful leaves had turned to a gray-brown carpet.

Maddie had no idea what she was looking for at this point. Part of her thought she'd find a clue, like a lucky detective: a footprint, a bit of dried blood, some hair, a shoe stuck in mud. She wanted to see what Nate had seen—the haggard man with the beard, the ghost of a dead girl, a serial killer stalking the trees, even his father. And then it hit her again, as it had many times in the past few days: an insane urge to *make something*. To get her hands on materials, fucking *primal* materials like stone, twig, mud, and metal. And to craft them into something alive, something that would help her.

But last time she did that—the last time she'd surrendered herself to the work—she'd summoned a serial killer. And then that same killer attacked her husband. Just as she'd brought the owl into the world, maybe, just maybe, she'd brought Edmund Walker Reese into the world, too.

That terrified her.

Art as vessel. Art as doorway. Do I control it?

Or does it control me?

She sighed and tamped down the urge. That mad spark to *make something* swiftly sizzled. Maddie glanced at her watch. It was time to meet Fig at the house.

"I think he's shady," Fig said, framed by the steam from his coffee cup. "I went to talk to him again yesterday. Just to poke around. I'm not a detective or anything but—Nate's a friend. And Maddie, the guy acted cagey as hell. His place was a mess. *He* was a mess. He'd been drinking, and I don't know if he was coming down off a hard drunk or getting ready to climb up one, but this was not the put-together guy from the party. He was short with me. He was quick to usher my ass out the door."

Maddie paced the kitchen.

"He just doesn't seem the type," Maddie said.

The story Jed told the police was a simple one: Nate was supposed to come over and have a drink. That was it. Nothing about the park, about serial killers, about crazy storms or folklore or any of that.

He also told them that Nate never showed up.

He'd said as much to Fig and Maddie, too. Jed said Nate never made it to Jed's doorstep. Which meant that Nate had disappeared somewhere between their two houses.

"I've talked to Jed," Maddie said. "He seemed . . . upset by it. Really broken up over it. Like he feels responsible, like he led Nate on some fool's crusade."

"So why didn't he call you that night? To let you know Nate hadn't shown up. Or why didn't he call Nate?"

"He said he assumed Nate forgot. Or that something came up. Jed's very friendly, very considerate—in his words, he 'didn't want to be a bother.'" She shrugged. "I don't know. I trust him."

"You don't really *know* him, though."

"No. I guess not. It's just—he's an author. A writer of books! I figured he had it together."

"I'd guess artists and authors are similar. Would you say that most artists are pretty good at keeping it together?"

She blinked. "Okay, point taken." She sighed. "He seems nice is all. Nate likes him, and Nate's always been a pretty good judge of character. And, for the logic of it, I have a hard time believing Jed could take Nate. Nate's pretty tough—and he had his gun with him."

"In a straight fight, you're right, but who knows how it went. Lotta ways to take the fight out of someone before the fight starts."

"And then what? He killed him?"

Fig shrugged. "Shit. I dunno. About three years ago, a teen girl went missing, and the mother was distraught, losing her mind. This was down the road a ways, not even ten minutes from here, okay?

The teen girl had some troubles, drinking and prescription drugs and whatever. The boyfriend—of the mother, not the girl—was a little weird, too, though. He had a rap sheet. Nothing big, a car theft, a credit scam. Everyone liked the mother. Everyone said it was probably him. It's always the guy, right? Always the husband or the father. The mom, though, she had an alibi for him, said he was with her the night the daughter went missing, and they said the girl liked to go into the city and maybe she just ran away. And the truth of the thing was, what? The boyfriend did it? He did. It was him. But it wasn't *just* him. It was the mom, too. This woman, the mother, had a good job as a business account manager at Bank of America. She paid her taxes, was liked by her neighbors. It was all a ruse. She was the mastermind, and she got her boyfriend to help her kidnap the girl and fake her disappearance. They kept her daughter in a root cellar in the woods outside their property. They sexually abused that girl for weeks. Filmed it. They used that poor girl up and when they were done with her, they cut the body up, left it in the cellar, and then the boyfriend—who worked construction—filled in the root cellar with cement. *Only* way they got caught was the mother had begun beating on him and threatening to kill him, too, and he cracked like an egg, told the police everything, because he decided it would be better to die in prison than to be at the mercy of this woman."

Maddie blinked. "Jesus, Fig."

"Yeah."

"Way to keep me optimistic."

He winced. "Sorry. I don't mean that's the kind of thing that happened to Nate. I only mean—look, you can't always be sure that what you think about a person isn't what they *want* you to think. Guy like Jed might have constructed a persona, like a mask. And maybe he's good enough at it to have fooled Nate." Fig hesitated. "You know about his wife and kid, right?"

"Yeah. Nate said they left him."

Fig made a face.

"That's not what happened?" she asked.

"Oh, they left him all right. They left the land of the living. He killed them in a drunk-driving accident. Jed was driving, crashed the car. He survived. Wife died on scene. The daughter died a few weeks later in the hospital while in a coma. Just a few years ago. Then he moved here."

"That's not what he told Nate."

"See what I mean?"

She'd grown comfortable with the fact Jed couldn't have had anything to do with this, but now . . . doubt formed a heavy weight inside her.

"Fine. You know, I wouldn't want people to know that story, either. That's dark." She threw up her hands. "With all the super-weird shit going on—the girl, the lightning, *Reese*—I don't feel good pointing fingers at someone we ostensibly trust. Do you?"

"No," he said. "I dunno." He sighed and rubbed his temples. "We'll find Nate," Fig said, obviously seeing the crestfallen look on her face. "State police are involved now. Contrino's on it—he's a prick, and I hate his guts, but he's smart. He's good at what he does. It's only a matter of time." He said it again, as if to convince himself: "We'll find Nate."

But will we find him alive? she wondered.

She ran it through her head again and again. If Nate was walking over to Jed's that night, and he went missing before he ever got there . . . he'd have left a trail, she would've thought. But they never found one. Though it was hard to, wasn't it? Their woods were all just leaves. Not a patch of exposed dirt to be found. But now she took it past that. Past their property. What if he *did* end up at Jed's place? Maybe they did go somewhere.

"It was warm that day," she said.

"Yeah."

"Then it got cold that night. Temperature dropped."

Fig seemed to think about it. "Yeah. You're right. Hard frost the next day. Hasn't warmed up since."

"If there were footprints, they'd be pretty frozen in place."

"We checked your woods."

"Cops check Jed's property? And the park?"

"His property, maybe. I didn't, but the others probably did. As for the park—he said they were going to check out the tunnel. That's paved from where he would've gone in. No footprints in asphalt."

Her brow furrowed. "But the park was closed by that point. Ramble Rocks closes after dark, right? And you two don't have keys."

"That's Parks Department. I'd just assume he'd have hopped the gate if that's where they went. Easy to go over it, around it, whatever."

"Around it would mean stepping on dirt."

"Okay, true."

"And," she said, thinking further, "I know Nate. They were going into that park for reasons . . ." *That were a little crazy.* "They wouldn't want to be seen, and I know Reese killed girls in the boulder field." *The actual rocks of Ramble Rocks.* "Maybe they went that way."

"Hunh." Fig seemed to think about this. "Lotta maybes."

"Maybes are better than nothing."

"It's a reach, but I'm good to check it out. I don't have much on my plate, since hunting season hasn't quite ratcheted up yet. Well, muzzleloader, but nobody uses them around here anymore. I'll take a look."

"Let's chart the path from Jed's place to the rocks, and then to the tunnel *in* the park."

Fig stood up, draining the last of the mug. "Listen, Maddie, you've already been through enough shit. I don't want to drag you out into the brambles on this—"

"I want to." She realized she sounded insistent, demanding, and so she softened her tone as she gently pleaded with him. "I *need* to do something or I'll pull my fucking fingernails out with my teeth. I'm maybe netting a few hours of sleep every night. Whenever I try to eat, I feel queasy enough that I stop halfway through and then throw the rest away. I gotta do something. I want to help. It's Nate, you know?"

He nodded. "Yeah, I know. And absolutely. Let's go out tomorrow. Bright and early, you and me. Sound like a plan?"

"The best plan. Thanks, Fig."

49

The Oliver Process

Jake was once Oliver. *An* Oliver, anyway.

He knew that, deep down. But for so long now, he'd called himself Jake—Jake for six years, Jake across branching timelines and universes, Jake to every Oliver he'd met. So much Jake that he had done more than accepted the name; he'd subsumed a whole new identity. Into each world he went he became someone slightly new to appeal to the Oliver of that place: sculpting himself into a key that fit into the hole in every Oliver's heart.

In many ways, he wasn't Oliver anymore.

Oliver was someone else.

Oliver was the boy with belt scars on his back.

Oliver was the boy with the broken ankle, the bruises from books he'd loved, the mother whose jaw was broken and wired shut and that never worked again.

Oliver died in the coal mine.

Jake was born in it.

The same Jake that stood here now, watching the old prick pace the space behind the ratty, saggy couch.

"Jake. Jake! He came again, you know," Jed said. "To my house."

"Uh-huh," Jake said, top lip hooked in a dismissive sneer. "Wow, come in, Jed, make yourself at home." The old fuck showed up just minutes ago, pounding on the door, *wham wham wham*, demanding to be let in. He'd maybe been crying, as his eyes were pink and puffy.

Or maybe he was just hungover; certainly the sour swamp stink of sweated-out vodka was hanging around him like a miasma. He looked like days-old stomped-on shit. Skin pale and thin. Hair every-where, like he'd forgotten that combs were a thing that existed. Fin-gernails bitten down to the bloody quick. Watching the man pace, he said, sharply: "Seriously, *sit the fuck down.*"

"Oh. Ah." Jed looked around, as if only just realizing where he even was. "Of course, of course."

He took a seat on the arm of the couch.

"Now, who came to your house, exactly?" Jake asked.

"The cop. Um. No. Not a cop. Nate's friend, the one from Fish and Game. Something Figueroa? Alex? No. Axel."

"So?"

"So. He—he's still sniffing around, Jake. He still thinks I had something to do with Nate's disappearance!"

Jake shrugged. "You *did* have something to do with it."

"But he's not supposed to *know* that."

"Honestly, who cares? He figures it out, he figures it out. He throws you in jail or he doesn't. Maybe you take that pistol I gave you, you shoot him. Maybe he shoots you." Jake smirked. "Maybe you shoot yourself."

"That's dark talk, boy. Dark talk."

"Dark talk? It's all going to be over soon. All of it. All of *this.*"

"That doesn't mean—that doesn't mean I'm a monster."

The old man was wobbly. He was on the precipice. That was a dan-gerous place to be. He could still jeopardize things. Everything was going well here—the demon was not pleased, no—it wanted things done *now,* it wanted them done *faster*—but Jake urged the beast to be patient. But all told, it was going as well as could be expected, given how different the circumstances were this go-around. So to have it all fall apart because this nervous horse got spooked, that would be a right goddamn tragedy.

Jake, eager and impatient, thought, *Well, fuck it,* and he idly considered just twisting his wrist and bringing out a blade or a pistol from the In-Between place, and opening the old fucker's throat or popping his brains out the back of his head. But that was risky, too. All the blood and the cleanup. No, thank you. That came with its own problems.

No, after six years of this, Jake was pretty good at managing people. Some universes let him tackle the situation all by his lonesome, but considerably more of them had him building a team of people— weak people whose damage made them vulnerable, but whose vulnerability, when exploited, when *pushed upon,* also made them incredibly loyal.

Time to push those buttons.

With Jed, it was easy.

"You're not a monster," Jake said. He put a steadying hand on the old man's shoulder. He put on a different Jake mask: softer voice, kinder face, the one he'd worn when he convinced Jed to help him the first time. When he showed him what was possible using the magic of the Book of Accidents. "You *were,* though, a monster— weren't you? Roaring and raging. The drink brought it out. Lost your senses. Lost your mind. Made you get in that car and start it up even though your family was there with you. They died that night, but that isn't final. Mitzi and Zelda are still out there, Jed. We do this right, you stay steady and hang with me, it'll all come around again. You'll see your family once more, *and* you'll get it *right* the next time. Because you'll be a better man than before. Right?"

Jed said nothing.

The knife. The gun. Kill him.

"Right?" Jake asked again, more insistent. "What do we have to do to fix something? Jed? When we fix something, we—"

He waited for the old man to fill in the blanks.

"Break it first," Jed said, finally. "Of course. I just . . . we're close now, aren't we?" Before Jake could answer, the old man kept going:

"With Nate out of the way, you can do this more quickly, you can just take the boy, take him to the park and—"

"*No.*"

That word, spoken like a word of God, from on high. A word with steel rebar threaded through it. The Book of Accidents sat on the coffee table, and it stirred when he said that word, *no.* Its impatience with him hummed in his bones. Jed watched the book, warily.

"I *told* you," Jake went on, "we do this on my timetable. There's a lot of wick on this candle, and it burns how it burns. The deal is the deal. I have to give Oliver a chance. A chance to do the right thing. You knew that going in. This Oliver . . . I have a real good feeling about him."

With Nate gone, he hoped Oliver had been pushed to the edge. Kid was vulnerable. *Exposed.* Jake had dangled the promise of magic in front of him, and now Oliver just had to reach up and take it.

But Jake had to admit: *This* Oliver wasn't like any of the others. He had no idea if the kid would react like he hoped. None of this was like in any of the other timelines. The Nates were *always* pieces of shit. Every last one of them, a failure in some way: a drunk, an addict, an abuser, a loser. Hell, half the time they were already dead or they'd fucked off to wherever, abandoning the Olivers to their fate. But this Nate didn't seem like that. Jake told himself it was just a carefully crafted illusion: *This* Nate, the one he'd sent into the maelstrom, was almost certainly a monster same as all the others. He just kept a tighter lid on it. Maybe a serial rapist, or a serial murderer, or he touched little kids before throwing them down in a well or something. Was no way that this Nate bucked the trend. He *refused* to believe that a man who underwent what Nate did—the abuse from his own father—would come out the other side okay. Abuse begat abuse. Hate made hate, pain birthed pain. It was the way of things. It was as Eligos Vassago had told him. Had *showed* him down there in the mine.

The Maddies—this one was different, too. Seemed stronger, somehow. The other Maddies were pill heads and wine drunks, mostly. Selfish shits who crawled so far up their own asses they practically died up there. Some were so anxious or depressed they spent most of their day in a fog or under a blanket, abandoning their family sure as if they'd gotten on a plane and never came back. Others were quote-unquote "lost to the art," ditching their family as they traveled the world, looking for inspiration, never home, never caring, never knowing what was up in their own damn house. None of them had it *together.*

Except this Maddie.

And as for the Olivers . . .

Oh, ho, ho.

They were all special.

They all had their ways of being different. Each a snowflake.

And each as easy to melt. A little heat, a little pressure.

The Oliver of 33 could talk to animals with his mind. He went mad, lost the ability to speak to people, went essentially feral.

The Oliver of 42 was a preening narcissist, an artist like his mother, one who claimed to be always lost in "deep thought," and, of course, liked to pull the wings off butterflies and the heads off squirrels and, inevitably, the dresses off struggling girls, the pants off drugged boys.

The Oliver of 71 was crushed by depression born of abuse from his own father. Jake understood him so well. Too well. It was easy. When he was truly in a black mood—and only then—that Oliver could move objects with his mind. Jake found he could use that. He used the boy's black mood to crush the boy's father with a refrigerator. Easy from there to show him the path forward. The way to break it all. The way to *fix* it all.

The Oliver of 98, the last Oliver that he'd met, was stubborn. That one took long, *too* long, and it made him all the more impatient now—*that* Oliver was a fucking brute. The Nate of 98 never beat that Oliver, not with fists or objects, no, but with a barrage of verbal abuse.

Diminishing and demeaning him at every chance. But that didn't squash the boy like a bug; rather, it just puffed him up, and he built for himself a wall of muscle and force that surrounded a hollow, vengeful center—and one day, that Oliver decided he would beat his father to death with his bare hands. He was physically gifted, stronger than any of his fellow students, and oh so defiant. Even to Jake. It took a lot for Jake to get him to the boulder field.

But he did.

And now he had this Oliver. The 99th Oliver.

The *last*.

All the dominoes had fallen except this final one, and they were all propped up against that last domino—and it was putting so much pressure on the universe. Some of the maelstrom was coming in, bleeding through the thinning walls, causing chaos. It put pressure on him, too, to get it done, to just fucking *finish* it, already. But he'd done right in the last ninety-eight; he wasn't going to shortcut it now. He had his code. He had his way.

"Is Nate dead?" Jed asked.

"No. I don't know."

"I'm glad," the older man said in a faraway voice. "But why? Why leave him alive?"

"Because I didn't want a body to deal with." *And because the demon wanted to show Nate something.* What that was, Jake didn't know. Didn't care. He didn't have to know the whole scope of the creature's plan. He only had to do his part, and he had to do it his way.

"But—" Jed began.

Jake silenced him with a twirl of his wrist. A bottle of whiskey spun into his hand. Jack Kenny American Whiskey, Blue Label. The brown liquor sloshed around the bottle as he handed it to Jed.

"Here, you deserve this. A reward."

"I . . . *oh,* I don't know this brand." His thumb traced over the embossed label showing a man in a bowler hat going over a waterfall in half a whiskey barrel. Gold text on a faux-distressed texture.

"It's not from here," Jake said.

"Not from here. You mean—"

"That's right. Bottle of whiskey from another reality, Jedward. That's the only bottle left. You hold in your hands a rare artifact—a prize that is unparalleled in its value. You could drink it all. The taste would be yours and yours alone. Or share it. I don't fucking care. Just take it, enjoy the spoils, and leave me to do what I need to do."

Jed was staring at the bottle the way a starving man stares at a chicken wing. Jake wasn't even sure the old man heard him. He did nod, but in an idle, distracted way.

A knock at the door brought him out of his reverie.

Jake went to the window and peered past the slat blinds—

It was Oliver. *Yes. Yes!*

Then he looked over to Jed. *No. No!*

"Shit," he hissed. Pointing at Jed, he said, "Tell me you didn't park out front."

"No. No! I—I parked at the far side of the park this time, like you said."

"Good. Now get the fuck out. Go out the back." The trailer had a door on the side and a door at the far end, past the single bedroom. "I *can't* have him seeing you here. Not now." If Oliver began to doubt . . .

Jed nodded, cradling the bottle to his chest like it was more precious to him than his own missing daughter. Which, truly, it probably was.

Pathetic.

Soon as he was gone, Jake opened the door and met Oliver with open arms. He invited him in. Again he thought of the knife and the pistol, but he tamped those down. *There's still time,* he thought. *Let the process work.*

50

Lamp in the Dark

Jake and Oliver walked in the cold away from the trailer park and toward Oliver's house. They went through the park—down the paved pathways, then down some hiking trails, back to the path.

Jake smoked a cigarette as they walked. He watched Oliver warily. Eagerness sang in the back of his ear, in the hinge of his jaw. Jake felt like they were close. *So* close. Oliver, standing on his tippy-toes on the edge of a cliff. The goal wasn't to push him, but to let him decide to jump.

"I feel sick to my stomach that he's gone," Oliver said, of his father.

"I get it," Jake said. "I mean, I don't. My own father—" *My own Nate,* he thought, almost comically. "Was a fucker. I would've been happy for him to die." *I was happy for him to die. I was happy to kill him.*

"I've been thinking."

"Yeah?"

Oliver stopped and turned to face Jake. Jake pitched the cigarette into a puddle, *tsssss*. He felt a crawl of termites in his chest. Eagerness and anxiety percolated there.

"I've been searching for Dad high and low, you know? The last three days I've been out, I've been with Caleb, and he and Hina were helping me look, up one road, down another, into the woods, into the park, and I yell for him and—" Oliver's voice cracked like a

Christmas ornament falling off the tree. Tears shone in his eyes. "Nothing. He's just gone."

"I'm sorry, man." *So. Close.*

"But that's the thing. He's gone. *Gone* gone. Like he just . . . disappeared. No trail, no evidence, no anything. Like he walked through the wrong door, a one-way exit."

"So?"

"The spellbook," Oliver said, finally. "Your spellbook."

"The Book of Accidents. What about it?"

Oliver licked his lips. "Maybe my dad being gone, it wasn't an accident."

Shit. That wasn't exactly the revelation he wanted from this last, most vital Oliver. *C'mon, c'mon, c'mon. Don't go there, kid.*

"Whaddya mean?"

"I mean . . . it's like those coal mine accidents. Some of them were intentional, a lot weren't, but all of them were because of a buildup of failures. Weakness. Like you said, entropy."

There. That was much better. Jake could work with that. He wanted to just blurt it out, put words in Oliver's mouth, but it was better to let him get there on his own—blah blah blah, lead a horse to water, can't make it drink.

Oliver continued on: "You said there were weak spots. *Thin* spots between the worlds. Maybe Dad fell through one. Maybe he got lost. Like I said, maybe he went through a door. A door that wasn't supposed to be there. And now he can't get back."

Jake faked being in thought, like he was considering it. "Wow. That could be, Oliver. I dunno, man."

"Mom said my dad was interested in the park. Real interested. And you said in your world it wasn't a park at all. You said there was a Ramble Rocks in every world."

"That's right."

"It's like a nail through the pages of a book. Present in every world. A . . . a constant." *A constant,* Jake thought. *Just like you, Olly.*

"You're right."

Wow, whoa, no way. He almost rolled his eyes.

"Is that where you came through?" Oliver asked.

"It is. The tunnel—the train tunnel, that's where."

"Do you think . . ."

Here it comes. The plea.

"Do you think we could use the Book of Accidents to find him? Maybe . . . maybe there's a spell. Or another vision? You have magic. You were trying to tell me that we can fix things—maybe this is one of the things we can fix. One of the things we can start with."

Jake almost burst out laughing. Not just because it was easy—it wasn't!—but because of the relief he felt that they were almost there. He showed the horse the water, and now the dumb animal was licking its lips and looking real thirsty.

Jake nodded. "Yeah. Okay. *Yeah.* You might be right, kid. I bet the book has answers. It's back at the trailer. We could go there. See what it can tell us. But you need to know, I think this is pretty big magic. I don't think I can do it alone."

"You won't have to. I'm here. I'll do whatever it takes."

"Whatever it takes?"

Oliver nodded.

Jake put out his hand to shake, but Oliver hugged him instead. It was a strange feeling—a hug from your own self. Eerily comfortable while at the same time possessing a deep uncanniness—a physiological version of déjà vu. Warm and sickening in equal measure.

Fuck it. Jake hugged him back. And he meant it, too. Because this kid may have just saved him a lot of trouble. May have saved everything—Jake, Oliver, this Nate, all the Nates, all the worlds.

Soon, it'd all be over. The wheel would be broken.

The pain would end.

"Let's go figure out how to get your dad back."

51

When the Maker Meets the Made

Spears of light stabbed through the trees in the cold November morning. Maddie met with Fig at sunup, and he had plotted one potential route that would take them from Jed's house and into Ramble Rocks, bypassing any of the official pathways into the park. The two of them walked about fifty feet apart. Fig said they'd do a light zigzag pattern, trying to cover as much ground as they could while still heading roughly in the direction of the old train tunnel at the heart of Ramble Rocks.

Now, she did exactly that—gingerly stepping through the woods, careful of where every foot landed. Her eyes were fixed to the ground, not the horizon, because they were looking for footprints, something to prove that Nate *and* Jed were here together.

Ten minutes in proved what a fruitless endeavor this was. The forest floor was thick with leaf litter and sticks—no way to see a footprint, much less make one. Maddie glanced over at Fig, who was also searching slowly and thoroughly for footprints as he slalomed left, right, left again.

An absurd, intrusive thought struck her like a rock:

Thanksgiving is coming soon.

Was just a couple weeks until a big holiday all three of them loved, because Thanksgiving had none of the trappings of the other holidays but two: food and family. No presents, no caroling, no songs, no snow, no tree to decorate or crowds to endure. Just one rock-solid day of gorging yourself (she preferred to make proteins other than turkey, because turkey was a fat fucking garbage bird) and then watching movies. They didn't have extended family, so it was always just the three of them.

Now, the two of us.

She had to stop. She put her hand out, leaning on a tree. Her knees felt weak, but she stayed standing.

Nate . . .

"You okay?" Fig called to her. He was already ahead of her by a ways; she hadn't realized. She forced a thumbs-up.

"Just shoulda had breakfast is all," she said.

"You wanna stop? Get something?"

"No. Let's push on."

The boulder field was so stark and so strange, it nearly took her breath away. This part of Bucks County, she knew, was rocky—a lot of homes had big boulders lining their driveways, or old forgotten stone fencerows marking property lines—but even still, seeing them all laid out like this, boulder after boulder, stone after stone? Seeing it felt like she'd found something rare—a precious, unparalleled place. And there was something more, too, a feeling she couldn't shake. As if the field pulsed with a kind of energy, dark and alive. Hadn't Jed said there was some kind of frequency here, or was she misremembering?

Maddie caught a glimpse of Fig—he'd veered off to the left. Her path went to the right.

She hazarded one last glimpse out over the stones—

And saw something out there. Something on top of a strange, flat, table-like rock.

It's a bird.

She blinked a few times.

No. It wasn't just a bird.

It was an *owl*.

The owl moved, as if to rebalance its footing. Or perhaps it was just impatient.

Her chest held on to her breath. Again that vertiginous feeling, but instead of falling, she was rising.

That can't be my owl.

The one I made.

The one that went missing. Can it?

She swallowed hard and walked straight into the boulder field. It was nearly impossible to find even, easy ground, so instead she went over, delicately stepping from rock to rock, moving toward the owl—an owl she *knew* couldn't be real. But as she got closer and closer, dancing quickly across the rock tops, she could see the owl for what it was. The colors of the feathers on the bird's breast were mottled, but it was not a pattern on its feathers, but rather the grain of stained wood. The eyes were delicately sculpted tree knots; its thrust-up ears were dark, dry leaves.

She slowed as she grew closer.

Don't scare it. An insane thought. Because she'd *made* this owl.

She held out both hands, half like she was trying to soothe a spooked horse and half like she was initiating first contact with an alien species.

The owl watched her. It turned its head with a creaking, juddering sound—the sound of an old tree swaying in winter wind.

"I . . ." she started to say, but no words fell after that first. What was there to say? *Are you real? I made you. Can you fly?*

Am I dreaming?

Am I dead?

The bird opened its wings and shook a little bit, the way a dog shakes its fur. Then it settled back down, wrapping its wings about itself. The "feathers," layered atop one another on the wings, were tantalizingly delicate. The fine texture of those feathers looked carved—perhaps with an X-Acto blade. A torturous, exacting task. It urged upon her a swell of pride. *I did that. I made you. And you're beautiful.*

The owl dipped its head. Then it did it again, as if Maddie wasn't getting its point—and only now did she realize it was gesturing toward the next boulder over, on which Maddie spotted a small cairn of stones: a larger, baseball-sized rock, and next to it, two flatter stones. Skippers, her father would've called them, good for skipping across a flat lake.

As Maddie regarded these bits of rock, the owl hopped over to the other rock, striking out with one of its taloned feet—

And knocking those skippers over with a clatter. They fell to the ground.

Then the bird dipped its head again. Almost impatiently. As if to say, *Pay attention to what I'm trying to show you.*

"You . . . want me to pick those up?"

The bird stared at her with its wooden eyes. Implacable. Like, *duh.* It hooted at her: *hoo, hoo.* Behind its voice was the sound of snapping twigs and the susurrus of a tree bough in a hard wind.

"Okay, settle down," she told her creation. "Let's see what you see."

She hazarded a quick look toward Fig. He wasn't watching. That was good. But she also wanted someone, anyone, to see. To tell her it was real.

Taking a deep breath, and hoping like hell the owl wouldn't dig its sharp wooden claws into the back of her neck as she went for the rocks, she scooched closer and bent down. She gathered up the rocks, and they clicked as she jostled them around like a pair of dice. They felt good in her hands. They felt *right.* Like they had a purpose she had yet to discern.

Then, beneath them, she saw something.

The space between the boulders was wider than most, and there she spied a footprint. No, a *boot*print, like her husband's boot.

"Nate," she said, her voice breaking.

He had come through the boulder field.

This is it.

Quickly she began to survey the area, looking for more gaps like this one, and here the stones seemed just a bit farther apart than they had elsewhere. She bent down, leaning across rocks, balancing herself on one as she turned herself to study the ground—

"Oh my god," she said.

Another footprint.

This one, a flat tread. Like a sneaker.

In the center of the tread, a half-smooshed Nike swoosh.

Jed.

They were here. Nate was not here alone. Jed was with him. Their neighbor had lied. "That motherfucker," she said aloud, standing up—

A rush of wings and branches breaking—

The owl, *her* owl, was suddenly gone.

She looked up into the morning sky and saw no sign of it.

That was a problem for Future Maddie to worry about. Now she hollered to Fig, told him she found the prints. Then she pocketed the rocks, because they seemed like very good luck, indeed.

Fig looked around, making a scrunched-up, frustrated face. "I can't believe they walked *through* the boulder field."

"Jed led him here. For . . . some reason."

"How'd you even find this?" Fig asked.

A little birdie told me.

"I just thought to look," she said, instead. "Something different about this place. I thought Nate might want to check it out."

"Well, you did good, Maddie. This is . . . well, let's just say you have your husband's cop instincts. I'll wait here; we have some staties coming by to plaster-cast the prints and then sweep the area for more evidence."

"And Jed?"

"Then we'll have a talk with him."

"A talk."

He must've heard the wariness in her voice. "They'll bring him in, Maddie, don't worry. He'll be in a room with a couple of detectives."

"What can I do? In the meantime."

"You did what needed doing. This is it. You did it. So I'd say—go home, have some of that breakfast you're missing. Relax a little, maybe take a nap—I know it's not polite to tell a woman she looks tired, but . . ."

"I look like a pile of laundry, you can say it."

He laughed a little. "Go home. And thanks."

"No, thank you. For believing in me. If we find Nate—"

"*When.* When we find him, Maddie."

"Yeah. He'll appreciate it."

"He'd do the same for me."

The discovery of the footprints led to Maddie's feelings growing more complicated, not less. Hope winked in and out like a pulsating star. On the one hand, it was a lead. Which might mean finding Nate and discovering the truth of his disappearance. On the other hand, it was a sign that something awful had transpired, that Jed was lying— meaning, he had *done something* to Nate, either as an accident, or intentionally, out of malice. And that led her to something else:

Raw, red anger.

Jed had lied to them.

She'd trusted him. *Nate* had trusted him.

On the way home, she walked back through the trees to the road. And there she saw Jed's house—his chalet, his authorial palace.

She knew the cops would be here soon enough to question him.

But there she stood, her feet fixed to the asphalt. A wind whipped, and leaves scraped past her feet like scuttling crabs. Maddie couldn't quite will her feet to pick up and carry her home.

Her hands flexed into fists so hard the nails bit into palms callused from her work. It formed little bright bits of pain there, pushing through the numbness. The anger wouldn't quit. It rose up in her. It *seized* her.

She marched up to Jed's house and knocked on the door.

House of Entropy

His car was gone, and the door to his house left ajar. Again Maddie paused, wondering: Should she really do this? She knew the answer in the same way anyone *knew* that they were committing an unhealthy, problematic action, the same way you knew you were eating too much at a meal, or drinking too much, or driving too fast. And yet, she offered an excuse to counter that answer in much the same way: *I need to,* and *I want to,* and *I think I'm going to do it anyway because it feels like I have to.*

The door opened wide with just a gentle push.

Inside, it looked like hoarders had been living in the once orderly home. Or maybe just a family of fucking raccoons. Blackflies thrummed around open pizza boxes and Chinese takeout containers—some of which still contained food and filled the air with a foul, moldy-foot stench. Books lay scattered on the floor, as if torn off their shelves in a rage. The only thing left untouched, it seemed, were framed photos—photos of a pretty woman standing with a teen girl, a girl whose eyes shone keenly with the mischievous pluck and intelligence of Jed Homackie.

A girl that Maddie knew was now dead.

Just like her own husband.

A small voice reminded her: *You don't know Jed is to blame. You don't know that Nate is dead.*

And another voice argued back: *He damn sure might be dead, Maddie. And we know Jed fucking lied to us, didn't he, precious?*

"Jed?" she called out, her anger freshly renewed.

No answer.

Him not being here destroyed her satisfaction. She *wanted* him to be here. So she could confront him. Yell at him, even. *Club him over the head with something and kill him,* a darker voice urged.

"Fuck," she said.

Emboldened and pissed off, she decided to look around the house.

The truth of a house was this: It became a home when someone lived there, more so when many had lived there, their lives adding a kind of texture, sometimes invisible, in layer after layer. It was present in the way a house smelled: like the food of family dinners, the stink of cigarettes on the wall, the ripe pickled rank of body odor in a teen boy's room. It was there in little dings and scratches, in the drywall dent of a fist someone threw, in the loving and loved dents found in a child's playroom, in claw marks from pets scrabbling around hardwood floors. A house was just a place. A home had soul. It lived many lives, had many ghosts. Maybe they were happy ghosts. Maybe they were sad. Maybe it was a home filled with laughter—or one wet with blood and tears.

This house was not a home.

It was a mess. It contained *stuff.* But the construction was fairly new; it didn't feel properly *lived* in. It was an uncolonized land, borrowed and passed through rather than settled, and as Maddie moved through it, she noted how many of the rooms seemed entirely unused. Of the four bedrooms upstairs, two were empty of everything but dust and the wispy webs of spiders in the corners. One bedroom was just *stuff*: boxes and boxes of it, dresses in bags hanging on racks, a wedding gown, a music box, a trash bag half open offering a glimpse of stuffed animals bulging out the top. It occurred to her: *This stuff belongs to his wife and daughter.*

Or, rather, belong*ed* to.

A moment of empathy sandbagged her: to lose a child? And to have it be your fault? She couldn't imagine it. It would crush her, her heart turned to crater. And it had plainly done something to Jed.

But she also knew she would never let herself bring Oliver to that kind of harm. She had her shit tight. She had her life on *lockdown*. The errors of her youth and the anxiety that drove it, she had it beat.

(Another poisonous voice: *Or so you hope, Maddie.*)

Of the two bathrooms upstairs, one was devoid of anything but, again, dust and spiders and a house centipede that stalked the shower. The other bathroom was the one attached to the master bedroom, and both of those rooms were rough—filthy, messy, pure chaos. Signs of madness and anger abounded: bedsheets braided with a comforter and left on the floor; a mirror, cracked; a desk in the corner heaped with notes and crumpled pages and a square void in the dust where a laptop may once have sat. The dresser drawers were all pulled out and emptied. A walk-in closet still had its light on, and stuff had been pulled off hangers, the hangers left scattered about on the floor and mattress.

Under the bed, a little fingerprint-lock fire safe had been pulled out.

It, too, was open and empty.

He's gone.

He'd stolen from her the chance to confront him. He wasn't here. Jed had packed his things—hastily, without care—and abandoned this place.

"Fuck!" she said to the spiders, the centipedes.

How long had he been gone?

Had she just missed him?

Fuck, fuck, fuck.

Back downstairs, she saw one pizza box closed. And on top of it, two things: a pen and the handset to a cordless phone.

Normally, she'd expect these days someone would use their cellphone to dial out. She and Nate didn't even bother with a landline. But Jed was older. Older folks tended to rely on their landlines. Which meant maybe he'd used this before leaving.

To call whom?

She turned on the phone, tried to dial *69, unsure if that call-the-last-number-dialed feature even *worked* anymore—

It didn't. Not because the service was done, but because the phone was dead. Battery drained.

She chucked the phone down on the counter. No time to charge it. She had to imagine the police would be here at some point soon. And her being caught in the house . . .

You should leave, Maddie.

The pen. A Bic clicker.

Her thumb traced along the texture of the pizza box. And there, she found it, like Braille: the indent of something. Handwriting.

A number.

Maddie's gaze darted around the room until she found a receipt stapled to the pizza box. She snatched it and pressed it against the indentation.

A quick swipe-and-scribble with the pen revealed a phone number.

She pocketed it and ducked out the door, hurrying back home.

53

The Gravity of Guilt and Vengeance

Maddie was on the highway before she even realized it. Like she was falling into this journey, with no way to stop herself.

It was an hour up 476 to get to 80, the interstate that split Pennsylvania in half like a crack in a basement wall. Before going west, Maddie pulled over at a McDonald's parking lot to text her son:

Olly I'm taking a trip.

She waited. She stared at her phone. Nothing.

Then: three dots.

A response from him bubbled up: fine

That wasn't like him. It was curt. *Too* curt. She knew he'd been hurting with Nate gone, and only now was she seeing how she'd been ignoring him and his pain. She was as lost as he was, but she hadn't shared her own pain with him, hadn't let him know he wasn't alone, hadn't offered to let him help find his father. *Fuck!*

She texted him back: You okay?

Him: yes just busy

Her: Listen, Olly, I'm sorry I haven't been there for you. I've been so wrapped up in finding your dad. I'll be better when I get back

Time passed. Thirty seconds, a minute, five minutes.

Is this what kids felt like when their friends or girlfriends or whatever didn't write them back immediately? That surge of worry and impatience? She had a very mommish feeling of *god, these devices are poison,* but then she remembered being in high school and staring at the cordless phone on her nightstand, waiting for some boy or friend to call. Maybe this was the nature of human communication.

We need each other more than we realize.

Growling, she was about to text him to answer her, but then she saw those three dots again—

Him: its fine I said I'm busy

Him: Ill see you when you get back

She responded with a heart emoji.

He didn't respond at all.

Fuck fuck fuck.

She wanted to say more. That she would make it up to him, that she missed Nate, that she was worried—*so* worried it felt like the worry was going to chew her to pulp, and now she was afraid of losing Oliver, too, and the whole thing made her crazy.

It was what it was. She put the phone away and got out of the car. There was one more thing to check—the violent, vengeful version of making sure she hadn't left the stove on. She unzipped the carry-on bag in the backseat and made sure that she hadn't forgotten the pistol she'd taken from Nate's collection.

54

Stars to Stones

"Turn that phone off," Jake hissed at Olly.

"Sorry. My mom is taking some . . . trip. Out of the blue. I dunno."

He had a moment of strange, raw, reflexive anger at Maddie. He couldn't see his own pain like he could other people's, but he could damn sure *imagine* it. Right now it was a writhing, roiling thing. His mother maybe didn't deserve his resentment, but he felt what he felt. Besides, she was right; she *hadn't* been there for him, not really. But then he warred with himself because had *he* been there for *her*? The stupidest thought went through his head suddenly: *Being human is stupid, because being human is really, really hard.* He came back to the room as Jake snapped fingers in front of him.

"We're trying to get your dad back, remember?"

"Sorry."

"You need to focus the fuck up. This is interference. Distraction. Okay?"

Oliver nodded.

The two of them sat on the floor of Jake's trailer.

The Book of Accidents lay splayed out between them, open to a page. The logbook entry at the top of the page said:

Found O'Grady dead at the end of 5th level, tunnel 8, the Muldoon
*   Seam. His throt was cut*

But then those words began to tremble.

"Concentrate," Jake said.

"Yeah."

Oliver did as asked. He focused on the sentences—

McClellan gone mad
Talking to the walls
Tunnel 8 collapsed
Posner said he saw something down here
an animal like a "giant crab"
Found bloody knife in Posner's gear wraped in cloth
Posner killed O'Grady
Closing Ramble Rocks indefinitely

And then those sentences all began to vibrate, like bee wings at the honeycomb. It even made that sound in the back of his ear, deep in the back of his skull, at the base of his neck: *vvvvvvvmmmmmm.* The book moved into sharper focus even as the rest of the room slid into a greasy blur. It seemed to rise as the room seemed to fall.

Jake whispered: "It's happening."

It was. Oliver could feel it. That feeling of falling once more.

The void rose up around him. Broken stars shined fractured light in this infinite hematoma. And he wasn't alone, either. Jake was in here with him, somewhere. But there was something else, too, moving along the margins like a shark swimming just out of view, behind a reef.

Then, suddenly, the stars began to move.

Or am I the one that's moving?

Oliver did not know for certain, only that the stars were getting closer—all of them, which meant they were coming to him, not he to them, because if he were the one moving, wouldn't some stars be closer, and others farther away? Did anything work like normal here?

The void began to shift and shimmer. The stars grew brighter and brighter, and as they closed in, he could more easily see the fractures in them: The light came through them at janky and improbable angles, as if cast through a cracked prism. The light hurt his eyes, made him queasy. He found his throat full of something wet, something that tasted of blood—

The stars became stones. Rocks, boulders, like the ones in Ramble Rocks. No, not *like* the ones, but the exact same—a scattering of stones next to each other, but these were different in that they, like the stars, were fractured. Split in twain. Darkness shining out in sheer-cliff bands. They moved and trembled like the words on the page and—

A whisper slid through the void. Not from Jake. But from somewhere—some*thing*—something else.

(The book?)

It whispered of pain and cancer. It hissed of trauma and scar tissue. *To kill the cancer, cut out the cancer,* it said. *To stop the pain, end the pain.*

Break the wheel, remake the wheel.

In the center of it all, a new stone arose—this one, unlike the others. A flat, table-like stone. Almost anvil shaped. He saw Jake on the other side of it. Hands out, almost touching it. Oliver touched it, too, felt the cool grooves in the stone, well worn as if they were made not by human tools but by the slow erosion of water

(blood)

and time.

He traced his finger along those grooves to the center of the table, which bore a hole worn down through it.

And as he touched it, his world contracted in a lightning flash. He saw something there in the pulsing white: a glimpse of his father splayed out on the table, a great sucking hole in the center of his chest, his heartsblood pumping out in erratic regurgitations, like a milkshake in a broken blender, slopping out the top. Dad's lips were purple. His eyes so bloodshot, the whites had gone all the way red.

He tried to say a word—"Oliver"—but the name was cut off in a bloody burp, and then, as the blood crawled out underneath him down those smooth grooves, eight grooves, their channels cast out like spider's legs, the light went out of his father's eyes and—

Oliver screamed. He backpedaled away. He contracted all of his body and folded in on himself, metaphorically at first but then literally, as he felt like an imploding galaxy, a reverse supernova. His scream echoed out and roared back, and it flayed the void to ribbons, it turned the rocks to dust, and he heard Jake calling his name, farther and farther away—

55

Eject or Die

It felt like being thrown off a bucking horse. Oliver tumbled backward, using the momentum to half-crabwalk away, his arms and legs scrambling to stop him from bowling all the way over.

He tasted blood. Closed his eyes for a moment and wished like hell he hadn't—because when he did, behind the lids, he saw his father there on that table, dying upon it, his chest blown open, *all that blood*—

Jake, already standing, staggered over to Oliver. He offered a hand.

"No," Olly said, waving it away. "Not . . . not yet. I just need to—I just need to sit."

Nodding, Jake sat back down.

"That was some shit," Jake said.

"Yeah. Yeah it was." His throat felt like he was trying to swallow a batch of dead, dry pine needles. "My father—"

"He's dead, Olly. I'm sorry to say that, but he's gone."

"You don't know that—it could be some other Nate, or just a vision."

"The book shows truth, Olly. You can feel that, can't you? Your pops, he's gone."

"I can't—I can't do this," Oliver said abruptly, standing up. For a moment, as he looked to the older boy, he *swore* he saw something there—something *moving* inside his left eye. A shadow. Like an eel, whiptailing across the shifting sea. He shook it off. That didn't make any sense, did it? He staggered to the corner of the room and dry heaved—there wasn't much to throw up, since he'd eaten very little over the past few days. A string of bile spit hung from his lip.

"Oliver, we have to go there," Jake said, insistent. "We have to go to Ramble Rocks. To the place we watched your pops die, man. Just to see."

"No," Oliver bleated. He wiped his chin and stumbled to the front door. "I have to go home. I can't do this right now."

"Right now is the time we have." That, spoken through gritted teeth. He heard the urgency in Jake's voice. It was a plea, but beneath it ran a deep river of something else: anger. Not that he could see it— even still, Jake's anger and fear were hidden from him. But he was sure he heard it in there. Why would Jake be angry with him? Why the impatience?

Oliver couldn't reckon with that. He didn't have the spoons. So all he could do was push his way out the front door and leave. Jake called after him again and again, but Oliver, dreary and dizzy, heartsick and gut-sick, kept walking. All the while thinking about his father, dead on that stone.

Eschaton

So close.

So fucking close.

Jake roared. He kicked over the coffee table. He twisted his hand in midair, pulled the knife that lurked in the In-Between, and stabbed it into the couch again and again and again, until foam bits were bleeding out.

The Book of Accidents, on the floor, murmured and stirred with a pulse of resentment and disappointment.

It had told him what he needed to do.

It had been right all along.

It was always right.

He spun the knife, and marched out into the dark. Oliver had a several-minute head start. But he'd catch up. And when he did—

He'd usher this world to its conclusion.

The Hunt

Late night, almost midnight. His bike was still bent, so Oliver walked home instead.

He was tired. He just wanted to lie down and go to sleep for a long time. The image of his father dying on that rock haunted him. He feared that sleeping would only bring it back in nightmare, but it was already here behind his waking eyes—so, best he could hope for was a black, dreamless rest. A respite. His dad, dying on that rock . . . was it real? Was it true? Could the magic of the book have been deceiving him? For a moment he thought about leaving the road and straying through the park—to find the field of rocks and stones, to look for the table stone. But he resisted.

Don't give in to it.

But another voice begged him to.

I can't do this. I can't handle it.

Just go home.

Get some sleep.

How much sleep had he had? How much had he eaten? Too little.

As he walked home, Oliver was so lost to his own thoughts that he did not see who was following him back there in the deep, endless dark.

The Lodge

It was after midnight when Maddie arrived at the Barn Fox Lodge. Though on the way she'd passed the hallmarks of rural Pennsyltucky life (bait shops, antique malls, KOA campgrounds, trailer parks), the lodge was no such exemplar of that world. It was a sprawling series of cabins on a massive estate—even in the dark she could see it splayed out in all its rustic modern majesty. Signs alongside the parking lot marked the directions to the spa, the pickleball court, the stables, the café. It wasn't chintzy like some of the resorts up in the Poconos, where you and your newly married loved one (or escort) could take a rose-scented bubble bath in a jet tub that looked like a giant Champagne glass.

No, this place was high class. And it was high dollar.

She went into the main office, where she met a young man in a twisty mustache, a flannel shirt, and, of all the hipster bullshit, a bow tie. There she fulfilled her reservation with a credit card and got the keys to one of the cabins.

"Oh, I have a friend staying here," she said, faking like it was an offhand comment. "He's a writer, his name is Jed? Though possible he's going by John Edward. Last name, Homackie. Do you know what room he's in? I might pop by in the morning."

But the young man wasn't having any of it. "Sorry. Lodge policy is to not give out any information about guests. But if such a person was staying here, I'd be happy to take a note, leave it for them."

"It's meant to be a surprise."

"You could text them that you're here."

She forced a smile. "Like I said, a surprise."

"Of course. Sorry."

Maddie nodded. "It's fine. Thanks for your help."

"You're in cabin thirty-four," he said.

"Right. Have a nice night."

He didn't even *you too* her. The little mustachioed prick.

All that meant she was going to have to do this on her own. She took the carry-on out of the Subaru and ditched it in her room first—taking only a moment to regale herself in the glow of a palace of ultimate comfort. Big four-poster bed. White bear rug. A personal fireplace. Bathroom with a massive two-showerhead shower behind frosted glass, and a spa tub replete with the fanciest of beauty products. Art on the walls. A little waterfall by a huge back window. A *second* loft bedroom up a set of wooden spiral steps. In a better world, she'd flop on the bed, arms out in a comfy Christ pose, and let out a barbaric yawp of pure relaxation.

But this was not that world, not that day. The night was long, her husband was missing, and the man who knew what happened was *here*.

She had work to do, so she got to it.

Jed drove a black Lexus NX SUV, and it didn't take long to find it at the far end of the lodge parking lot, near a series of larger, more luxurious cabins. Problem was, those cabins were nestled together five at a time, laid out like the petals of a flower surrounding a central courtyard—whose fountain was turned off for the season but festooned with twinkling white Christmas lights.

Impatience itched her every nerve, but Maddie knew she couldn't go pounding on doors and staring in windows. Were she caught, *she'd* be the one on the hook for it.

No, she had to do this right.

As much as she wanted to retire to the lap of luxury that was her cabin, she had to stay out here instead. In the car. In the cold. Sipping cold coffee she'd picked up at a Sheetz gas station.

It's like a stakeout, she told herself.

Jed would come out eventually. And when he did, she'd have him.

Thump thump thump.

Maddie gasped awake at the wheel of the car. She blinked, her eyes gone blurry, slowly adjusting as she figured out what was making the noise.

Shit, I fell asleep!

Thump thump thump.

A shadow darkened her. Someone was at the window, the driver's side, and she turned to see who was there—

It was him.

It was Jed.

He peered in through the glass, one eyebrow raised in a curious, even sinister arch. Then he held up something else. A gun. No, not just any gun—the revolver she'd brought with her, the one from her bag. He showed her the bright whites of his teeth (*veneers,* she thought madly), and then he pressed the barrel against the glass of the window as she crawl-leaped over the center console toward the passenge-side door—

The gun went off and she felt the bullet go into the back of her skull—

Bang.

She heard the gunshot, loud as anything in her ear, and she lurched awake at the wheel of the Subaru. Daylight bled in, washed in winter gray (even though it was only November). Her eyes felt sticky. Her mouth felt dry. And the back of her skull throbbed with the memory of a gunshot.

The *dream* memory of a gunshot, she told herself.

Just the same, she had fallen asleep and—

The sound, the gunshot, she realized suddenly, that was something. Something real, creeping into her sleeping mind.

A car door closing.

Because just ahead of her, the black SUV came alive, its taillights red as demon eyes as it began to back out slowly from the space. The glare on the window prevented her from seeing who was driving, but she knew who it had to be. As the SUV left the parking lot, she started her own car and eased it out onto the road, following Jed Homackie.

I got you, she thought.

59

Another Way

Behind him somewhere, Oliver heard the sound of something popping underneath a tire—a hickory nut, maybe. Popping with a crunch. But no headlights washed over him. All remained dark.

His pulse quickened—his awareness was not concrete or complete, but rather just in the *feel* of things. Something was off. Was someone out there? Following him?

He turned to look behind him.

Nothing at first, but then—

Sure enough, a good ways back, he could see something—a silver mercury moon gleam. Light on metal. A car.

Its headlights, off.

"Shit," he said, the word coming out in a puff of visible breath.

Headlights came on, bright and terrible as God's own judgment.

There came a few beats, tick, tock, tick, tock, as if Oliver and the car were regarding each other—

Then the tires spun, squealing as the car surged forward, the bright lights like a pair of fireballs roaring down the ribbon of road.

Oliver cried out and tried to run, and he managed a few steps, but his foot caught some loose gravel and next thing he knew, he tumbled forward. His hands caught his fall, the palms stinging. He got his legs underneath him and launched forward anew—

A car sped past him, then cut hard in front of him. Oliver cried out as he again braced himself with his bleeding, stung hands, this time against the silver paint of a new Mercedes.

The door to the car whipped open, and out stepped Graham Lyons.

"Graham—" Oliver said.

Just as Lyons pistoned a fist into his stomach.

Oliver *oofe*d and doubled over.

"I saw you out here walking. And I figured, why not pay my good friend *Oliver Graves* a visit? Besides, we have unfinished business."

And now, the memory of being held facedown in a ditch puddle by Alex Amati surfaced anew, and his knees nearly buckled at the memory of it. But something else surfaced: Oliver's anger.

"You see this?" Graham said, shoving his busted right hand in Oliver's face. Still, after two months, it remained splinted. "I went in yesterday for surgery and you know what happened? They said I had two tendons, not one, damaged. Flexor and tensor, whatever the hell they are. And that means I'm out. Out of baseball. I won't get in for my second surgery until after Thanksgiving. Then it'll be three months of recovery. Plus physical therapy. December, January, February. Maybe I can rejoin practice in March, but they said I might not have full movement back for a *year*. A year!"

He popped another fist into Oliver's middle.

Oliver summoned some strength—enough, at least, not to puke from being punched in the stomach. He sucked up a string of spit that had been dangling from his lip. "Too bad," he said weakly. "Guess you'll actually have to *learn* some stuff for once to get into college."

Graham roared, spun Oliver around handily, and slammed him up against the side of the silver Mercedes. He placed his busted hand under Oliver's jaw, grabbing it so hard, Oliver could feel the pressure on his teeth. But he also felt something else: the finger brace. It bit into Oliver's skin.

The pain in Graham surged: a black shape, coiling and uncoiling like it couldn't get comfortable. It filled most of him now, like it was feeding on itself, a mad emotional infection on the petri dish that was Graham Lyons. Growing and swelling until he was nothing but pure anguish and anger.

"You snotty little prick," Graham hissed.

"What do you want from me, Lyons?" Oliver choked out. "You did this to yourself. Thing is, I think you know that. And you hate it."

At that, the pain in Graham Lyons *twitched*.

"You know what I want from you?" Graham grabbed Oliver's hand, then started to bend back the pinky and ring finger, sending a fresh twist of agony corkscrewing up his hand, his wrist, his arm. "I want you to hurt like I hurt. I want you to know this pain. Maybe your tendons will pop. Maybe I'll just *break*"—and here he ratcheted the digits back, forcing a cry from Oliver's lips—"these fingers like a couple of fucking pencils. Unless you have something else I can take away from you? What do you cherish most, Oliver Graves? Your daddy? He's already gone, isn't he—"

Crying out, Oliver drove a knee into Graham's crotch. Lyons squealed, and Oliver wrenched his hand free. With Graham doubled over, Oliver took his knee again and popped it hard into Lyons's face—the other boy's nose mashed like a soft potato. Oliver gave him a shove.

Graham fell over, alongside the tire of his car.

He whimpered, panting.

His ski jacket was open, his shirt pulled up, showing his ribs.

The light from inside the Mercedes dimly highlighted the dark bruises there, and the fresh scar tissue. Graham, seeing Oliver staring, quickly pushed his shirt back down over the injuries. Which only seemed to confirm for Oliver what he was looking at. Graham's pain recoiled, as if hiding from the light—or maybe hiding from the revelation of what Oliver had seen.

It's alive, Oliver thought. The pain itself was alive.

It was inside Graham.

A part of him.

But *given* to him. Like a parasite. An invasive species.

I can . . .

An idle, incomplete thought. Can what? The idea began in Oliver's head but did not end there. It simply hung like a hook on a wall with nothing dangling from it. He felt compelled to take a step forward. At which Graham shuffled his body backward, saying, "Get away."

He's scared of me.

Oliver took another step.

"I'm sorry," Oliver said.

He offered a hand.

Graham looked at his hand like it was a piece of dog shit. But Oliver didn't pull it back. Instead, he gave it a little impatient shake, as if to say, *Shut up and just take the hand.*

The other boy rolled his eyes and said, *"Fine,"* before reaching out and grabbing onto Oliver. And as Oliver pulled Graham up—

The pain in Graham Lyons recoiled again. As if the pain itself were a living thing, and had been hurt—and boy, did that ever bake Oliver's lasagna. Causing pain *to* pain? Was that even a thing? How? It was crazy.

The other boy stood, but Oliver didn't let go.

"I'm sorry about your finger," Oliver said. The pain flashed, from dark to bright, like an electrical shock. "I'm sorry that it makes you worry about who you are and what you're worth."

"You don't know what the fuck you're talking about—" The pain shuddered again, writhing.

"I'm sorry you're in pain and that somebody hurt you, but it doesn't have to define you, Graham."

"Fuck you, Oliver." But Graham didn't pull away. His grip softened. His knees dipped a little as they nearly buckled. The thick mucus of misery in his middle contracted and pulsed. "You don't know *anything.*"

"I do," Oliver said, and it wasn't a lie. How he knew, he wasn't sure.

Maybe it was being so tired, so stripped down to the wire. Maybe it was seeing that vision of his father on that table stone. Maybe the book had awakened something in him, for good or bad.

But he suddenly understood things in a way he never had before.

Oliver let go of Graham.

And then he reached inside of him.

Or that's how it felt, at least—he felt his hand grab hold of something, something that thrashed in his grip. It was the pain inside of Graham, the misery, the fear, and it shrieked like a rabbit under the claws of a cat—

Oliver felt his gaze tumble backward into his own skull, and the space between them, above his nose, suffered suddenly an *intense* pressure, as if he were lying back on a bed and someone had just balanced an entire table there by its leg—it felt like concrete in his sinuses, like a *fist* pressing into the fore of his brain, and a flood of awful feelings rushed in. He felt a belt whipping him in the side. He remembered a fastball pitched at him so hard it took a bone chip out of his hip. He remembered crying into a pillow that wasn't his, in a bedroom that wasn't his, in a house that was not his. He heard the names and accusations echoing in his ear: *Nancy, faggot, waste-of-space, you got the yips, keep your eye on the ball, are you stupid, are you slow, are you some kind of retard, you're a disappointment, Graham, that's all you are, one big disappointment, you've crapped on my legacy*

you're not a winner

you're a loser

loser!

LOSER

Oliver's hand burned like it was on fire, and he cried out, his fist closing on the thing that squirmed like an eel.

He squeezed—

It began to bulge and distend—

Graham screamed—

The inky black thing *popped*, wet and viscous—

And then it was gone. All of it. None of it remained—at least, not physically. Graham tumbled backward again, back onto the ground. Oliver nearly fell himself, bracing his fall against the car and the passenger-side mirror. He gasped as sweat poured out of him, soaking him through. Then he turned and puked. This time, something came out—a flood of dark matter and oily liquid.

For a while, all was quiet. Just the sound of wind through winter-dead branches—a papery, crisp whisper. Oliver wiped his mouth. The barf-taste stuck to his tongue. But he tasted blood, too. And sickness.

"Graham," he moaned, standing up.

Graham was flat on his back. His eyes empty. Mouth agape. He looked feverish. Inside him now, the pain remained—but it was small. Manageable. Like most people's, it was just a little thing

(like a baseball)

sitting at the center of him.

Oliver stared. He wanted to say something, but had nothing to say. The thought ran laps around his head: *I killed him. I killed him. I killed him.*

And then, Graham gasped loud, lurching upright—the gasp was a keening, sucking breath, a howl that made Oliver clench up.

Then he looked around, his gaze eventually falling to Oliver.

"Hey," Graham said, his voice small, his expression dazed.

"Hey."

Silence filled the space between them.

"Something just happened," Graham said.

"Yeah." Oliver coughed a little. "Are you—are you okay?"

"I feel . . . kind of amazing."

"You do?"

"I do. Yeah. I feel . . ." Graham seemed like he was searching for words. "Lighter, somehow. Clear." Another pause. *"Calm."*

"Oh. That's good."

Graham grunted as he stood up. Again Oliver helped him, though this time there was no reach out with his hand to touch the other boy's forehead. Graham thanked him and said, "Do you need a ride?"

"A ride."

"Yeah, like, to your house. Your home."

"S . . . sure."

Graham, still half-dazed, said, "Hop in."

"I'm sorry about your dad," Graham said, as he pulled into Oliver's driveway. The ride was a short one—just five minutes—and in it, neither really said much. Graham mostly watched the road, and Oliver mostly watched, well, *Graham*. But now? This.

"It's okay."

"It's not. It's not cool. I knew he was missing and I couldn't see past my own bullshit to be nice to you for five minutes about it. And I said something awful to you. Like I was happy to hurt you. God, that's fucked up. What was wrong with me?"

He eased up next to the house, and left the engine idling.

"We all have bullshit to deal with," Oliver said.

"Yeah, but this was something else."

Pain like a parasite. Pain that was given to him.

Oliver decided to take a risk and said: "I'm sorry about your dad, too. I don't think he's very good to you, Graham."

"Yeah. Yeah." Graham tapped the steering wheel with index finger and thumb, a little distracted drumbeat. "My father is not a good guy. And I think I've always known that, but I also think I convinced myself otherwise. That he was some kind of hero. Truth is, I think he's a failure himself, didn't live up to his own standards—or maybe the standards of my grandfather—and so now he's putting all that weight, that pressure on me. Because it's easier for him to push it off on me. Does that make sense? God, it sounds like it makes sense. I'm talking a lot. I feel like I'm high."

"I don't think you're high." Oliver shrugged. "I think maybe you're just . . . having a moment of clarity."

"It's definitely clarity, but it's more than a moment."

"Maybe that's good."

Graham finally turned toward him. "You did this to me."

"I'm sorry."

"Don't be. I'm okay."

"You're sure?"

Graham smiled. "Yeah. *Yeah*. I, uhhh. I'm better than okay. I feel good. Like you said, *clear*. Whatever you did, it was something special, man. I feel like I just had a splinter taken out of me. You're a weird kid, Oliver. I'm sorry I made your life kinda shitty."

"It was okay. It all . . . worked out. I really am sorry about your hand, and I hope it doesn't impact your future."

"Maybe you were right. I can't play ball forever. I think I was just mad about things in my life I didn't control and that not getting to play baseball meant I didn't know who I even was anymore, and with my father breathing down my neck and calling me dummy and beating on me I just wanted to control *something,* and so I guess I chose to punish you instead of owning my own problems, a sign of my power at a time I felt I had none, *aaand* I think I'm saying all my thoughts out loud. Again, am I high? Is this therapy? This feels like therapy." He laughed and craned his head back. "Oh, fuck, Oliver, this is weird."

Yeah, it's weird for me, too, Oliver thought.

"Thanks," Oliver said.

"I hope they find your dad."

"Me too, I miss him."

"I bet you do." A sad look settled on Graham's face. "I miss mine, too. He was okay, once upon a time. Or maybe I just hadn't seen who he really was."

"What happens now?"

"Between him and me? I don't know. I'm not gonna let him keep doing what he's doing. Which will be hard. But I have to own that and make a change. As for you and me . . ."

"Yeah."

"I'll just see you at school."

"Okay."

"You're different than everybody else, you know that?"

"I don't think I really knew it before tonight."

"See you, Olly."

"See you, Graham."

Oliver got out of the car, and watched it pull away. All the while being entirely unsure what had just happened, or if it had even happened at all. He didn't know whether to laugh or cry, whether to be afraid or excited, or if he should just give in to all of it and go mad.

One thing he knew, though: He was fucking *hungry.*

He ate like a fiend. Frozen pizza. Bag of chips. Made himself a milkshake with some old vanilla ice cream in the freezer, and he didn't have much milk so he used heavy cream and it was *thick* and *impossible to drink* and totally amazing. He was *still* hungry so he found a bag of carrots and ate them like a starving rabbit.

He *still* felt famished, but he held off, certain he'd make himself sick.

Just like earlier, he thought. He remembered himself puking on the side of the road after he . . . took something out of Graham Lyons.

No. Not something.

Pain. He took his pain. Not all the way away—but he pulled something out of him. Like a cancer that was excised. It left some part behind—some healthy part, or healthy pain, maybe. Pain that looked like everybody else's. But the multiplicative, consumptive pain that was in him? It acted like a poison, or a disease. And Oliver took it out. A bloodletting to let out the rotten, sick blood.

The Book of Accidents—what had it told him?

To kill the cancer, cut out the cancer.

To stop the pain, end the pain.

Break the wheel, remake the wheel.

He had done that. And now Graham was . . . different. Better.

Fixed, he thought. He'd taken the parasite inside him, pain delivered unto him, and he'd ripped it out. Then he thought, if he could get his father back, could he do the same to him? Could he grab all that pain, all that fear and anger and terror, and rip it out?

60

The Splinter

Come morning, Oliver waited outside, in the chill of November. He stood in the driveway, and Caleb's shitty sedan pulled up alongside him.

"Olly. Get in."

Oliver still felt buzzy from the night before. Like, he knew his father was missing, maybe dead. But what if he could get him back? With Jake's help—maybe he could. And then he could help his father the way he'd helped Graham. Who else could he help? He felt like a fucking *superhero.*

He felt almost literally like he was flying. Buoyant, unanchored. Sitting there in the passenger seat, he just kinda *babbled.*

"I dunno, Graham Lyons and I had a moment last night, I think—like, I think we understood one another for the first time. We saw each other's pain and we dealt with it." He did not mention that he also seemed to pull out part of the boy's pain—some kind of evil eel? "Not trying to excuse the way he is, I just mean, some of the way he is was because of what was given to him, or put in him, or whatever. And it made me happy to connect with him on that level. Which is fucked up, right? Because my own dad is gone. And I'm sad about that. Really sad. But I also feel happy about having talked to Graham. Is that weird? That I feel both things? Happy and sad?"

"Nah, Olly, dude, listen. Life's fucked up. It just is. It's got ups and downs and I say it's worse not appreciating the good things, because then what's the point? It's like the Native Americans used to say, right? *Gotta use all of the buffalo.* Life is a whole damn animal, and you can't waste any part of it."

"Thanks, Caleb. That's actually . . . really smart."

"That's me, man, stable genius." He laughed. "Want more genius-level shit? I dunno if you should be trusting Graham Lyons far as you can throw him—or, haha, I guess far as he can throw a baseball now. *Yeah, that's right, I said it.* Him with his busted-ass paw. Don't trust Graham. Don't trust Jake."

"I don't know, either. Jake and I have a . . . complicated relationship."

"Yeah, well. Just be cautious. Don't trust too easily."

Olly nodded as they pulled into the school parking lot. "I'm feeling pretty good right now. I feel . . . like people are more trustworthy than they are not. Like they're more *good* than they are *bad.*" And maybe sometimes when people were bad, they didn't mean to be.

Closing the door and locking it by hand, Caleb said, "I'm just saying, Olly, don't be surprised if you step in that school and Graham Lyons drags you into the bathroom, dunks your head in a urinal."

"I really think Graham and I had a moment—"

Someone passed by them in the parking lot. It was Alice Handelmann, one of the jazz band geeks. Big eyes. Ginger locks. She said, "Are you talking about Graham?"

"Yeah," Caleb said, giving a little chin-lifting nod.

"It's fucking *crazy,* right?" she said, shaking her head. She whirled past them. Oliver and Caleb stopped about twenty steps from the entrance to school. Kids streamed in, but slow, real slow. Some came back out. Something was up.

"Yo, hold up. You get a weird vibe from everybody?"

Oliver looked around, and at first, he didn't get it—but then, he saw. People coming together and talking, and people wore faces of confusion, shock, sadness. A girl, Shveta Shastri, was full-on *bawling.*

Pain bloomed in them. Passed from person to person, like a gift—or a curse.

Caleb caught someone's elbow—Dave Turner, photographer for the school paper and the yearbook. "Dave, hey. What's the deal?"

"You didn't hear?" Dave asked in a low tone.

"Hear what?"

"Graham Lyons killed himself last night. But not before he took his father with him."

The day's classes were canceled. Midday they held a short assembly where Principal Myers said without detail what had happened, and they had a short presentation—a slideshow with some video and audio clips—of Graham Lyons. At dances, or laughing in the hallway with friends, or, most often, at a baseball game at bat or sliding into home plate. Coach Griffin, the baseball coach, spoke. So did Norcross, the gym teacher. One of the English teachers read the A. E. Housman poem "To an Athlete Dying Young."

Afterward they made available all the guidance counselors, plus a community grief counselor and a local Presbyterian minister, for anyone who wanted to talk out their grief. The remainder of the day was mostly a kind of slow, dreamy chaos. Nobody knew whether to honor him or revile him: He'd taken his own life, which was sad. But he'd killed his father first, which was murder. Stories popped up about how his dad beat him, or how maybe the abuse was sexual in nature, and then those stories became worse—just guesses and lies that threatened to become true, *Oh I heard his dad pimped him out to all the Richie Riches around here* or *I heard Graham was a choir boy at St. Agnes once and you know what that means* or *Maybe it's like those stories about politicians diddling kids and peddling underage ass in pizza shops.*

All Oliver knew was:

This was his fault.

Somehow, it was his damn fault.

What he'd taken from Graham had done something. Emptied him out, but maybe didn't fill him back up again. He didn't know, didn't understand. He broke the wheel, like the book said—but somehow, that turned Graham crazy. Turned him into a killer.

I did this to him, Oliver thought. And now Graham was dead.

61

The Things We Carry

Maddie followed Jed to three different places:

First, a used bookstore just outside the one-stoplight town of Falls Creek. It was a square brick building with a sign out front: FALLS CREEK BOOKS. A bright pink piece of poster board hung in the window, and someone had written on it in marker: *Certified pre-owned literature!* In the window, a plump tabby-cat slept in a pile of itself.

The bookstore parking lot was small and gravel lined, and she was afraid she'd be spotted there. So Maddie parked down the highway a ways, but close enough to keep the store in sight.

Jed came out after about a half hour, carting an armload of big books, maybe old textbooks, maybe dictionaries.

The second place he went was a burger place called Jack's. Looked old, like it was once a walk-up counter that someone had built a restaurant onto. Still had the patio and the outdoor seating, but Jed went inside and stayed in. She parked in the back of the lot, and could see him sitting alone in a booth. He had a hamburger, some fries, and a big, thick milkshake. He seemed to relish it. Head back. Eyes closed. Long pauses between bites marked by a gentle cleanup with a napkin of his mouth, his cheeks, his chin, his fingers. It was now she noted that he had cleaned himself up. Jed looked put-together. A new man.

You sonofabitch.

On, then, to the third and final place:

The hardware store.

An Ace Hardware, on the corner of that one-stoplight intersection. He went in and came out pretty quick, a plastic bag of something or somethings in his hand. She couldn't see what everything was, but one thing stuck out the top of it, at least—

A bundle of rope. Nylon cord the color of Mountain Dew.

Her heart nearly leapt out of her chest.

She thought: *I need to call the cops.* It was time to let this go and let *them* know where Jed was. That was the responsible thing to do. But, at the same time, she reminded herself—there was a lot more going on here than she could casually explain to the police. She hadn't even told Fig all of it. How could she? Ghosts and sculptures come alive and freak storms . . .

No, she had to see Jed first. Herself. Without anyone else there.

But the good news was: If he had rope? Then he needed it to tie someone up. Which meant maybe, just maybe, he had Nate.

Alive.

62

The Fox and the Fucking Grapes

*G*otcha.

Maddie watched Jed park. She watched as he got out, taking the stack of books in his arms, the hardware bag balanced precariously atop it. She saw which cabin was his as he made a beeline toward it. At that she thought, *Now is the time.* Maddie tucked the gun in her waistband and got out of the car, following far enough behind so that he didn't think to throw a casual glance in her direction. She stalked him, a lioness on the veldt hunting her prey. He went in through the cabin door, closing it quickly with a kick. It slammed shut even as she reached for it. Her pulse quickened as rage and impatience ran roughshod.

That frustration made her want to stand firm, shoot open the knob, put bullets in the hinges—*It's a door all right,* she remembered Nate saying to her, the first day in their new old house. *One knob, two hinges.*

But that would attract attention.

She could knock. Soon as he answered, she'd stick the gun in the gap, force her way in. Then it came time to question herself: Would she really kill him, if it came to it? The answer came too easy, so easy she dared not give it any further thought. (Some dark corners needed no light.) Better instead to focus on her strategy: This cabin sat in a courtyard with four others. At any point someone could come through as she was jamming a gun through the open door.

Around this enclave of five cabins was a tall hedge, which itself was hemmed in by tall pine trees. And the hedge—some kind of evergreen boxwood—left a substantial enough gap between it and the cabin to give her room to maneuver. Maddie quickly sidled along the edge of the cabin, deciding the best way in would be a window— maybe, just maybe, they were unlocked. How good was the housekeeping staff at closing and locking all windows? At a luxury place like this, she had to imagine good—too good for her to have much hope, but still, best to check.

Lo and behold, around back?

One window, already cracked open.

Heat from inside the cabin bled out, warming her hands.

She peered in the window and saw a bedroom—one similar to the bedroom in Maddie's own cabin. No one was in the room. Had Jed opened the window to have some cold, crisp air at night? Or was it something else?

Maddie used her thumbs to gently ease the window open. She hooked her elbows over the ledge and hauled herself up and over, onto a soft cork floor. Her body made a *fwud* when it landed, and she instantly coiled up, pulling the gun.

The door to the bedroom was ajar.

On the bed was his suitcase.

From outside the room—the living area, she guessed—she heard a thumping. Like something being stacked up. *The books?* she wondered. But why? Another sound followed: a *vvvip vipp* like the sound of a kid walking in snow pants, and then the crunch of knots being cinched up. He grunted, breathing loudly at times.

He was occupied.

Now's the time, she thought.

With that, Maddie stood, taking special care not to knock anything over. Gingerly she crept toward the bedroom door. The doorknob was cold in her hand—

And here again her mind went somewhere else. Some memory

slipping quick into shadow. Another door, this one in her mind, closed, locking before she could open it.

Maddie drew a breath, then let it out. *Now's not the time to be crazy, Maddie. Just open the fucking door. This one. The real one in front of you*—the doors in her mind could wait.

She eased open the door—

John Edward Homackie was up off the ground, standing on the stack of books he'd just bought—with a noose made of neon-lime cord around his neck, the other end tossed over an exposed log beam and tied to the bone-white antlers of a wooden elk sculpture hanging over a massive stone fireplace.

The rope was nearly taut.

Jed and Maddie locked eyes.

Then he moved his right foot, and used it to knock the stack of books over. The tower toppled, and Jed dropped far enough for the rope to tighten, for the noose to pull snug around his neck. Instantly his arms stiffened and his legs kicked. He swung. The man's eyes bulged and Maddie felt frozen in a panic—her gut constricted even as she thought, *Good, fuck you, hang, you bastard,* and it took pushing through that to realize she hadn't found her husband, or any information about him at all. Jed couldn't die. Jed needed to *live.*

Maddie gasped, gun still in hand, and rushed to grab his legs and lift him up. He wasn't a big man, but he felt heavier than she expected—and she was strong, strong enough to heft logs and haul a chainsaw around. So she was able to lift him, taking the pressure off the throat-closing noose. Groaning, she worked to take her hand—the one without the gun—and reach up to loosen the rope. But Jed started smacking at her, pushing her. Words gabbled out of his mouth, a panicked gush of nonsense.

"Stop it," she hissed. *"Stop struggling—"*

"Nnngh," he grunted.

Both of his hands grabbed her shoulders and *pushed.*

Her heel caught on one of the books—

Maddie lost her grip on him, and next thing she knew, she was down on the ground, the air horse-kicked from her chest, and again Jed was dangling, his body jerking in the spasms of his encroaching demise.

Time seemed to go sloppy, slippery—her body felt like it was trying to jump up out of mud. She sucked in a hard breath and grabbed at his ankle to pull herself up—only realizing a second later that pulling *down* on the man's body was *killing him faster*. It was pure reflex, and one that was too late to bail on now, so she got her legs under her and launched up beneath him once more, hoisting him high. His legs bucked in her arms. Again he pushed at her. Gritting her teeth, she took the gun and slammed it hard against his side, into his kidneys. He tightened up, ceasing his assault long enough for her to get her hand back to the rope, opening the noose loop wide enough that his head slipped through it.

Together, the two of them tumbled to the ground.

Him, gasping.

Her, launching back to her feet, standing astride him, her chest heaving, the gun at her side.

"You should've just let me die," Jed babbled, bridges of spit connecting his lower lip to his upper. He sobbed without tears.

"There'll be time enough for that," she said. "Get up. I need to know what you did to Nate. *Where is my husband, you fucking monster?*"

Oliver paced in front of Jake, talking a mile a minute.

He went through it all: He told how when he'd left there the night before, Graham Lyons had followed him. They fought. And then . . .

"It wasn't just that I could *see* all the . . . all the nasty shit inside him; it was like, suddenly? Suddenly I could *touch* it. It felt like, I dunno, like you realized that not only could you see the world but now you could interact with it, you could reach out and *move something*," he said, the words falling out of him faster and faster. "I could affect it.

Touch it. Change it. And I did. I reached in. I took hold of that awfulness inside. It was terrible, Jake, it was the worst thing, like a . . . like sucking out a drain clog with your mouth and then throwing it back up, but also? Something worse. Something deeper. Like I could *feel* what his father did to him. And I could feel how much he hated that, and it all came out of him, into me, and then it was . . . gone. Just *gone*. And I thought things were okay. Graham seemed *okay*. I was okay, too." Tears threatened to break. "But then—"

"I saw the news," Jake said. "That's fucked up."

Jake sat on his couch, a half-drunk bottle of Mountain Dew pinched between his legs. Oliver stood before him now, plaintive, almost pleading.

"What happened?" Oliver asked. "Why did he do it? I did like the book said. I broke the wheel. I stopped the pain."

Because Oliver needed answers.

About something. About *anything*.

Jake sighed and shrugged. "I don't know, Oliver, I'm no expert—"

"You're the only one who even knows I can do what I can do. You—you have magic! You have the *book*. Please."

"Maybe . . . maybe you didn't go far enough."

A gross, ugly laugh came up out of Oliver—bitter and mad. "What? What do you mean?"

"You broke the wheel. But you didn't remake it. You just scooped him out, like a pumpkin—and then that pumpkin rotted. Listen, man, Lyons was built from what his father did to him, good or bad. He was full of bad wiring. You can't just rip that shit out and expect the place not to go dark. Or worse, catch fire and burn the hell down."

Panic throttled Oliver. He felt his chest tighten. "I didn't mean to—I didn't *intend for*—"

Jake stood, then blocked Oliver's frenetic pacing. "Listen. You did the best thing for him. Graham was fucked up. And he was made fucked up by an even more fucked-up father—a guy who beat on him and called him names and held him to impossible standards.

Guy like that was never gonna be anything more than a bully, a serial predator. A rapist, a wife beater." Jake offered a vigorous, uncaring shrug. "Now, they're both gone."

"No. *No.* I believe in second chances."

"This *is* their second chance."

"That doesn't make sense."

"It makes perfect sense. Graham saw it. He must've. You didn't fix shit. The father was still the father. Daddy Lyons wasn't gonna have some *come to Jesus* moment. He'd hurt Graham even more. Or . . . Graham would hurt him, instead. It's like cancer. Best thing you can do is—"

"Cut it out," Oliver said, his voice distant. The book had told him as much. Told them both. Maybe Jake had a point. *Shit shit shit.*

Jake put both hands on Oliver's shoulders and stared hard into his eyes. "Graham is better now dead and gone than he ever was alive. He's equal parts hometown hero and cautionary message. And his father . . . well, people will see that guy for what he was. All that will come out. Graham took control of the story. That's the real power."

Could that be?

Did that make sense to Oliver?

He didn't know. He felt so confused. Dizzy and lost.

Oliver pulled away from Jake. "This is all too fucked up. I can't believe I'm saying this but . . . I wish I could see Graham again. That I could keep talking to him. Talking him *through* this. I wish I could stop him."

Jake was silent for a while, until finally he said: "There's a way, Oliver. There's a way to bring him back. And to bring your father back, too. There's a way to undo all the harm, all the pain, to not just break the wheel, but to remake it." He lifted Oliver's chin, and Oliver looked him in the eyes. "Go with me. To Ramble Rocks, to the stones. I'll show you."

The world felt like it was spinning off its axis—like a twenty-sided die spinning on one of its points like a top, but never landing on a number.

"Do you trust me, Oliver?"

Slowly, Oliver nodded.

"Good. Because I trust you, too."

The hand towel hit Jed in the face.

"Clean yourself up," Maddie said, leveling the gun again after pitching the towel at him. "Towel off. Blow your nose. Clear your stupid throat. Then tell me everything."

He swallowed and nodded, honking as he blew his nose, then he coughed into it. Jed wiped his face afterward—a messy, clumsy order of operations, but Maddie didn't give a shit. He used the wet cloth to dab at his cord-burned neck, too, wincing as he delicately dabbed at it.

"You have to know that I'm sorry," he bleated.

"Fuck your apology."

He nodded. "I deserve that."

"What you deserve is to hang, like you wanted, but I can't let you have that yet, Jed."

An iciness flashed across his face—a dark shine in his eye. "Admittedly, this is a strange play, Maddie Graves. Pointing a gun at me to stop me from killing myself is not perhaps your wisest move."

"Oh, I get that, *Jed*. You want to know my play? My play is that I'll hurt you first. Smash your fingers, bang the gun against the bridge of your nose. Put a pillow over a kneecap and fire a bullet into it. It's death you want, then I'm going to make you *really* fucking want it, John Edward. And I'll keep you from it. Tantalizingly out of reach, like the fox and the fucking grapes. All until I get what I want."

She heard the words out of her mouth and she wondered:

Maddie, is this really you?

"Where is my husband, Jed?"

He wetted his lips with a gray-pink tongue. "What I'm going to tell you, Maddie—it's not going to sound sane. I know that. I understand—"

"I don't care how it sounds, just say it."

"He's gone. I took him to the park, to-to-to the tunnel. It was a trap—you need to understand that. I knew what it was going in. But it had a purpose, a grand design, it's not to be *cruel* or to be *vicious,* because I like Nate, I didn't want to see him hurt—"

She cracked him across the top of his head with the side of the gun. The cylinder dug into his skull—a black bruise spread fast, and blood ran through the trough of his wrinkles like water down a dry creek bed.

"Speak plainly. Is he dead?"

"Yes? No. I don't know."

She raised the gun again to hit him, and he held up his hands.

"Wait, wait," he cried. "I mean I can't say—he . . . disappeared, you see? He fell between worlds, lost from this one to . . . a place I'm assured is not safe, Maddie, not safe at all. Past the interstices, you see, past what I believe is known as the In-Between and to the collapse of all worlds—"

She growled. "None of this is making *any sense,* Jed."

"It was the boy."

"Boy? What boy?"

"*Jake.* I led Nate into that tunnel where . . . Jake sent him away."

"Jake—Oliver's *friend* Jake?"

"Oh, Maddie. It goes a lot deeper, and a lot stranger, than that. But yes. The one and the same."

She tensed up. "My son. Is he in danger?"

"Of the greatest kind, my dear. Of the greatest kind."

Darkness settled over, and then into, Ramble Rocks park, the trees and ground soaking up night like blood into a sponge. Oliver and Jake walked the north side of the park, heading toward the black-maw train tunnel. As they approached the tunnel, Oliver asked: "We don't have to go in there, do we?"

And Jake shook his head. "No."

Good, Oliver thought. Because that place suddenly radiated a special kind of darkness: a blackness thicker than shadow, bleak and foul and thick as a melted tire.

"We're not allowed to be out here at night, I don't think."

Jake chuffed a laugh. "Olly, dude, only you could be such a cop that you're worried about getting caught. We're talking about doing magic. World-bending magic. So maybe worry a little less about the laws of mortal man, yeah?"

"Yeah. I just—"

"You trust me, don't you?"

"I—yeah."

They came through the woods, and suddenly the tree line was gone, and the moon shone bright in an open sky—the expanse of the heavens spread out over a massive field of craggy, uneven rocks.

"We're almost there," Jake said. "Just a little farther."

Oliver sucked in a deep breath. When he spoke, he saw his breath, and it felt like watching little parts of himself leave—puffs of soul, a mist of who he was. His voice trembled with sudden fear as he said, "I just want to tell my mother where I'm going." At that, he pulled his phone out to call her. He saw that he had a text from her, but before he could read it, Jake snatched it from his grip.

"Hey!" Oliver protested.

"No phone," Jake hissed. "This place is a convergence of signals, kid. Sacred, magical signals. You bring that phone in here, you run the risk of us doing this for no reason at all. We, and your dad, and Graham? We'll all be dead, and *for nothing.*"

"I need that," Oliver insisted. "I saw a text—"

"You'll get it back. *When we're done.* Your mother just said everything was fine, she'd be home soon."

"I want to talk to her. I want to tell her—"

"No. You do that, then what? She'll call the cops. Or send your dad's buddy, that Fish and Game guy. No. No way, Olly."

Jake twirled the phone in his hand—

And it disappeared. Going, as Oliver suspected, to the In-Between.

There was *something*, though. Something curious that Oliver had not seen before: When Jake made the phone disappear, there was the briefest burst, a *dark glimmer* of sorts, around his hand. Like a spray of liquid shadow. It appeared around his hand, a black, wet halo, and then it contracted and was gone when the phone disappeared.

What the heck was *that*, and what did it mean?

On the screen, the text to Oliver read:

> Oliver, something is wrong. I found Jed. He said Jake is dangerous. Stay away from him, Oliver.

Then a second text:

> STAY AWAY FROM JAKE

Jake read that after telling Oliver the bullshit about "sacred signals" and whatever. Then he magicked the phone into the In-Between. Spin, poof, gone. Because he couldn't have Maddie, *that bitch,* interfering in this.

They were *so close* now. He'd thought he'd lost the thread, that Oliver had strayed too far afield—he'd gone out after him last night to grab him, drag him by his hair if he had to, into the park. But what did he see? Oliver, fighting with that jock. Graham Lyons. Then he'd watched as Oliver did something else—he reached deep into Graham Lyons, into the other kid's *fucking soul,* and pulled out, what? Some kind of eel, some serpent, some oily black worm from hell. Some crazy shit.

And that's when he'd thought of a new plan. He'd snuck into Graham's backseat, went home with him. Then killed him, and his father. Hoping that it would send Oliver over the edge. Now, he realized only in retrospect, he maybe could've let it go. If what Oliver did was break the other boy's pain, he could've used that, too. Turned out, killing Graham hadn't been necessary, and perhaps overcomplicated everything.

But, oh well. He'd enjoyed it just the same. And used it, too.

So he really, *really* didn't need Maddie—and Jed, that craven old cocksucker—ruining what was already a delicate situation.

So, so close.

This was the night.

The message said it was both received and read.

Maddie stared at her phone.

Stared *through it.*

Waiting, waiting. Looking to the phone, then to Jed on the floor, then to the phone. Oliver didn't answer. *Oliver, Olly, Dude, please answer me.*

Nothing.

She slid the phone back into her pocket with her free hand. Again she drew the gun and pointed it at Jed. None of this made any sense, and she was spiraling. "Keep talking. What does any of this mean? Why is Jake a danger to my son? What does he want?"

"He wants to end it all, my dear. Immanentize the eschaton, to quote Eric Voegelin. And he's not Jake. Not really."

This is getting deranged.

"Then who is he?"

"He's Oliver. An Oliver of another time, another place. Older. Considerably more broken. But he has a plan, Maddie. Oh, does he have a *plan*." Then Jed told her what exactly it was.

*   *   *

Jake danced atop the stones, leaping bands of moonlight and shadow. Oliver followed slowly behind, winding his way. The way Jake moved—like he was happy. Eager and excited.

But why?

Oliver felt queasy and confused. His head was a mess. Like he couldn't even think straight anymore. But something about this—it settled into his stomach like a lead weight.

He wished his father were here to tell him what to do.

But that was both the problem and the point, wasn't it? And it was the reason they were here.

"There!" Jake said, pointing.

Oliver followed the line of his upthrust finger, and ahead he could see one rock standing up and out above the others—a rock that, in profile, looked more like an anvil of black stone than did any of the other stones.

Even before they approached it, Oliver knew that it was *the* rock—the one upon which he'd watched his father die. Up close, it seemed larger, darker, heavier. More real than in the vision. The top of it was less anvil-like, not as narrow or as angled—it was, instead, more like a table. He swept his flashlight across it and saw a series of eight grooves radiating out from the center—shallow furrows that again Oliver felt compelled to touch, but that also frightened him. He moved his hand toward it—

But then the stone seemed to flicker with darkness deeper than the night. Oliver pulled his fingers away before skin touched stone. He realized too that the channels did not run from the center out, but had a slight decline to them—they ran inward *toward* the middle of the table, not away from it. In the center of the stone was a hole. A slit, really, narrow like the pupil of a serpent's eye. Like the slot where a sword blade would stick, were this one of the Arthurian legends.

Jake spread his arms out wide, as if to encompass something that should be obvious. But Oliver didn't understand.

"Here we are," Jake said, his teeth shining in the moonlight.

Oliver peered through the dark. "I don't see any sign my father was here. I don't see any blood—"

"Who said it happened here?"

"But, the vision—"

"This rock is like the park, Oliver. It's one of the—what did you call it? One of the constants. Like a nail through the pages of a book."

Again the table stone seemed to possess an inner darkness that grew, a corona of shadow that swelled before shrinking once more. Oliver again reached his hand out. He wanted to touch those grooves, grooves that seemed smooth, not rough, almost as if polished—

His finger grazed along one and—

Oliver kneeling on the rock, a gun in his mouth, boom, a red spray out the top of his head

Oliver crying out, his arms and legs struggling fruitlessly, bound to the rock, skin rubbed raw with rope, the gleam of a sharpened pick-ax

Oliver sleepily crawling up on the table rock, vomit crusted to his black T-shirt, eyes half-lidded as he curls into a fetal position

Oliver with his wrists vented and weeping

His skull bashed open like a clay pot

A gunshot

A noose

Oliver with long, shoulder-length hair

Oliver with hair shorn to the scalp

Oliver with a buzz cut and a foot turned inward

Oliver with a cleft lip and green eyes

Oliver with braces, Oliver with clean straight teeth, Oliver with blue eyes, brown eyes, freckles, a mole over the lip, a mole on the cheek, this way, that way, dozens of variations, one after the next, a Sims character tweaked just a little each time, circus mirror versions, and each is dead and dying, always on this rock, and never, ever alone.

Never.

Ever.

Alone.

Oliver gasped. He backed away from the table stone, nearly catching his heel on the rock behind him. His breath came in short, ragged bursts. "I . . . no, no, no. What did I just see?" He put his fists against his temples and pressed in hard. *"What was that?"*

Jake leaned forward. "You okay, Olly?"

"You."

"Me. Me what?"

"You were always there. And you—" Oliver's voice nearly lay trapped in his own throat, but he forced it out. "You're not you."

Jake's face crept into a smirk. "Oh?"

"You're *me.*"

That one eye, robed in scar tissue, gleamed. "Who told?"

Oliver's head spun. "You've done this before. Again and again. You led me—other versions of me, other versions of *yourself*—to this stone. You convinced them to kill themselves here. Or you just killed them yourself. But they all died. They died here on this—"

"Go on," Jake said, the smile dropping off his face, replaced with an eager sneer. "Say it."

"It's not just a rock. Not a table."

"Do tell."

"It's an *altar.*"

The Nature of Human Sacrifice

The room spun around Maddie. Tinnitus rang in her ears like a dial tone. Jed was talking, even as she stood above him trying like hell not to hyperventilate, or fall down, or pull the trigger and put a bullet through the bull's-eye she imagined on his forehead. "Human sacrifice has power," he said. "The world has long understood that, but now it pretends to know differently—ohh, we're all so buttoned-up, pretending we don't *do* those things anymore, even though we sacrifice the homeless on our cold streets, or migrant children at the border, or the poor at every turn."

"Stop talking," she said in a small voice.

But he didn't.

He was lost to it, lost in the throes of what he was saying. "In Japan, it was *hitobashira,* women or children buried in the foundations of buildings in order to afford them, ah, *mystical protection.* Retainers were sacrificed alongside their dying pharaohs and Mesoamerican chiefs and Mongol warlords. Many went willingly—the Lindow Man, bound and drowned in a bog without any fight, all to meet some ancient pact with the gods. The power was in the blood, you see, *the blood,* as with the taurobolium of the cult of Cybele, where one would stand underneath a bull as it was sacrificed to let the blood rain fortune upon him. Not always a bull, too, if the more sordid histories are to be believed—shades of Elizabeth Báthory, there. And of course there's the Binding of Isaac, lest we believe our own God—"

"Shut up," she hissed, backhanding him. He cried out. Blood drooled from a split lip. Maddie felt torn in two. Her son was in danger. She had to get to him. But this man, here before her, knew where her husband had gone. And from him she had not yet extracted a sufficient answer. She pressed the gun against his temple. She checked her phone again. Nothing from Olly. *Shit, shit, shit.* "You will tell me where my husband went. Now."

"I don't know, Maddie. He went through the tunnel and now he's gone. He went to wherever Jake came from. And I helped. Oh, god, I helped send him. All to see my wife and daughter again. But maybe if it all resets, if it all breaks apart and begins again, you can see your Nate again—"

Whap. Another backhand. Then she pressed the gun barrel into his knee instead. "This is insane. *You're* insane. I don't want him back that way. I want Nate back now. In front of me. I want him pulled back from the place you sent him." It wasn't just that she needed him. It was that *he* needed *her.*

"I—I'm so sorry—"

She used the barrel of the gun like she was trying to hammer a nail—driving it like a piston into the flat of his knee. He cried out in a ragged moan, rocking back and forth. "*You* helped facilitate this, and now you're going to tell me how to get him back. You say you're sorry? Then you can fix it. You can help me. How do I get him back, John Edward? You're *smart.* You're *academic.* I know you've got ideas"—she twisted the barrel into where she'd just smashed it, digging it in like she was turning a screw into tough wood—"in that *big brain* of yours."

Again, he cried out. "Please. *No.* Please, I can't help you."

"Is this what they'd want from you? Your wife, your daughter? You killed the both of them, and want to hide from it. You want to turn back the clock, rewinding to a time they don't know what you did? What a weak, small man you are," she said, condemning him. "Ready to help destroy everything just to hide what a pathetic piece of shit you really are. What you did to them was an accident. But all this? It's not. It's murder."

It was like a little bell ringing—he stopped. His eyes lost their focus, and he went inward. She suddenly understood that hurting him physically *wasn't* the way forward. Hurting him this way? Sticking a metaphorical knife in his heart, his mind, his guts? That was the trick.

Guilt.

And shame.

What mighty motivators they were.

"I . . . I didn't mean to get into that accident."

"No," Maddie said, softening her tone. "But you did. And you don't fix it by rewinding the tape. You fix it by going forward and learning to be better than the man that you were. But this, what you're doing? It's worse. And the guilt you carry from that day in the car may be no match for the guilt over what you did getting them back." From guilt and shame she moved to pluck other strings: doubt and distrust. "Besides," she continued, "what if it's all a lie? What if you're just a prop? A pawn in this monster's game. What if you wake up and it didn't work? What if you burn it all down only to find that your wife and daughter are still in their graves and you're alone in a world you helped to destroy? What then?"

He took a shuddering breath—the gasping spasm of a child after a long bout of crying. "You're right. Oh, god, you're right. I'm a fool, Maddie. An old fool, a drunk, a hopeless fuckup." He wiped his nose with the back of his hand, leaving a long slug's trail of snot across it. "I wish I knew what to tell you, Maddie. I wish I knew how to tell you to get back there. And stop Jake. And get Nate back. I wish I knew something, anything to help you to save your son, and save the world."

"A sacrificial altar," Oliver said.

Those words traveled on a puff of cold breath.

Jake gripped the side of the stone, his muscles tensing like he was either carefully mitigating his rage—or his excitement.

"That's right, Olly. And you're right. I am you. We're a constant. One of the pillars holding up the cosmos. There's always you—or me. *Us.* There's always a Nate and a Maddie. There's always a Ramble Rocks, though as noted it's not always a park. And in it, there's eternally *the altar.*"

"This is insane. I'm leaving."

"Slow your roll," Jake said, holding out his hands. "We need to talk this out. You and me, we've got the power to rewrite history. *Literally.* You and me, we're the last. This is the last world. When we do this, it all ends. And it can all begin again. Better than it was before."

"You can't be serious."

"I am. Your dad's gone. Graham's gone. This world is fucking busted, man. You can feel it, can't you? The grand scheme is all *screwed up.*"

"I don't . . . I don't care about the grand scheme!" Oliver screamed in indignation and horror. "I just care about people. I don't care about, about all of that, I just care about people and their pain. I just want to help them—"

"This helps them. We can end it. And it ends their pain. You'd do that for a sick dog. Or a . . . an ailing parent. Right? The world is on hospice. This is . . ." Jake's voice rose to a fevered pitch. "This is *mercy,* Oliver, why can't you fucking see that?"

"No. No. I can't—"

"Shh, shh, listen, *listen,*" Jake said, pleading. He spun his hand around, and a container of pills appeared in his hands with a maraca rattle. "I can make it easy. So easy. Think of me as your *suicide sommelier,* okay? We can do it peaceful like. This is a mix. An artisanal bespoke blend of happy life-enders. Ambien, Xanax, Oxy. Take a few of each and you can go off to sea, a peaceful sleep as the world ends and everything resets."

"Suicide? I—I don't want to be here anymore," Oliver said in a small voice. "I just want to go, Jake. I'm going to go." He tried to back away, but found himself trapped by so many rocks. A sudden worry twisted up inside him: *If I really wanted to run, could I?* He couldn't. It would almost be impossible to extricate himself from this place with any speed. But he had to try. "I'm sorry, Jake. I'm really sorry."

"Really?" Jake sucked air between his teeth, a disappointed sound. "Olly, buddy, I'm disappointed in you. Not as disappointed as your dad . . ."

"Fuck you."

Oliver turned to make his way back through the stones.

"Don't you at least want your phone back?"

He turned to see Jake twist his wrist—again came the faintest flash of darkness around the tips of his fingers as the phone appeared.

"I don't know. I don't care."

"Jesus, just take it. Call your mommy, have her come pick you up." Jake tossed it into the center of the table.

Oliver reached for it.

And as he bent forward, grasping the phone in his hand—Jake moved, and moved fast. Both hands came together, and a little thunderclap cut the air as something appeared in his grip: There was a gleam of moonlight on metal, and a swish of something cutting the air—

Oliver called out, tried to recoil—

But it was too late.

The point of the pick-ax came down through the back of his left hand, through the phone, and into the altar stone.

"My son is in danger," she said.

"Yes. I believe so."

"This boy, Jake, wants to hurt him."

"Wants to *kill* him. Sacrifice him there in the felsenmeer."

"And what happens when that happens?"

"This world ends. And, if you believe Jake, we're the last world left.

Bobbing in the chaos like driftwood. Everything clinging to us. If we fall, all of it falls. Sinks back into the primeval dark, the true dark." He stared, unblinking. "It's why things have gone thin, gone strange. Like your ants spiraling. Or the man Nate's been seeing. I think they're the effects of the worlds all—" Here he softly clapped his hands together. "Collapsing into each other."

She checked her phone again. Sent another alarmed text. This time, it wasn't even marked delivered. It just hung there.

Waiting, waiting.

"The park. They're going to the park? That's where this happens?"

Jed nodded.

She grabbed him by the neck, shoved him toward the door. "Let's go. My car. We're going."

"Maddie, please don't make me—"

"Shut your fucking mouth." As she pushed him against the door, she grabbed her phone and called Fig. He was the only one she trusted.

The dull crunch of it throbbed in Oliver's hand, reverberating all the way to his elbow, then his shoulder—a lash of lightning. He panicked, bracing his knees against the altar and trying to free his hand, but it wouldn't budge—and every movement sent new sparks of pain through him. With his other hand he grabbed the metal head of the pick-ax. Most of the tool was crusted with rust, but the tip was burnished to a gleam and, stranger still, whittled down so that the heavy, churlish rock-breaking end was now more a long, lean spire, like an ice pick.

"Struggle, struggle," Jake said, pacing back and forth, watching Oliver thrash and cry and bleat as he tried and failed to extricate himself. "That's life, isn't it? Struggle. One big long fuckin' struggle, dude. *All life is suffering*. Buddha, right? Whatever. Go on, you keep working at that trap, mouse. Let's see how it goes. It's okay. We have time, you and I."

I just need leverage. He had none, the way he was positioned. Oliver grunted, trying to launch himself up onto the altar in order to push his shoulder against it, but his knee slipped—

And the weight of him tugged hard on the embedded pick.

The pain was white-hot and all-consuming. He heard a terrible sound, like wind keening through a broken window, and soon Oliver realized he was the source of that wretched noise.

Panting, he slumped against the table. Trying to stay standing as he was bent forward. Drool slicking his chin. Tears blurring his vision.

"You piece of shit," he hissed through his own spit, his voice gushy.

"I'm disappointed in you, kid. I really thought you were smart enough to see what I'm trying to do here." Dismissively, he waved his hand at Oliver. "Look at yourself. Fight's already going out of you. It's like a fish on a line—you just have to let 'em tire themselves out and then it's all done." He shrugged. "That's what people do. They struggle. Even when they're in a death spiral, they just keep on spiraling, thinking they're heading in a straight line and not down the fucking drain."

Oliver's mind went to the image of those ants in his bedroom, what felt like a lifetime ago. Whirling about, a carousel of starvation and death.

"I hate you. I *hate* you."

"I know. And I'm sorry. I'm not just saying that, either, Oliver. I mean it. I don't enjoy this. There's a part of you that knows it. There's a part of you that *feels* how right I am—things have gone wrong. The cruelty in the world, it's too much. Evil's having its day, a beast off its leash. And we can change that, Oliver. All of the religions and the spiritual teachings show us the way—a path of cleansing, a fuckin' *deluge* to wash away the sin and remake the world, the wheel turning, one age yielding the next. But that wheel needs a push, Olly. *And I learned how to push it.*"

"Just let me go." It came out *Jush lemme guh.*

"And when I give it a push, it all starts to turn, faster and faster and fuckin' faster, until it pops off its axle and—crash, boom, bang." He threw up his hands. "I confess I don't understand it all myself. I learned it in the Book of Accidents. Given to me by . . . a *friend* named Eli. It's all about the . . . what did you call them? The constants. Break the constants, break the world, and each world you break adds up and up and up until it's all chaos and all starts over. The constants, well—" Again he leaned forward on the altar, this time on his elbows like he was at a slumber party confessing a secret crush. "They exist at every level, through every timeline. Like you said, a nail through a book, the hole in every page. Or like this pick—" He reached up and touched the top of his finger to the top of the pick and gave it a wiggle-wiggle. Oliver screamed behind his teeth. "The pick is through your hand, through the skin and the muscle and the bone, through the phone, into the stone. Oh, that rhymes, look at that."

"I won't kill myself for you."

Jake's head rocked back on his neck and he pressed his fists into his eyes, as if frustrated. "It's my fault, really. I thought I understood you. But you don't care that the world is fucked up. You just care about people. And I can't do anything with that. I need you to see the forest and all you see is the *fucking trees*. So I guess I'm gonna have to do this the old-fashioned way."

His wrist twisted, his fingers snapped—and in a little pulse of liquid darkness, a revolver appeared. He spun the chamber, and from the air snatched six bullets, one after the next.

Oliver grunted and struggled. Told himself to calm down. To breathe. But it was impossible. Panic throttled him.

Jake went on: "You know, the Aztecs understood it. All this. They told stories of the Five Suns. Each Sun was an age, an era. The First Sun died when Quetzalcoatl knocked it out of the sky with a club, and jaguars ate all the people. Quetzalcoatl became the Second Sun, but had to step down to use his magic to stop people from being monkeys. The Third Sun was Tlaloc, who was sad and mad and jealous because his wife had been seduced by another god, and first he gave the earth a great drought, and then as the people begged for rain, he gave it to them—as a rain of fire. And the gods made a new world from the ashes." He thumbed open the revolver, began slotting them into the cylinder, one by one. *Click, click, click.* "Fourth Sun? Tlaloc was cruel to his *new* wife, told her she wasn't worth shit, so she wept blood. So much blood she drowned the world in it. And finally, the Fifth Sun—our sun, now. They say that once human sacrifices stop, the stars will eat the sun, the sky, and all the people, and a great earthquake will shake apart the cosmos."

"You're insane. Those myths aren't yours. They're not even real." Still Oliver struggled with the pick. It hurt bad enough he had to will himself not to black out. *Push through. Push through. Push through.*

Jake finished loading the gun. He jerked his arm to the right, snapping the cylinder shut.

"Every mythology has its tale of apocalypse—god, even that word, Oliver. Apocalypse. It means *revelation*. It's an epiphany. An awakening, not an ending. You'd see that, if you learned the way I did. Down in the dark. With a most excellent teacher." Jake sniffed. "By the way, you can stop struggling. That pick won't move. I made sure of that. Magic."

The pick won't move.

By now, the hole had widened. He could see the light of the moon glistening in the wet red meat in the back of his hand.

If the pick wouldn't move—

"See you on the other side," Jake said. He raised the gun.

Oliver yanked as hard as he could—

Not on the pick.

But on his *hand*.

He hauled back his shoulder, and the tip of the pick ripped through the skin of his hand, bursting through the muscle and bone between his middle and ring fingers—blood sprayed as he tumbled backward.

Jake discharged the revolver.

Bang.

Oliver fell between two stones, and quickly wriggled around so he was right-side up, on his knees. Hurriedly, he darted through the boulders, staying low as two more shots rang out, the tops of stones near him singing with the whine of bullets ricocheting. A spray of stone chips dusted the air in front of him. His hand ached.

Jake roared, and idly Oliver thought, *Maybe the difficulty of escaping the boulder field can be an advantage.*

He dropped even lower, down to his belly—

A shadow fell in front of him.

It was only then he remembered coming here in the first place, and watching Jake gambol atop the stones like a dancer.

A hard boot connected with Oliver's face, knocking him sideways. His nose felt like concrete. His skull pounded. His hand gushed blood.

The other boy stood over him, lording over him.

The barrel of the gun leveled toward Oliver, staring as ruthlessly and malevolently as Jake's own impossible eye.

"You don't get it," Jake said, his voice thick and sticky. The gun did not waver in his hand even as the rest of him seemed unsteady. "You don't appreciate the grace of this. It's not just me killing you. It's me killing *me,* too. I end you and it all goes away. It's not just your sacrifice. It's mine."

Oliver, resigned, rested his head on the rock behind him. "One big cosmic murder-suicide," he said, bitter and sad.

"Beauty in cataclysm, power in destruction. Now get on the fucking table, Oliver."

Wearily, weakly, Oliver stood. He stepped across stripes of moonlight, toward the altar. There, though, he saw that the pick-ax was no longer stuck in the stone. It had fallen. *When I escaped it, I broke that spell,* Oliver thought. Magical logic. *Mad* logic. But true just the same.

He leaned across the table.

He heard the revolver draw back. *Ca-click.*

And then he did the only thing he could do. His hand curled around the wooden handle of the ax, and he spun around blindly—

Thuck. The gun went off, then clattered away. Oliver's ears screamed with the sound of the gunshot. Jake staggered backward through moonlight, the ax stuck indelicately in the meat around his collarbone. Jake let loose a stream of wordless invective, vulgar despite it being a guttural, profane roar.

Oliver thought, *Kill him.*

Kill him now.

End this or it never ends.

But his middle tightened. Could he? Would he?

Instead, he turned the other direction, and he ran.

It was at the edge of the park, near the road, that he saw the flashing lights. Not red and blue, but the flashing yellow of a Fish and Game truck. He saw Fig pulling gear out of the truck and Oliver tried calling to him, finding his voice was lost somewhere in his throat, and all that came out was a gargled whisper. So he staggered out of the brush, knowing that somehow Jake would be right behind him with the ax, with the gun, and he knew as soon as he got to Fig the man would die, shot in the chest, but none of that happened. All that happened was that Axel Figueroa saw him coming, and caught him just before he fell. Then everything went dark.

Interlude: Jake and the Demon

The Oliver that would one day be Jake sat in the living room, criss-cross applesauce, watching his favorite cartoon, *Audric and the Warriors of the Wheel*, where the young hero Audric—with the help of his friends, Stormbringer, Ulysses, Shadow Cat, and Marisol—battled the evil fungus empire of Sawblade the Spore Boss. Each side fought with cars and trucks as their weapons: Audric's cars were cool muscle cars and military-style trucks, and Sawblade had a bunch of organic postapocalyptic vehicles (that looked a little like veiny poops, to Oliver's eye). Sawblade's tank fired out, well, sawblades, which was presumably what gave him the name.

Oliver had a few of the toys in front of him: Audric's Firecharger, Shadow Cat's Leapwheel, and Sawblade's Spore Boss tank.

He was nine years old.

The show was one he liked very much, because it depicted a clear battle between good and evil. Audric was unabashedly good and heroic. Sawblade was grotesque and evil. Easy.

But the show was also troublesome for Oliver, because it came on at 3:30 in the afternoon. As he watched, the clock on the living room wall tick-tocked its way toward 4:00 P.M., and the boy's stomach grew tighter and sicker, and his head felt like a knocked-over beehive of worry and fear. It made him want to get up and run, but also, he liked this show very much, and didn't want to miss a moment of it.

Sometimes when the clock struck 4:00, he would hurry out of the room and hide in his bedroom. Sometimes under the covers. Sometimes under the bed. He wasn't supposed to do that, though, and he knew it only got him in worse trouble.

No, he was supposed to be ready and waiting for his father. Dad came home at 4:00 every day, promptly, and when he did, he sometimes had tasks for Oliver. These tasks were often random. Dad would tell him to dig a ditch in the backyard. Or hammer nails into a board for an hour; if he filled the board, he had to pull them back out and hammer them again.

Sometimes Dad was actually doing something like repairing a fence or fixing a clogged sewer pipe in the backyard and so he demanded Oliver accompany him, drinking a beer as he asked Oliver to fetch a certain tool—a $3/16$ wrench, or a Phillips-head screwdriver, or linemen's pliers. If Oliver got it wrong and brought back the wrong one, his father would hit him. Sometimes a slap across the face, sometimes a punch to the stomach.

So then Oliver started to bring over all the tools—if Dad wanted a $3/16$ wrench, he would bring an armload of wrenches just to make sure. But that made Dad even angrier, because it was "a waste," and it would earn Oliver another slap, punch, maybe even a kick to the knee or hips. Dad would say that the size of the tool was written on the tool itself, but Oliver often found this wasn't true—the tools were old and rusty, and seeing if a wrench was a $3/16$ or a $5/8$ was difficult. Sometimes he'd find the numbers on the metal and try to read them like they were in Braille, but it was no use. His newest thing was to simply try to memorize which ones were which, but even that was fraught—because he became so upset and so frazzled that he often brought the wrong one anyway. Sometimes he went into the barn and looked through the tools in the toolbox, and doing so made him so queasy he'd throw up in the corner and cry. Dad hadn't found his puke in the corner yet.

Oliver feared what would happen when he did.

The time now was 3:55 P.M.

He heard the telltale sound of gravel popping under truck tires.

The show was almost over. But the cartoon screen glitched. Some images on-screen froze in place, while other pixels seemed like they were melting, a spray of animated garbage growing more indecipherable by the moment. Bands of white static threaded across them. Rage and disappointment filled Oliver. The one good thing he had and it was now gone!

The TV went dark.

Moments passed.

Soon, though, a new image appeared:

The TV showed his father, outside. As if filmed by a camera high up, in the trees. He got his lunch bag out of the car, and a toolbox.

Oh god, he's home, oh no, no no no.

Then the man stopped, frozen. Or almost—it was like he moved by an inch, then moved back an inch. Forward an inch, back an inch. Caught there, paralyzed in a moment of time.

Oliver didn't understand what was happening. He looked to the clock on the wall, saw the second hand doing the same thing—a gentle twitch back and forth, never forward more than one second.

A face appeared on-screen. A cartoon face, and for a moment Oliver thought, *Oh good, the show is back on,* but he didn't recognize this person. Dark ringlets of greasy black hair hung around a pale face. The nose was long and comically crooked. A little pair of golden spectacles sat perched at the end of that nose. Underneath it, a marker-scribble mustache.

"Hello, Oliver," the cartoon man said, grinning big.

And it was then that Oliver knew him.

His name was Eli. He didn't know how he knew that, though.

"Do you remember today, Oliver?"

Oliver blinked. Was he supposed to answer the TV man?

Eli, also known as Eligos and Vassago, said, "It's okay, you can answer, Oliver."

"I . . . I don't remember today." He afforded another glance at the

clock on the wall. The second hand continued to twitch, as if straining to move time forward once again. "How can I remember a day
that hasn't happened?"

Eli smiled. And then went away.

On the television, a new scene appeared, again in the same cartoon style as *Audric and the Warriors of the Wheel*. But what was por-
trayed was not the Firecharger racing toward the Spore Boss, but
rather the very living room in which Oliver sat. And in through the
door came his father—in the cartoon he was brawnier, duskier, his
beard a series of jagged lines like upside-down mountain peaks.

On the TV, his father said: "Where's your mother?"

"Upstairs," Cartoon Oliver answered. And it was a true answer,
because that's where Mom was. As she often was at this time of the
day. Upstairs. In bed. Asleep, or half-asleep, or maybe just softly crying.

"I heard from a friend today she's been making some calls."

"Okay," Cartoon Oliver said, clearly not sure what that meant.

But Cartoon Dad explained: "She called a divorce lawyer."

"Oh."

"Means she wants to leave me. Leave *us*," Dad said. And now real
Oliver, the one watching this unfold, thought, *Is this true? Did this
really happen?* A strange pulse of hope flashed in Oliver because
maybe she wasn't leaving them but just leaving *him*. Maybe she
would take Oliver with her.

"You wouldn't leave me, would you?"

"No, sir," Cartoon Oliver lied, and real Oliver knew it was a lie.

The Dad on-screen patted his son's cheek. "Good boy. Now I need
to go have a *talk* with your *mother*." Both this Oliver and the one on
the TV knew what that meant. It wouldn't be a talk. It would be a
screaming match. And it would end the way it always ended: with her
crying. Almost certainly bruised up. Probably bleeding.

And now Cartoon Oliver was, for one moment, like Audric: His
hand darted out and caught his father's wrist as the man started to

head upstairs. It was a defiant gesture. The boy stuck his chin up and made a face screwed up with cartoon courage.

The dad on TV looked down at the boy grabbing him, an inky scribble of anger forming above his head. Steam arose from reddened cheeks.

"No," Cartoon Oliver said. "You leave her alone."

That did it.

The father on the TV grabbed his son, threw him against the television. It fell over, the screen gone spiderwebbed. The father pulled a crumpled cigarette pack out of his back pocket, tapped one out, plugged it into his lips as he pawed around his front pockets for a lighter. The boy tried to scramble away, but Cartoon Dad planted a foot on the base of his tailbone and pushed down. The boy grunted and wriggled, crying out.

Cartoon Dad lit a cigarette. Little clouds puffed from the tip.

"I know we're not churchgoers," Cartoon Nate said, "but I do remember a passage from the Good Book about how if a hand offends me, thee must cut that hand off or some bullshit." Cigarette hanging from his lips, he pressed his body weight on top of the boy, animated nicotine clouds still hanging above his head.

Then he grabbed Cartoon Oliver's hand.

Held it out.

Took that cigarette out of his mouth.

And—

Tssss.

Pressed it into the back of Cartoon Oliver's hand. The boy thrashed. And screamed. Little red devils arose from the boy. Gathering on the father's shoulders before finally fading like ghosts.

And now, Oliver, the *real* Oliver, felt a sudden surge of pain in his own hand—and when he turned it over, he saw a little scar forming. Old, more pink than red, but still raw.

The cartoon went black.

Moments later, Eli appeared again.

"That's today," Eli said. "You remember now?"

Oliver swallowed. "A little."

"That's about to happen."

"I know."

"It's happened before."

A new scene on the TV replaced Eli: a young boy, not Oliver, not a cartoon, on the ground. Faceup, this time. Pinned there by a jowly, stubble-faced man in a sleeveless shirt once white, now yellow with sweat. The boy's wrists were pinned underneath the man's knees. He had a cigarette—no, a little cigarillo, with the plastic mouth tip—bitten between his teeth, and he popped it out of his mouth and jabbed it into the boy's collarbone.

Now, Cartoon Dad, *his* own father, was back on the screen. He pulled back the collar of his flannel and showed a little scar there on his collarbone.

"See, son," Dad said, in a voice that was his, but that was also somehow Eli's voice. "Happened to me. Happened to you. Wheels turning. Cycles and cycles. What has come before will come again."

He grinned with black, shining teeth, and then was gone once more.

On the wall, the second hand continued to twitch, twitch, twitch.

On the TV, a Ferris wheel appeared. Calliope music going, *doo-dah-dah, doo-dah-dah.* Then it was night, and the Ferris wheel was on fire. The riders were on fire. And screaming. Some of them jumping off, flames trailing them, as they plummeted to their deaths.

A series of images flashed one after the next.

A school bus crashing into a line of schoolchildren at a crosswalk. It doesn't even try to stop. The driver is asleep. Kids are dragged under tires.

A woman on a round wooden board spinning at a circus, surrounded by hatchets stuck in the wood—one more is thrown and it hits when it should've missed, cleaving her head like a cantaloupe. *Sssthunk.*

A girl disemboweled on a rock by a smiling, handsome killer—he's boyish, like a salesman, and he's looking at the screen like he knows he's being watched, and he likes it. Her guts bulge, burst the way ticks do after they've gotten too fat on blood. On her cheek, Oliver sees something strange: a number carved there. The number 3.

The images came faster and faster. Animals dead and rotting in a field. Flies on a dead girl's face. Thin, sick captives in raggedy pajamas pressed against the wire at a concentration camp. Men in ditches, trampled by men on horseback. A soldier in a trench struggled to shove a gas mask on his face as his skin bubbled and his eyes ran like egg yolks down his face. Starving children, bellies swollen. Women loaded into a van with sacks over their heads. Machine-gun fire at a concert, barely audible over the music, people in the crowd going down one by one, little arcs of blood spraying up with each hit to the head, *bang, bang, bang, bang*. A hallway at a high school full of dead, shot kids. A sick little girl dead in a tangle of barbed wire at the border. War. Disease. Starvation. Torture. Death. Oliver watched it all because he could not look away, and he was not sure how long it went on, maybe a few minutes, maybe weeks, maybe years. He felt filled up by it, like it was a living thing, a series of images made into a serpent that wound its way around his neck before pushing into his mouth, choking him. He cried but made no sound. And the tears did little to hide what he saw, did nothing to blur them out, like they were somehow delivered to him in a way that was not entirely visual, but like they were pictures hammered into the wall of his mind with bent, rusted nails.

Eli's face appeared again. This time, not animated. No cartoon for him, oh no. He was all too real. His face pale and pasty. Eyes bloodshot. Lips the blue of a drowning person. He said, his voice so loud that Oliver could hear it inside his head, his teeth rattling like coins in a car's cup holder, "Do you see, Oliver? Do you see what the world has become?"

"I do."

"Is the world a good place, Oliver?"

"I . . . I don't think so."

"You don't think so?"

"I *know* so."

"Yes. You know it. Cycles turning. Wheels and gears. And the machine keeps spitting out the same suffering, the same prepackaged bricks of misery. Your great-grandfather comes back from war, takes it out on your grandfather, who carries that rage and trauma forward like shit in a bucket, sipping a little to quench his thirst, and then he passes it to your father, and now your father to you. Like a disease, like a cancer, both contagious and inherited. Do you want to pass it down to your child?"

"No."

"No, of course not, Oliver. Of *course* not. So what do we do?"

They said it together:

"Break the wheel."

In front of him now was a hammer.

The clock on the wall resumed, *tick-tock, tick-tock.* The door opened and here came his father. He said as he did on the TV before, "Where's your mother?" but then his eyes fell to the hammer on the floor. "That my hammer? You been fucking around with my tools again, Oliver?"

Oliver reached out and took the hammer.

He gave his answer without any words.

The strike was clumsy. He leapt up, swinging hard for the old man's face. It clipped him in the temple, staggering him. He remained standing, though, and reached up with two fingers to touch the slick little patch of blood there. His fingers came away sticky and wet.

"Why, you little piece of—"

Oliver smashed him in the mouth with the hammer. His teeth shattered like the end of a porcelain sink. Bits in his mouth. Gums gone to ambrosia salad. He gargled and choked on those bits and that blood, and Oliver climbed him like a tree, bashing him in the head and neck with the hammer over and over again. The hammer falling until the man's head was soft and losing its shape, a dodgeball losing its air, a rotten stump kicked in, and he kept hitting and hitting until he couldn't see through the blood and hair that matted in his eyes, until the man fell, and until Oliver fell with him.

He stood astride the body. Hammer dripping.

The walls began to bleed. Not blood, though at first that's what he thought. Just water. Wet water, slicking the wooden walls of the house, wetting the floorboards, turning them so dark that they became like stone. And then they truly turned to stone, and the darkness of the inside of the old coal mine filled the room until it was no longer the room at all.

The memory of it all rushed back to him—running away from home to the old Ramble Rocks mine, then sinking in the mire until he ended up here. In this mine. If it was even truly that.

The last thing left of the house was the television, and a black shape, ever-gleaming, slid out from the screen like a snake through an open window. Then the TV, too, was gone. The demon remained. It stood tall, taller than it ever had, stooping low, its liquid shoulders hugging the roof of the mine. "You are ready," it said, its voice deep and wet. It reached for him with a long, languid arm—five claws dead-ended it, dripping with glistening liquid, white in the dark like drops of bad milk. The arm moved quickly, slashing the boy across the eye—

He staggered back, and felt his face bulging and swelling around that eye socket. He clutched at it, feeling the bones shifting and distending. Cracking, then re-forming. He could feel *something* slithering around in there, like an eel in a shoe. And then he saw it all laid out—a circle of boys who looked like him, but who were not him, one after the next. In the center of them, a table—no, an *altar*—from which radiated slowly spreading cracks, and one by one the cracks took each boy and drew him down into a roiling sea of chaos. Oliver saw the way forward.

And when he opened his eyes—

He could see properly out of only one. Through the other eye, he saw many colors, ever-shifting. He saw endless possibilities. He saw blood and fire. He saw a hundred doorways and a thousand paths to each. He saw the doorways into the hearts of humans, too—weak places, soft places, their sins burning a hole in them.

And out of that mad eye, he saw both inside and out of the mine—its many twisting tunnels and its hungry entrance and the coal silt mire beyond it. Then he saw himself standing out beyond it, alone. In one hand, he held the coal pick. In the other, a ratty book—the Book of Accidents. He felt something at his wrist, a tickle, a tingle, and when he clutched the logbook tightly, his wrist crackled with cavitation, and the book was gone somewhere *else*. (And yet, he could still feel it out there, somewhere, too.)

A voice in his head said:

You have my gifts.

You have my mark.

You have work to do.

And that's when the bird crossed in front of him, a hunter chasing it with his gun raised.

PART SIX

MAKERS, BREAKERS, AND TRAVELERS

Was Edmund Walker Reese a serial killer born of the abuse visited upon him as a child, as many such monsters were? Was he schizophrenic? Or are those excuses too easy—or lazy!—to provide the basis for this villain's origin story? Perhaps something stranger is true: Reese was made vulnerable by what had happened to him, but it was only through his exposure to the supernatural that he had found an outlet for his rage. So fascinated was he by the folkloric legends of the area—Ramble Rocks in particular—that he either invented the creature known as the demon, or was truly met by some diabolical being who had come through the "thin places" that Ramble Rocks is known to possess. And during an era of Satanic panic, this demon real or imagined was able to convince Reese that the rage he felt and the pain he experienced were ample fuel for a crusade to kill little girls. And in killing those girls, he would be able to vent his rage and diminish, even erase, his pain. Certainly others before him had found themselves subject to abuse and misery, and many others were able to live healthy lives in spite of that. But few were like Reese. And few others had been transformed in such a way by the delusional invention of—or a true encounter with—a demon in the dark. Whatever is true, we must all be glad of one thing: that he was unable to finish his Satanic crusade. May we all wrestle with our demons and win.

—from the final chapter of the book *Sacrifice at Ramble Rocks: The Satanic Murders of Edmund Walker Reese*, by John Edward Homackie

Orpheus Looked Back

With Oliver in his bed, half in, half out of consciousness, he heard his mother and Fig talk in a low murmur.

Fig: *There was no body, Maddie, I'm telling you. Blood, yes. Oliver's phone. No body. No pick-ax, no gun, nothing.*

Maddie: *Then he's still out there.*

Fig: *They're on it. I talked to Contrino. He said they'll find this Jake kid.*

Maddie: *They won't find him. There's more going on here than you know, Fig.*

Fig: *You can tell me. And if you told me too where Jed was—you said you found him. And we found his car at that fancy lodge upstate.*

Maddie: *I don't know where he went from there.*

Fig: *We'll catch them both, Maddie. I promise. For Nate.*

Maddie: *Nate's gone, Fig. Don't do it for him. Do it for us.*

Thanks for Ramblin' By!

The fall was short, but hard. He landed flat on his back, the air horse-kicked from his lungs. He tasted blood.

Nate lurched to his feet. Pain shot through his arm, and the memory of Jake swinging the bat resurfaced. He could move it, at least. Arm wasn't broken.

Where the hell am I?

The tunnel. He was still in the tunnel.

In the distance, he saw the entrance, a half moon of gray light. Looked like daytime. Maybe early morning. Was he asleep? He wanted to believe what had happened was exactly and only the nightmare that it felt like at the time, but . . . all this seemed pretty damn real.

Nate pulled out his phone. He tried to call home, but had no signal. *Must be because I'm in the train tunnel.* Nate used the phone's flashlight—

Shining ahead, he saw tracks.

Which was a helluva thing, because the old tunnel had long ago removed its train tracks, hadn't it?

Shit, I gotta get out of here. Gotta get home. Get to a hospital.

He turned off the flashlight to save battery, and then staggered forward. The exit was about a hundred yards off, so he put a little pep in his step. As he left the tunnel, morning light washed over him, blinding him for a moment—

And then his vision resolved.

At first, it felt as if he were surrounded by great beasts—skeletons and fossils. But he blinked and saw that they were not beasts, but rather the architecture of amusement. A roller coaster. A Ferris wheel to his right. Dead ahead, concession stands, and a carousel, half-collapsed, three of the horses broken off their pistons.

"What the . . ."

Nate turned and looked at the tunnel.

A big sign framed the top of it: THE TUNNEL OF TERROR.

Each letter, an old light box of broken bulbs. The *o* in *of* was a cartoonish woman's screaming mouth, her eyes garishly painted, her cheeks half-rotten.

Nate looked down the tunnel from whence he came—

And now he saw that the tracks were the tracks from the Tunnel of Terror ride. A face popped out of the wall on an accordion extension, so broken than it was little more than a rusted skull. Farther down, raggedy white ghosts hung on wires. And beyond that, other shapes and shadows, unidentifiable.

Nate spun back around.

What *was* this?

Had his nightmare truly, finally come true? Or was he dying, and this was his brain's last gasp?

It certainly *felt* real. Realer than any dream. The air, though, had the same wrong feeling as it had in the tunnel. But now it didn't feel thin so much as heavy and oleaginous. Like he could grab a chunk of it, squish it between his fingers.

Past the bones of the roller coaster, the sun was just a smear of light. Rheumy clouds gathered in the slate sky.

A howl split the air off in the distance.

But it was not the howl of an animal.

It was, he was sure, the howl of a man. A raw, throaty sound. Desperate and mad.

Idly, he felt for his holster—

But it hung empty. The gun had been knocked out of his hand before he sank into the asphalt mire, hadn't it?

I have to get out of here, he thought. *Wherever "here" is.*

He stormed forward, feeling a fearful itch at the base of his neck. Nate moved past a row of concession stands, on which were spray-painted messages:

THE NUMBERS MAN GONNA GETCHA

BEWARE THE WHITE MASK

THE TRESPASSER COMIN

WASTIN' AWAY AGAIN IN 'RONAVIRUSVILLE

And then, most troubling of all:

WELCOME TO THE END OF THE WORLDS

On that last one, the *s* had been painted on by someone else—the first message was in white paint. The last *s* in WORLDS was in red.

Nate ran, then, past the concession stands, through the skeletal shadow of the roller coaster, over the broken carousel horses, until he found the exit—or, rather, the entrance. Above which hung a sign:

RAMBLE ROCKS AMUSEMENT PARK

THANKS FOR RAMBLIN' BY!

A cowboy clown was painted beneath it.

Someone had scratched out its left eye, hit it with white spray paint.

Nate headed toward the gate, knowing he had to get to a hospital, or find home—when he heard the distant whistle of something cutting through the air and then—

Pok!

Something clocked him in the back of the skull. He yelped, reaching back but blessedly finding no blood. At his feet lay a stone.

Small. But sharp.

His eyes scanned the park—

It didn't take long to see who had thrown it.

They were crouching behind a rust-wrecked bumper car. He

glimpsed shoulders, tousled hair, and a mask of some kind. Like a Halloween mask, maybe. As they peeked out, it looked like the mask might be an animal face, a cherubic Easter bunny without the ears—

And then whoever the person was ducked down farther.

From the other direction, he heard the scuff of a shoe—he turned to see a second individual. Big fella. Fat in the belly, but with small legs and arms, almost birdlike. No mask on this one, but rather a hood. Made from a tote bag with the eyeholes scissored out.

Nate spied a number on the mask. A slash-through zero in red, drawn in what looked to be dripping paint.

The man had a weapon: an aluminum baseball bat.

Nate searched around for his own weapon, but found nothing.

Now, Bunny Mask stepped out from the bumper car. The cartoony mask had round cheeks, a pink triangle nose, whiskers—with the ears cut off in jagged slashes. This person was short and lean. Too lean, as if starving. A weapon dangled in their hand—like a handmade machete. A piece of metal, like from a car door or metal roof, bent and crudely sharpened. The handle was just a swaddling of electrical tape.

Same number painted on their mask, too. Zero with a slash through it.

To hell with this, Nate thought. He pivoted on his heel and broke into a hard sprint toward the exit. But two more figures stepped in his way, blocking the way out.

One was a woman. Tall. Skinny. Her one hand ended in an arthritic claw. She wore a cheap plastic baroque butterfly eye-mask, like from a masquerade ball. Her pink sundress was ragged and torn with rust-colored stains.

Next to her, a boy. Younger than Oliver, maybe twelve or thirteen years old. Blond hair so pale it was almost the color of sun on a white-sand beach. He wore no mask. His cheeks were ruddy red, and the rest of his face was speckled with red dots, like hives, or measles. He wore dirty corduroy pants, a moth-eaten sweatshirt, and black leather gloves.

The woman had a red snow shovel. The boy held a rock.

On both faces, the same zero. Carved into their literal cheeks, into their skin. *Numbers,* like from Reese's victims. But these people were alive. And how could anyone be Victim Zero?

Nate cracked his knuckles. He was going to have to fight his way through this. He turned to check on Bunny Mask and Baghead— they were creeping up on him now.

The boy and the woman were his easiest way out. A snow shovel was unwieldy, and the boy was just a boy. He could barrel his way through—

Whud.

A camera flashbulb behind his eyes as another something struck his head. He staggered sideways, looking down at the rock that now lay at his feet. His hand went to the back of his head and came away wet and red. The boy at the one side no longer held a rock in his hands.

Absurdly, Nate thought, *Helluva throw, kid.*

Bunny Mask broke into a hard run, bolting toward him, the blade in their hand up in the air, swiping through, *swoosh, swoosh.* Woozy, Nate had little chance to move out of their way. He held up his arm in front of his face just as the blade sliced a ribbon of meat out of his arm. He yelped, and fell onto his ass. Pain climbed his spine as his vision went double. Big Boy was on him now, and the man's crude boot sunk into Nate's ribs, and he felt them *give.* He did all he could do: double over, onto his side, curling into himself as the kicks came.

The kicks stopped.

"I know you," came a familiar voice, growing closer and closer. A creaky voice, like an old door.

"No," Nate said, his vocal cords like raw meat.

"I *know* you!" Edmund Walker Reese said with no small delight.

He licked his thin lips and pushed a pair of eyeglasses up a bent nose. "You tried to take Number Thirty-seven from me. She almost got away from me, that one. But I rode the lightning and I found her again, didn't I? I did, I did. Found her in the Ninety-nine. I found her in *your care,* you little robberfly."

He held a hunting knife in his hand. It gleamed: a well-kept blade.

Reese pressed a filthy sneaker against Nate's chin. "I gifted you with a scar. I could give you another. You'd look fetching with a zero carved into your face meat, wouldn't you?" The masked ghouls around him nodded; the young boy, sans mask, chuckled and whooped. "These are my friends. My *zeroes.* I have many friends. Those who fell between worlds, or whose worlds fell, come to me. And they join me, or they die. What say you? Will you come with me? You arrived in my kingdom, traveler. My tunnel, my park. You're basically my property already . . ."

Nate grabbed the man's foot with his one good hand and tried to twist his body, bringing him down—but Reese pulled away, and someone's boot connected with Nate's face. He grunted dully, and it felt like some of his teeth had come loose. Blood drooled. He groaned, tried to turn over and get away. Hands found him, started to drag him away. Splinters bit through his clothing, into his skin—

Choom.

The roar of a gun filled the air. One of the attackers, maybe Bunny Mask, pirouetted backward, blood fountaining up from their bent neck. Nate saw Bunny Mask hit the ground next to him, the dead eyes of the Easter rabbit staring at him, and through the little pinprick holes he saw *real* eyes, human eyes—three blinks and then no more. *Choom.* Someone cried out, gargling on their tongue. Nate tried to get up, but found his legs had gone to rubber. His caved-in ribs felt like they were freshly breaking. *Choom.* A woman screamed.

Nate flopped over onto his back. His breath coming in shallow, whistling gasps. Darkness wicked away the light. Someone moved over him and past him, a long boxy gun in hand, like an army .45. The person wore a gas mask and dirt-caked jeans and a T-shirt the color of bad liver.

Nate closed his eyes. He felt hands grab his heels, start to drag him. And that's when the river of unconsciousness swept him away in its current.

66

One More Shot at the Goal

Out of the hospital, Oliver could see the anger moving in his mother like a bully looking for a fight. She packed both of their suitcases with rage at every fingertip, flinging clothes in, almost as if by punishment. Oliver didn't help because she told him the doctor said he needed to rest his hand. So he watched her, instead, and watched her pain. For a moment he wondered what would happen if he reached out, as he did with Graham, and took that pain from her? Could he? Was that something he could replicate? Would it save her? Or doom her? Did we need pain? Was some pain good, and some of it bad? Some of it ours to keep, and some of it invasive? He didn't know. And so he was afraid to do anything at all.

So when Maddie turned away from the bag and toward him, he looked at her and said: "I'm so sorry."

Her pain and anger receded. "Sorry for what, lamb?"

"Sorry I got involved with him. Sorry I fell for it." He felt tears burning the edges of his eyes. "Sorry I didn't have the guts to kill him. Now Dad's gone and—"

She swept him up in her arms then. Almost dancing with him, swaying back and forth. "No. No, no, *no*. You don't do that to yourself. You don't be that way. You're a good kid, Olly. A damned *beautiful heart,* and don't let anyone tell you that's a bad thing." She grabbed his cheeks and pointed his face at hers. "You listen to me. That kid— Jake, that fuck, I know you think he's you, but he's not. And neither are any of those other Olivers who died on that table. You are your own creature. This is your life, and you will face it how you must— and run when you have to."

He nodded.

"Is that why we're running?" he asked.

"We're running until we figure out how to not run anymore."

"I love you, Mom."

"I love you too, baby."

They sat in her Forester, Fig in the passenger seat, and Oliver curled up in the back across the seats, under his jacket as a blanket.

Maddie told Fig everything. *Everything*. It was time. She needed his buy-in if she was to get from him what she wanted.

"Maddie," he said. "This is all . . . insane. I wish the two of you wouldn't go. I wish you'd stay. We can keep you safe."

"Jake is Oliver from another universe. Or timeline or what-fucking-ever. And he wants to end every universe, and to do that, he has to kill my son. I assume he sent Nate away in order to get to Oli-ver, but I don't know. And I'm not sure it even matters. Nate is gone. Probably dead. But who *isn't* dead is that kid—Jake. And I need a place to hide. So. How about it?"

"Maddie, we have to call someone. Get you into protection with the cops, maybe even the feds—"

"I said, how about it, Fig?"

Fig sighed. He reached in his pocket and gave her the keys. "The cabin isn't much, okay? It's, like, a little fishing cabin kinda thing. North of Lake Wallenpaupack by about ten miles. No internet ser-vice. Meager cell service. There's a landline, but it's spotty. There's a TV with an antenna. Woodstove for heat and for cooking. Pantry isn't stocked right now, but there's a little general store two miles south back down the road. They have enough to get by, even in the winter, because there's ski opportunities not too far. But it's all yours, with Zo's and my blessing. We're gonna be busy with the little one coming soon, anyway. No time for the cabin."

"Thanks, Fig."

Fig was quiet for a while. Then, he unholstered his gun and tried to hand it to her. "Go on, take it."

"Don't need it." She popped the console between her two seats and drew out a Glock. "I can take care of myself. Nate asked I carry it."

He laughed a little.

"Fair enough. I'd like to hear from you. Maybe . . ."

"Honestly, Fig, you should take Zoe and get out of here, too. Find a place and lay low for a while."

"I . . ." A look of conflict and confusion twisted up his face. "I don't know that I can do that."

"You're not a cop. Not really. You don't owe anybody this."

"Ouch."

"You know I don't mean it like that."

"Fine. Yeah. But maybe I can help. In my way."

"If you say so."

"Stay safe, Maddie. If you need to reach out, please do. I'll be waiting. And I'll help however I can." He leaned between the seats. "You too, Oliver. Your mother's a tough cookie. She'll protect you. But you gotta protect her too, okay?" To that, Oliver nodded.

"Thanks, Fig," Maddie said.

He popped the door and was gone. Maddie started the car. She saw Fig in the rearview, watching them go.

67

Tell Me, Doctor,
Where Are We Goin' This Time

Nate awoke, gagging. He rolled over and dry heaved. Pain cut across his midriff like someone was cutting him with a pair of scissors.

He looked up and blinked.

My room, he thought.

Literally. His old room. From when he was a kid. Water-stained ceiling bowing in. Spiderwebs in the corner. A Lamborghini poster on the wall, peeling, most of the color drained out of it. There were other, more notable differences, too: a stack of rifles and shotguns in the corner. An ammo box next to them. Boards hammered across the windows. And next to him, on the end table, a bottle of some strange brand of bleach (Hygeen) surrounded by a clumsy circle of paper towels and gauze wads.

He sat up with a groan, the effort causing him to pause and catch his breath. The pain that sawed across his ribs dulled.

There, on a frail dining room chair, sat his father. In his left hand, a spoon in a bowl of cereal. And nearby, a .45 ACP. *The ghost,* Nate thought. *The one I've been seeing.*

And yet, this was no ghost. Whoever he was, he sat there, real as anything. Plain as day.

It was his father, but also, not his father. The left-handedness marked him as different, yes, but he looked tougher, too. Like a strip of weathered leather. This was not a man dying from cancer. This man wore vitality like a mantle. He looked up at Nate with clear, blue eyes.

"Nathan," the old man said.

"It can't be." Nate's voice was so raw it sounded like a rock scraping against the sidewalk.

His father, or his doppelgänger, sniffed. "It is. And it isn't." The old man bent down and picked up something: a dingy coffee mug, chipped around the rim. On it was an orange cartoon cat Nate knew to be Heathcliff, who mopishly declared in a word bubble: I HATE MONDAYS. Wasn't that Garfield's catchphrase? "Here."

Nate winced as he reached across, taking the mug.

In the mug was water. He took a sip. It tasted . . . off. A sharp mineral tang slicked his tongue. But it was refreshing just the same. He pushed past the taste and swallowed it all in a gulp—which he immediately regretted. His guts cramped up and his esophagus spasmed.

Carl said, "Should've sipped it."

"Yeah. I get that now, thanks."

"You're probably also hungry."

"I don't feel hungry."

"That's because you're so far past hungry you're pushing into feeling sick again. Say the word, I'll get you a can of something. Won't be warm, but it'll be food. Hopefully you'll keep it down this time."

Nate furrowed his brow. "This time?"

"Last couple times you rolled over, upchucked it onto the floor."

Last couple of times.

"How long have I been unconscious?"

The old man shrugged. "You been in and out."

"I don't remember being in and out. How long?"

"Couple weeks."

His body tensed. *Oliver. Maddie.* They were in danger. From Jed, from Jake. "I . . . can't have been out for a couple weeks, that's not possible, I have to get back—"

"Believe me or don't, Nathan, I don't care."

"Not Nathan. Nate. *Nate.*"

His Not-Father nodded. "Nate. Okay. I cleaned your wounds," he said, gesturing to the bleach.

"With bleach?"

"Best antiseptic around."

Nate remembered how his own father used to sometimes get poison ivy, and when he did, he'd take a penknife and scrape open the blisters, then splash bleach over them.

Was this man his father? Or some strange version of him? "Who are you?"

"Carl Graves."

"You're not my father."

Carl sniffed. "No, I suppose I'm not. Just as you're not my boy."

"Your son. He went by Nathan, not Nate?"

"That's right."

Nate dropped his legs off the bed and let his feet plant on the floor. The boards complained under even the gentlest weight. And his body complained, too—fresh pains and aches. That *hit-by-a-truck* feeling ran through his bones.

"You an abusive piece of shit to your Nathan, Carl?"

The old man hesitated. Then he reached across and abruptly took the mug from Nate. "I'll be downstairs. You want to come down, come down. I'll find you some food. Or you wanna stay up here and rot in bed, that's on you."

It took awhile for Nate to get up and go downstairs. It wasn't just the pain, or the aches, or the cramping stomach. It was the reality, or rather the unreality, of his situation. His world had already started to fray before all this, and then came that day in the tunnel. With Jed and Jake. Was Jake really his son, Oliver? Yes and no. Just as the man downstairs was and was not his own father, Jake was Oliver—only not *his* Oliver. He was *an* Oliver, an Oliver of another time, another place. His son was good and kind; this boy was a vengeful, venomous wretch.

And now, because of that wretch, Nate was here.

In his house that wasn't his house.

With his father that wasn't his father.

A world, or many worlds, away from his own son and wife.

Nate stood, pushing through the pain. He went downstairs.

The two men ate in silence. Each of them had a can of food in front of them. Nate had something called Golden's Spaghetees, which was basically like SpaghettiOs except with short little spaghetti noodles. Otherwise, the sauce was roughly the same. Carl ate something called Tremblaytown Turkey Stew. Looked not unlike dog food, but it appeared in fact to be for humans. It looked to contain . . . pickles?

Nate didn't say much. He just ate, his eyes wandering around. It was the same house he grew up in, but it looked worse for wear: walls stained, some boards bowing, and, given the lack of electricity, the shadows were longer, darker, deeper. It was light out, and the curtains were open, but the windows were still boarded up. The light came in through bands and angles, like bright knife slashes across the opposing walls.

"Not surprised you picked that can," Carl finally said.

"Why's that?"

"You always liked it as a kid."

"Not me. Him. Nathan."

Carl blinked. Like for a moment, this was news to him. Then he nodded and covered it up with an awkward laugh. "Yeah. Sure. Sure."

"I did like SpaghettiOs, though." Nate paused. "Pretty similar. We don't . . . have this brand, where I'm from. Or when I'm from. Whatever."

"How did your world fall?"

Nate stiffened at that. The question was so stark, so strange, it felt like a glass of ice water poured down his back.

"I don't know what that means."

"You're a traveler, aren't you?" the old man asked, as if this question somehow clarified the previous one instead of muddying the waters further.

"A traveler."

"You didn't come from here, like you said. You came from somewhere else. Some*when* else. I've met other travelers."

"The other man called me that. Reese."

"Edmund Reese," Carl said, nodding. "Yeah. *That* one. He doesn't belong here. He came here one night during a bad storm. Been a plague ever since." Carl licked his lips. "I met him once. Out there, while hunting. He was there alone. Said I could join him. When I told him when and how and how many times he could go fuck himself, he laughed, said I was the same old Carl that he knew, even though I wasn't. He said because we 'knew each other,' that he'd leave me be. I was miserable enough as it is, he said."

"He has friends."

"Brain-dead sycophants. Yeah. Folks who hunt for him. You're lucky I was out salvaging."

"Thanks for that."

"Sure."

"How did they get back? The travelers, how did they go home, I mean. To where they came from."

Carl looked taken aback, like someone had just dribbled a little bit of piss into his turkey stew can. "Get back? Home is *gone*. The worlds all crashed together when they fell, Nathan. *Nate*. There's no home anymore. There's just . . ." Spoon in hand, he gestured broadly. "All of this. This melting-pot apocalypse, this . . . well, *stew*." He tapped the spoon against the can.

"My world didn't fall. It's still—it's still there. What does all of this mean?" Nate could feel the panic rising in him like mercury in a hot thermometer, but he couldn't do anything to stave it off. "You're talking nonsense—worlds crashing together, travelers, apocalypses . . ."

Carl stood up suddenly, the chair skidding out behind him. He licked clean his spoon. "C'mon. I'll show you."

The march up the stairs into the attic was agonizing. Every step made Nate's head and ribs throb, and he needed a moment on the second staircase.

Carl let him, then said, "You got a fractured rib, I figure. Not sure about a concussion. Good news is, I didn't see any kind of infection in there. Infections happen real easy now, and antibiotics don't work so good no more."

"Another part of the apocalypse?" Nate asked.

"You bet." Carl picked some stringy stew meat from his teeth. "All right. Enough rest. Up and at 'em, tiger."

That, a thing his own father used to say to him.

Usually said in sarcasm, to accuse him of being lazy. *I see you on that bed, pretending to be asleep. C'mon. Time to work. Up and at 'em, tiger.*

So when Carl said it, Nate damn near punched the old bastard in the back of the head, but he held his fist and continued up the stairs.

"The hell am I looking at here, Carl?"

The wall was, to put it mildly, a Crazy Conspiracy Wall. He imagined a commercial playing out, *C'mon down to Carl's Crazy Conspiracy Wall! We got corporate logos! We got creepy clown masks! We got mysterious medical documents! And we got all kinds of string to connect them together. Who needs a corkboard? Our new patented steel-point thumbtacks will stick right in the wooden paneling on the wall, tickity-tack.*

"Some of the ways the world has ended," Carl said, plainly.

"Last I checked, there was only one world."

"Last you checked, you had one father, Carl Graves, and he wasn't me. Last you checked, you lived in a land that wasn't this one."

"Fair point." Nate swallowed. "Explain this to me, if you could."

"Sure. Best as I can, mind you; some of this is just guesswork. But it's like this: There are worlds other than yours. I don't know how many. Dozens. Maybe hundreds. Maybe there's a finite number, maybe there isn't. I'm guessing they're, howdoyoucallit, alternate dimensions. Timelines or whatever. Things are similar, but different. In each world came a boy, a boy named Jake, and in each of those worlds he took—" And here, Carl's voice broke a little. "He took my grandson, Oliver, took him to Ramble Rocks, and either made the boy kill himself or . . . or just murdered him. And that act, that awful act, it did something. It *opened* something up in each world, unleashing the end there. And in each world the end came differently, not Four Horsemen, but Fourteen Horsemen, or Forty, or maybe an infinity of Horsemen, each bringing their own kind of Armageddon. The end came in ways you might expect the world would end: disease, or global warming, or some supervolcano opening up and choking the air with soot. Other times it was . . . worse. *Weirder.* Intelligent computers launching nukes or . . . or monsters coming out of holes in the ground, eyeless things, things with wings. In one, I heard a comet passed over, and that was the end of death—those who died got right back up again, hungry as a starving dog for whatever meat, blood, brains they could find."

Nate's gaze glanced over the crazy wall of images, items, and documents. "How do you know all this?"

The way Carl looked at him, it was more like he was looking *through* Nate, instead. Off at some faraway, infinite point. "I've put it together the past few years. Like I said, met some other travelers like you—refugees, if you will, of their own fallen worlds. They tell their tales. And sometimes the . . . atrocities or horrors from those other places, they show up here. Because here is there now. Like I said, the worlds fell, and they fell together. Like the floors of a collapsing building, each on top of the last. So it all falls together, son."

"I'm not your son."

"So you've said."

"The other parts. How'd you know about Jake and Oliver?"

"I saw it happen here with my own eyes. To my grandson. But others saw their own versions happen, too. You aren't the only traveler." His voice broke again. "Like I said."

Nate suddenly understood. "Some of those other travelers, they weren't just random people. Were they? They were versions of your family."

"That's right, Nate. That's right."

Back downstairs, Carl explained more about how things were now in this world. He said that everything was broken, or breaking. The bugs were mostly gone, though some remained: ticks, flies, cockroaches, mosquitoes. In some places, fungus took over: Plants stopped growing—you couldn't grow food—but fungus was having a field day. In other places even *that* had stopped: Dead stuff didn't rot anymore. A fallen tree or a corpse would just lie there, breaking down at one-one-hundredth normal pace, if at all. He said it was always warm, sometimes hot. It was February now, not that it mattered. He said sometimes storms came through, and when they did, they left chaos in their wake. They'd pass by and bring down trees, and he said the trees would scream, literally scream, like a woman or a child being murdered. Sometimes they'd turn puddles of water into gasoline—he was grateful it hadn't poisoned his well, yet. Sometimes the storm would turn all the animals inside out, their guts steaming after the rains passed. ("It's why when a storm comes," Carl said, "you make sure you're *inside,* not out. Unless you like your insides gone outside.")

Carl went on and said, "You're welcome to stay here, Nate. I won't turn you out. I fed you and watered you and cleaned you up best as I could, and though you're not my son I feel some recompense is due to you. But if you stay, I ask that you help out here. We'll need to scavenge, and that means going farther out. We can always head into town and trade with the handful of folks in the fort set up in the middle of town. I need help making sure nothing dies in the well, hand-pumping water, and so on. And then there's committing to the general defense of the house. I've got a few guns around, some ammo. As for things like the bathroom, you can just piss outside, of course, but for the other thing, there's an outhouse I built—"

"I can't stay here," Nate said. "I have to go back."

"Back? Back to *what*?"

"Back to . . . where and when I came from, Carl. I have family."

"Could be that their world will crash into ours and you'll see your Maddie." He narrowed his eyes. "It is Maddie in your world, right? I didn't figure there'd be any deviation from that—I've met a few Maddies already."

"It's Maddie. But you're not understanding me. My world *didn't* fall, Carl. Oliver is alive. Jake is there, and my boy is in danger. I need to get back there. I've already—" His jaw tightened. "Been gone too long."

"How do you figure on getting back?"

"I . . . don't know."

He really didn't.

And with that, he wept.

68

Hiding by Hanging Over the Edge

Time passed at the cabin. Days spun into a week, and that week birthed a second. Oliver and Maddie, at the edge of the world.

They shopped. The little store at the end of the gravel lane didn't have much, so they made trips to a Walmart outside of Honesdale. They had to be frugal; Mom said they would run out of money eventually.

The cabin, a three-hour drive north, wasn't much to look at—rustic, but not so rustic it felt like just a box in the woods. It had plumbing, so no outhouse necessary. The kitchen was a dinky little galley kitchen, and the old stove was the color of pistachios, like something out of the 1950s. The fridge, on the other hand, was the color of old avocado meat—that, from the 1960s or '70s. (And it smelled like a wet dog in there.) One bedroom had a queen bed, but there was a pull-out couch, and that's where Oliver slept, night after night. Or tried to sleep, anyway.

When he managed it, he dreamt of his father. They were good dreams, sometimes, which were worse than bad dreams, because Oliver would wake up thinking that Dad would be there with them, that he was alive and not dead. Other, far worse dreams were of Jake—Jake, who Oliver knew was himself, or some otherworldly version, anyway, an alternate reality doppelgänger who, night after night, chased him through nightmare forests and down phantasmic Walmart aisles and into twisting mine tunnels; those dreams always ended up at the same place, at Ramble Rocks, at the felsenmeer, upon the altar stone.

Mom helped him chop wood for the stove to heat the cabin. It was hard going—Oliver wasn't exactly cut out for physical labor. Didn't help that his left hand was half ruined. The stitches tugged and hurt; Mom told him not to even try to chop the wood, but he was mad at the world, mad at himself, and decided that he liked the pain. Or, at least, deserved it.

The first several times he mostly just got the ax stuck in the wood, and then Mom had to pick it up and slam it down to split the log.

"You're good with that," he said. "Especially for a city girl." The words came out more venomous-sounding than he meant them to be.

She rolled her eyes. "I'm a city girl but let's also not forget, I'm a fucking *badass*." The ax fell again, cleaving half a log into quarters. *Thwack.* "Your father grew up rural, and I can do stuff your father never could. I can weld. Can he weld? Solder? Carve trees into art?"

"It's not Dad's fault," Oliver said defensively.

"No, I know—I didn't mean—" She sighed. "Shit."

"It's fine." He sucked at his lower lip. "I just miss him."

Inside her, he saw a sudden bloom of pain. Like blood in clear water, *whoosh*. She set the ax down and leaned on it—not casually, but like she needed to. A crutch, lest she tumble over.

"I miss him, too."

"I saw a vision of him. He was dying. Dead."

Mom stared off at nothing. "We don't know that was real."

"I guess not. But it felt real." He kicked at some dead leaves. "You think he's still alive?"

She handed Oliver the ax and started gathering up logs to take inside. "C'mon, Dude. Let's get inside. It's getting cold."

69

Up and at 'Em, Tiger

Nate awoke sharply at some point in the night, sure he had heard something but too slow awakening to realize what it was. The darkness around him was impenetrable, and so was the silence: It occurred to him that in his old life in his old world, there was the ever-present white noise *hum* of modern life. The distant buzz of power lines and traffic, the gentle crawl of an airplane somewhere far away, the hum-and-tumble of an air conditioner or a heater or a ceiling fan. But all that was gone. *This* world was still and dark and quiet, and it made him feel all the more alone. Lost in the void.

Then: the sound. Somewhere outside, a human sound. Something that was halfway between a laugh and a scream.

It went on for a little while, then cut short.

As his heart raced, his mind wandered to the thin, bearded man in the woods. The one he'd seen so many times. The one he'd *chased* to Jed's. He wondered who that person was. A traveler, like him? Someone who fell through the cracks of a breaking, or broken, world?

He eased out of bed, his bones snap-crackle-popping as he pushed past the pain in his side. Nate knew this house like the back of his hand, and so as he gently stepped down the stairs, he knew to walk toward the edges of each step to lessen their creaky complaining.

At the bottom of the staircase, he found the old man peering out the glass in the door.

A rifle, held fast in his hand.

He didn't startle when Nate came up. His face, bathed in soft moonlight, turned toward Nate. "You heard it, too."

"I did. Do I want to know what that was?"

"If I knew, I'd tell you. Some freakshow out there, probably. Or maybe just some animal."

"Didn't sound like any animal I know."

"Sure, that's because it wouldn't be any animal you know. Most of the critters are gone. I see a possum once in a while. Maybe a raccoon. But other times . . . animals appear that aren't right. Saw a whitetail deer with six legs. Saw a feral pig once, too, had worms hanging from its face like black spaghetti."

"You think this could just be some animal?"

"No. Probably not."

"Maybe the masked bastards who came at me. Reese's zeroes."

"Could be. I think maybe they come out of that tunnel at Ramble Rocks."

The tunnel. Ramble Rocks.

"I came from the tunnel. Tunnel of Terror. Though where I'm from, it used to be a train tunnel. Part of a park."

"Yeah. In this world it used to be a covered bridge."

"Does it just . . . change? Become something different?"

Carl shrugged. "Seems so. Lately it's been the amusement park. Before that it was an old shopping center. Some of the travelers I've met say it was a coal mine, too, or a park-park, or even a prison. But there's always a tunnel. And there's always a boulder field. And it's always, always called Ramble Rocks."

"And in that boulder field, I'm guessing there's always that stone. The one that looks like a table."

"It's an altar. That's where Oliver died. Or dies. Again and again."

Nate's blood turned to cold slush. "That's how I get back."

"How's that? The stone?"

"The tunnel. I came in via the tunnel. I can go back via the tunnel. A friend of mine—" Nate started, then corrected himself. "Someone

I knew said the wall between worlds there was thin. Thin like old skin, not like a wall at all."

"No. That place isn't safe."

"I don't see I have any other choice."

"You stay here. With me."

"No." *I left before. I have to leave again.*

Carl sniffed and stiffened. "Well, you won't get any help from me. You're on your own there, Nate."

"Yeah. No help from you. There's the father I remember."

The old man turned, indignant. "Oh, go to hell. I saved your life, if you'll recall. Fed you, put water in you, cleaned up your shit and your puke. And as you pointed out, you aren't even my son. You're just a . . . traveler. A *stranger* to me. I was doing you a kindness, and that kindness is now over. You wanna go disappear into the dark? *Up and at 'em, tiger.*"

"Fuck you."

"Uh-huh. Yeah. Fuck me, sure."

Nate crept back upstairs, waiting for morning to come. He didn't hear the mad scream-laughter from the woods anymore. And somehow, that was worse.

The next day, Ramble Rocks amusement park stood before him. Or, he stood before it, maybe—he felt small in its presence. Like a little kid at a museum looking up at the T. rex skeleton. Spears of crepuscular light stabbed through the struts and tracks of the roller coaster, as if fixing it in place.

Moss and vines hung from the parts. Everything in decay, disarray.

But he saw no one. Heard no howls, no mad laughter.

He had one weapon: a long-handled splitting ax. He'd hoped to bring a gun with him, but he'd expected that Carl wouldn't give him shit. And at first, that was true. The old man wasn't there when Nate went out the door. He was up in his room, door closed. But Nate only

got about fifty feet before Carl came calling after him. He handed
over the ax, said, "I got two. Take it. You'll need it."

And that was all the goodbye he got.

Carl went back inside, Nate hit the road.

And now, Nate was here.

He didn't have much of a plan. It was hard to plan for a batshit
universe like this: Nothing made sense, so why make a plan? Best he
could do was decide to go to the tunnel and check it out. Just see
what he could see. Go deep. Look around.

Nate picked his way through the amusement park, and again his
eyes wandered to the spray-painted messages. One was scrawled
across one of the roller-coaster struts:

DON'T EAT THE BLACK APPLES.

He didn't know what that meant, and didn't see any apples to eat.

Idly, his eyes strayed upward, up, up, up, and it took him a moment to realize that the out-of-place thing his gaze had found was a
body. It dangled there from a rope—a noose around the neck. It was
high up there, almost to the tracks. The body hung perfectly still. Its
face was a mess of white, crusted tubules—no features could be seen.

He hurried on.

The yawning void of the Tunnel of Terror loomed. Nate stood at
the edge of the light, and it felt more like he stood at the ledge of a
mountainside cliff. Bits of it crumbling away, threatening to drop him
to his death. His ears rang. His pulse quickened. Every part of him
screamed to turn back, run away, forget about it. But he told himself,
That's what it wants. It wants you to run. So push on. He didn't know
how he knew that. Or if he knew it at all—it was absurd to think that
this place was somehow alive.

And yet, that's suddenly how it felt.

It was alive. Or as close to it as a place could be.

Just inside the tunnel was a body. It was long decayed, its face like an October pumpkin left out till February. It had the cut of a farmer: overalls, work boots, muddy knees. Was it real? He feared that it was. In the curled-up monkey's-paw hand he saw something gleaming—

A lighter.

Nate stepped into the dark. He quickly darted in and stole the lighter from the corpse, half-certain it would suddenly get up and lurch for him.

It didn't.

The lighter was cold in his hand. He flicked the Zippo and summoned a flame.

The tunnel, he knew, should be a circuit. That's how amusement park rides went. You boarded. They went around and around, and then you got off them in the same damn place you got on. But the Tunnel of Terror was not like that. It made no sense, in fact, because it seemed to Nate to be a single straight line into darkness. On and on it went. To where? He didn't know. But as he walked along the tracks, he noticed a gentle, downward grade. Maybe ten percent at first.

Then a little steeper.

The light from the stolen Zippo danced on the walls. It highlighted mechanical zombies on accordion armatures, meant to spring out at riders. He saw speakers that likely once played creepy music or recordings of screams, and warped, wavy mirrors that would freak riders out as they looked over and saw mutated and twisted versions of themselves. Fake rubbery limbs still dangled from the ceiling on chains and cords. A foot, a hand, a head—

He froze. The head.

It wasn't comically gory, like the foot and the hand, the bone sticking out, the red of the exposed muscle gone peach-colored. The head was smaller. Puckered. The skin was sucked tight to the skull, crispy and dry like jerky.

It's a real head, he realized.

The chain holding it dead-ended in a gaff hook, and that hook was stuck into the severed head's temple.

In the dry meat of the head's forehead, in the center of a curtain of brittle dead-straw hair, was a number:

19.

He eased past it, staying on the tracks, lest he fall into the standing water that ran parallel to it.

The Zippo flame illuminated a seemingly endless tunnel. Ahead, shapes stood pressed against the wall—clown mannequins frozen and posed against the curve of the tunnel. Horror clowns, one with a machete, another with its eye hanging out of its head.

Past them, the tunnel kept going, and going, and going.

He turned around, saw that the entrance was a good ways away now. Maybe a quarter mile, already.

A shadow passed in front of the entrance. Like a vulture flying in front of the sun. And then, the tunnel rumbled—down through the top, and to the tracks beneath his feet. *Thunder,* Nate realized.

A storm.

Not here yet. But . . . maybe soon.

Carl had said storms sometimes came through, and when they did, they brought hell with them. *Chaos* was the word he'd used.

Another distant rumble. Made his teeth hum.

And now, a choice. Nate could leave. He could try to get ahead of the storm, head back to Carl's—assuming the old man would welcome him back. Or he could stay here and take shelter until it passed. *Or* he could turn and go deeper still. See where this thing led. If this place was truly somehow . . . transitive, if it could take him to another place, maybe back home, then didn't it stand to figure that he should press on?

What was the saying?

The only way out was through.

That decided it. He'd go deeper.

But before he could turn around and head into the dark—

"Once upon a time," a voice sang, down in the deep. "A young man named Eddie Reese found himself in a train tunnel, angry again at being told *no*—no from another girl, no from another boy: *No, Eddie,* they'd say, *I won't go out with you, I won't touch you, I won't look at you!"*

Nate wheeled to face the darkness. He saw nothing there, though the shadows felt oppressive. He eyed the horror clowns on the wall, half-expecting them to come alive—and come at him.

"Stay back," he cautioned the darkness.

But the voice continued:

"But that day, our young, intrepid Eddie—a fan of numbers, he was—found himself in that tunnel counting first the number of times he had been told *no*, which, for the record, was twenty-one, and then counting the number of erratic, uneven bricks in the tunnel. Which, for the record, was seven. But Eddie found suddenly that he was not alone, just as you are not alone now. That is when Eddie met the demon."

"Fuck off!" Nate said.

"The *demon*, Eligos Vassago, the Archfiend. Above and below, was he. Loyal not to the legions of Hell nor to the filth of Heaven. And he told Eddie that were Eddie willing to undertake a quest, a grand quest, he could break the worlds and become a god, and in doing so, no one would ever tell him no again."

Now, Nate could see the shadow of Edmund Walker Reese stepping through the dark. A blade gleamed, despite the lack of light.

"Ninety-nine girls," came a whisper and a giggle from the walls. Had it come from one of the clowns?

"Ninety-nine for the ninety-nine!" came another whisper, across the way.

"Yes," Reese said, his voice not necessarily loud, yet somehow *everywhere*. Like serpents slithering up the walls in every direction. The echo of them was slow and deliberate, a crawling voice. "Eligos said to kill ninety-nine girls, *pure* girls, girls who were young and chaste, not yet sullied, and if I sacrificed them, then at the culmination, *all would fall.*"

"But you *failed,*" Nate called. "Didn't you? The fifth girl, Sissy Kalbacher. She got away. Thanks to my wife."

"Your *wife.*" Those two words, hissed with great venom and rage. "Doesn't that just figure. Yes. I failed. Perhaps it was always a fool's parade to even try. But try I did, and rewarded I was for my efforts. I was saved from the chair by the lightning—and the demon put me here. Put out to pasture, perhaps. But *oh,* what a nice pasture, Nate. So many victims for the taking. And once in a while a young woman winds her way into my web. Though for now—it's just you, isn't it?"

Nate could feel the tension rising. The air buzzed with it. He had to get out of here. Had to leave. But he wanted to kill Edmund Walker Reese *so damn bad.* If he wasn't going to get home, at least he could take this murderer with him . . .

No, he told himself. *You're not ready. You're injured, Nate. Still.*

"It's all fine now," Reese sang. "My work has been resumed by a more capable candidate. The boy: Oliver. Oliver killing Olivers killing Olivers, dominoes toppling one after the next until the world dies. And when it does, they all come here." These last two words, he growled, an inhuman sound: *"To me."*

He laughed, a mad stuttering whoop.

Edmund Reese surged forward, his hunting knife slashing the air, sparking against the walls. He roared forth, seeming to have not two arms, but four, then six—and his shadow grew larger, stranger, and as he ran it was not just the sound of footsteps in the dark but the wet sound of something slithering, like a clot of infinite worms pushing through the tunnel. And at that, the clowns on the wall began laughing in time with Reese—

Thunder boomed, but Nate saw no choice—he turned tail and hard-charged fast as he could down the tunnel, back toward the entrance. Braving the storm was chaos. But chaos was better than *this*. He couldn't take Reese down. Not here. Not now. He had to *run*.

Nate dared not look behind him, and he kept his eyes fixed ahead. The half circle of light indicating the exit to the Tunnel of Terror dimmed. What was blue sky had gone to an eerie, jaundiced green. A sick sky, stirred up by the coming storm. And like that—

The sounds of footsteps behind him were gone.

Don't look. Don't look. Don't look.

He looked.

Reese stood far back. Flanked now by the outlines of the clowns, who had pulled themselves off the walls, swaying. Something wet gleamed behind them and around them—worms slithering upon the inside of the tunnel. The clowns had stopped, about a hundred yards back. He could see their silhouettes standing there. Watching. Reese was no longer with them. He had returned to the dark. To the tunnel.

Even *they* dared not go out into the storm.

Good.

Into the storm he ran.

Hail hissed around him as the sky grew grayer, and greener. It fell against the broken amusement park with the cacophony of glass beads pouring from the heavens—and they stung him just the same, pelting him with the sting of stones whipped at his head, neck, shoulders, and back. Nate buried his head under the meager shelter of his arms as he raced through the park, past the concession stands and the burnt-out Ferris wheel—

Lightning throttled the sky. White and bright. Filling everything up. And when it was gone again, and Nate was left blinking the streaks of starshine from his eyes, he saw that he was surrounded.

By his son.

So many versions of his son.

"Oliver," he said, his voice cracking.

Oliver, gunshot between his eyes, long wet hair plastered against his cheeks. Oliver, throat open like a steamed envelope. Another Oliver, wrists slit, oozing rust-water blood. This Oliver, bloated like a body from a river, that Oliver, half-dissolved pills stuck to the inside of his lower lip like sugar confetti on a cupcake. Another shot in the chest. One with guts spilling out. Some decayed to the point of being barely recognizable. Some pink-skinned and freshly dead, others gray, dead for weeks but not yet decayed. All of them opening their mouths in concert. Humming and gurgling. Blood pouring out. River water pouring out. A cascade of splashing bile.

Their horrible hum-song resolved into a word—

"Dddaaaaadddd."

Something slammed into him. Nate whirled on it, ax up—

It was Carl. Eyes wide as moons as he looked upon the Olivers all around them. "Jesus Christ," Carl said, loud over the hissing hail. He gestured with the .45 pistol in his hand. "We have to *go,* Nate, c'mon. *C'mon!"* He pulled on Nate, and Nate ran with the old man—he closed his eyes as they moved through the crowd of his son's corpses, knowing that he couldn't look, not again. When he opened them again they were gone, or behind him, and he knew not to look back.

The two of them hurried toward the park exit, now in sight.

"Almost there," Carl called over the cacophony of cascading hail.

Lightning filled the sky once more. And this time, the bolt struck the ground in front of Nate like a hammer—it knocked him backward, flat on his back, and ahead of him he saw Carl, or the shape of him, trapped in the roaring channel of electricity. Nate could see his skin, his bones, all of it turning black and flaking away like fire burning parchment.

The lightning was gone.

And so, too, was Carl Graves.

70

Carving Birds

What a grand spread.

Maddie beheld the feast—sorry, "feast"—before the two of them.

Canned cranberry sauce: a classic.

Canned sweet potatoes: She preferred to make her own most years, but okay, this would do fine.

Cheap Martin's potato slider rolls: a piss-poor substitute for biscuits, but Maddie did what she could, toasting them over the woodstove; now each had the char-black crust of the Devil's heart.

Lunch meat turkey in jarred gravy: the *pièce de résistance*.

Oliver poked at it with a fork, glumly elevating the meager meal to his mouth with a fresh pout for every bite. A little spike of resentment shot through her, and she wanted to rage at him: *You know, a lot of kids in this country get a lot worse, and you could appreciate the effort I put into giving us some kind of Thanksgiving in the middle of this tornado of shit.* But she bit her tongue, because she knew it was unfair. It wasn't that Oliver didn't like the food (though, why would he, ugh). It was that his dad was missing. It was that their lives had been overturned. They were on the run, alone, in the middle of nowhere. He'd almost been killed, and not by some rando, but apparently by *himself*. Plus, he was still taking antibiotics for the hand injury—and that left his guts unsettled.

Kid had been through the wringer.

So have you, she told herself.

And that's when Oliver said, "So when does this end?"

The question hit her like a truck.

"What?"

"When does all this stop? Jake is still out there. They're not going to find him. He has magic. He'll get away, or outwit them, or maybe kill them. And then he'll come for us here." He wasn't just looking *at* her, but *through* her, like he had speared her with his gaze. "What's the endgame? What's the plan, Mom? You always have plans."

It felt like she was falling, like someone had pulled a lever and opened a trapdoor underneath her chair. She felt cold. Then she was hot. Could barely catch her breath and she thought, *Is this menopause, is this a heart attack, is this a fucking aneurysm?* but of course, she knew, it was panic. Sheer, bloody-fanged panic taking a hard bite.

I'm someone with lists and goals and plans, always knowing what to do, but here she was and she had nothing. No answers. No direction. They'd just removed themselves from the world, as if they'd died and gone to this interstitial place, this *limbo,* this cabin at the end of the world.

What was the end?

Was there an end?

"You okay?" Oliver asked, no longer watching her eyes, but now looking toward her middle. Toward her heart. *What does he see?*

"Yeah," she lied. Then, the truth shouldered its way to the front of her mouth: "No! God. Fuck no." She gasped in a sudden sob, and wept hard for ten seconds—ten nearly eternal seconds. Wiping her eyes, she cleared her throat and said, "This dinner is rat food. It's shit, and I'm done with it."

"Oh—I didn't mean—"

Standing up suddenly, she added: "Come on. Let's go do something."

Bewildered, he asked, "What? Why?"

"Because, my boy, when the time comes, when your head's just full of . . ." She gesticulated wildly, her fingers scribbling madly in the orbit of her skull. "*Nonsense,* the best way to machete the weeds and drown out the static is to go make something. So that's what we're going to do. We're going to go and make something. For us. For the world. We make."

For the first time in weeks, she saw her boy smile.

It gave her life.

They sat on the cabin's narrow front porch in the burgeoning cold, under a porch light that was just a bulb inside a large mason jar. Beyond the meager light was the muddy-rut parking lot in front of the cabin, and a long driveway that cut through a fence of dark pines standing sentinel. Above was a clear, star-sprayed night. The moon was just a thin shaving of white bone.

Oliver's joy at the idea of creating was hampered by his difficulty actually *doing* it—he struggled to hold wood in his ruined hand and carve with the other. Mom must've detected his frustration, and instead did most of the carving—she just let him decide what they'd look like.

They'd found a crude knife in the kitchen drawer that Mom was using to carve bits of softball-sized firewood into owls. She gritted her teeth and whittled the pair of ears into their final points before handing it to Oliver. The owl he held in his hand felt substantial—not light and airy, but heavy in a way that almost seemed impossible. He lined it up on the wooden porch railing with the other two she'd carved. Each was a little different from the one before it. It felt almost like they were watching him. He guessed that's what was cool about being an artist: the feeling your work was more than what it was. Like you gave it life. Imbued it with some spirit.

"Hand me the next chunk," she said, and he reached down into the pile of firewood they'd chopped. Oliver did as she asked and she said, "Screech owl this time? Barn owl? What?"

He laughed and shrugged. "I don't know. Like, um, one of those frogmouth owls?"

"The tawny frogmouth is not an owl," she corrected, gesturing with the knife.

"How do you know that?"

"Kids aren't the only ones who can watch YouTube, buddy."

"Fine, fine. We just did a horned owl, so yeah, I guess, screech?"

"Good choice, kiddo. Pull one up on the phone for me, we'll get a photo for reference."

He nodded and got to work.

"Why owls?" he asked.

She smiled. "You know, when I was a kid? I had an owl. Er—not a *real* owl, but not a toy, either. It was this little tchotchke that my dad bought for me on some trip upstate one time. Something for a shelf, a decoration. It was an owl, and it was made from coal. Carved from it. I don't know that I ever thought much about it but . . . it sat on my dresser, night after night. Watching over me."

"Maybe these owls can watch over us."

"Maybe, Dude. May. Be."

As she talked and worked, Oliver noticed that the pain and rage inside his mother had ebbed once more. He'd watched it peak during dinner—while they were talking, a maelstrom of frustration had danced up inside her, like a desert twister. It filled all parts of her with whirling, flensing darkness. But now it was smaller. It had shrunken down to a small, pulsing thing. Was that good? It felt good. But again, Oliver grappled with questions over the nature of pain. Was it better for the pain to be made small, but allowed to remain? Or was it like an infection that needed healing? A bad tooth that demanded extraction.

I could just reach in and take it from her . . .

"As to your earlier question," she said suddenly, "I don't know."

"What earlier question?" he asked, even though he knew.

"What the plan is. How long this lasts. All of it." She idly spun the knife in her grip. "I don't know. I don't have any answers."

"What if he comes for us?" He didn't have to say who.

"I dunno, Dude. We have your father's pistol, and he taught me how to use it long ago. We're way out of the way, in the middle of nowhere. There's a gate at the bottom, and we have the key. It's pretty defensible and, worse comes to worst, we could escape into the woods. Highway's only a few miles north of here."

"Wouldn't it be better to be . . . like, near people?"

"*No.*" He watched the pain in her bloom at that, like black smoke. "We can't trust other people, Olly. You trusted Jake—look how that went. Dad trusted Jed, too. It's best if it's just you and me."

"You know where Jed is, don't you?"

Mom narrowed her eyes in suspicion. "Why do you ask?"

"You said you found him. And then you let him go again."

"Uh-huh."

Oliver felt her gaze crushing him into paste. "What?"

"Don't act all incredulous. You looked at my phone."

Gulp.

"Well. I mean." He hated lying. *Hated it.* "Okay! Yes, yeah, I was looking for games, like, anything, even Candy Crush or some other old app because I was bored and . . . then I saw the text and . . ."

It was a text that said, in all caps because that was apparently how old people texted, HOPE YOU AND THE BOY ARE OKAY. IF YOU NEED ANYTHING AT ALL, TEXT THIS NUMBER. I'M SURE YOU DON'T TRUST ME, AND I UNDERSTAND THAT, BUT IF EVER THE NEED IS DIRE, I'M HERE.

If ever the need is dire . . .

Mom shrugged. "We haven't talked much. He doesn't know where we are."

"Do you know where he is?"

"Nope."

"So, why even talk?"

She sighed. "They're only a few texts. He was just checking in."

"Maybe because he's still working for Jake."

"That could be. But I don't think so."

"Why?"

"I don't know." Irritation had crept into her voice. Again the black smoke stirred inside her. "I think I got through to him. I think I found a doorway into him and walked him through it. Does that make sense? Fuck, it probably doesn't." She looked down at the lump of wood, pre-owl. "He's a man with a lot of pain, and that pain got the better of him. I don't forgive him. Not at all. Your father was a man of great pain, too, and he never let it guide him, or at least, it didn't control him." Grunting, she stabbed the wood into the porch railing, *kachunk*. "I wish your father were here. I was good at managing a whole lot of things, Olly, but this? All this chaos and crazy shit? Your father was always a rock in the storm—unperturbed by crisis, able to manifest the coolest calm and fortitude. And I fucking miss him."

"Me too. I wish he were here."

"Same, kiddo. Same."

They sat like that for a while. The cold of November crept into Oliver's bones, and he shuddered. "I think I'm ready to go in."

"You go ahead. I'm gonna stay out here for a while. Maybe keep up the whittle-work for a while."

"G'night, Mom."

"Night, Dude."

Maddie was three beers in, and thirteen owls deep.

The beer was a particularly vicious Russian imperial stout named after Old Rasputin. She'd picked it up at a distributor next to the Honesdale Walmart. She couldn't feel her lips, and she *could* feel her teeth. Both a sign she was not yet all the way shit-faced, but she was on her way.

As for the owls, well, by the fifth she'd stopped caring what kind of owl they were, and by the tenth they'd started to look maybe a little derpy, but she still liked them. *My weird little owl family,* she thought. Guardians and hunters.

She poked at one with the knife, and it wobbled on the railing.

"C'mon," she urged it. "Blink. Flap your wings. Hoot at me."

Poke, poke, poke.

"Screech! Fly! Claw my eyes out! Get to fucking work!"

Still nothing. Each just a dead piece of wood.

"Ah, fuck off, then," she barked, and swept them all off the railing.

And again she felt sure she was missing something. Some piece of all of this. Some piece of *herself.*

What was she doing here? What was she hoping to accomplish?

She'd been right. She missed Nate. Yes, she was the one who had plans inside of plans inside of plans. But in this kind of uniquely fucked-ass situation, *he'd* know what to do.

And I fucking miss him.

Me too, she heard her son's voice say in her head.

I wish he were here.

She chewed the inside of her cheek. Looked down at the knife. Looked down at the owls. Her mind flashed to the memory of making Edmund Walker Reese without even meaning to—a mad, nasty automaton come to life, trying to kill her.

She wished Nate could be here.

But then she wondered.

What if he could?

What if she could bring Nate here?

Maddie started to plan.

71

Travelers

Nate rocked himself up to a sitting position, trying to blink away the wave of white in his vision. Slowly, the wall of light began to disintegrate into lava lamp blobs of it. He stood, stung by hail, looking at the charred ground where Carl had been only moments before, when lightning . . . took him? Burned him? Was that char mark him?

"Carl!" Nate called. He swallowed hard, wondering what to do next. Go back to the house? Run back into the park? He felt dazed.

Then all the hairs on his neck stood. The ones on his arms, too. Everything tingled—the air felt alive, like burning ants.

And then it was like a silent thunderclap: a chuff of air, a rush of wind. Carl appeared in front of him, standing still, staring off at nothing. Then he disappeared again, only to reappear a half second later. Like he was a glitch, a skipped image. His voice stuttered this second time:

"Ate—am I—ight—ning—"

Nate rushed to him, grabbing his hand and pulling him away. A static discharge between them made a loud snap: It was like getting pricked by a thumb tack. But then Carl, shaken, seemed to remain.

And it was Nate's turn to say: "We have to go, Carl. C'mon. *We have to get the hell out of here, now.*"

By the time they stepped back into the house, weary and wild-eyed, the storm had already passed. The day went back to being as it had before: muggy and warm, the air thicker now with clouds of gnats and mosquitoes.

Inside, they both sat down hard at the dining room table.

Neither looked at each other for a while. Neither did much of anything, really. They sat there, numb. Shell-shocked.

Finally, Nate said: "Thanks for coming to get me."

Carl's gaze flicked toward Nate.

"Of course. You're not my son, but . . ." His words died in his mouth.

"The lightning," Nate said. "I've seen it before. It took you away. Somewhere else. Didn't it?"

"I saw myself dying."

Nate paused. "Okay."

"I thought for a moment I *was* dying. That I was having some kind of . . . what do they call it, an *out-of-body* thing. I stood in the corner of my bedroom, watching another version of myself on the bed. That version of me looked like hell. Paper skin. Yellow like pus. I was dying. Maybe even dead. And you, or some version of Nate, were there—"

All the while, as Carl spoke, the realization settled into Nate.

"You crossed over," Nate said.

"What? Like that old show *Angel of the Night*?"

"I don't know what that is. I just mean—you were a traveler, Carl. You went to *my* world. You saw . . . you saw me. And my father, my version of you." The words were hard to summon, but he managed to keep on talking. "Carl, my father died of cancer. I was there when it happened. I hated him. I wasn't there to provide him with . . . comfort or kind words. I wasn't looking for closure. I just wanted to watch him die. And I did. But then I saw . . . I saw *you* there. Standing in the corner. Gun in your left hand. I thought you were his ghost at the time but . . ." He rubbed his eyes with the heels of his hands. "You were *you*. Not a ghost. You were real, I guess."

"Uh. I'm having a hard time wrapping my head around all that."

"You and me both, Carl."

Carl patted him on the arm. "Go clean yourself up, son. I'll get out the whiskey. Because I need a drink or three, and I figure you do, too."

The whiskey wasn't fancy. Royal Crown Canadian—Nate pointed out that in his world, it was Crown Royal, not Royal Crown, but otherwise, the packaging and branding remained the same. Further, his own father drank the stuff, too.

An hour in, they were both pretty sauced. Not fall-down-and-puke-on-yourself drunk, but for Nate, nothing hurt, everything felt like a warm bath of Epsom salts. Carl was telling a story about a "fella he worked with" at the plastics fabrication plant where he worked for most of his life, a guy named Keith. Keith, he said, was always playing the lottery. Every day, every week, every scratch-off ticket, every Powerball. Keith was fond of saying, *God helps those who help themselves, that's from the Bible. You gotta meet God halfway and he'll meet you the other half. Can't win if you don't play, Carl, no sir, no you can't.*

"So one day," Carl went on, coffee mug full of whiskey in hand, "the daft shitbird left his fool lottery ticket on the desk. And we're talking Powerball, the big payout—it's gone bigger since, but at the time it was the biggest damn jackpot they'd had, some five hundred million or some such. And Keith, he was like clockwork every day, and he went off to the bathroom to take his morning dump, stink up the damn place, and so I snuck over to his desk and quickly—" Here Carl mimicked the action. "Scribbled down the numbers he'd picked. And I went back to my desk, kicked back with the newspaper, and whistled a Willie Nelson tune.

"Now, like I said, Keith was clockwork. They did the lottery drawing every night at eleven P.M., but Keith couldn't stay up for that—we had to be at work by five in the fuckin' morning, right? Sure. So he'd come in, put his lunch in the fridge, take his morning constitutional, then come out, look for the newspaper, and check the numbers. *Every day.*

"But on *that* day, I had the paper first, so he came out of the bathroom smelling like the air freshener he used as if, uhh, as if it were cologne—and by the way those bathroom air freshener things don't work, I'll tell you—"

Nate laughed. "They just make the bathroom smell like shit *and* vanilla instead of just shit."

"That's right! That's right, they do. So he comes out smelling like—well, I don't know if it was shit and vanilla but maybe shit and marigolds or some such, and he's looking for the paper—but then he sees I have it. And he asks for it and I say, here, I'll read you the numbers, and all the while I'm dragging him a little, I'm saying to him, Keith, you'll never win. You'll never win! Quit playing, for chrissakes, and he's saying, *God helps those, meet God halfway, can't win if you don't play* and all that happy horseshit.

"But you see, I know his numbers. So I'm reading off to him, real slowly like, I'm reading off *his actual numbers* from the little Post-it Note where I got them written down, you see? So I read them one by one, number by number, and as I go along his eyes get wider and wider. And by the end he thinks he's won! He thinks he's won *five hundred million dollars.*"

"What did he do?" Nate asked, laughing.

"Oh, what did he do? Nate, I'll tell you. He was spending that money from the first thirty seconds. Gonna buy a hot tub. Gonna buy a Ford F-350. Gonna buy a house in the Florida Keys and make Jimmy Buffett himself come and write a song for him about, who knows, parrots and pirates and cheeseburger bullshit or what-have-you. And he's not planning on sharing it with us, ohh no. Not us, not charity, nothing. But what about God, I asked him? Wouldn't God want him to help feed the starving children? And he said, I swear he said this, *God helps those who help themselves, Carl.* Next thing we know he's already starting to practice his resignation speech—he was gonna give it that day! Gonna walk right into the boss's office and tell him to fuck right off, all: *I'm rich now, sayonara, you prick.* So he started to march to the boss's office and we let him get to the door before we stopped him and told him the truth. Ohh, man. He was mad, boy! Steaming mad. His face got red like a beet and—" Carl started laughing so hard he was wheezing. "Oh, it was something. That goddamn fool."

The two of them laughed themselves hoarse, then Carl poured more whiskey for the two of them.

Carl said, the humor gone from his voice, "You ever, ahh, you ever do this with your father? Sit and drink and shoot the shit, I mean."

"No." Nate tensed up. "Definitely not."

"Your father was a real piece of shit, huh?"

"A real turd, Carl. A real turd."

"Mind if I ask . . ."

"You wanna know how bad he was."

Carl didn't answer, but the look on his face was plain enough.

"Okay," Nate said. "I don't talk about this much, but Dad, *my* dad, *my* Carl Graves, he would beat the piss out of me. He'd slap my mother around. I don't know. It sounds . . . hollow when I say it like that, like it's mundane, but I can't tell you how it felt growing up in a house like that. It wasn't even that he beat me on the regular—some days he seemed like he was trying to make up for it, like he was trying to do better, but somehow, that was worse. Because it was like, well, it was like today. A sunny day that hides a surprise storm coming. From calm to chaos. Made it so I couldn't trust a single moment. One minute he'd be laughing along with some TV show or watching some cowboy movie and the next he'd be laying into me, or into my mother, maybe over something small or dumb, maybe over nothing at all. Maybe over something he imagined. He drank. He smoked. He beat us."

Carl was quiet for a bit. "I'm sorry to hear all that."

"Yeah. Well. Was what it was." Now Nate leveled a piercing gaze toward the old man. His voice was thrust through with ice when he said, "How about you, Carl? You beat on your boy? On Nathan?"

"No."

"You sure about that?"

Carl let out a breath and gave a lazy nod. "I'm sure. But that don't make me father of the goddamn year, either. I wasn't there, Nate. I wasn't home. I was at work, and then after work I was at the tavern, and then after that I was probably whoring it up with some waitress or whatever."

"And Nathan? What'd that do to him?"

"The chain has a couple more links than that, Nate. Me not being there was bad for my wife, Susan. Susan was . . . a drinker." At that, Carl stared down into his own whiskey like it was an oracular pool. "She was a bit of a mess, and instead of helping her I just ran away, and in my absence, her pain and her misery grew, and so did her drinking. *She* beat on our son. And I think it's worse when a mother beats on her son, because fathers, as men, we're just . . . angry, just tornados of pain, but women are nurturing, or supposed to be. They're the ones who hug away your pain—"

"Don't do that. Don't make it okay that men are monsters. If we are, we need to own that. It's not better or worse when one of your parents is an abuser and the other isn't, Carl. It's awful either way."

He tried to imagine his own mother being the monster in that family. Fact was, Nate held some blame for her over what happened to him. She didn't protect him. She didn't protect herself, either. All his life, and even now, he warred between feeling so sad for her, and so mad *at* her, too. He knew she was a victim, same as he was, but he was a little kid, and she was an adult. She could've taken him away. Couldn't she?

Blood under the bridge, he supposed.

"You're right," Carl said. "Point is, I abandoned the family and she had no one there to help her course-correct, and she took it out on Nathan. And Nathan grew up . . . you know, he was a raw nerve, that kid. Always getting into trouble. Getting into fights. Got into drugs in high school, somehow managed to graduate despite all that. He was a mess. Sometimes he'd start to right the ship and then another hard wind would knock him adrift again, and then came Maddie, and Oliver—an accident, that kid, but by then my wife had passed away from liver disease and I was settling down, so Oliver lived with me as many days as he lived with them. Then, ahh—"

Here he stopped for a moment. Once more staring into the turbid depths of the middling whiskey. He sniffed, as if summoning some resolve, and then slammed back the glass.

"Then Nathan overdosed one night. There was a note. So. Maddie and Oliver became a bigger part of my life and I tried to do them well, but . . . the ghost of my son lived on in Oliver. And then that boy Jake came along and . . . that was that. Just a train chugging along on a bad, broken track. The crash was inevitable, I guess. So much goddamn wreckage along the way."

Wreckage. That word stuck with Nate. *So much goddamn wreckage.*

"I'm sorry," Nate said. "For whatever that's worth."

"It's worth something. Not everything, but something." Carl blinked a shine from his eyes. "Lemme ask you: How'd you do it?"

"Do what?"

"Keep it all together. My Nathan was screwed up by what me and my wife did to him. And we were . . . I guess screwed up by what was done to us. My own father kicked the shit out of me on the regular. Her mother was a drunk. The apple don't fall too far from the tree, as they say. But you—unless you're selling me a book of tales, you kept it together. How?"

Nate chuckled softly. "I just did. I just kept it together. Not even together—I kept it behind what I called my seawall. Like a storm-tossed ocean held at bay by a strong, strong emotional wall."

"You ever worry that something like that, something that bad, won't stay behind the wall? A hurricane might bring it up and over."

"I do worry about that. Or did, anyway. I worried that the wall would break. Or the ocean would rise too high, too fast. And I feared I'd one day break. I'd drink too much. Or choke my son or hit my wife. I knew deep down I wouldn't, but sometimes you get a thought in your head and you just can't shake it no matter how hard you try." He sighed. "My Oliver, we took him to therapy. I should've been the one in therapy. I was almost jealous of him but didn't really know it at the time. Just to have someone like that to talk to . . . to help, I dunno, bring it all out."

"You ever hear the saying that oxygen is the best antiseptic?"

"According to you, I thought it was bleach." Nate waited, then slowly cracked a smile.

Carl laughed again, a big, sudden whoop. Then they were drinking again. They drank until the bottle was gone and night had come.

Sleep that night was a restless shade, stirring amongst the graves. The whiskey helped him sleep at first, but after some unknown amount of time he woke up again, restive in the dark. Feeling like he could hear Reese out there, whispering about demons and numbers.

My god, how fucking insane all of this was.

Insane *and* unreal.

Maybe it wasn't real. He comforted himself with that. Maybe this was all just a deranged vision—he'd gone into a coma, or he was dying and this was what played across his mind in the last few seconds of his life. *Or* this was all some kind of . . . *Matrix*-level simulation that had glitched so bad it had gone off the rails, and the end of the world was just the degradation of data, a breakdown of systems, a cascade of unhappy accidents.

Just like Carl had glitched out of existence.

Bzzt, and then he went elsewhere. And else*when,* too. Lightning. Same way that Reese came and went.

Holy shit.

Nate sat up in the dark.

Carl went to Nate's world. He left Nate—and still ended up with Nate. And not in sync with time—he showed up to before Nate had even bought the house. This fallen world, comprising all the ruined timelines, did not match up with the one that remained—the one from which Nate came. All this time he'd been feeling like he was racing the clock, like if he didn't hurry back, he couldn't save Oliver. Like he was racing Jake for the life of his son—and to stave off the end of his world.

But if the timelines didn't march together in lockstep . . .

He could go back. He could fix it.

Carl went back.

If only for a moment.

Maybe that was the way. The storm. The lightning.

Maybe that was the way.

72

The Winnowing

I have to go somewhere," Maddie said to Oliver the next morning. Already a little Moka pot was brewing coffee, which she quickly poured in a thermos to take with her. (And oof, she needed it; last night's Old Rasputin had come back from the dead and was haunting her brain in the form of a persistent, if mild, hangover.) "Get up. Jacket on. Shoes. We'll grab breakfast on the way—sandwiches from Wawa or something."

"We're in Sheetz country. No Wawas up here, remember."

"Ugh. Fuck. *Sheetz*. Fine. Let's roll."

"Where we going?"

"I dunno. Walmart, probably, but . . . we'll drive around. I need some things."

"What kind of things?"

"You know. *Things*."

Seemed it was his turn to act suspicious. "You're being weird."

"I have a project I want to work on." She thought about telling him, but Oliver had it hard enough already without his own mother dumping this in his lap. *Hey, Dude, didn't I tell you that sometimes the things I make come to life? I have magic powers, like your friend Jake! Cool, right?* It felt like a betrayal not to tell him, but wouldn't it be better to *show* him?

"I . . . don't wanna." He blinked at her, bleary and weary. Hair all in a tangled, half-frozen tidal wave. "Can't you just go?"

"What do you mean? We stick together."

"I just, I dunno, I just woke up. I'm tired. And over the last week we've kinda, well, seen a *lot* of each other and—"

"You want time alone."

He didn't answer, but she could see it on his face. And of course he did. He was a fifteen-year-old boy trapped in a cabin with his mother.

"Olly, I don't know."

"I'll be fine."

"If Jake comes—"

"He could show up while you're here, too."

"But if I'm gone—" She stopped short of saying, *I can't protect you.* "I want to make sure you're safe."

"There's a phone."

"Fig said phone service is spotty. And there's weather coming—"

"So, leave *your* phone." Oliver didn't have a phone anymore, not since Jake put a pick-ax through it. "If something happens, I'll call Fig."

"Fig won't be able to get here. It's hours to this place."

"So, 911 then."

Maddie paced. *The kid needs his space. He's been through a lot.*

"Fine," she said, finally.

He flopped back on the bed. "Thank you."

"You're going to be okay?" she asked him.

"Yes, Mom."

"You promise me?"

"I promise."

Maddie left in the Subaru.

That's when the first snowflakes started to fall.

It's just flurries, Oliver told himself. He ate cold turkey from the night before, looking out the smeary glass of the cabin window. Mom had said there was "weather" coming, though it wasn't supposed to be here until tonight. It was winter—well, almost—so they could expect some flurries here and there. It was normal. No worries.

He took a walk for a while, just wandering the woods. Slate-gray sky above, whorls of flurries. Oliver tried chopping wood, but his left hand hurt too much—the cold stuck in there like an icicle splinter, so he thought, to hell with this, he'd go back to the cabin, maybe read some more of the Robin Hobb book he'd brought.

But as he headed closer to the cabin, he saw something in the window. A flicker of light and shadow.

Movement, he thought, and suddenly he cursed himself:

The phone was still in there.

Oh, no. No no no.

Fucking Walmart.

Maddie was a snob. She knew it. She felt it in her bones, all the way down to the marrow. She would've preferred to have been anywhere else but a Walmart—it felt equal parts dystopian and apocalyptic, like this was the last big-box department store operating in the end times. Those who haunted the aisles and shelves were a motley mix: camo-clad doomsday preppers with their ass cracks showing; old white men who wore cowboy hats because apparently that was still a thing here in upstate PA; chunky girls with too-tight glitter-script spandex swallowed by hungry, hungry butt cheeks, their hair teased higher than the Tower of Babel; shuffling housewives haunted by the ghosts of regret; pock-cheeked teenagers in their Walmart vests, pushing a mop over mysterious spills. Fluorescent lights buzzed and snapped above. Somewhere, a baby wailed.

But it was what it was, and what it *was* was the only damn place around that had anything close to what she needed.

Maddie was a desperate woman, and though she would've preferred to tackle the *making of a husband* with the highest quality tools, parts, and assorted *reagents,* she did not have access to them.

But they had chicken wire.

Which meant *she* had chicken wire.

She bought that, wire snips, needle-nose pliers, a bit of gardening wire, a pair of textured gloves for grip, and two rolls of duct tape. Because duct tape was *real* damn magic.

While there, she also re-upped some of their supplies: food, bottled water, some clothes, cleaning materials.

Maddie paid, and headed outside—

Only to find that it had really started snowing like a sonofabitch. *Maybe just a squall,* she thought—it was blowing this way one minute, and then the next, shoving hard the other direction. This wasn't in the forecast. Her middle clenched up again, thinking of the mad storm that had besieged their home just last month. *Strange weather.*

Well, she figured the Subaru would handle it. The Forester was an all-wheel-drive, all-weather badass. She got in and hit Route 6 to head back to the cabin. *It'll be fine,* she told herself, even as the snow came down like punishment from a vengeful god.

Gently, quietly, Oliver urged open the cabin door.

Across the room, on the far side of the pull-out couch, he saw that the television was turned on. Black-and-white static hissed.

It reflected in the window glass.

That's all it was, he thought, letting out a sigh of relief. Just the static. Not movement of anything other than the interplay of light and dark.

But then, the real question got its hooks in:

Why was the TV on? He hadn't turned it on. They couldn't get crap for channels here. And he didn't want to watch PBS.

Oliver stepped inside and kicked snowmelt off his shoes and shut the door behind him.

Then: *kkksssshhh,* the volume of the static hiss rose to a roar. He clamped his gloved hands over his ears—

Just as the static went black.

And in the black, a face appeared.

Red demon eyes stared through the curtain of white. That's what they looked like, all the brake lights lined up ahead of her. Maddie slammed the pedal and stopped the Subaru short. The vehicle settled into a skid—*No, no, no!*—barely coming to a halt just before hitting the rear bumper of a beat-to-hell Chevy pickup. No impact, *whew,* but ahead, she saw the ghost of a shape through the squall: a tractor trailer, unceremoniously jackknifed across every single fucking lane. Quickly she pivoted her head, popping the car into reverse—and already her ears picked up the hiss of braking tires sliding on slush and snow as cars skidded toward her.

She braced for impact and—

Still nothing. Thank all the gods in all the heavens, but already there were cars behind her, and cars behind them, and this thing was locking up tight. She had no room to move, nowhere to reverse. And no way to go forward. Maddie reached for her phone—

Which, of course, she did not have.

Olly had it.

Olly had the damn phone.

She steadied her breathing. It was fine. This wouldn't be forever. They'd get this truck out of the way and she'd be back at the cabin inside the hour. Maddie was sure of it.

On the TV, the darkness resolved into a face Oliver momentarily recognized as his own—that is, until the spray of pixels continued to sharpen into the grainy, sneering face of Jake.

"Oh," Jake said, almost playfully. "I didn't see you there."

Oliver stood perfectly still. *I fell asleep and this is my nightmare,* but no, this was real.

"I fucking *hate* you," Oliver seethed, standing behind the couch.

"Then don't you really hate yourself?"

"We're not the same."

"I know," Jake said, the note of bitter disappointment sung like an off-note. "That's where I went wrong. I thought we understood each other. I thought, deep down, there was enough of me in you—and you in me—that I'd get through to you. But sometimes a nail needs a hammer."

Oliver gasped and slid down behind the sofa.

"You can hiiiide," Jake said, singsongy. "That's okay. I can still talk. And you'll still listen because you're a reasonable kid, Olly."

This is what he wants. Don't listen.

He thought about running to the door—throwing it open and fleeing into the cold, into the snow. And yet, he found himself staying put. Even as he willed his legs to stand him up, his feet to carry him out the door . . .

And yet, he remained.

"Turns out, I had my sales pitch all fucked up," Jake said. "Here I thought with your *limitless empathy* and you being an antenna for the world's pain, you'd want to fix it all. You'd want to stop all the school shootings, reverse climate change, just stop the whole ride so we could remake it. A better vision of the future. And then with your daddy sent away—fucking *Nate*—I thought I did it. Killing Graham Lyons and his fucking asshole father, I figured *that* clinched it. That was it! Game over, I won. I almost had you, didn't I? Give me the ego boost, Olly. Tell me I was at least *close.*"

"You were never close," Oliver lied.

"Whatever helps you sleep at night, kid."

"Maybe you should just *give up.* Maybe this world is the one worth saving, not the one you destroy, you piece of shit."

Jake *hmm*ed at that. When he spoke, the static crept into his voice, hissing sibilance behind every syllable. "Too late now, Oliver. The rest of the fallen worlds are all leaning *hard* on this one. Crushing it.

Corroding it. Things from those worlds will come into this one. Already have. The machinery here is all starting to break down. We're in the death spiral now. And it's time for me to finish it. I figured out what'll get you here."

Oliver kicked off his shoe, put it in his hand, and stood up, ready to let fly. He was going to break that screen and send Jake's image back to the darkness of a shattered cathode-ray tube.

But his hand froze.

There, on the screen, was Caleb.

Caleb, tied to a chair. Mouth sealed behind a clumsy stretch of duct tape, that swatch of tape slicked with dark blood. Blood trickled from his nose, and down his brow, too. Even from here, Oliver could sense his pain—real pain, *physical* pain welling up like boiling water.

Jake's face appeared again with a snap of his fingers.

"Got your attention, did I?" Jake asked.

"Please . . ." Oliver said, feeling his throat tighten.

"You care about people. The little people. *Each* person. You don't care about *humanity*—" That last word, Jake said theatrically, big and booming, an opera in eight letters. "You care about humans. And I thought, gosh, I have a human right here I know you care about. So, the deal I'll make is simple: You get here to the altar stone by midnight tonight, or I'll start cutting parts off him. I'll bleed him. Whittle him down to sticks. And then he'll die eventually, Oliver, because as I'm sure you know, people can only endure so much trauma. But good news, you can stop it."

Oliver swallowed a lump of fear and rage. Somehow, logic persisted, and he thrust his chin out, defiant. "But you say it all has to end anyway. I come there, I die on the stone, then what? Caleb dies just the same."

"But you don't come, you'll know I'll hurt him. Won't even kill him, because death would be a mercy. The pain I deliver unto your friend will radiate off him and reach you in that little cabin you're hiding in." Detecting Oliver's shock and silence, Jake *tsk-tsk*ed him. "Of course I know where you are. Could I come and get you? Sure. But this is less work for me."

"Don't you hurt Caleb any more than you have."

Jake smiled. "You love him? Like, got a thing for him? You seem like you like boys and girls, both. A little Caleb, a little Hina. Maybe after Caleb, I'll find her, too. Make her hurt, too. Hurt so good."

"You fucking asshole—"

"And after I've killed them, leaving their corpses behind me in a bloody wake, if you still don't come, we'll come for you. We will hunt your mother like a dog through the woods. Her, I'll make hurt for what she did to me, Oliver. I'll cut off her fingers and toes and tits; I'll put starving worms in all her cracks and crevices and secret places. I'll stuff her up with so much pain, Oliver, before she finally expires. As for you, well, you get the Taser, or drugs, and we'll make you *watch*. You'll watch it *all*. And somewhere, there in the dark of your own closed eyes, it'll snap into place. You'll see that everything is bad and everything is broken, and it won't just be you wanting to escape that singular pain. It'll be you wanting an escape for everybody, from *all* the pain, and you'll want to take the whole world with you. For your mother and your dead friends and your gone-world father— you'll want to help all the worlds, all the timelines, find peace."

Oliver swallowed. "Is that what happened to you? You just wanted an escape from all the pain? Can't hack it anymore?"

"I can hack a lot more than you, be sure of that."

"I *hate* you."

"Feeling's mutual, kid."

And then the TV went dark.

An hour now. An *hour* of sitting here in the Subaru. Maddie let the engine idle long enough to warm up, then cut it again to save some gas. Once in a while she saw people milling about outside as the snow lightened. The squalls came and they went—sometimes it was just a speckling of flurries, white dots on gray; sometimes it was a full whiteout, swallowing the world in nothing.

Eventually she got out when she saw some folks wandering. She caught up with a round, jowly fellow in a Marty McFly vest and a John Deere hat—he stood outside a Chevy Blazer from the late nineties. Marines sticker on the back next to a DON'T TREAD ON ME Gadsden flag.

"Hey, excuse me," she asked him.

"Hi there," he said. "Helluva thing," he added, gesturing up and all around him, indicating the weather.

"Yeah. It's pretty weird out there."

"Out there, out here, out everywhere."

"You know what happened up ahead?"

"Trucker lost control—ground was just slick enough and the truck jackknifed. Then a couple cars from the other side slid into it, lost some of his load, I guess—nothing exciting, sadly, just construction material. Rebar, I think. Tell you, one time I saw a truck spill on I-80, whole trailer tipped over, and you know what came out? Oranges. Just a shedload of oranges, all rolling out. Tasty ones, too, I am glad to report."

"That's uh, that's funny. Can I ask you a favor?"

He shrugged and smiled. "Never hurts to ask, but if you need somewhere to pee, I'm all out of empty bottles."

At that, she really did laugh.

"I don't think I'm peeing in a bottle unless it also comes with a good-sized funnel. No, I could use to borrow a cellphone—mine's out of commission and I need to call my kid, let him know why I'm late."

He gave her a look like he was sizing her up. "Sure. Besides, where you gonna go with it?" From his jeans he dug out a flip phone, because apparently they still made those, and handed it over to her.

She thanked him, and took a few steps—not far, so as not to worry him—and called Oliver. It rang, and rang, and rang.

C'mon, kiddo. Where are you?

Finally, an answer.

"Hey, Mom," he said. Voice a bit broken up.

"Olly, Dude, it's snowing pretty good out here. Guess the weather we were supposed to get tonight is already here. I'm stuck on the road—jackknifed truck, and not sure when I'll be headed back."

"Okay." She heard worry in his voice.

"It'll be fine. You're good. You've got my phone, the gun, got wood for the stove, food in the fridge, even though the fridge smells like damp ghost farts—" She expected a laugh, but none came. "It'll be okay."

"I know."

"I love you."

"I love you too. Sorry, Mom."

"Sorry for what? Not your fault I'm out here."

"I know. Just . . . sorry."

"See you soon, Dude."

She handed the phone back to Jowly John Deere. "Thanks," she said.

"Your kid all right?"

"He's . . . okay. He's had a rough go of things." *And that,* she thought, *was the understatement of the year.*

"Lemme guess, teenager?"

"Yeah."

"I have one of those. She's nineteen. Sucks out there for kids. We squandered all the good we got and left them with the empty bag. But yours will be all right—it's clear you care about him. Willing to do whatever it takes. That's parenting, good parenting. That, and trusting them. You trust your son enough to leave him alone, but you also would do whatever it takes to get back to him. That right?"

"That's about right," she said.

"Then that's all you need. Trust and hard work."

They shook hands, and she thanked him again.

"Fred," he said.

"Maddie," she answered.

And then, like magic: The snow squall thinned once more to flurries, and she saw the red and blue strobe of a police cruiser ahead. The air shrieked with the squeal of hydraulics as the tractor trailer blocking the road started to move.

It took time.

A lot of pacing, a lot of thinking.

Oliver assured himself that he wasn't going to do what he wasn't going to do. He told himself that he couldn't give in to what Jake wanted. But he also asked himself, what choice was there? Jake would do what he said. He was committed. He'd hurt Caleb, hurt him bad, then kill him. Then he'd go for Hina, too. Probably come for Mom, do all the awful things he said he'd do. In the end, what choice did Oliver have?

He took his mother's phone, pulled up her contacts, and made the call. Oliver wasn't sure how much longer she'd be gone, but he had to do this before she got back—and before the weather got worse.

He wrote a hasty note.

He took the phone.

He took the gun.

Then Oliver walked out the door, past the scattering of thirteen owls on the ground (each now covered in a little mound of white fluff). The boy hoofed it through the snow, down the driveway, toward the end.

73

Better Remember,
Lightning Never Strikes Twice

Nate told Carl the next day, and Carl thought he was fucking nuts and said as much. But he also said he'd help. So they got to work constructing a lightning rod. Carl knew the principle, said they'd had one at the plastics plant where he worked. A lightning rod was just a long metal rod, ideally copper, mounted atop a building, with a wire leading from the rod to the ground—so lightning would strike the rod, and then go to ground, leaving the building unharmed.

In this case, though, the wire wouldn't necessarily have to go to ground...

It could go to *Nate.*

"Which would of course kill your hiney dead," Carl said.

"Yes, in any other universe. But you . . ."

"What happened to me was crazy, Nate. These storms aren't predictable. And so, I'd wager, their results aren't either. I don't guess it would be reproducible, but what do I know."

Nate shrugged. "I don't have any other ideas. Do you?"

"I don't."

"Then this is the idea."

Carl had copper pipe in the walls. The house's plumbing relied on a well pump—which itself required electricity—so the pipes weren't doing anybody much good. He and Nate ripped some out and fashioned a rod out of it. Spooled some coils of wire from the cellar around the rod, and then used the ladder to get to the roof. Nate said he'd go up, and Carl said he could fucking handle it, by god, and instead told Nate to stay on the ground with the rifle. Just in case.

As the old man clambered up, some of the slate shingles cracked and broke—pieces skidding off and shattering as they hit the ground. Nate ducked a few bits of debris.

"You all right up there?" Nate asked.

"I'm fine, and quit asking. I'm old but I'm not *old*," Carl barked.

Nate couldn't see much. Just heard lots of banging and rattling and slate chips surfing down. Carl suddenly hollered, "Fuckin' hell!"

Slinging the rifle over his shoulder, Nate hurried up the ladder—

He peered over the bent and rusted gutters. Now he could see Carl straddling the peak of the roof, riding the house like a horse. Blood streamed down his hand as he shook it.

"Hell, Carl, are you all right?"

"Fine, *fine,* just—cut the meat of my palm on the flashing up here. Sharp tin shit." He pulled off his shirt and wound it around the bleeding hand. The blood soaked through fast. Nate said he'd come up to finish, but Carl said, "No, hell, I'm already done. I was just fixing the flashing around the chimney here so it doesn't leak. I'm done, I'm done, just head back down the ladder and give me some room."

Nate, reminded of his own father's stubbornness, knew better than to wrestle this old oak tree. So he stepped back down the ladder, made some room. Carl scooted over to the edge—

And his rear end slipped off the roof, hitting the gutter—which broke away from the house as Carl tumbled through the air—

Nate called out—

And then there was a rush of air, a smell of ozone—

In midair, Carl simply *disappeared.*

"Oh, shit," Nate said.

He knew how fast the old man came back last time, and so he hurried to right where Carl had fallen, trying to guess at his trajectory. He stabbed out with his back heel to brace himself, opening his arms—

Just as there was another puff of air. Carl reappeared, and this time, Nate caught him. Or, rather, "caught" him—because he was bowled backward, slamming his ass bone against the dirt, and suddenly the two of them had sprawled into the unkempt lawn. The two of them groaned and rolled around in pain, but had no real injuries. Carl finally sat up, holding his cut hand under his armpit. "That sure was something," he finally said.

"What happened?"

"What happened? You saw what happened. I went away again."

"Where? And when?"

"I . . . well, I don't know when, Nate, I just know I was suddenly standing up. Looking out the attic window of this house. And I was watching . . . you, I think. You and your boy. On the driveway. The boy with a busted bicycle from the looks of it."

Nate nodded. "I remember that. I remember seeing you up there."

"Jesus. Ain't that a thing?"

"Sure is, Carl. Sure is."

Carl stood, shaky, his knees popping as he did. "Tell you one thing, though, Nate. I know he wasn't my grandson, not proper, but it was good to see Oliver again. Real good."

I imagine it was, Nate thought. And that's all he could do. Imagine.

The first sign something was wrong with Carl came a few nights later. Nate awoke, finding Carl standing there, the beams of bright moonglow coming through the boarded-up windows of the room, painting him in the zebra stripes of light and shadow.

The gun was in his hand. He pointed it at Nate.

"Identify yourself!" Carl hissed. "Wake up, you piece of *shit.* You can't squat here. Who are you? Where'd you come from?"

"Carl," Nate said, calm as an unstirred lake. "Carl, it's me. It's Nate."

"This was my *son's* room. He's coming back. You can't sleep here."

"Of course he is, Carl. I can sleep downstairs, if you'd rather."

The old man seemed staggered by that. "Okay," he said, finally.

Then he tottered out of the room. Somewhere down the hall, a door slammed. And that was that. Nate figured it was just the old man sleepwalking, or suffering from the vagaries of age. Just in case, though, he went downstairs and slept on the couch.

He hoped that was the end of it, but really, it was just the start.

Days went by, and Carl didn't mention it. Neither did Nate. Only real change in the old man was that he seemed a little draggy, a little unfocused. Said he was dealing with a cold, maybe. "Feeling a little achy today," he said. "But I'm good," he added, and life seemed to resume. They hunted, they scavenged, they waited for a good storm to come, but none did. It was a week later—seven scratches in the wood—that it went to hell.

Nate was sitting outside, rifle across his lap. He'd taken to leaving out scraps of food gone bad for the squirrels, because squirrels were dumb as paint and would cape for a moldy kernel of corn quick as they would a fresh one. One well-placed shot to the head and that was that. Squirrels were easy to skin, too—Carl showed him that all you had to do was lift the tail, cut a slice "right above the shitter" (his words) and then across the legs, and then step on the tail, grab the paws, and *pull*. The skin peeled right off. Maybe you had to use the knife to cut a few more bits away, but that was it.

After that, it was imperative to get the squirrel into a stewpot and over some fire pretty quick. Carl said back in the "good days" you had a few hours at least, and could extend that time with ice. Now, they went rotten fast. Rancid in under an hour. ("Whole world's gone rotten," Carl had taken to saying, and Nate flinched whenever he heard it.)

There Nate sat, waiting. Waiting for a squirrel much as he was waiting for a storm. Waiting for *anything*. Outside he was calm and still. Inside he was a maelstrom of worry and impatience. *I just want to go home,* he thought, before there came a crackle of brush, and the movement of weeds and grass. The front lawn to the house had obviously grown wild, turning to a rangy, mangy meadow—but where he placed the moldy corn, he stamped down the grass and weeds in a straight path for his line of sight.

A squirrel danced into view. Skinny, but they all were. Looked healthy, though. Wouldn't get much meat off it, but it could flavor the stew well enough. Nate hugged the rifle against his shoulder, pressing his eyes against the scope. He pinched that squirrel right between the crosshairs—

A door slammed. The squirrel bolted.

"Shit," he said, and turned to see Carl coming out of the house. The old man staggered out like he was deep in his cups. He had a cigarette in his mouth, unlit.

"Gone rotten," Carl said. The cigarette fell from his lips.

"Carl, what the hell, I had a shot lined up—"

Then he saw: Carl had the gun. The .45 pistol. It was slick. Barrel dripping with gun oil. Each drop hit the ground with a little *pat-pat-pat.*

"Carl," he said, more gingerly this time. "Put down the gun."

Slowly, Carl turned his head toward Nate.

"Nathan, that you?" the old man asked.

He didn't know how to answer. He'd heard tales of friends having to deal with parents suffering from dementia or Alzheimer's, and they always seemed to tell the truth to try to steer the parent back to reality—but in those stories, the parent never had a gun in their hand. "Sure, it's me."

A shadow of uncertainty passed over the man's face. "No. Are you? It's gone rotten, son. World ruined. Everything's in danger. It's Oliver. You see? Where's Oliver?"

Then he pointed the gun at Nate.

"Carl—uhh, Dad—"

"What did you do to Oli—"

He disappeared.

One minute, Carl was there. The next, gone. With that came the little *chuff* of air and a stink in the air like chlorine and rain-slick roads.

Nate knew where the old man went.

He remembered the night: Carl appearing behind him at the house on the night of the storm there. Clocking him with the gun. Calling him *Nathan.* Telling him the world was ruined and rotten, that danger was coming . . .

And then, like that, Carl appeared once more.

Sweat-slick and dizzy, the old man teetered. Nate reached out to steady him—and to snatch the gun out of his hand. The old man relented easily. He woozily stumbled toward the same chair Nate had been sitting on while waiting for a squirrel. Carl plopped down on it, legs splayed. He seemed lost for a moment, staring at the grass.

"I went somewhere again."

"I know, Carl. I know where you went."

He licked his lips. "I think I . . . I hit you. With that." He dipped his head toward the gun in Nate's hand.

"Don't feel too bad, it healed up okay."

"I wasn't just gone . . . physically. I was gone up here too."

Carl tapped his forehead.

"I know that too."

"I'm sorry, Nathan." He hissed, as if mad at himself. *"Nate."*

"It's okay. It's fine, don't wreck yourself over it."

"Could I trouble you for a spot of whiskey? I got a taste in my mouth like . . . like a bloody nose, you ever get that?"

Nate wasn't sure whiskey was the best medicine, but given that they had *no* medicine, what could it hurt? He nodded and went inside to fetch one of the bottles the old man kept under the sink. Only problem was, they didn't seem to have anymore. He did find a bottle of something called Oberon's gin—had a label with a scruffy-looking

Irish wolfhound on it—and he figured that would be good enough. His own father used to say of gin, *Tastes like Christmas,* and that was that. (And here Nate's insides twisted up. Wasn't it almost Christmas here? Or there? Or somewhere? He'd already passed Thanksgiving, hadn't he? If he could get back there . . . No. This was something to worry about later. Right now? Carl.)

He grabbed the bottle of Oberon's and twisted off the cap. He grabbed a couple of coffee mugs on the way out, one finger through the ceramic loops. They clinked and clunked together as he headed outside—

And saw Carl wandering out into the grass. He faced away from Nate. His head was bent. His arms, slack by his sides.

"Carl! Hey. No whiskey, but I found gin—"

The old man tumbled forward into the grass.

Shit!

Nate set down the bottle and mugs and bolted toward him. He got his arm around the old man's middle and eased him back.

Carl's face was a tangled mess. Black, wet tendrils hung from his face like rotten vines. Red-black worms pushed up out of his nostrils, dangling from his lips; one even pushed out from the corner of his left eye. He made a fluid sound in his chest and then gagged. Nate backpedaled as Carl retched, loosing a gush of black threads from his mouth in a bile-yellow froth. They spattered against the ground. Still alive, the worms clumped in a pile.

Carl locked his arms and heaved again, letting fly with fewer worms—just a handful now. Nate reached over and helped him pull some away from his face, careful not to break them. He took off his own shirt and used it to wipe the old man's face and mouth before helping him stand quickly and back away from the writhing mess in the weeds.

"Jesus," Carl said, followed by a despairing groan. "Christ on a . . ."

"You're okay. You're okay. C'mon. Got something to help you . . . uhh, wash out your mouth. Disinfect, too."

He advanced ahead of Carl, fetching the gin and handing it to him.

"Here. Go on."

Carl took it greedily in both hands like a toddler clutching a juice cup. He plugged it to his lips and drank. First round, he swished and spat. Second round he just drank. Three hefty glugs.

"There you go," Nate said. "You're okay."

But Carl shook his head. "I'm not okay."

"You don't know that."

"I know it. I know it like I know rain. That—what just happened, it wasn't good. The, the worms are in me. I've seen this before, Nate. Eggs, cysts, the worms, I dunno, but I'm pretty sure I can *feel* them in there, son."

Nate was about to reassure him once more, but something moved across Carl's eye. A black worm. Little, like a baby worm. Its tail flagellated in a whiplike motion, swimming across the surface of his eye, from one corner to the next, before disappearing again.

"What is it?" Carl asked.

"I . . ."

"I'm not going to be okay."

Nate shook his head, feeling the blood drain from his face.

"I think you're right, Carl. I'm sorry."

The old man made his wishes clear. He said he did not want to die here, but rather he wanted to die where Oliver died. He was to meet his maker on the altar stone. For he was, in a way, a sacrifice too. Nate told him he couldn't do it, wouldn't do it, but Carl objected, said, "You have to, Nate. This is what mercy looks like. I don't want to lose my whole mind—my *brain*—to these things. You end me now. Before I'm not me anymore."

The grim irony of all this was not lost on Nate. Before, all he wanted was to see his father die. And in the deepest, darkest chambers of his heart, he wanted to be the one to kill him. Watching him die of cancer was second-best, a silver medal, not the gold. And though this man was not his father, he also *was*. Or had become, at least.

Carl, *this* Carl, saved Nate. Helped him. Taught him things. Like a father did. And now Nate wanted anything other than to watch him die.

Worse, anything other than to *help* him die.

One version of Carl Graves he wanted to kill, and couldn't.

This Carl Graves he wanted to save, and couldn't.

It was what it was.

He took the pistol, and together they walked to the boulder field.

When it was done, when Nate said how thankful he was to the old man for helping him, when Nate told him he was glad to have met him—a better version of him, anyway—and when Nate and Carl wept together before he pointed that gun and pulled its trigger, Nate sat down on a broken boulder, facing away from the altar stone where Carl's body lay draped. He looked toward what was once Ramble Rocks amusement park but now was just trees. What Ramble Rocks had become, he didn't know. A park, a mine, a quarry. From here it was just trees. He looked down at the gun in his hand. It stank like rotten eggs—the smell of expended powder, of the bullet that ended the man who was not his father, but who also was. He set the gun down next to him.

Just as the sky rumbled in the distance.

A storm was coming.

74

Enjoy Your Wintry Tomb

Maddie straddled the mad line between weary and excited, enervated and energized. She was bone fucking tired from what this morning she'd hoped would be an easy journey. Took that tractor trailer another half hour to shimmy its ass back onto the highway—and then the snow and all the traffic turned her ten-minute drive back into an hour. But now she was here, and a toothsome thrill pushed back the fatigue: She had a plan. A crazy, batshit, cracker factory plan, *but a plan.*

She stepped inside the door, kicking snow off her shoes and dropping the chicken wire on the ground. On the way home, she decided something else, too, that had to be a part of her plan: coming clean to her son. She had to tell Oliver who she was and what she could sometimes do. It was wrong of her to deny him the truth, to fail to give him the whole side of the story. They each had their parts to play, and if she was going to do this, she wanted him to be there. To see it.

"Olly?" she called.

But already she could sense his absence. The emptiness of the cabin had its own weight, its own presence. The TV was on. It showed static.

"Kid? Dude?"

Nothing.

Huh.

She turned around, headed back outside. The snow was really roaring now, coming down like the static on that television. She called for him outside, too. "Oliver! *Oliver.*"

Maddie scanned the ground for footprints.

Nothing fresh—

But she found the faintest shallow divots. Each a little bowl in the snow where his feet would've fallen. One after the next. Leaving the cabin and going down the driveway—or the reverse, coming back up?

Decision paralysis fixed her like a nail to a board. Go after him outside, or check back inside? Any chance he might just be . . . sleeping?

Maddie scanned the dark pines behind the waves of white and didn't see anything or anyone. Darting back inside, still calling for him, she didn't even bother taking her shoes off—she tracked snow everywhere looking for him. Not that the place was huge, not that there was even anywhere for him to *hide*. Was there a basement? An attic? Some insane memory reached her, tickled at her brain stem, the memory of a strange house and a basement . . .

There. On the pillow of her bed, a note.

No, c'mon, Olly—

She snatched it up. The note was simple:

> *Mom, I'm sorry. I don't know what else to do. Jake has Caleb. He'll kill him, and Hina, and eventually you too.*
> *So I'm going to kill him first. I have your phone and the gun.*
> *Please don't follow I don't want you to get hurt.*
> *I love you so much. I'm sorry again.*
> *Olly*

Before she even had time to process the letter, she snapped into crisis mode. *He had to get a ride somehow.* Because he wasn't walking, was he? How long ago could it have been? An hour, maybe an hour and a half. Out there, in the storm . . . she rushed back out the door, keys already in her hand.

Car. Keys. Ignition. Tires spinning on snow and she chided herself: *Calm the fuck down, Maddie. You have to be even-keeled, just ease the pedal,* so that's what she did. It took everything she had to be gentle with the pedal—but a slow press and the Subaru urged forward in the snow. Down the driveway she went.

Outside the windshield of the car, the snow was picking up again. Oliver thought it looked like they were traveling through hyperspace—the falling snow forming streaks of starline white. They made their way west on the highway before turning south around Carbondale. It was slow going, but Jed's Lexus SUV seemed to handle it okay. Said he had weather chains on the tires, and they'd be all right.

"Good thing your mother had my number," Jed said.

"Yeah," Oliver said. Guilt galloped through him. *Mom* . . . he'd left her. He'd taken her gun. Her phone. He was on his own. But that meant *she* was on her own, too. And here he was in a car with the man who'd sent his father away. Pushed him out of this universe and into another.

Jed must've seen the shadows of doubt clouding his face.

"Do you trust me?"

"I don't know. I don't think so."

Jed nodded. "I don't blame you. I wouldn't trust me either. I just want you to know, I fell under his sway. Jake's. I won't call him Oliver because though he may be you from another world, he's nothing like you, is he?"

I hope not, Oliver thought.

Jed went on: "I lost my wife and my daughter because I made a mistake, and instead of trying to live with that mistake and find peace, he offered me a way to undo what I had done." His voice broke a little as he was talking, and Oliver was compelled to look at this man and the well of pain he was carrying with him: a dark ocean with hard tides crashing against its margins. As he spoke, the waves rose higher and higher. "But that's not right, is it? We can't just paper over it. We can't just walk it back. We gotta live with what we've done, gotta carry your weight. Like in that book *The Things They Carried*. You probably haven't read it, but—well. Let's just say it's about men at war carrying more than just what's in their hands and on their backs. About what's in their heads and their hearts, for good and ill."

The dark waves in him rose and fell. Shadow tides, roaring. Oliver thought, again, *What if I took that out of him?* The man was a boat taking on too much water. What if Oliver chose to bail him out?

"If you're not sure about this," Jed said, "I could take you back."

"No. We have to go forward. I don't know what else to do."

Jed nodded and gripped the wheel. "When you're at rock bottom, you can either dig down or clamber your way back up to the light."

"I don't know which direction I'm headed. Down or up." *Dark or light.*

"Can't say I know, either. But I think you're doing the right thing."

"Thanks for picking me up."

"Of course, son. I owe Nate for what I did to him. But your father is gone. So now I owe you."

Flashing lights ahead. Yellow lights, not red and blue. Maddie threw open her door and hard-charged toward the cop whose SUV sat parked across the highway entrance. He was hunched down, his dark jacket already peppered with cold white sky dandruff, as he put out traffic cones next to the emergency barrier.

"The hell is this?" Maddie asked.

"PennDOT and the PTC are closing the highways. Turnpike too."

"Why?"

In the glow of the lights, she saw him make a screwed-up face like, *The fuck?* "I dunno if you noticed, lady, but the sky is puking snow."

"Right, but I need to get on that highway—"

He lifted up his boot as if to demonstrate. The snow was already up over the front, and he shook it off. "This is just since I got here. We're getting an inch or two an hour. This thing came up fast and there's already accidents *everywhere*. So, they made a decision, and here we are."

"My son. He's out there. He's a kid—just fifteen years old—"

"And he's driving in this without a license?"

"What? No. *No.* He's . . . I don't know who he's with—"

"Then how do you know he's out there? You should probably know who your son is with, ma'am."

"Don't tell me how to parent."

The cop grunted as he reached for the last cone. "Lady, I'm sorry, I am. But I can't help you. If your son is really missing, you're gonna need to call 911 or go to a station to fill out a report."

"What if I just go? What if I just blow past you, drive over those cones, and hit the highway?"

He barked a laugh. "Go for it. Got accidents all along this corridor. Then you'll be stopped again when you try to get on 476, and that one? It's *closed* closed, because the toll booths are blocked."

"There's another way. There's 191—I could take that south—"

"Good news is, that one's not closed, but bad news is, it's barely a highway. It's two lanes and no plow trucks are gonna be out there now or later. You get stuck, you're fucked. *And* there are accidents there, too."

"Fuck."

"Yeah, fuck. Lady, go home."

"I can't. My son."

"*Go home.* Call 911. You're no good to him stuck in some snow-bank, frozen to death."

"I still have to try."

"Enjoy your wintry tomb!" the cop yelled after her, but she was already in her Subaru and turning her ass around.

Highway 191 was slow going. But it wasn't ice, wasn't slick, and her Forester was a fucking workhorse. *Go, car, go.* Onward through the waves of white and the wall of flakes she went. *Please, Olly, be okay, be okay.* She'd already lost so much time dicking around with this trip. And she wished like hell she still had her phone. Still, she felt hope: She was on the road now, and maybe Oliver was caught in traffic or behind an accident—hell, she'd even take him being *in* an accident, long as he survived it. A broken arm was a small price to pay for him not having some kind of misguided confrontation with that little monster, Jake.

Then she thought, how fucked up was that? Here she was, wishing for him to be in an accident? Her brain felt upside-down.

And a little voice spoke in the words of the man she'd met earlier today: *Willing to do whatever it takes. That's parenting, good parenting. That, and trusting them.*

Trust. He wasn't even sixteen yet. She trusted him enough, but not on this. He was wrong to leave. He wouldn't survive his confrontation with Jake—that other boy was a snake, a scorpion, a vicious little liar shit. Killed her husband. Wanted to sacrifice her son.

No, she thought. *Keep going, keep going, you're going to make it, you're going to save your son . . .*

But even as she felt a surge of hope, she saw something ahead, something that started to crush her heart in a vise. It couldn't be—

She pumped the brakes, easing the car to a stop as tears threatened to again spill over.

The Subaru's headlights speared a tree that had fallen across the road. Some big pine tree, toppled across both lanes. Even in the coming dark she could see its massive roots ripped up from its mooring, leaving a snow-filled crater behind. Maddie got out, churning through snow that was already halfway up her calves. She got to the tree, tried to imagine driving over it, but it was too high. She thought absurdly about getting under it and lifting, like she had some kind of magical Mom strength—but it was *huge,* a mature eastern hemlock, a hundred feet tall. Didn't leave any room to go around it, either. And with that, Maddie felt hope wither inside her, a dying thing. She fell to her knees. She buried her head in her gloves and screamed.

They'd gone south enough that down here, the snow was just fat flakes that didn't stick to anything but grass—the roads and parking lots were wet and clear. Oliver and Jed stood in the parking lot outside a Wawa convenience store. A quick bathroom trip was necessary.

"You say you see it?" Jed asked.

Oliver bit his lip and nodded. "Yeah."

"What's it look like?"

The boy tried to describe it. "I think it's both different and the same in everyone. Yours looks like an ocean. An angry sea."

"Like in a storm."

"Maybe. But also, it's not water. It's poison."

They'd gotten to talking earlier, and Oliver told Jed what he could see, and what he now realized he could do—that he could not only see the pain inside people, but that he could pull it out. He didn't even have to offer it to Jed: Jed wanted in. He explained to Oliver, *What we're about to head into, I don't want to bring anything with me, no baggage, no anything, no pain for him to grab on to and exploit. Maybe he doesn't know it, Oliver, but Jake is real good at finding the pain, same as you are—but he doesn't pull it out. He twists it into knots. He uses them like puppet strings.* Oliver said he knew. That's how Jake almost got him to die on the altar stone once already.

So, when Jed asked if he could have his pain taken away . . .

Oliver said okay.

And now, here they were. In a parking lot. Ready to do it.

"So, I got an ocean of poison inside of me."

"Seems like."

"And you're going to drain it dry?"

Oliver shrugged. "I think so. I did it before, with Graham Lyons. I thought it caused him to hurt himself and his father, but then I found out Jake did that. So maybe I really did help him. And maybe I really can help you."

And then maybe, if I survive this, I can maybe help Mom, too.

If only he could've helped his father.

But would he survive?

He didn't know.

With a clap of his hands and a jaunty two-step stomp of his feet, Jed nodded. "Let's do this, then, son. I've seen some truly weird shit in this life, so I am a whole-hog believer. And," he said more despairingly, "I ache to have this gone." His eyes glassed over, and in a hesitant, mouse-squeak voice he asked: "It won't take them away, will it? My Zelda? My Mitzi?"

"No. At least, I don't think so."

"Well. Then onward we go, my boy. Let us proceed with light and with love and with the hope that we can put all this pain behind us."

Maddie found herself back in the cabin, another hour past. Her throat was raw from screaming, her eyes red and puffy from crying. With no hesitation she stormed over to the phone and said a small prayer to all the gods who might be listening that she *just needed a dial tone.*

She picked up the handset, expecting that the storm had taken yet another option from her—

A dial tone buzzed in her ear.

Quickly she punched in Fig's number. His wife answered. Zoe.

"Zoe, it's Maddie."

"Maddie, oh my god. Are you—"

"I'm okay, I'm okay, but I don't know that Oliver is. I need Fig's help. Can you—"

"I'll put him on."

"Thanks, Zoe."

A rustle over the phone. Mumbling. Then, his voice: "Maddie."

"Fig."

"Where are you? You at the cabin?"

"Yeah. I need you to come get me."

"Maddie, aren't you in the middle of a blizzard up there?"

"Yeah. Aren't you down there?"

"It missed us, mostly. We're getting some wintry mix business, little rain, sleet, snow. None of it really sticking. But that's beside the point—Maddie, what's wrong? Why do I need to come get you?"

She told him. Told him everything she could: Oliver left her, took a gun, and now she was stranded in this storm. "I think he's going home. He's going to . . . deal with Jake."

Fig drew a deep breath and paused. Finally he said, "Maddie, I need you to stay as far away from this as possible. We'll handle it."

"We? We who?"

"The police."

"You're not police."

"Yeah, I know, but you can trust them to get this done."

"I don't trust them for shit, Fig. I trust me. I trust you. So go to your car and *come get me.*"

"Maddie. Listen to me. You're hours north in a blizzard. I won't make it in time, if at all. Don't worry, we'll find Oliver. We can intercept him before he gets in trouble. You think he's going . . . where?"

"I don't know! I don't know. Jake's place. Our house. Jed's. I don't know. But I know where they'll end up. They'll end up at Ramble Rocks. At the boulder field. Where Reese killed those girls."

"Stay put, Maddie. Lemme go and do my job."

"Fig. *Fig*—"

"Maddie, do you trust me?"

"Fig, yes, of course, I just said I fucking trust you. This isn't about trust. This is . . ." She growled. "This is motherhood! This is me knowing my son is in danger. Physical danger. Emotional, moral, *cosmic* fucking danger. And at no point am I just going to . . . just gonna hand that responsibility over to you." She paused, her breaths coming in rough, untidy gasps. "I can't. Not after everything. I can't lose him, too, Fig. Not Oliver."

"If Oliver needed surgery, you wouldn't pick up the scalpel yourself, would you?"

"You're goddamn fucking right I would."

"Maddie."

"Shit!" Maddie pulled the phone away from her ear and pressed her forehead to it. As if it were an object of prayer. A saint's reliquary. A deep, centering breath gave her clarity. He was right. Fig coming *here* meant that Fig wasn't *there*. And by then it might be far too late.

She put the phone back to her ear. "Okay. Fine."

"I'll keep him safe. We'll send somebody for you soon as we can."

"Find him and don't lose him, Fig. Don't you dare."

"I promise, Maddie. I promise. You just plan to stay put, stay near that phone, and I'll call you."

Maddie hung up the phone.

She sat on the edge of the bed, and wept until the tears had run dry.

And then, when they had run dry, she was left with nothing but a kind of cold, mad clarity. What was it Fig had just said? *You just plan to stay put.*

Plan.

She'd had a plan this morning, but it had gone all *fuck-shaped*. Once more she cast her gaze to the bail of chicken wire on the ground, and the bag next to it—pliers, snippers, and such. Maddie had nothing else but this one thing, and so she crawled over to them, fit her hands into the gloves, and began to unroll the wire, snipping its bindings, shaping it with hard tugs and shoves, using her own head as a model for Nate's head, and as she used the snips to cut wire and the pliers to shape features she kept thinking, *It's going to happen any minute now—I'm going to fugue out, going to slip and slide into unconsciousness as the act of creation overtakes me, and when I come to, he'll be there—Nate will be here with me and it'll all be better,* but it still wasn't *happening* and she gritted her teeth and bore down and made an arm and then part of a hand and she pushed harder and harder, she thought *Any second now, it's coming,* but it was *not* fucking coming, it wasn't happening at all, and it felt like thinking about sleeping when you were trying to sleep, like thinking of *breathing* when you were trying to breathe and all you ended up with was a feeling of drowning in your own lungs, of being in air too thin to fill your chest, and now her heart was beating and she heard her blood in her ears and *c'mon c'mon c'mon, you fucking bitch* and she worried what if the phone rang while she was fugueing out and *this isn't working, just like the owls out there in the snow* and *please, Nate, come to me* and *please, Oliver, be okay* and once more she knew she was missing *something,* some memory, some part of her, *think, you stupid bitch, try to use your brain* but nothing came, NOTHING, and she again let out a scream that burned her throat like stomach acid, then she punched her fist into the face of the wire creation and pitched it against the wall as thunder boomed outside and lightning flashed.

It wasn't happening.

It wasn't working.

She'd lost. She'd failed. She pulled the gloves off with her teeth, found that one of the wires had poked through, made the palm of her hand bleed. Even spilling blood hadn't worked. It was over.

Maddie stood up, and that's when she saw the man's face at the window.

75

So Take Me Away, I Don't Mind

It was a helluva thing, getting struck by lightning. Even *trying* to get struck was an exercise in madness. Nate toyed with hurrying back to the house and winding the wire around his hand. But these storms were fickle. Last time, it never got up to the house. It stayed here. Over this place.

So he went forward, back into Ramble Rocks.

It had changed. No longer an amusement park, it was an overgrown field with fallen trees. It was weeds and thorn-tangles and bits of spice bush so that when he pushed through it, it left the air fragrant with something not too far from the smell of sarsaparilla. The storm swept in fast, painting the sky in a black-lung phlegm. The rain that soon fell hammered the ground, and moving through it took effort, like it fought Nate, trying to push him back.

But onward he persevered. He found the tunnel framed by white logs built into the earth, each of them wound tight with ivy in the way you might loop barbed wire around a fence post. Above it was a sign: RAMBLE ROCKS NUMBER EIGHT. Was it a coal mine? It looked to be.

Even from here he thought he saw something standing there in the black. Wet and glistening. Shaped like a man.

Edmund Walker Reese.

Waiting for him.

He held the gun in his hand, pointed it at the shape. He knew he could go over there. *Should,* even. And he could end that man once and for all.

But that, he reminded himself, was not his task here. Reese was out to pasture. This was his world, and his death would help it. But Nate had another world to save. His own.

Be seeing you, Reese, he thought.

Then Nate turned around and stared up as lightning laced the corset of the sky. The rain fell harder. He felt like a turkey looking up at the storm. Wasn't that what they said turkeys did? Stare up at the rain, beaks open, drowning themselves? Probably an urban legend, but that's how he felt. Like a dumb turkey, drowning himself in the rain.

And then the wind stirred up real good, gave him a hard shove forward. He staggered, almost lost his footing, and—

Everything lit up white.

The world turned to ash around him.

He didn't know where he was. It was dark. He couldn't see. He walked forward, nearly tripping on something. Thorns scratched his face. His shirt was wet and cold; he pulled it off, over his head, and tossed it to the ground. Nate saw lights. The lights of the house—dim, but present, like the house was a little bit alive, a little bit awake, and so he moved toward it, sure that what had happened to Carl was just a dream. A *nightmare.* He knew now that Carl would be in there, waiting for him. Alive and well.

Fireflies whirled about him. He put out his arms and they came to him. Circling and diving in the air before him. They preceded him as he walked. Some landed on his shoulders, his face, in his beard. They seemed to glow brighter when they did.

To the door, Nate went, and he peered inside, and he saw Carl looking back at him—

But it wasn't Carl.

It was himself.

A cleaner-shaven Nate from an unfallen world, from before every-thing went to hell. Before they'd all met Jake.

It worked. I'm here. The lightning took me away.

And then, one more thought—

And I'm the bearded freak on my front fucking lawn.

And next thing he knew, he saw himself coming for him.

Nate—Nate Prime, Original Nate—was hard-charging toward him, and he didn't want that. Didn't want to meet his earlier self. What would that mean? What would that *do*? A little part of him wondered if he could warn himself of what was to come, but what if it broke everything? What if it made things worse, not better? He remembered how this had played out and was suddenly the one making it play out that way—he turned tail and bolted through the woods, and it happened just as he remembered it. Ending up on Jed's lawn. Nate coming. Gun up. Fat flies swarmed him—summoned by what, he did not know. Summoned the way the fireflies were, maybe. Or maybe just by the pickled smell of his sweat and the sudden sores on his arms and chest. They were on him, on his face, a mask of them—

Then the world went white and pulled him away once more.

There came the sense of riding, of traveling, like he was a fizzing spark sprinting down a long loop of dynamite cord. He knew intui-tively where it led him—it would detonate, and he would be thrust once more into the storm in the fallen worlds. But that wasn't an op-tion. He didn't *want* to go back. He had work to do here, and so he focused inward, concentrating every ounce of anger against Jake *and* the love he had for his family into a white-hot ball inside him, and he used that energy to jump away like one of Oliver's old Matchbox cars popping off its racetrack after going too fast.

And then—

He was watching himself. On the front lawn. Staggered in the storm by Carl appearing suddenly with the .45, knocking him on the head. And then sure enough, here came Jed. His neighbor, *that betrayer,* came out the front door, and his eyes first beheld the fight between Nate and the old man—but then, his eyes wandered to the *other* Nate, the one watching this all happen from the woods, the one with the haunted eyes and the scraggly beard—Nate the traveler.

Nate saw the glint of recognition in Jed's eyes.

Jed *knew* who he was.

Knew he was Nate, even as he saw the other Nate now on the ground.

Motherf—

Again, white light. Again pulled away. Again he struggled against it. Thrashing, twisting, working like hell not to go back. *My wife,* he thought. *I need to see Maddie. Or Oliver. I need to* warn them *of what's to come . . .*

Whoosh. The rush of air. A baby thunderclap.

No, no, no—

It wanted him back—

Back to the altar stone—

Back to the fallen worlds—

He could see them now, the broken rocks of the boulder field, the pouring rain, the mouth of the coal mine, the house, the ocean, the black diamond gently rotating in the sky, and Carl's body draped across the altar stone like a rag doll tossed clumsily across a child's nightstand . . .

No!

A room with pink walls. A dresser with a My Little Pony on it. And something, too, made out of ceramic—like a mug, but made by a child; it had a sloppy drunken lean to it. And in front of all those was a coal-carved owl, its wary gaze pointed toward her neatly made bed, ever vigilant.

Night waited at the windowpanes.

A little girl sat on the floor with a pair of scissors, and a black Sharpie marker at her side. He watched her cutting into a big cardboard box. The scissors made short, imprecise work of it.

She startled suddenly when she saw him.

"Oh," she said, her eyes going from glazed over to keenly aware, looking him up and down. She opened her mouth as if to scream—

Nate put his finger to his lips to shush her. "Maddie. It's me."

"I don't know you," she said. "You're a stranger."

"Just a traveler," he said. He sat down on the bed. "And I know you. You're making a Box Man, aren't you?"

"I think so. I don't know."

"You're doing it to help that little girl. The one who's missing."

She hesitated. "Yes." Then, in a voice that he recognized as distinctly Maddie's—a voice that rose in pitch when she got frustrated, especially with a creative project. "But I don't know how to get the Box Man there to help her. He's a hero, but he's here. Not there, with her."

"You can make things, Maddie. You're a maker, aren't you?"

She shrugged.

"I think you are. You can make doors, I bet."

Little Maddie gave him a quizzical look. "But how?"

"I dunno. All I know is: two hinges and one knob. That's what makes a door. That's all you need. You told me that when we moved into our house. Or . . . I guess you'll tell it to me one day."

While sitting on the floor she looked away like she was thinking very hard about this. She looked to the window, then to the wall, then to the stuff atop her dresser. She started to say something, and Nate couldn't hear her—

And then the world began to vibrate around him. The hairs on his neck stood up and his fingertips burned and—

Bzzt.

*   *   *

A filthy window. Laced with the webs of cellar spiders. He peered into it. Saw through a rancid, foul kitchen with food on the floors and flies on the counter, pots piled high. Past that, he saw two little girls.

Maddie and Sissy Kalbacher.

Behind them in the wall was a door just their height—crooked and strange, as if drawn in awkward chalk. The doorknob was a My Little Pony doll. The hinges were strips of duct tape. The girls looked to him.

They waved.

He waved back.

They went through the door as lightning stole him away once more.

He closed his eyes against the searing white light, and in his mind's eye he thought of Maddie, Maddie, Maddie—he willed the lightning to take him to her, to let him be there, to let him stay.

76

A Face in the Glass, a Message in the Snow

Nate," Maddie said, her voice barely above a whisper.

The face in the window was her husband's—she was sure of it. Haggard and worn, his face stretched thin. Eyes haunted. His lips moved as if he were trying to speak—*I have to help him*—so she leapt up off the floor and nearly broke her neck throwing open the door and storming out into the snow, snow that now mounded up around her knees. She pushed her way through it, her legs churning, unable to truly run. Maddie called for him, calling his name again and again with a voice that threatened to give out. The corner of the cabin wasn't far, and when finally she rounded it, she saw him kneeling there, the snow up to his middle, his hand extended outward, finger thrust as if pointing—

Nate! she thought, her world coming alive—

Then she smelled something like burning wires. The hairs on her neck rose like the restless dead and—

Lightning filled the air. White and hot, a thunderclap following swiftly after. She cried out, and kept moving even though everything in her vision had been washed out. Slowly the real world bled back in, intruding upon the starry smears of light in her eyes. But even as it did, new memories flooded back, as if the lightning did more than strike the earth here; it was as if it struck something deep inside her, an electric shock and pyroclastic lance melting all the locks keeping her memories sealed tight.

She remembered being in her room, at home, as a little girl.

Hearing about the missing girls.

Wanting to find them.

Pink walls. My Little Pony. The owl of coal. Bad dreams. Then, a burst of light, and *he* was there. A stranger then. Her husband now. He showed her the way, and that's when she remembered being in Edmund Walker Reese's house, and offering a hand to Sissy Kalbacher, and then she remembered *how* she did it, *how* she got there, *how* she saved that poor little lost girl, the taken girl, the girl marked literally for death by a number on her cheek.

And as she came back to this place, to the *now* outside the cabin, she saw that Nate was gone once more. But he had been here. The snow was disturbed where he stood and where he knelt. And there in the snow too was something else: a message, written with his finger.

TWO HINGES

ONE KNOB

MAKES A DOOR

You can make things, Maddie.

You're a maker, aren't you?

I think you are.

You can make doors, I bet.

"I'm a maker," she said aloud to the night. "I make things. And I can make a door." That's when she looked up and saw something else, too: thirteen owls, wooden owls, crudely carved, all perched in a line on the snow-heft hemlock branches all around. They blinked at her and shifted restlessly in place, eager to get to work.

PART SEVEN

SACRIFICES

Real magic can never be made by offering someone else's liver. You must tear out your own, and not expect to get it back.

—Peter S. Beagle, *The Last Unicorn*

77

The Promise

"You can't do this," Zoe said to him.

But Fig told her he had to. "Zoe, I can't fail these people. They've been put through hell. They're going through something I can only barely begin to understand."

She grabbed his hand, then his wrist, and gave it a sharp squeeze—a move Zoe said she'd learned from her own grandmother, a woman who, when she needed to get her way, did some kind of witch-fingered death grip on the soft space between the two bones of your wrist. Zoe always said, *With that wrist pinch, Me-Maw could get you to sign over your life savings, kick a puppy, and pee your pants—I mean fully soak them—in public. All in one go.*

"Fig," she said, her voice firm, her hand contracting. His knees nearly buckled. "I'm pregnant. Five months now. I need you *around* for her."

He swallowed and nodded. "I get that, Zo. But I also need to be able to look her in the eye and tell my baby girl, *I did my best for the people who needed me, and I didn't turn my back on them.* Because that's who I am. If I'm not that person, then who am I to our daughter?"

Two tears crawled simultaneously down Zoe's cheek.

She let go of his wrist.

"Okay," she said.

He kissed her. "I love you."

"I love you too."

"By the way, that vise grip would do your Me-Maw proud."

Zoe grinned. "Damn straight."

Night. Closing in on ten P.M. The weather remained perfectly shitty—it was damp and cold, spitting an inelegant mix of rain and ice and snow down on them. The Quaker Bridge PD had a temporary HQ set up under some tents down on the vacant lot off across from Lake Holicong, a lot that used to house a local Mennonite shed builder, one that went out of business in the 2008 recession. Chief Roger Garstock gave the briefing, explained that they'd stake out the park primarily, plus have units stationed around a series of other locations: Jake's old house, since abandoned; Jed's house, also abandoned; Alex Amati's house, too, though that boy was nowhere to be found. Plus they had staties looking out for the Graves boy, Oliver, to ideally intercept him before he could get close. Though Fig knew that'd be tricky—they had no idea how he was even getting here, or from what direction, or even *when*.

When the briefing was over, Fig fought through the crowd of dispersing cops to catch up to Garstock. "Chief. Chief!"

But someone stepped in his way: Deputy Chief John Contrino, Jr.

He put out a hand, caught Fig in the chest. "Whoa whoa whoa, Figueroa, the fuck you think you're going?"

"I want to talk to the chief. Your boss."

"Not doable. He's busy." Contrino lowered his voice. "Besides, don't you think you've done enough? You maybe led your buddy Nate astray, huh? Maybe helped get him killed."

"Hey, go fuck yourself, Contrino. And Nate's not dead yet. We don't have a body, you'll recall."

"I'm *Deputy Chief* Contrino, get it right. What's your title again? Oh, right, right, you're Fish and Fucking Game, not a boy in blue like me." Contrino smirked and then laughed a little, a kind of shitty *heh-heh-heh*. "I'm just fucking with you, Figueroa. Chief wants you involved, just not *all the way* involved, you feel me? He's putting you in the Graves house."

"I wanna be at Ramble Rocks."

"And people in Hell want popsicles."

"Like you said: I'm Fish and Game. I get to carry a piece. I'm good for it. Let me help in a real way."

Contrino whistled. "Look at you. Big man with a gun. Hey, I didn't give you the assignment—if it were up to me I'd have you nowhere near this thing. But Chief said, Figueroa knows the family, he knows the house. So, you go there. You wait in case the kid shows up. He trusts you, yeah?"

"Yeah. Definitely."

"Ta-da."

Fig knew they had a point.

He wasn't a cop.

And he knew Oliver *and* the house.

"Shit." He nodded. "Fine."

"See, I knew you could be reasonable, Figueroa." Contrino clapped him on the back hard—too hard—and nodded. "Now move your ass."

All remained quiet. It was cliché, but for Fig, it felt *too* quiet. He wandered this house—the house of his friend's family—and everything felt eerily still. Nate and his family being gone felt as much a presence as an absence, like the silence and stillness added an uncomfortable weight. A thickness to the air, a fly-wing hum in the deep of his ear.

He tried to occupy himself. He listened to the police band to see if anybody had seen anything at all. They did hourly check-ins; nobody saw anything. (They didn't ask him to check in. But he did anyway. *I'm a part of this, damn it.*)

And that was what bothered him most. He wasn't a cop, not really. He hadn't honed his instincts on this sort of thing, so he knew he was being a paranoid idiot. But the lack of anything felt too much like an indication of *something*. Maddie had seemed so worried. Oliver was gone. It meant they had all missed it—whatever *it* was, they weren't seeing it. Maybe Jake wasn't here at all. Maybe Oliver wasn't coming. Could be they were off somewhere else. His fear was that his eye was on the wrong ball, that they'd find Oliver dead a hundred miles away, in a place they didn't imagine, in a situation they didn't understand.

He called Zo. Told her he was okay. He made it a habit that whenever they heard their hourly check-in, he made a check-in of his own. She said she was fine, too. Had heartburn so bad it felt like she'd swallowed a book of matches. Had a craving for a cookies-and-cream milkshake.

He tried calling Maddie, too, to update her—

But the number he had just rang and rang. That made him worry she was out there, in the mountain snow, trying to get here. But he couldn't control her. He could only control this situation. He had to remember that. It was like when he confessed his worries about the world to Nate—and Nate reminded him he needed to watch over his own child, not watch over the whole damn world. *One thing at a time, Fig.*

One hour at a time.

One hour, then three, then five.

Midnight gave way to one, then two, then the clock closed in on three o'clock in the morning.

Downstairs, he heard something.

No—not in the house. *Outside* it.

He drew his gun, and radioed the others. "This is Figueroa. I got something here at the Graves house. Sound outside. Probably nothing, but checking it out. Over."

As he crept down the steps, he awaited their response.

But no response came.

Chills ran over him like spiders.

Outside, the noise—like heavy footsteps—came closer.

He neared the front door of the house, and again said in the radio, this time in hushed urgency: "Repeat: This is Figueroa. Hearing something outside. Footsteps. Do you copy? Over."

No one copied. All that came over the radio was a gentle hiss.

Something *thudded* against the door.

Fig drew the pistol. His pulse ratcheted.

Another *whud* against the door. It rattled in its frame.

Then, a voice through the door: "Fig! *Fig.*"

It sounded familiar, that voice. He'd just heard it—

"Figueroa, you in there? I need help. *Help.*"

It was Deputy Chief Contrino.

"Okay, shit, hold on," Fig called, holstering the gun and hurrying over to the door. Soon as he opened it, Contrino damn near tumbled inside, like he'd been leaning hard on the door. Fig caught him, stabilized him.

And saw he was covered in blood. Head to toe.

"Jesus," he gasped, grunting as he kept Contrino from falling to the floor. "John. Goddamn. Are you all right? What happened? Are you hurt?"

Contrino put his head against Fig's chest. "The others. They're not okay. Fig, I . . ."

"It's okay. It's all right, Contrino. The blood—you're hurt?"

The other man looked up at him. The blood streaked his cheeks. He blinked through it. "The blood? It's not mine."

"What?"

Contrino grinned.

Then he jabbed a knife into Fig's middle.

What Fig would remember most about the knife thrust into his guts was this: The blade felt longer and colder than it could possibly have been. It wasn't pain that hit him first, but that saline thrust of ice, like he'd been stabbed with an icicle. He half expected the blade to go all the way through him, opening him up like a sack of deer corn. But as he staggered backward, the knife coming back out of him, he

was surprised at how small the hole was. Contrino stood there, the
hunting knife dripping.

Fig reached for his gun.

But he was slow. He felt like he was operating in a bad dream—
the way sometimes you run but it's in wet concrete. The gun was in
his hand, but raising it felt like raising a sledgehammer—and by the
time he had it up, Contrino was on him again, backhanding him and
pulling the gun out of his grip in one move.

Fig fell backward. He clutched at his middle. The red spread.

"Don't worry, you got time," Contrino said. "Getting gut-stuck
won't kill you, not right away. And the kid, he wants you alive."

"The kid . . . Jake . . ."

"That's right."

"Wh-why?"

Contrino licked his lips—a lurid act given how bloody he was.
"He saw who I was. Saw *all* of me, Figueroa. He's got a plan, and I'm
his man."

The Altar Stone

This, Oliver knew, was the end. What that meant was not precisely clear, not yet. But he knew, as he and Jed came upon the boulder field in the hissing cold rain, that this was the culmination of things. There too was the reminder that this was the culmination of *all* things, that a great cosmic weight weighed heavily upon his shoulders, for, if all of what Jake had said was true, this could be the end of this world. And the end of this world would mean the end of all worlds. The piece of driftwood that the other worlds clung to would break and sink, and all of reality—the reality of all realities—would disappear into chaos. Into the void. Into nothingness.

And then, according to Jake, it would all come back again.

A great reboot. A cosmic, psycho-spiritual *reset button.*

If he was right.

And Oliver did not believe that he was.

Moreover, he did not care. Because he had no intention of letting this world go. It contained too much that he loved. Broken as this machine may be, it was his machine, and in it was his mother, and his friends, and their mothers, and their fathers, and all the good people, and broken people who needed fixing, and the bad people who could be made better.

Oliver cared nothing for the cosmic battle.

He cared only about all the people who had to fight it.

*   *   *

Together, Oliver stood with Jed at the edge of the felsenmeer. The moon and stars were gone, hidden behind a ratty curtain of clouds. The rain had slowed, and was now just cold spittle. On impulse, Oliver flexed his left hand, and it throbbed with fresh pain behind its gauze, beneath its stitching. As if it remembered what happened here the last time Oliver came to the altar stone. The pain, a warning.

They could see the altar stone from here, despite the dark. Because on it sat a small electric lantern, its yellow glow diffuse in the mist. It was not the only lantern, either—a ring of them were set in a circumference about it. At the edges of the circumference, Oliver saw people standing. Just shades, from here. Three of them, at least.

A voice rang out over the rocks.

"Oliver!"

Jake's voice.

One of the shadows gave an almost friendly wave.

"Good to see you," Jake called. "Someone there with you? That's all right. More the merrier! Come on. Come closer now."

Jed said in a low voice. "Are you ready for this?"

"No."

"That's probably fair."

"Are you?" Oliver asked.

"I am. Now. I feel clear. I feel . . ." He drew a deep nasal breath and held his hands to his heart. "Unburdened."

"I'm glad." Taking the pain from Jed had been even harder than when he robbed Graham of his. It was like grabbing an ocean with your bare hands, an ocean whose acid waters burned your skin. But then he was able to find the drain, and once he did, all that dark water poured out on its own. Like it wanted to leave. Like Jed wanted to be free.

In an even lower voice, Jed said, "You still have the gun, right?"

Oliver hesitated. "Uhh."

"Oliver," Jed said again. Almost like a warning from a parent—a reminder that Jed had been a parent, once. Until his daughter died in a drunk-driving accident he caused. But some of that remained, it seemed.

"I . . . don't have it. I threw it away when we got to the park. Kind of on impulse. You said that we had to proceed with light and with love. And a gun wasn't going to do any of that." He'd been thinking about it the whole car ride. The gun. The violence. The poison inside people. He thought now, as he did then, of his father's words about bullies. And about power. Who had it, who didn't. Who used it for good, and who used it for harm. How some people had holes inside them. A gun was power, but the wrong kind. A gun made pain. It made holes—bullet holes, yes, but emotional ones, too.

And bullies make bullies . . .

Jed chuckled. "Okay. You *are* full of surprises. Unsurprising, I suppose. You are your father's son."

"I hope so. You're not mad?"

"I'm trusting you, is all."

Oliver nodded.

Jake, again, from across the boulder field: "You're not getting cold feet, are you, Olly? C'mon already. Time's wasting, kid."

"You *do* have a plan?" Jed asked.

"Maybe. Part of one." It wasn't a lie. Not exactly.

Another chuckle. "Better than 'no,' I suppose. Shall we, son?"

"Yeah. Okay."

Together they crossed the felsenmeer.

As they entered the circle of lantern light, Oliver saw who waited for him at the altar stone. Jake stood tall behind the altar, his chest puffed out, a fox's grin on his long face. That one eye of his seemed to radiate its own eerie light in the mist, a light that swam and shifted as if through pond water, through brackish sheen and algal bloom. To the left stood Alex Amati. He looked pale and pasty—almost as if sick, like a flu had taken him, turned him ghoulish. His arms bulged. A gun quivered in his hand. The lantern light came up underneath him, distorting his features and turning the scowl on his face into something like you'd see on a Halloween mask. Or maybe it was the rage: twisting him from the inside out. Oliver was both shocked and not shocked to see him. Jake must've gotten to him—promised him that with all this, he could get his vengeance upon Oliver *and* bring Graham back.

(Did Alex love Graham, he wondered? Was it something he held down and repressed? Was it something that had been repressed for him?)

Off to the right was someone Oliver didn't recognize: a man in a police officer's uniform, covered in—

Blood, Oliver realized.

Someone else lay down on the ground, slumped against a boulder.

"Fig," Oliver said, moving suddenly toward him through the stones. But the cop, he held up a hunting knife, then grabbed Fig by the collar, hoisting him up toward the blade.

"Uh-uh," the cop said. "Stay there, kid. Or I stick this in his neck."

"Please," Oliver pleaded. "Don't."

Jake held up both hands. "Olly. Don't worry. Fig'll be all right. He's insurance. Just like your friend here."

With that said, Jake moved aside.

There sat Caleb. Head hanging low, chin dipped to his chest. The lantern light reflected off a stream of bloody drool hanging from his lip. Jake smacked him on the cheek, and the other boy snorted and startled awake.

"Tell him you're fine," Jake said. "Go on, Caleb."

"Olly, man," Caleb said, eyes wide, his words half mush. "Run. You gotta *run*, get the fuck outta—"

But already Jake was unwinding a bit of duct tape, *vbbbbbt,* and clumsily swaddling Caleb's mouth with it. "Shush, little baby. That's enough out of you." Now, to Olly, arms wide, he said, "You do your part, this can end today."

Oliver swallowed. "And if it ends today, do your theatrics even matter?"

"Would you have come if I hadn't?"

"No."

"Then there it is, Olly. The hammer and the nail."

It was Jed's turn to speak up. "I see you've got new friends."

"Alex just wants his friend back, isn't that sweet? You could take a page out of his book, Olly. And Officer Contrino—sorry, *Deputy Chief Contrino*—he's someone I've had dangling on the hook for a while in case I needed him. Isn't that right?"

The cop, Contrino, shrugged. "I saw the light. What can I say?"

"What he saw was a world that was changing, and he didn't like that. I gave him a way to change it back." Jake turned to face Jed. "I gave *you* a way, too, John Edward, you old drunk. But you turned on me, didn't you? Not before you sent Nate away, though. You okay with that, kid? Partnering up with the man who did your dad dirty like that?"

"He's turned around," Oliver said.

"*And* I'm not drinking anymore," Jed said.

"Oh, that's nice. That's real nice. I'm sure your wife and daughter wish you'd made that change while they were alive, instead of fuckin' dead in a car accident you caused, you old goat, but hey, hindsight is twenty-twenty, huh? Whatever, thanks for bringing me the kid."

"I didn't bring him. He brought me."

"Potato, tomato. We gonna do this, Olly?"

Oliver nodded. "On one condition."

"Let's hear it."

"Fig, Jed, and Caleb get to leave here alive. And you leave my friends alone, and my mother. Everyone goes free."

Jake whooped with sudden laughter. "Boy, Olly, it's like you got shit in your ears. Or worse, you don't have faith in me. Because if you die on this altar, we *all* get to go free." He spread his arms out wide, grinning big.

"Let's say you're wrong. They still get to go free."

Jake's grin did not fade, but it tightened up—a skull's rictus of a smile rather than one of genuine pleasure. Through his teeth he said, "I'm *not* wrong." At the ends of his arms, his hands were clutched into miserable fists. "But fine. Fine! *Fine.* If for some reason this doesn't work, the magic fails, the machine keeps on *chugging* . . . they go free. You have my word."

Oliver swallowed.

"Okay."

This is it.

He stepped forward toward the altar stone as Jake leaned on the edge of it, leering. Oliver now saw that rope had been wound around the bases of two neighboring stones, cinched under ledges. As Oliver approached, Jake took one end of one rope and brought it up to the lip of the altar.

"Ropes," Jake said. "Just in case you decide to get *squirmy.* Something to keep your arms and legs inside the vehicle."

"I won't move. You don't have to tie me up."

"Eh. But I *want* to. Besides, it really gives it that *old-school sacrifice* vibe, right? Some ancient entreaty-to-the-gods shit. A satanic bargain."

Don't do it. Fear churned through Oliver. No, not just fear. Panic. Existential panic. Like the moment atop a roller coaster before it goes down that first big hill, except times a thousand. A million. A million plus infinity. Every molecule in him wanted to bolt. And yet, he stayed the course. He measured his breathing. He thought again about his parents.

I miss you, Dad.

I'm sorry, Mom.

Oliver got up onto the altar.

* * *

Jake cinched the second rope tight around Oliver's wrist—his left, the arm with the bad hand. "Too tight?"

"It hurts," Oliver said. It wasn't a lie. It felt like it was abrading his skin. The cold air stung both of his wrists as he lay, flat on his back, upon the altar stone. His heart directly above the cleft in the rock where Jake had once stuck the coal pick.

"Sorry."

Oliver laughed—a small, humorless laugh. "Huh."

"Huh what?"

"You meant it."

"Meant what?"

"You said sorry. And I think you meant it."

Jake stopped to consider. "I think I did."

"Why? You hate me. You want me to hurt. You shouldn't be sorry."

From off to the side, Alex Amati barked, "Don't listen to him, Jake. He's just fuckin' with you. Kill him. *Kill him.*"

But Jake shushed him with a foul hiss. Then, back to Oliver: "I don't hate you. I say that, but I don't. That's just . . . that's just a *part* of me talking. But I don't hate you, Olly. You and me, we're the same, even as we're different. I'm like a . . . more evolved version of you. Older. Wiser. Maybe there's a part of me that is angry at who you are because it's who I was, once. You know? Someone who didn't know the stakes. And maybe I hate you a little bit, because you had *such* a better life than I did."

"You're full of pain, aren't you?"

Jake hesitated. In the lantern light—the lantern now placed between Oliver's knees—it was easy to see the taller boy wrestle with this. His jaw working like he was trying to loosen a seed from between his teeth.

"Yeah, I am," he said, his voice breaking.

"And you just want it all to end. That's what this is. You're killing everyone and everything to kill that pain inside of you."

Jake chuffed a laugh. "So what if I am? What do you know about pain anyway, Olly? Like I said, your life? Nothing compared to what I endured. But I learned what to do about it down in the dark of the old coal mine. I was shown the way forward. I was given a path. My pain gave me clarity."

"I have pain, too. Pain you gave me."

"Did it give you clarity, too?"

Oliver swallowed. "I think so."

"Good. Then let's end our pain together."

And with that, Jake snapped his fingers and twirled his wrist—

Since meeting his older doppelgänger, Oliver came to believe that the reason he couldn't see Jake's pain was because Jake and that pain were one and the same. Oliver didn't know what his own anger and fear looked like, and so why would he be able to see Jake's? But then, whenever Jake pulled something from that nether-realm, that interstitial In-Between place, Oliver saw *something*.

Just a glimpse of it. A glimpse of darkness leaking out.

A flash of fear, a shine of something worse.

Pain.

Pain that could not be contained.

Jake kept his pain hidden, not like Oliver's father, no. That pain was kept to the same place where Jake kept *all* his hidden things—

That interstitial place, the In-Between.

He either wanted to keep his pain so badly, or he was so afraid of it that he banished it to another place entirely.

And so, when he snapped his fingers and twirled his wrist to bring out the implement of sacrifice—once again, the coal pick—Oliver saw that flash of pain. Then Oliver did as he had done with Graham Lyons, and as he did only hours ago with Jed Homackie.

He reached out, not with his hands, but with his mind.

He grabbed hold of that pain.

And he fucking *pulled*.

The coal pick appeared in Jake's hand, but something came with it. Whenever he pulled something from the In-Between, he always felt a strange little rush, equal parts pleasurable and awful, and it came this time, too—but this time, the feeling remained. Clung to him like oil and sweat. And it deepened, thickening, expanding, filling him up, soaking him through. With it came memory, and loss, and pain. *So much pain.* Memories of his mother crying. His father beating him. His father hugging him after. The stomp of the old man's feet. The scampering of his mother up the stairs as the old man chased her with a metal ladle. In these memories Jake wasn't Jake. He was Oliver. That Oliver. *His* Oliver.

No, no, no, no—

He didn't want any of this.

Put it all back.

Take it away.

Those thoughts were pleas sent into the ether, to Eli, the demon Eligos Vassago, the black shining thing from the mine. That day the demon scarred his face, took his eye, and filled him up and then was gone.

But not really gone, he knew. It spoke to him through the book, didn't it? The Book of Accidents: a vessel, a hymnal, in the demon's own tongue.

And now he could *taste* the pages of that book—papery and sick, the bitter tang of pen ink and the copper-slick stink of blood.

Why is this happening? he screamed inside his own head—the texture of the coal pick felt rough against his palm, and cold, too. He tried to bring it down into Oliver's heart, but his arm felt noodle weak. It wouldn't move. The ax should've felt powerful and mighty, but instead felt cold and heavy, a grotesque burden. His fingers wanted to relax. To let it *go.* He imagined the pick dropping away from his hand, clattering to the stones and—

He focused on Oliver's face. Oliver, whose eyes were closed. His chin, out. A look of struggle warred on the boy's face, like he was doing something—even though he was tied to that rock, he *was* doing something.

But what?

Jake suddenly understood.

The little prick was pulling this stuff *out* of him. Just as he'd done with Graham Lyons that night on the road.

Wincing, *roaring,* Jake—*I'm Jake, I'm not Oliver, not that little weakling, I'm Jake*—hauled back with the coal pick even as he tried to recall the feelings down into the dark, where they belonged—

He swung the coal pick.

Down into Oliver's chest.

Through his heart.

Except.

Except.

The pick buried into the cleft of the altar. It did not find skin, or bone, or meat. The tip found only hard stone. *Tink.*

Oliver was gone.

Whatever just happened, Jed didn't know. He stood there, watching with agony as Oliver put himself in a place of the greatest vulnerability—strapped down to an altar, in front of an older version of himself. Presenting himself willingly as sacrifice. And yet, even as he did it, Jed had a distant feeling that this was all part of the plan. That it would all be okay.

And then, Oliver—*poof*—disappeared.

Like he was never there. The ropes fell away, sliding off the edge of the altar. Jake looked staggered and winded, almost as if slapped across the face. The monster was left, goggling at the altar in horror.

So was everyone else.

The other boy with the gun.

The police officer with the knife.

Caleb, bound to the chair amid the jagged rocks.

All eyes watching the altar.

Now's my chance, Jed thought.

The boy with the gun was the most dangerous—

So that's where he went.

Jed rushed the one called Alex Amati, tackling him into the stones. The big lumbering idiot was top-heavy and went crashing down into the boulders. The gun in his hand went tumbling away.

Jed laughed.

Gotcha, you big gorilla, he thought, madly. *All part of the plan.*

This is not part of the plan, Oliver thought.

He was not on the altar anymore.

He wasn't in the boulder field, or in the park, or in Pennsylvania, or maybe even on the planet.

It was questionable if he was even in *reality* anymore.

He *knew* this place. It was the void: the land of contusion, empurpled and endless, bruise-black with broken stars, rocks, teeth.

All around him, this great void filled a seemingly infinite expanse. Stars—smeary and strange, as if seen through a window smeared with Vaseline—hung at the margins. Colors danced there, too, around those stars, and between them. Colors and shadow, too. Shadow like the shadows he saw inside people: liquid and elastic, flowing here and there. Shadows like pain.

Something floated by him: a bottle. Brown liquid sloshed inside. The label read JACK KENNY WHISKEY. It gently spun through the air—or "air"—past him. Then another thing: a book, like a ratty old notebook. Oliver snatched that with a swipe of his hand, and he knew instantly what he had. It was the same book Jake had before. The logbook. That heretical tome.

Also, his spellbook.

The Book of Accidents.

Oliver did not stop to read it. Instead he began to tear out its pages, one by one, more furiously with each rip—the pages spiraling away from him gently, in slow motion, as if underwater.

The void around him rippled.

Something down deep stirred. A great shadow moved in front of a patch of stars, blotting them out as it passed.

I'm not alone in this place, Oliver realized, with horror.

"Motherfucker," Contrino hissed. He gave the hunting knife a vicious twirl, staring off at the old man who'd tackled the other kid. "You stay here," he said to Fig, tapping him on the head with the flat of his knife.

Fig felt death behind him. Like a great gray shadow, waiting. Idly, he wondered if that's what it was like to be standing in the path of a coming tsunami—a churning wine-dark wave rising up and then waiting before it crash down upon you, pinning you to the beach and turning all your bones to broken pottery before dragging you back out to the hungry sea. But the wave, the shadow, had not fallen upon him yet.

He still had something in the tank.

So when Contrino began to stalk away—

He did the simplest, stupidest thing he could think of.

He tripped the bastard. Just reached right out, grabbed his foot, and pulled backward as hard as he could. Contrino called out as he pitched forward, smacking hard into the rock ahead of him. He moaned in pain. It did little to diminish Fig, and in fact, filled him with sudden, profound purpose.

Fig growled, and clambered atop Contrino before he could get up, and started beating hell out of him, even as his gut wound pumped fresh blood. Contrino writhed beneath him, shouldering him backward, and the two tumbled between a set of stones. The knife stuck into Fig's bicep once, twice, then a third time through his forearm, and a fourth between his ribs. He felt the air go out of him. But as his one last act—

He reached up, grabbed the bastard by the ear—

And slammed his head into a rock.

Contrino twitched once, then stopped moving.

Fig heard a gurgling whistle from his own side as he tried to catch a breath. But his breaths were half breaths, just hollow gulps of what they should be. He laid his head back on the cold, damp ground. That great gray wave rose up, blotting out the sky, taking away the rain, and stealing his breath before finally falling hard upon him.

Reduced to torn pages and ribbons, the Book of Accidents was streamers and confetti. And with that, the void boomed and turned black. The darkness spread like ink through parchment.

The shadow rose up before him, a murmuration of blackbirds, then a tide of snakes, then worms, now spider legs. Its body was darker than everything, but also brighter—light played along its surfaces like a living thing. It swam before Oliver, and its voice swam alongside it, slithering into his head like the taproot of an invasive weed.

You do not belong here, boy, it said.

"Neither do you," Oliver said. He was afraid. And the thing roared at him—all its tendrils and limbs thickened and swelled, pointing at him, surrounding him. The air filled with the pure noise of unbridled *rage.* Above it all, Oliver cried: "You can't hurt me. You can't scare me. You need me. You need me to die out there, don't you? On that stone!"

The thing recoiled. Back to its slithering, writhing mass.

You do not understand. The wheel must be broken. The axle, snapped. God made this a broken place. I will show you. And then Oliver's head filled with viciousness: atrocities and murders and suicides and mass graves, but Oliver bore down and bit the insides of his cheeks until he tasted blood, and he pushed back with images of his own: his mother and father, his friends, kids playing, all the stars around a bold full moon; and he further remembered all the good things he'd seen people do for one another: someone helping a homeless man stand and get food and shelter; a Pride parade on TV; flowers to people in nursing homes like his mother used to deliver.

I will remake the world! The thing howled. *I will fix what God has broken. You will not stop me, you foolish, trivial microbe.*

It lashed out anew, capturing Oliver in tendrils of tightening shadow.

And then, an absurd moment as something floated between them. A bizarre, almost comical interruption, as a human eyeball—its optic nerve and attendant meat trailing behind—bobbed slowly from left to right.

It was then Oliver understood.

That single stupid absurd thing, and he understood it all.

"This isn't some In-Between place," he said aloud to the demon. "I'm inside him, aren't I? This isn't a void. *This* is where he's keeping all his pain. All of it, including you."

You BEDBUG. You MOTE of DUST. You understand NOTHING.

"I get it now. You're a parasite. An infection," Oliver said woozily. "You and the pain are one and the same."

The great beast filled the void once more.

It came for Oliver, all its limbs turned to blades, no longer caring if he died out *there,* eager and impatient to see him die in *here.*

A fist crashed into Jed's kidneys like the moon pulled out of the sky and slammed down upon him. Alex Amati lorded over Jed as he fell.

"I don't need a gun," Alex growled. He grabbed Jed, lifted him up, and dropped him hard against a boulder. Jed's ribs gave way. His chest felt like broken glass. His breathing felt like knives. His hands scrabbled against the ground, reaching for something to hold on to—

Alex grabbed him again, and once more hauled him up, higher

than last time. He spun him around and showed Jed a manic, twisted visage: His neck tendons were tight like tree roots. His jaw was so clenched it looked like his teeth would crack like corn.

As for Jed, well.

Jed started laughing.

Alex's eyes widened farther. "What's so funny?"

"You lost your gun," Jed said, still laughing, and with every laugh came a hundred stitches of pure goddamn anguish.

"So what?"

"I found it!"

Then he pulled the trigger of the gun in his hand. He pulled it not once, but as many times as he could, and with each bullet, Alex shuddered like each bullet was a fist striking him in the chest.

And then the giant fell, taking Jed with him. A tree toppling: *whoom.*

Jed lay there, still laughing a little, and weeping a little too. His triumph, however, was short-lived.

He felt the presence behind him. The boy. His former . . . master. Reviewing his relationship to Jake in a literary manner, he realized that he had been Renfield to the boy's Dracula, hadn't he? The bug-eating freak, all the more pathetic and pitiable than the monster, for at least the monster was simply doing what the monster must. But Jed had always thought Renfield was so much worse than Dracula. And that is what he had become. Jake had seen something in him, seen his weakness. Knew it from snout to tail. And he used it to turn Jed into something unrecognizable.

Not any longer. His pain was gone. He felt free.

Jed stood up wearily, grunting as he did. He turned to face Jake.

The strange-eyed boy was shaking. As if cold. Sick and trembling, as if staving off a fever, or a seizure. The coal pick turned again and again in his grip.

"Jake," Jed said. "Or should I call you Oliver?"

"I'm *Jake.*" When he said it, his teeth chattered audibly. Jed saw then that the many-colored eye had settled on one color: red. Crimson light burst from it. "Jake!"

"Well, whoever you are, you don't have me anymore. Oliver saved me. No matter what you do to me now, it doesn't matter. He saved me."

"He didn't save shit. You're weak piss, old man. A sad fucking shriveled killer. A *failure*."

"Seems you're the one that failed, my boy. You may not think you're Oliver, but you are. He's inside you, somewhere. Isn't he?"

Jake raised the coal pick.

Jed closed his eyes.

And then—nothing.

Jake said, "You're right. By god, old man, you're right."

He grinned. And Jed knew then that something was wrong.

The knives came. Oliver knew they'd cut him apart. This demon, this *parasite* living inside Jake's mind, had lost its sense. It was the one who'd taught Jake to end the world, Oliver knew, but its rage had overtaken it, and now it would kill him. He didn't want to die, of course. But he at least knew that dying here ended the machinations of Jake and this creature. It canceled the apocalypse. Because Oliver would die *here*, and not on the altar stone.

And then, as the beast rushed upon him, throttling through the void with a thousand knives pointed at him—

A hand appeared out of nowhere.

It grabbed Oliver by the throat, and—

It pulled.

The rush back to the world was disorienting. Vanishing from the void left Oliver reeling, his vision blurry, his guts coiling and uncoiling. Jake held him fast, hand around his throat. His trachea tightened as he fought for breath. His legs kicked as Jake lifted him—

And slammed him down on the altar. Stars burst behind his eyes.

Jake pinned him there, one hand on his throat, the other on the coal pick.

Oliver heard Jed call out, saw a blurry streak as the man rushed toward Jake—but with what air Oliver could muster, he called out:

"Jed, no."

This is on me, he thought.

I know what to do.

Again the pick rose. The sharp point gleaming in the lantern light. Oliver's hand darted out, his fingers forming a claw.

He grabbed for Jake's eye.

Except, it wasn't Jake's eye at all, was it?

That, Oliver realized now, was the trick. Every magician had their tricks, and every trick had at its core misdirection, and this was that. As his fingers sank into the puffy scar tissue surrounding that chameleon orb, he knew that what he was grabbing was not Jake's eye. Because Jake's eye? *It was in the void.* It was there in that In-Between place inside him. If the eye was in there, what was in his face? What was that chimera's eye in his eye socket?

It was a cork in a bottle. Put there by that *thing* inside him—the creature, the demon, whatever the hell it was. A parasite. Jake was its egg case, its ootheca, its tumor, its *home.* And the eyeball was the lock on that door, keeping it all inside.

With one hard tug, it wrenched free from Jake's face with a wet, ripping sound.

Jed watched it happen. Oliver, appearing out of nowhere. Jake, with the other boy by the throat. Slamming him down on the altar. Raising the pick. Jed hurried forth, knowing he had to stop this, had to kill Jake before he sacrificed Oliver on that literally godforsaken stone—

Then Oliver took the other boy's eye. One clawlike motion—up, and in, and *out.* That ruined eye *burst* like a rotten grape.

Oliver shook something wet from his fingers as he scrambled backward off the altar stone.

The other boy just stood there for a moment, as if in shock. His mouth opened and closed, and only the barest hiss came out. The hole in his face was a dark, black thing. Lantern light played along its wet rim.

"Jake," Jed said softly. He took one step toward him, in case—well, in case of what, he didn't know. In case he had to restrain him. Jake was, after all, still a monster. Wasn't he? Still capable of anything, he knew.

Jake shook once in a teeth-clacking spasm. *Tacka-tacka-clack.*

His neck stiffened. Followed by his back.

Then his head snapped back, eyes toward the sky—

And from that open eye socket came a geyser of black fluid. Like oil. Like blood. Jake wailed. Lights, bright lights, came out with the disgorged fountain of darkness (and later Jed would realize that there were ninety-eight such lights, shooting off like fireworks loaded with ghosts, *foosh, foosh, foosh*). A bottle launched up and out, too, shattering on the rocks, *kssh*. Pages of some book caught on the wind, slick with red, spattering down. A baseball bat clattered. A gun spiraled away. Old photos. A lump of black coal. A wedding band. And with each, the boy's screams got louder and louder, shriller and shriller, until—

Until something *else* came out.

Something very big, and very angry.

The parasite.

The demon.

It's here, Oliver thought.

Legs and tendrils thrust up out of the geyser and anchored against Jake's cheeks and forehead, using that to gain leverage. The boy's face swelled up impossibly large as the thing came out of him. And it *just kept coming*. A huge, wormlike body. Swelling as it emerged. Wings unfurling. Bones bubbling up from its surface. A thousand ants rising from the muck of its flesh, pouring off in scattered, skittering streamers.

Jake's body fell over, limp. The beast was free.

It turned toward Oliver. A hundred mouthparts forming, all its gleaming chelicerae clicking as it spoke in a guttural susurrus:

"You almost won. So close, little speck."

Oliver turned and tried to crawl away on his hands and knees—

But something slithered around his middle, and slammed him back up onto the altar. A single tentacle reached out, grabbing the coal pick that had fallen. It gave it a casual little *flip* to get it in the right direction.

"You can't end the world by killing me," Oliver said, defiant. "It has to be him or me doing the deed. You won't get what you want."

"No," the demon hissed. *"But I can still find joy in your death."*

Somewhere behind them came a sound—and with it, a burst of light.

And then, moments later, shapes. Shapes with wings. The sky, moving. *Owls,* Oliver thought, and thereafter, he knew: *Mom.*

79

The Fatal Bellman,
Which Gives the Sternest Good Night

Later, Oliver would describe it to his mother this way: He'd say it reminded him of the time he was little, maybe seven or eight, and he threw that rock at that old wasp's nest that he'd seen hanging in Fairmount Park. Except it wasn't an *old* nest so much as it was a *quiet* nest, and one that still contained, in his mother's words, "a metric shitload of wasps." They swarmed him, and they hit him one by one, each wasp dive-bombing in, looking for its own patch of skin to sting. (And many did; he came away with twenty-three stings that day, some of which left little pockmark scars across his body.)

The owls hit the demon much as the wasps had hit him that day, one after the next, but not stinging, no. Rather, their talons were forward, and they tore chunks out of the thing—clots of viscera, bits of shadow. They went away with those pieces, though to where, Oliver didn't know. But they returned again and again, eerily silent as they disassembled the demon. Oliver couldn't help but watch as these owls—who were not made of feather and talon but rather carved of wood, by his mother's hand and partly by his own—reduced the monster, piece by piece, until most of it was gone. But it was not the owls who ended it.

Underneath all that muck and all that shadow waited a face: a human face, skin as white as bone and porcelain, a bent hammer-claw nose, a little pair of glasses. This shifted, too, the topography of its visage moving from face to face, from Graham Lyons's face to that of Nate Graves, to others that Oliver did not recognize—though some that he feared might even be his own. It lurched toward him, reaching for the coal pick that it had dropped. But the pick was gone. When the demon turned, hearing a sound, it would find itself face-to-face with an enemy, the one who beset upon it these thirteen birds, owls black in beak and claw. Maddie Graves stood there, in front of a door made from thatch and twig, with two hinges made from skipping stones and a knob born of a baseball-sized rock. In her hand was the pick. The demon hissed at her, she gave the pick a spin—

And then she embedded it in the demon's skull.

It turned to flies and skittering things.

Oliver blacked out.

80

The Sin Eater

It was over, except of course, it wasn't.

Things like this had a way of living on, passed down and around from one person to the next. Love and pain, trauma and hope, light and dark. Around and around they go, some given as gifts, others as curses. The whole machine, whirling on its own axis. A cycle of something made, something broken, and hopefully something made again.

A day came that June, a hot day, a breezy day, the air as thirsty as a desert dog, when Oliver found his mother outside the house, planting marigolds. ("A desperate act on a day like this," she'd said before she went outside, "but one must have some *fucking* optimism.")

Oliver asked if he could help. She said of course, and told him to get his gloves from the work shed, which he did. Upon returning, he assumed the job of sprinkling the little fertilizer pellets—"Flower vitamins," she called them—into the holes before she plopped a plant into the space.

"I've been thinking," Oliver said.

"Ohh no," she joked. "That's never good."

"Shut up, it's fine. This is fine."

In a stage whisper she said, "Spoiler warning: It wasn't fine."

"Will you just hear me out?"

She rocked back on her heels and said, "Shoot."

"It's three things."

"Oh, Jesus, give me strength. *Three* things? Can't it just be one?"

"Nope. Things come in threes. It's like a, I dunno, a cosmic law."

She winked a bit of dirt out of her eye, and then it fell to her cheek, which she brushed away with a thumb. "Go ahead, Dude."

"Thing number one: I want to go see Jake."

Maddie felt a rush come to her cheeks. "Olly, we talked about this—"

"It's safe."

"He's in prison." As, she knew, he should be. That teenage prick had run a cult. Led a campaign of terror and murder against her son. Disappeared her husband. Wanted to end the world. To this day, she had a hard time reckoning with how much she saw—and did, and how much happened—was real. She knew in her heart *all* of it was real. And yet, it was so strange, so impossible. It felt like something out of a dream, as if the mere act of acknowledging it made it slip farther away. "And he should rot there," she added.

"He *is* going to rot there. I just think . . . I should talk to him. He's me. Or was? I dunno. Maybe I can help him. A lot of what was in him is . . . gone now. I think. I hope." That night in the boulder field, the Jake that was left behind was alive—and a trembling, gibbering wreck. He was, in Olly's words, "hollowed out." Oliver explained it to her by saying that Jake had relied on the demon inside him for so long—even as it too relied upon him—that without it, he was lost. The pain filled him up. Gave him shape, life, purpose. Without it, he was a puppet without its hand, or so it seemed.

"There has to still be a person left in there, Mom. They'll allow visitation, and I've already gone and seen Jed—"

She sighed. "Okay. Just one. But *I* drive you, not Caleb."

"Deal."

"Good."

"Second thing, turns out, is kinda related to the first—"

"Lord give me strength."

"I want to learn how to drive."

A bark of laughter rose up out of her, unbidden. "Oh, Olly. Sweet summer child. I don't know if I'm ready for *that* stress. I think I'd rather face down another potential apocalypse."

"C'mon. I turn sixteen next month. And I can already get a permit and—"

"My child. Driving. Ohh, fuck."

"*And* I am very responsible, and honestly it would get me out of your hair, plus it would stop me from relying on other kids—those naughty, tricksy, unreliable teenagers—"

"Caleb drives you now, and we like Caleb, remember?"

"I can't rely on Caleb forever."

"Ugh. Christ. Am I old? Oh shit, I'm getting old. Olly, you had to do this to me today, didn't you? A sixteen-year-old son. Driving. Driving!"

"You're not old. I'm just . . . getting older."

She stuck the trowel she'd been using into the dirt, *kiff*. "Time moves forward for all of us, Dude. God, fine. That's two out of three. That's a good ratio. In fact, why don't we stop now? We'll give up on the third thing; you can mention it to me in a year or three."

"I know exactly where you can teach me to drive."

And just then, as if on cue, a truck came ambling up the driveway. Fig's truck.

"Hold that thought," she said, and stood up. She waved Oliver along and the two of them went to meet Fig. He parked, then hopped down out of his truck, wincing a little—the injuries from that night in the park had damn near killed him. In fact, Fig had thought he *was* dead that day—he even told a story of him looking up, and seeing what he described as a battle between the Devil and God's own angels happening all around him. Great swooping flying things tearing at a black, writhing mass.

Maddie hugged him. And he stopped to shake Oliver's hand.

"On a lunch break. Thought I'd stop by, share the news."

A grin spread like a wildfire across Maddie's face. "I swear, Fig, this better be *baby news,* or I will shit."

He laughed. "The baby's running a little late, so we're scheduled tomorrow for a C-section. That's the news. But not all of it. We were kinda hoping, me and Zo, that Maddie, you'd be our daughter's godmother?"

At first, she said nothing. She just stood there, quaking a little. And then, Maddie made a sound like—well, like if happiness were itself a living thing, and this was its mating call to summon some other happiness in order to mate in the hopes of spawning *even more happiness.* She wasn't sure she'd heard herself *squee* before, but these days, given everything, she was embracing as much joy as she could muster.

In horror's wake, hope was a bountiful garden.

"I guess that's a yes," Oliver said, smirking.

"I am down to be your child's spiritual advisor," Maddie said with a mad gleam in her eye.

"We're not too interested in the *spiritual* part, just the part where you're there for her when she needs you. Also, no teaching her curse words."

"No fuckin' promises," Maddie said.

"And you," Fig said to Oliver. "You wanna be the kid's sort of . . . honorary adopted uncle?"

Now it was Oliver's turn. He didn't make a *squee* sound, but he beamed. Glowing bright like the morning sun. "You can count on me. I'll be a good uncle. A *great* uncle. I mean, not a *great*-uncle because that would mean I'm the uncle's uncle, but you know what I mean, I'll be a really excellent uncle—"

"Thanks, guys." Another round of hugs came. "Zo would be here to ask you but she's already feeling completely whackadoo over this birth thing tomorrow. But if you wanna come by? We're doing it first thing in the morning, so maybe come by the hospital in the afternoon—but maybe call first, just in case. Napping and all that."

"I've got a gallery showing to prep for, but that's early. So we will bring only the softest and most adorable stuffed animals and a robust supply of cloth diapers," Maddie said. "Count on it."

Fig nodded. "Thanks. For everything."

"You too," she said. They embraced for a while. It felt good. He asked if they were both okay, and they said yes. They were, finally, as good as they could be. Which would never be good enough, Maddie knew, without Nate.

Soon Fig was gone again, his truck pulling back down the driveway.

Together, she and her son stood there, out front of the house, watching him go. "Okay," she said. "The third thing. Spit it out, dude."

"I want to take a road trip with you."

She snorted. "A road trip. Okay."

"I . . ." This one was hard for him, she saw. She watched him summon his strength. "Mom, I'm not like other kids. Or adults. Or . . . uhh. People."

"I know."

"You know how I can see people's . . . pain? And deal with it, sorta?"

She arched an eyebrow. "As you've explained to me, yes." He told her not long after the events of that night what his power was. She'd always known her boy was special, and when he told this to her, she wasn't exactly surprised. Dr. Nahid, who he still saw every month, often over Skype, said that his empathy was off the charts, and that would never change. But the good doctor didn't really know *how* off the charts it was.

The day came, a month or so after the battle of Ramble Rocks, that Oliver said he once thought about trying to help Maddie with her pain. But he said after that night, her pain changed. It lessened, but more important, it seemed different. Not as angry. *Less like a bull in a hall of mirrors,* were his exact words.

"I want to go out there. In the world. And maybe try to help people. See if I can . . . take some of that bad stuff out of them."

"Excise their pain."

"Y . . . yeah."

"Dude, you know that some people want their pain, right? Maybe even need it. Pain is a part of who we are. You can't destroy it, and you can't hide from it." *As we've learned all too well,* she thought. "It's like Jake. You took something from him, and better or worse, he needed it."

He nodded. "I know. But sometimes it goes bad. Like a cancer, how good cells turn against each other. Like what was in Jake. And sometimes it's pain someone else gives you. As if someone has, I dunno, poisoned you. That's the wrong kind of pain. It's like an invasive species. It hurts you. And it can hurt other people."

"Like with Jake," she said again.

"Yeah."

Christ, my kid is smart. Too smart. She wished he wasn't. It made him vulnerable. All those big thoughts. And that big heart. *Fuck.*

Putting him out there like this, it was, or would be . . . dangerous, she feared. It entangled him with other people, and worse, it tied him up in their emotional lives. And that was fraught, forbidden territory. He was young yet—so young. She was barely ready to let him drive, much less put him in the path of other people's misery.

"I dunno, Dude . . ."

"We can drive and just see. You can teach me how to drive, and I'll meet people and just, who knows, see what I can see."

"Olly—"

"I can *help* people. Like you said. You're a maker—you make things. I want to do the thing *I'm* good at now."

He said it with such force, such certainty, she was shocked by it.

He wasn't angry. It didn't come from rage or ego. But there was a confidence there that felt unusual for him. What else could she say?

"Okay."

"Okay?"

"Don't make me say it again, it was hard enough to say the first time." She shrugged. "I have some money saved up, had some good gallery sales. We can afford a little trip, as a treat, so let's do it. *After* my next showing, which is in a few short weeks. Okay?"

He hugged her. She *oofed* from the vigor of the embrace. She hugged him back. They stayed like that for a while.

"Your father would be proud of you," she said. "He was then, and would be now. You're going to end up a better man than he was, and he was the best man I knew, kid."

"Thanks, Mom." He pulled out of the hug. Then he stopped and looked down at the space between their feet. "Do you think he's still out there?"

"Your dad?" Her answer came with no hesitation. "I do. I'm sure of it. I don't know where. I don't know *when,* even. But if I know him, he's out there, and he's trying like hell to get home." And she'd been trying like hell to bring him back, too. Every day since that day she made the owls, she made a new door. She tried in different places, in different rooms, in the woods, in the road. Different materials, too: wood from fallen trees, stones from Ramble Rocks, bits of his clothing, bone from a dead whitetail she'd found in the woods. She even used pieces of the house: bits of trim, radiator knobs, and spigots. Some she painted. Some she fixed to the walls in their own home. Others she built in their backyard, just sticking up out of nothing.

Not once did any of them open.

Not in a way that took you anywhere except to the other side. Wall or tree bark or open air. No other worlds.

And no Nate.

But, she knew, they made a nice collection. The doors formed the focus of her next show. And a little part of her hoped that when the show was all done, when she gave the world her doors, that she'd be standing amongst them and then, in concert, they'd all open at once.

And in one of them, she'd see her husband again. And Oliver would have his father. And their broken home would be unbroken once more.

Epilogue: The Numbers Man

Every day at his job at the pigment plant, the janitor went through the numbers. He counted the minutes. He counted the *shushing* pushes of the broom in his hand. He did his best to count the bristles on that broom. He counted the words spoken to him, the cracks in the concrete floor, the metal shavings on the floor that inevitably came off machinery like the high-shear mixer and the masterbatch dispersion machines and the can cutters.

(How many people spoke to him in a day was inevitably the lowest number of them all. The other employees didn't like him. He knew it. He could sense it. And truthfully, he didn't like any of *them*, either, though he tried very hard to be nice and pleasant to them so it didn't upset them. Never upset the normals. But he idly pondered what it would feel like to take them all out to the boulder field, lay them out one by one, and cut each of them open. Especially that big-haired blond secretary. He'd like to split her open, taint to tits. Stem to stern.)

When each day of running the numbers was over, he'd punch out. Sometimes he'd go by Ramble Rocks on his way home. In this place, this world, it was an outdoor amphitheater. They held concerts here. Community concerts mostly, nothing really big. The tunnel was there, part of an underground area where they stored equipment and such—it was locked up, always. He'd snuck in there one time, in the hopes it would call him home—that there in the dark of the tunnel he'd find the demon waiting with open arms and breath of carrion. But it was not to be. The staff of the park simply shooed him out under bright fluorescent lights.

The boulders of Ramble Rocks were there, too, far behind the rear of the amphitheater, nestled amongst wisp-needled evergreens. He wandered the rocks from time to time, like a worm crawling between broken teeth. One thing was missing: the altar stone. It was gone. Nothing existed in its space, just a blank, dead spot. No rocks. No life. Nary a bug or a weed. Just a patch of dead, cracked earth.

Home was just an apartment over someone's garage.

He lived quite sparely. Canned food and one pot. A cot. A toilet. He didn't need much more. He knew that one day his landlord—an old mummy who didn't bother him at all, except when it came time to pay the utilities, and even then he bothered him with notes slipped under the door only—would demand money back given the way that he'd ruined the walls in here. So much writing, so many thumb tacks, so many red threads.

All the photos and the calculations and the pages torn from library books on demonology. The demon, he knew, was gone. It no longer spoke to him, nor he to it. He'd lived a life of crass, grotesque comfort in the fallen worlds, poaching whatever came his way, greedily feeding, lazily hunting. He had acolytes and he had victims. It was a good world. And then it all went away. Or rather, it went back to the way it was, regurgitating itself back into a normal universe, but this one was not the one he came from. It was different. The brands were strange: the car he drove was a used 1998 Yorisaga Chevalier. Korean brand, but made in Kentucky. There weren't even two Koreas, here, no North-South split. Just one united Korea.

This was not where he came from.

This was not home.

And so, the plan was the plan once more.

He'd selected a series of young girls. He hadn't hurt them yet, hadn't even taken one—but he had watched them carefully, taken photos at a distance, written extensive notes. This time he had to move more quickly, all at once. Farming them too slowly was what got him in trouble last time. The man had chosen some of his victims already. He had twenty-two of them so far—they were part of the equation. *Ninety-nine, and the world would die.*

All the worlds, he hoped.

So he could leave this place and return, not to the world in which he was born, but the world to which he fell—the one where the lightning took him. His hunting ground. His true home.

So now he sat, admiring the photos. Touching them. Imagining the wet splash of blood. The hungry slop of guts on the rock.

He wondered if he would first have to make a new altar stone. One more thing to think about. It gave him a headache behind his eyes.

Then: a knock at the door.

"Go away," he said.

But the knock came again. More insistent, this time.

He cursed himself for having said *Go away,* because now whoever it was knew he was here. He had to maintain a normal appearance. Anything odd, it might spook the herd once more. Playing it *normal* was key. Normal man. Job as a janitor. Apartment. A life. Nothing to fear, no sir, nothing to fear. Everything's aboveboard here, yessir! We're all normal here! Ha ha!

Grumbling, he moved to the door and opened it.

"I'm sorry, I'm busy right now," he started to say, but then stopped short. A man stood there. A strange man, he thought at first. But then, no. Not strange at all. Familiar, once you saw past the changes. "It's *you.*"

"Edmund Walker Reese," that man said, stepping through. He looked different to Edmund. Cleaner cut. Beard trimmed all the way. Hair, too. The scar across his head would never go away, though, would it? That gave Edmund a small smile, at least. The smile didn't last, though, when he saw the gun: a small snub-nosed revolver, its blue-black barrel gleaming.

"How did you find me, robberfly? How did you get here?"

"Fate put us in the same world," Nate answered. His thumb drew back the hammer. "Ain't that something? Same town, even. One day I saw you. Saw you watching girls at Rosie's ice cream shop downtown. You know, it's funny, where we came from, that place was—"

"Rosalita's ice cream," Edmund said, with a small smile.

"Rosalita's was better."

"It was. I liked their rum raisin."

Nate shot him in the chest. Edmund fell backward—not a hard fall, but a gentle, slow drop. Blood slicked his shirt and he could feel it below his waistline, oozing down his groin. The other man, the killer's killer, turned around to leave. Edmund Walker Reese's last thought was that the front door had changed. A different knob, and a blue door, not red. The hinges looked strange, too. Like they were made by hand, not by machine. Like someone took Altoids mint containers and hammered them into the shape. And the knob: Was it the face of an owl, carved out of wood? Nate seemed surprised by this, too, and stepped through it. Darkness swept over Reese as death found him, finally, across time and space.

Edmund Walker Reese left this world.

Perhaps, so did the other man, too.

AFTERWORD AND ACKNOWLEDGMENTS

I tried writing this book three times.

First time was—jeez, who knows how long ago? It was one of my five so-called trunk novels—in this case, meaning novels that were so bad they deserved to be thrown into a lead-lined trunk which was then dropped into an ocean fissure, lest the existence of these very bad novels in the world lead to some kind of Airborne Toxic Event. It was a different book, then, very different, but it had a few of the touchstones: a creepy coal mine, monsters down in the dark, bullies bullying and abusers abusing. It failed for a lot of reasons, likely—at that time I was too young, too unsure of myself, working too hard to make the book too many things and sound like too many other authors.

Second time was . . . I'd guess around eight years ago. I didn't even finish it. Got about 77,000 words into it before it kinda unspooled like a ruptured testicle. (Sorry, in case you didn't know, testicles unspool. You're *welcome*.) This one was a little closer to what you just read: a family under duress, a bearded weirdo in the woods (based in part on a strange dream I'd had), coal mine. Also had some other stuff, like a haunted Nazi pistol? Shit, I dunno. It's strange—I found the draft of the story and tried reading it and I literally don't remember writing any of it. I chalk it up to the fact I write so damn much, but maybe also that book just wanted to be forgotten. Maybe it *needed* to be forgotten, so this one could be written. Maybe this book has gone back through all the other universes, assassinating all other iterations of itself. Who can say?

But thankfully, it was not *so* forgotten—some part of it lived on inside the dead bird's nest I call a heart. And somewhere recently it began to twitch anew, struck with life once more. Which meant it was time to have a run at a third and thankfully final iteration of the story, which is the book that you hold right now. (Physically, digitally, or in your ears.) This version demanded to live, to crawl out of the tunnel of the Ramble Rocks and be the story that it is—one about, well, I dunno. Cycles of abuse and other versions of ourselves and emotional seawalls. About spirals, and families, and mistakes, and *love,* and *empathy* and and and . . .

Well, I guess serial killers and ghosts-that-aren't-ghosts and interstitial liminal voids.

So, now that you've read it, I can put in the caveat that this book gets a lot of things wrong, and it does so largely on purpose, because you're reading a book that represents just one reality, one where things are maybe a little different from our own. (And if this helps forestall any surly emails about how there's no Fish and Game in PA and actually it's two commissions, the Game Commission and the Fish & Boat Commission, then this afterword was worth it.) Though I'm sure I also messed up some stuff without meaning to, but if you're feeling charitable, chalk it up to ALTERNATE REALITIES, please and thank you.

This draft by itself took its sweet time too, coming to life—it was a book with lots of big ideas and took many moons to wrestle into shape. So, there are many drafts here sealed up behind the walls of this novel, trapped with the ghosts of the first two not-so-useful iterations of the story. That's how books are, sometimes.

Writers should know that, I think, going into writing their own stories—sometimes a story comes out fast and bloodless, like unsheathing a blade. Sometimes a story comes out slow and in a gush of red mess, like removing shrapnel with a soup spoon.

And sometimes you're just not ready to write it. Sometimes that story isn't done baking. Or sometimes the story is ready, but you, the writer, aren't the writer you need to be yet. That's okay. It feels discouraging at the time but it's a good thing. It needs to be that way. Every story is its own animal, unique and without partner—a true rare bird in the wild, the last of its kind. And you tempt it with food only it will eat, and you tame it with tricks that only work on that one beast. It's like in a video game, how you just aren't ready to tackle that part of the map yet.

More to the point, sometimes you aren't ready because you don't have the right people with you. That's a thing, too: a book is written by one person, but built by many, most times. And for that, some thanks are owed.

First up, Tricia Narwani, the editor of the book, who politely listened as I pitched this random-as-hell tale in a sloppy, slapdash gush of story-babble. I must've said something right, because she believed in it, bought the ticket, took the ride, and without her steady editorial hand, *The Book of Accidents* would've landed on shelves a half-formed, wobbly-legged thing. (Think if you will of that wailing horse fetus in *Eraserhead*.) Thanks, too, to Alex Larned, editorial assistant, for offering smart, empathetic thoughts as to how to make the book better. And of course, my agent, Stacia Decker, who has a sharp mind for story and knows how to stick a knife into its soft, unformed spots. Thanks, too, to friends and fellow authors like Kevin Hearne and Delilah Dawson for letting me talk about this book and try to make sense of it sometimes.

And of course, thanks to you for reading this book *and* this silly bit at the end.

May you find peace and stay safe in this peculiar time, friends.

ABOUT THE AUTHOR

CHUCK WENDIG is the *New York Times* bestselling author of *Wanderers, Star Wars: Aftermath,* the Miriam Black thrillers, the Atlanta Burns books, and *Zer0es* and *Invasive,* alongside other works across comics, games, film, and more. He was a finalist for the John W. Campbell Award for Best New Writer and is an alum of the Sundance Screenwriters Lab, and he served as the co-writer of the Emmy-nominated digital narrative *Collapsus.* He is also known for his popular blog, *terribleminds,* and books about writing such as *Damn Fine Story.* He lives in Pennsylvania with his family.

terribleminds.com
Twitter: @ChuckWendig
Instagram: @chuck_wendig

ABOUT THE TYPE

THIS BOOK is set in Arno. Named after the Florentine river which runs through the heart of the Italian Renaissance, Arno draws on the warmth and readability of early humanist typefaces of the 15th and 16th centuries. While inspired by the past, Arno is distinctly contemporary in both appearance and function. Designed by Adobe Principal Designer Robert Slimbach, Arno is a meticulously-crafted face in the tradition of early Venetian and Aldine book typefaces.

DON'T MISS THE EXHILARATING SEQUEL TO *WANDERERS*

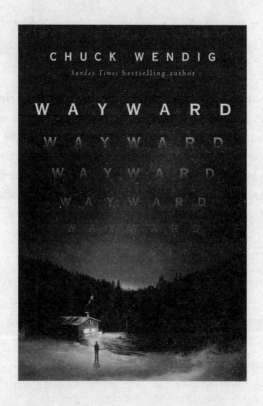

COMING SUMMER 2022